Wishing On A Star

WISHING ON A STAR

by

RAYNETTA MANEES

Print ISBN: 978-1-7321342-1-8
eBook ISBN: 978-0-9855324-2-0

Please visit www.RManees.com for additional author information and appearances

DEDICATION

This book is dedicated with love and gratitude to Linda Diane Swanson, the most loyal, supportive friend a writer could ever have.

ACKNOWLEDGEMENT

Love, thanks, and warmest memories to my dear friend, the late Dennis Pitts, beloved former principal of the Detroit Fine and Performing Arts Academy, for his invaluable input on musical issues.

CHAPTER 1

WORKING GIRL

The PA system crackled to life, "Ladies and gentlemen, we are now beginning our approach to Los Angeles airport, and should arrive right on schedule in twenty-five minutes. It's a beautiful day in LA, with the temperature currently at a balmy 79 degrees. The captain is turning the seat belt sign on again at this time. We hope you enjoyed your flight."

Shay looked out the window with a sense of vertigo...not from the height but from the series of abrupt changes in her life that had put her there.

She fastened her seat belt, and leaned back, crossing her long, slender legs and looking about at her surroundings. *The back of the plane gets there at the same time,* she thought with satisfaction, *but first class is certainly a lot more comfortable, especially when you're not paying for it yourself!*

Out in the lobby, a chauffeur was waiting, holding a sign that read "MS. LOGAN" in big red letters. Shay introduced herself and he led the way to the waiting car while informing her that his partner was already in the baggage bay, collecting her luggage.

As they walked through the terminal, a young woman of about twenty approached Shay, "Excuse me, but aren't you Natasha Logan?"

Shay still wasn't used to being recognized by "fans," although it was happening more and more frequently of late. *Mercy!* Shay told herself contentedly, *this thing is really putting your name on the map, girl!* She smiled at the girl, "Yes, I am."

"I just love your books, Ms. Logan. I'm in the middle of *The SuperStar's Lady* now. I've got it here somewhere..." she was rummaging through a backpack as she spoke. "*Here* it is! Would you sign it for me, please? My name is Tameka."

"My pleasure, Tameka." Shay signed the book, handed it back, and said goodbye just as a young man approached them.

"Who was that, baby?" Tameka's companion asked her as Shay walked away.

"Natasha Logan," Tameka breathlessly told him.

"Natasha Logan?" The guy shrugged his shoulders. "So who's Natasha Logan?"

Well, that's your *reality check for the day, honey,* Shay laughed at herself.

In no time at all, Shay was settled into the back of a sleek white stretch limo, breezing along the freeway. She looked at her watch. The meeting with Woody Hollister and his manager was set for one o'clock, but she'd agreed to meet Marty half an hour earlier, to go over last minute strategy.

Shay moved her watch back from 3:05 to 12:05, and called to the driver, "I have a meeting at the Riverwalk restaurant at 12:30; is it far from here?"

"Yes, ma'am; it's a pretty good piece away. But we can make it if we go directly there. I can drop you off at the restaurant first, and then deliver your bags to the hotel, if you prefer."

"Thanks. That would be fine," Shay told him. She pulled her mirror from her purse, to give her make-up a fast check. Her slightly slanted dark brown eyes stared back at her. No major damage from the flight, but her lipstick could stand refreshing. With a not quite steady hand Shay carefully applied the lipstick to her full, pouty lips and then needlessly fluffed her shoulder-length black curls.

Shay ran her hands over her smartly fitted suit. She had selected her outfit for this meeting very carefully. Marty had told her, "We don't want to look naive or needy. I want you looking like just what you are—a highly successful and sought after author."

After much consideration, Shay had decided to wear her black and white tailored suit. The white fitted bodice with black collar and lapels and the slim black skirt looked crisp and professional but showed off her tall, curvy figure to best advantage. The three-inch black leather pumps accentuated her height and the length and shapeliness of her legs.

Shay arrived at the restaurant smack on time. Blair Underwood and several companions were leaving just as she entered the door.

Shay caught her breath, but told herself, *Stay cool, girl; if all goes well, you're gonna to have to get used to this kind of thing now,* and just gave them a friendly nod. Intent on her appointment, she didn't notice one of the entourage turning to give her an appreciative glance as she walked past.

Marty was waiting and leaned over to give Shay a quick peck on the cheek as soon as she sat down, "I see you made it in one piece. If it hadn't been for my appointment in San Francisco yesterday we could have flown out together. Welcome to Hollywood, girlfriend! You're sho nuff in the big-time now!"

"Marty! You look fabulous, as always, but I almost didn't recognize you! What have you done to yourself *this* time?"

"*You* should talk! Half the men in here got whiplash checking you out just now. As for *moi,* ten pounds less here..." she patted her hips, "...and fourteen inches more here," she added, stroking her long elegant braids. "What do you think—am I the Weave Queen, or what?"

"I think they weaved those things into your *brain,* that's what *I* think," Shay laughed.

The waiter came then, and they ordered drinks. "Ice tea for me," Shay told him.

"Me, too," Marty told him. "For now," she said to

Shay as soon as the waiter had left. "I need to keep a clear head."

"So..." Shay said, "are the enemy still set to arrive at one?"

"Now, now...that's no attitude to start an important negotiation. They're not the enemy, Shay. After all, we all want the same thing; for Woody Hollister to buy the movie rights to *SuperStar*. It's obvious he really wants it—and why not? It's a natural: a pop superstar having a covert love affair with a woman executive. I can't wait to see the movie myself!"

"Yes, but *you're* the one who said they won't be all that enthusiastic about my terms."

"Well, that's why you've got me, sugar," Marty shot back with a devilish twinkle in her eye. "We'll just make them an offer they can't refuse."

"We *are* still talking about the movie deal, aren't we, Marty?" Shay queried with a raised eyebrow.

"Of course, honey. You know when it comes to business I don't play around. But Woody Hollister is famous, rich, sexy, cute, *and* single." She winked at Shay, "So what's wrong with a little playing around *after* business hours?"

Shay just laughed, but Marty had handled her business affairs since her first book contract and was now one of her best friends as well as her agent. She knew Marty could switch from her usual light-hearted persona to a hard-headed business woman in the blink of an eye, whenever the situation required.

About ten minutes to one, they were joined by Gabriel Lamont, Hollister's manager. Marty had dealt with Lamont before. She had told Shay, "He's a tough cookie, but a straight-up dude. He won't try to pull any fast ones on us; that's not his style."

Shay was expecting a man of about their own age, so she was surprised when the slim, dapper man of about 60 in a three-piece pinstriped suit stepped up to Marty. "Martha, my dear," he took her offered hand and, bending from the waist, lightly kissed it. "You're looking lovelier than ever."

He looked over to Shay, "Gabriel Lamont, at your service, Miss Logan." He bowed to Shay, "I *must* say...stunning as it is, your book's cover photograph hardly does you justice."

"And *I* must say, sir," Marty declared with a laugh, "you're still as elegantly full of it as ever. Now that you've schmoozed us both with that famous Lamont charm, won't you have a seat?"

"Did you have a pleasant flight, Miss Logan?" Lamont asked Shay as he sat down, "...or may I call you Natasha?"

"A very pleasant flight, Mr. Lamont, although my book signing ran late, and I had to take a later plane. I just arrived an hour or so ago. But please call me Shay. I hate Natasha. Too many 'Boris and Natasha' jokes when I was a kid."

"I can relate to that. I've dealt with my share of 'angel' jokes, too. Call me Gabe, love."

The three of them began to exchange generalities, it being tacitly understood no negotiations would begin until the fourth principal arrived.

A few minutes later, Shay, who was sitting with her back to the entrance, became aware of heads turning and a slight rise in the buzz of conversation around them. Suddenly there was someone standing beside her. She looked up into a face she'd seen a hundred times—on television, and in the movies—but was surprised to find herself so shaken by his physical presence.

In the past ten or so years Woody Hollister's multiple talents had elevated him to the pinnacle of the entertainment industry. Along with the rest of the world, Shay had watched him progress from a stand-up comedian, to an actor in dramatic as well as comedic roles, to a director and producer of films, gambling all his newly earned fortune on his first movie. It had been a critical as well as box office success and Hollister hadn't looked back since.

Although he now had investors falling all over themselves to finance his movies, Hollister still preferred to go it alone. "I don't want to lose content approval," Shay remembered him saying in one interview. "I want my movies to *accurately* portray black people and our culture and lifestyles. I won't attach my name to any movie that doesn't."

But now this icon stood before Shay, wearing a black shirt and a charcoal gray suit, looking like an extremely successful businessman. *Well, that's what he* is, Shay mused. But business-like demeanor or no, the brilliance of his eyes gave away the genius behind them.

"Afternoon, ladies; Gabe. Hope I haven't kept you waiting."

"Not at all, Wood," Gabe replied, looking at his watch. "In fact, for once in your life, you're actually smack on time. Have a seat, and let's get this show on the road."

Hollister pulled out the seat next to Shay, flashing his famous lopsided grin. "Hey, man," he said to Gabe as he sat down, "I thought we were meeting with an author and her agent. Either of these lovely ladies could *star* in the movie."

"We can discuss *that* right after the movie rights are settled, Mr. Hollister," Marty said with a smile, extending her hand. "I'm Martha Tibbs." Shay noticed Marty held their handshake a beat longer than was customary. "But you can call me Marty; almost everybody does..." she leaned forward a little, "long as they stay on my *good* side. After that, it's *Miss* Tibbs."

Hollister laughed, "I'll try to remember that." He turned to Shay, "And this is our author."

In spite of herself, Shay felt her breath quicken under his gaze. She was intensely aware of his closeness.

Woody Hollister wasn't "drop-dead" gorgeous, but he was unpretentiously handsome, nonetheless. His light brown eyes seemed to sparkle with humor. In spite of herself, Shay felt like a tongue-tied groupie.

"You're a fabulous writer, Miss Logan," Hollister went on, "I guess that's why we're all here. But let's drop the handles; I'm not much on formality. Most people call me Woody or Wood...or Hollywood." He grinned ruefully, "With *this* name, I guess *that* was inevitable...Natasha."

"The lady prefers 'Shay,' Woody," Gabe advised him.

"Then 'Shay' it is." He looked deeply into Shay's eyes. "But that's a pity. 'Natasha' suits her—beautiful and mysterious." When Shay didn't respond, he added mischievously, "Your writing's great, but so far you haven't *said* a word. You do *speak*, don't you?"

That snapped Shay out of her reticence. She fixed him with a look, "Yes, I do..." she smiled sweetly, "that is, whenever I have a chance to get a word in edgewise."

Woody looked startled as Gabe and Marty burst out laughing, and then started laughing himself, "Ouch! Set myself up for that one."

"Now that we're all on a first name basis—and before my client puts his *other* foot in his mouth," Gabe prompted, "let's get down to business. First off, I'd like to thank the ladies for flying out. It would have been difficult for Wood to get too far away just now. He's doing his one-man show in Vegas."

"No problem, gentlemen," Marty answered. "I *need* to get away from New York every once in a while. And we don't mind *too* much having limos and luxury accommodations forced on us. We have to thank *you*; the arrangements are quite lavish indeed."

"And I've been traveling quite a bit lately, anyway," Shay volunteered. "I just left a book signing in New York."

"And doing an interview shot on Wendy Williams also, I hear," Woody put in.

"Yes, that's right," Shay replied, wondering how he knew.

"That's great," Gabe said. "Any publicity your books get will spill over to help the movie—assuming we can come to agreement. "Now...what about our offer, Shay?"

"Well, Gabe," Shay started guardedly, "naturally I'm thrilled at the prospect of *SuperStar* being made into a movie. To tell you the truth, I don't think the reality of it all has actually hit me yet. I'm still in a state of shock over how successful my novels have been."

"That's understandable," Gabe acknowledged. "But you've got talent. I've read your books; you can write. Don't worry about the business end of it; that's what Martha and I are for. And I don't need to tell you that my client here..." he gestured to Wood, "is the best; as an actor, comedian, *and* as a director."

"So we know we all want the same thing, fellas," Marty put in, reprising what she'd said to Shay earlier. "The questions to be settled now are the terms."

"I think our initial offer was quite outstanding," Gabe responded.

"I'm not as concerned about the money, Gabe, as I am about my story," Shay told him. "*SuperStar* means a lot to me. I put a lot of myself into that book. I've seen other books made into movies that had little more in common with the novel than the title."

"I understand your concern, Shay," Woody joined in, "and in addition to your quite justifiable feelings about your work, it sure wouldn't do your career any good to have your novel made into a botched up movie. But I'm producing this movie, as well as directing it. *My* reputation—and a lot of my money—is on the line here, too. I wouldn't hire a screenwriter who couldn't do your novel justice."

That was Marty's cue, "Who *do* you have in mind for the screenplay, Woody?"

"I've made no commitments, but I'm considering

several people, including Taylor Washington. He co-wrote 'The Works' with me. And I've also thought about just doing it myself. *SuperStar* should be a breeze to adapt as a screenplay. A large part of the dialogue will convert directly to the screen as is."

Marty leaned forward again, "What about *Shay* doing it, Woody?" she said purposefully.

Gabe looked a long moment at Marty, then at Woody, then at Shay. "So *that's* the situation, huh? You ladies have been holding out on me."

Gabe turned to Shay, "I gotta be honest with you, my dear; I don't think there's any way we can go for that. After all, this *is* only your second novel, and darlin', you don't have any experience writing screenplays at all!"

"My second *published* novel," Shay corrected him. "The third one is due to be released in a couple of months. And remember, Gabe, before *Heart Song* I didn't have any experience writing *novels* either."

Marty took up the fight, "Shay *has* written plays, although none have—yet—been published. And you know her bio. Woody plans to make this a musical, right? As well as being a gifted writer, Shay's been a part-time singer and actress for years."

"Yeah..." Gabe leaned back in his seat, "and three years ago she was a full-time junior high school teacher. No offense, Shay, but those are hardly the credentials we're looking for in a screenwriter. This is a big budget production here. We can't take any chances—and *you* shouldn't want us to. As Wood just said, *your* rep is on the line here, as well as his."

"Woody also just acknowledged the novel will easily adapt to a screenplay," Marty countered. "And Shay would be willing to work with a co-writer..." Marty stopped cold. Her eyes lit up. Shay knew that look—and braced herself for whatever bombshell had hatched itself in Marty's enterprising brain.

"Hey! Wait a minute! Wait a *minute!*" Marty exclaimed. "How about Shay and Woody writing the screenplay...together?"

Shay stared at Marty thunder-struck, not saying a word.

Gabe held up his hand, "Now wait a minute, Martha, we don't..."

"No, *listen* to me!" Marty insisted. "Woody said he was thinking about himself and a co-writer. Since he's directing and producing the movie, who better to collaborate with Shay on the screen presentation? And since *Shay* wrote the original story, where could he find a better partner?"

"But, Martha..."

"Hold up, Gabe," Woody interrupted him. "Shay," he turned to her, all the humor gone from his eyes; he was all business now, "you've gotten quiet on us again. I know Marty wouldn't have proposed this unless you two had discussed it first, but I want to hear from you directly. How do *you* feel about this idea?"

"I told Marty I wanted a shot at the screenplay," Shay said warily, "but to be honest, I'd never considered *co-writing* with someone..."

Woody examined Shay a long moment, and then said—very deliberately, "Consider it now."

"Hey, Hollywood," Gabe began anxiously, "I think you and I should discuss this privately before we commit to..."

"We will, man, but I want to hear Shay's answer first." He turned back to Shay, "Well?"

Shay studied Woody, then said tentatively, "I...I'd be willing to try it."

"Great!" Marty said. "All right, then, why don't we set up another meeting in a day or so," she suggested, "and..."

"It won't take that long," Woody said firmly. "Gabe, let's you and I go into the bar. That'll give the ladies a chance to talk this over privately as well."

Gabe gave him an unreadable look but didn't speak as they left the table.

As soon as they were out of earshot Shay turned on Marty. "Have you lost your *mind*?"

Marty looked at her in wide-eyed surprise, "What?"

"Marty! I've never collaborated with anybody before! I don't even *know* Woody Hollister. What makes you think I can *write* with him, for goodness sake?"

"Now look here, girlfriend," Marty told her, "*you're* the one who wants to play Tyler Perry. *I* was all set to take the movie rights deal and run. I told you from the outset you had two chances for doing the screenplay: slim and none. There's no way they're going to let you do it solo, Shay. In fact, I was flabbergasted Woody showed an interest in the collaboration notion." Marty flipped one of her braids back over her shoulder, "*That* was a stroke of pure genius if I do say so myself."

"All right, then, Ms. Genius, so what do we do now?"

"Wait to hear if Gabe is successful in talking Woody out of it—which I doubt—then see how this changes the offer. Are you still willing to take less for the movie rights, if it comes to that?"

"Well...yes...but..."

"But me no buts. Just sit tight, look bored, and leave the haggling to Mama."

"I'm twenty-seven; you're twenty-nine. Just when did you become 'Mama?' "

"When *you* decided to be a screenwriter. Now pipe down. Here they come."

"Well," Gabe began, looking back and forth between Shay and Marty once they reclaimed their seats, "it looks like we may have a deal. I gotta tell you, I still have reservations, but Woody thinks this co-writing idea might be doable."

"Shay..." Woody scrutinized her face, "I don't know you, but I know and respect your work. I hope you feel the same about mine. This is an impetuous idea, but some of my best work came from impetuous ideas. I can see where *this* one has possibilities.

"But I have to make one thing clear from the jump," the comedian was gone; he was dead serious now. "*I'm* the boss. As director/producer, I have final script approval. I'd demand that of any screenwriter. If you and I disagree on a section of script, my decision is final. Can you live with that?"

"Yes. But *I* need to make something clear," Shay countered. "I won't be involved in name only. I respect your experience; I'm willing to defer to your judgment if need be. But I expect my ideas and my input to be taken seriously. Can *you* live with that?"

Shay held her breath while Woody searched her face yet again. "Yes," he finally said, "Yes, I can." Woody broke into a grin, "I wouldn't be so foolhardy as to try to dis *you*. I can already see you're a force to be reckoned with..." he smiled as he offered his hand, "partner."

Shay reached out also, but Gabe gently pushed both their hands down, saying, "One moment. Now that you *artistes* have come to a meeting of the minds, there's still the meeting of the pocketbook to be settled."

"Yes, indeed," Marty agreed. "Now...we're willing to accept your offer for the movie rights as tendered, but how much more are we talking for Shay's services as a screenwriter?"

"My dear Martha," Gabe came back, "you misunderstand me. We're making a concession here, in giving Ms. Logan the opportunity to expand into screenwriting."

All of a sudden we're back to "Ms. Logan" again, Shay noted wryly.

"We expect something in return," Gabe was continuing. "Seems to me since we've acquiesced to this request, a *reduction* in the amount offered would be in order, not an increase."

Marty stared him down, "You're *getting* something in return—a fine screenwriter. An inexperienced one, true, but you can't tell me you gentlemen haven't decided Shay could be a real asset to this project. Otherwise, you'd have never even considered it."

" *'Could'* is the operative word in that sentence," Gabe countered.

Shay tried her best "look bored" as Marty had advised, but was beginning to feel more and more like a ping pong ball.

"Yes, we agree she has potential as a screenwriter," Gabe went on. "But Ms. Logan is untested in this area. As you well know, not every novelist can make the transition to screenwriter. They are two related, but completely distinct arts."

"Agreed," Marty came back. "But this is a completely separate agreement that has nothing at all to do with the value of the work as a film property. And as *you* well know, many novelists become spectacular screenwriters. You obviously feel Shay may be one of them. There's no way I'd allow her to take on that much responsibility—and that much work—without appropriate compensation, and...."

"Look," Woody interrupted, "I know you're each trying to get the best deal for your client, but let's cut to the chase. I'm excited by this project, and I want it.

"So let's say the movie rights offer stands as is. And…" he turned to Shay again, "you back up your faith in your ability by taking one-half percent of the movie's net profits for your contribution to the screenplay, instead of an upfront cash payment."

Before Shay could reply, Marty began to slowly applaud. "Very nicely done," she said. "And with so little time for Gabe to rehearse you, at that."

Both men looked somewhat discomfited, but Gabe

gamely answered, "Okay, you got us. That's what we agreed on before we came back. But nevertheless, it *is* a mutually advantageous deal, Martha."

Marty looked both men over before saying, "I concur. Throw in a non-refundable ten thousand dollar advance, and as far as I'm concerned, it's a deal." She turned to Shay, "But you have the final say…'Ms. Logan.' "

Shay didn't know *what* to say, until Marty leaned over to whisper, "Woody's last movie made seventy-seven million dollars—net."

After a little quick math, Shay silently offered Woody her hand, and they shook on it, this time with no interruption.

"Good," Gabe said firmly. "Well, now that we've got the business all squared away, let's eat. I'm starving. And let's break out the champagne. We've got some celebrating to do!" He motioned the waiter over.

Champagne flowed liberally during the meal. Shay had had a demanding day, and a bit of jet lag was starting to set in, as well. She definitely felt the champagne's effects as they rose to leave.

"Whoa!" Woody put an arm around Shay as she wobbled a bit upon standing. "I think my new partner may have celebrated a little bit *too* much."

"I think you're right," Shay replied, putting a hand to her forehead. "I'm not much of a drinker, anyway. I should have known better." She hadn't realized how tall Woody was. She was five-eight and had on three-inch heels, but the top of her head barely reached his chin.

Woody offered his arm, which a grateful Shay took, and they all walked to the entryway, waiting for the valet to fetch the men's cars.

"I'll drop our guests off at their hotel, Gabe," Woody told him. "It's on my way."

"And if it wasn't, you'd *make* it on your way, wouldn't you, my man?" Gabe retorted with a grin.

"You'd better sit up front with me, partner," Woody said as the valet opened the door to his silver Bentley Continental GT Speed, "...so I can keep an eye on you."

"*Both* eyes, I'd wager," Marty whispered to Shay before she slipped into the back seat, as Woody said goodbye to Gabe.

In a few moments, they were on the freeway. "Feeling better now, Shay?" Woody asked attentively.

"Yes. The fresh air seems to help."

No one spoke for the next several moments. Shay was aware of Woody repeatedly stealing sidelong glances at her. *Bet he thinks I'm going to upchuck all over his leather dashboard,* she thought.

"I wish I could take you," Woody began, "...*both* of you..." he quickly amended, glancing hastily over his shoulder at Marty in the back seat, "out to dinner tonight, but I gotta beat it back to Vegas in time for the nine o'clock show. Hey! Maybe you'd like to fly over with me and *see* the show."

"Well...I don't..." Shay began.

"We'd *love* to, wouldn't we, Shay?" Marty playfully— but not exactly lightly—punched Shay on the shoulder. "After all, now that we've TCB'd, it's time for a little partying."

"I thought that's what we just did," Shay remarked dryly, rubbing her shoulder.

"And anyway," Marty obliviously went on, "this will give you two a chance to get to know each other a little better. You might as well start now."

"You've been on the go for months, Shay. Why don't you take a break for a couple of days?" Woody urged, glancing over at her. "The rest would do you good."

I have *been on the go for months, but how does* he *know that?* Shay pondered. "But I just got *here*." she protested aloud. "I haven't even unpacked yet!"

"So much the better; you don't have to *re-pack* to

leave" Marty put in. "Our business is concluded here, girl—at least mine is." Marty leaned back and crossed her legs, "And I'll be damned if I don't get in some R and R before I go back to that rat race they call New York!"

"You're going to need to find somewhere to live, Shay" Woody pointed out. "You wouldn't be comfortable spending months here in a hotel suite. My real estate agent can start looking for something for you if you can tell me what you'd like," he offered.

He looked over at Shay and smiled that famous grin again, but there wasn't the same self-possession behind it this time; he seemed a little unsure of himself, almost shy. "And if you stay over a couple of days, we can at least start discussing how to begin on the screenplay."

He really *wants us to go,* Shay realized with surprise. *And I thought he was just being polite. Well—why not?*

"Looks like I'm outnumbered," Shay said. "I've never been to Las Vegas—and I could use a couple days rest—and I don't have any appearances for another week—and it *would* give us a chance to start laying a framework for the screenplay, and..."

"Hey, Shay, what is this—'Conjunction Junction?' What a string of 'ands!' " Marty said in exasperation. "Shay, if you wrote like you talk, none of us would be here now! So does all that conjuncture means you're going?"

Woody didn't say anything, but it looked to Shay as if he was holding his breath.

"Sure, why not?" Shay finally said. "It should be fun. I'd love to go, Woody, and it's really sweet of you to invite us."

"Well, hallelujah!" Marty said. "She's finally come to her senses!"

"Great! I'll call ahead, and reserve a suite for the two of you." There was nothing tentative about Woody's smile now. He was beaming. He pulled out his cell phone to tell his assistant to make the needed arrangements. "Glad you're coming," was all he said as it was ringing, but his eyes had a look that said more than "glad."

I hope I know what I'm doing, Shay thought, as the car sped down the freeway.

CHAPTER 2

VIVA LAS VEGAS

"Can you believe this?" Marty exclaimed, lounging on the gold lamé quilted spread covering the enormous round bed.

"Yeah..." Shay said, picking up with thumb and forefinger the two-inch-long black silk fringe on the genuine ostrich leather pillow at her elbow, "if the decorator was going for the *Biggest Little Whorehouse in Nevada* look."

Shay touched the seat cushion next to her on the black leather sofa, "Domesticated it ain't..." she ran her hand across the butter-soft fabric, "but at least it's real."

"Of *course* it's real! Shay, do have any idea how much this suite must cost a night?"

"Oh, you mean they don't rent it by the hour like those no-tell motels with cars parked in back at lunchtime?" Shay asked naughtily.

Marty rolled over on her stomach and put one hand under her chin. "You are absolutely hopeless. How can a woman who makes a living with her imagination not get a kick out of this place! It's so...wanton! So deliciously decadent!"

"Well, since *I* am neither..." Shay stood, giving the sofa one last lingering caress, "I think I'll go to my bedroom, take a shower, and change for dinner."

Having had a light snack on Wood's plane, they'd decided to delay dinner until after the show. Woody said he was always too keyed up to eat before a performance, anyway. Shay was nervous, too—but not for the same reasons.

"For dinner...and the *show*," Marty said purposefully, seeming to read Shay's mind as she swung her legs around to sit on the edge of the bed. "I'm sure Woody arranged the best seats in the house for us—I mean *you*."

Shay stopped in her movement toward the door, and turned to face Marty, hands on her hips, "And what's *that* supposed to mean?"

"It means our esteemed host wouldn't notice for at least an hour if *I* didn't show up. All the way here on the plane... He didn't ignore me—he's too nice to do that—but his attention was centered on *you*."

"Marty, you're...you're imagining things. Anyway, *you* were the one who had designs on the fine Mr. Hollister, not me."

"Yes, I know," Marty sighed. "Alas, it was not to be. Guess I won't be adding an actor to my doctor, disc jockey, and Congressman."

"*Congressman!* Marty, when did you start seeing a..."

"Don't change the subject. Shay, be honest. A woman knows when a man is interested. He's interested, and you know it."

"I guess he is," Shay conceded worriedly. "It...it took me a while to believe that's where he was coming from, but I finally had to admit it to myself."

"Well, excuse *me*. I didn't know having a man like Woody Hollister interested in one was cause to rend one's clothing. What's wrong with you, woman? That man is Grade A Choice!"

Marty stood up, "And don't try to tell me you're not attracted to him, too. I know better, though you've done an admirably good job of trying to hide it."

"Yes," Shay sank down on the bed. "Yes, I *am* attracted to him," she moodily acknowledged.

"I must be missing something here." Marty held her hands palms up, "He likes you..." she gestured with one hand, "you like him," and then the other. "That's a problem?"

"Of course it's a problem! I'm going to be working with him, Marty. On a project that's important for him *and* for me."

"Which means you'll be seeing a lot of him. Considering your mutual captivation, isn't that at least marginally better than being a few thousand miles apart, like you'd otherwise be?"

"Marty, what woman *wouldn't* be attracted to Woody? If we weren't going to be working together, I'd be thrilled to pieces. But neither he nor I need this complication *now*. I'm worried that it's going to affect our working relationship."

"Has it occurred to you," Marty said slowly, "that it might serve to *improve* your working relationship? After all, the story you two will be working on *is* a romance. Maybe a little romance between the two of you will help, not hurt."

"But, Marty..."

"Shay," Marty sat down next to her on the bed, "I don't mean to belittle your uneasiness. In your shoes, I guess I'd be anxious about it, too. All I'm saying is don't go assuming. The work comes first. You know that, and Woody knows it, too. So just hang loose. Don't go borrowing trouble."

Marty gave her a little shove, "Now, go get dressed. We want to make an entrance, but we don't want to be unfashionably late."

In her travels, Shay had learned to be prepared for anything. This wasn't the first time she'd had an evening affair thrust upon her out of nowhere.

Among the casual shorts and slacks she'd brought with her, she also had a black velvet sheath cocktail dress. The dress was strapless, sprinkled with sparkles of silver. She added to the ensemble black suede pumps that were merely a circuitry of straps holding the wafer thin soles to her delicate feet, the three-inch heels made of completely transparent Lucite.

Shay swept her hair up into a loose chignon atop her

head, leaving a myriad of willful curls loose about her face and neck. Then she added the final touch; diamond stud earrings and a modest diamond pendant necklace—two of the splurges made possible by her new found affluence.

"Well, look at you!" Marty exclaimed when Shay walked out of her bedroom into the suite's living room. "Girl, how do you expect the poor man to concentrate on his act with that cornucopia of yours spilling out of the top of that dress?"

"My bodice may be a bit abbreviated, but honey, is that a dress you're wearing or a fringed napkin?"

Marty spun around. Her dress was simply one row of red fringe cascading over another, ending several inches above her knees. "Since I'm not as well-endowed at the top, Ms. Logan, I'm showing off my *lower* half to its best advantage. As the old commercial used to say, 'Nothing beats a great pair of legs!' "

The maître d' apparently agreed. When Shay and Marty arrived downstairs at the showroom entrance, he practically fell over himself leading them to their seats, which were, as Marty had predicted, front row center.

The room was huge, and in Shay's opinion, much more tastefully decorated than their suite. It consisted of a series of white leather booths, raised in sequence approaching the back of the room. Each booth held a spray of real flowers and a small lighted taper.

"Now, this is the life," Marty said, raising her glass in return to an unknown admirer across the room that had so complimented her.

"Why are they staring at us?"

"Because we are two beautiful, unescorted, young black women getting the gold card treatment, you idiot." Marty giggled, "They probably think we're $5,000 a night call girls!"

"Oh, joy, rapture," Shay said dryly. "My life's ambition—to be mistaken for a hooker."

A gray-haired woman in a sequined dress rose from a nearby booth and approached them. "Excuse me, dear," she said to Shay eagerly, "but aren't you Natasha Logan?"

"Yes, I am," Shay replied, surprised at being recognized there.

"Oh, I knew it. Edgar said you couldn't be, but I knew it!" Edgar was apparently the bald gentleman chewing on a huge unlit cigar sharing her booth. "I just love your books, hon. I've got one right now up in my room. I wish I had it here for you to sign, but would you mind signing this?" With a hand covered with rings whose stones most certainly looked real, she handed Shay a pen and a cloth napkin. "My name is Judy Feinstein," she added.

"Uh...sure," Shay signed the napkin, foolishly feeling guilty for aiding and abetting this woman's pilfering of the hotel's linen.

"Thank you, darling!" Mrs. Feinstein gushed. "The girls back home will never believe I met you! What are you doing here..." she lowered her voice, "doing research for your next book?" she asked, as though Shay was on a covert mission.

"Actually..." Marty leaned forward to whisper, looking right and left, as if to make sure she wasn't being overheard, "Miss Logan is Woody Hollister's guest. He's making a movie of her last book, you know."

"My agent," Shay flippantly introduced her, "Martha 'The Lip' Tibbs."

"Oh, how thrilling! I can't wait to go see it! But don't worry, I won't tell a soul!" Mrs. Feinstein replied, thinking she'd been let in on some great showbiz secret. Although, when she got back to her table, she proceeded to tell the couldn't-care-less Edgar, her waiter, the people at the booth next door, and anybody else within earshot.

"Just thanks a whole heap, Marty," Shay shot her way.

"You're welcome. Now hush! The show is starting!"

A chorus line of very scantily clad young women came

out and began to dance about the stage while singing the
song "One" from—what else?—"Chorus Line."

Having warmed up the audience—especially its male
members—at the end of the number the dancers lined up in
two parallel rows from the apron of the stage to the back,
and each gestured with one arm in sequence to the short
flight of steps at stage rear. The curtain at the top of the
stairs began to rise, and there stood Woody, looking laid-
back debonair in a navy blue double-breasted suit.

Now this was the Woody Hollister Shay was familiar
with; center stage, smilingly in command and in control.
Still, it wasn't hard to reconcile this Woody with the man
she'd chatted with about this and that on the plane coming
here. She realized Woody's on-stage persona, at least when
he was doing stand-up, was very close to the person he
really was off-stage: funny, charming, and down to earth.

Two chorus girls mounted the stairs. Wood took one
on each arm, and as they escorted him down the stairs. The
other dancers vanished, after placing a microphone in a
stand and a stool bearing a bottle of water near the front of
the stage.

Just as the trio reached the front, each of the girls gave
Woody a kiss on the cheek and departed.

"Hey, where are you going? Aren't you going to stick
around for the show?" Woody called after them. He looked
ruefully at the audience, "Story of my life, ya'll...the finer
they are, the faster they run." This got brought a laugh
from the audience.

"So how's everybody doing? You all enjoying yourself
in Lost Wages...I mean Las Vegas?" This got a big laugh,
along with a lot of applause and cheers from people who
were apparently enjoying themselves very much indeed.

"Well, glad you're having a good time. But don't
forget you gotta go back home when you leave here. That
is if you still *have* homes when you leave here..." This got
another laugh. "Don't go putting that mortgage payment on

the roulette table, or you may not have a *spouse* when you leave here, either!"

The audience laughed again. A guy near the front called out, "No wife? What's wrong with that?" The woman next to him, who presumably *was* his wife, didn't see the humor. She frowned and gave him a not very gentle elbow in the ribs.

"Hey, man, I'm not getting off into *that*," Woody shot back at him. "In thirty-two years, never took the plunge myself. And your old lady's already on the verge of smacking *you*. I don't want her coming up on stage after me, too!" Even the guy's "old lady" had to laugh at that one.

"I have a couple of very special guests in the audience tonight..." Woody began.

He's not! Shay thought, aghast. But he was.

"With us this evening," Woody was continuing, "is best-selling romance novelist, the lovely Natasha Logan." Woody gestured to where Shay was sitting.

A surprisingly loud wave of applause followed. "Stand up and take a bow!" Marty whispered to Shay, smiling through clenched teeth.

When a spotlight hit her, Shay decided she had no choice, so she stood, faced the back of the room and waved. She was astonished to see several women, including the ever devoted Judy Feinstein, standing. And there were more than a few wolf whistles from men who appreciated the writer's looks, even though they'd never read her work.

"And with her," Woody added as Shay sat back down, "is her agent, the equally lovely Miss Martha Tibbs."

Shay didn't have to tell Marty to stand. Marty popped right up and flashed the room a dazzling smile. She got not quite as big a round of applause but had a slight edge in the whistle department.

"I hope these two ladies don't run off on me, like my recently departed companions," Woody said as the applause died down. "It's not often a man gets to take *two* beautiful women to dinner—without having one of them ready to clobber him! And speaking of dinner, can you believe the stuff these fast food joints are selling these days?" And he was off into his act.

Shay had always thought Woody a brilliant comedian, and tonight was no exception. His humor was fresh, off-beat, and insightful. Shay was even more impressed than before because, on the plane on the way over, he'd told her he wrote most of his own material.

He was on for about an hour, bringing a lot of the audience to tears with laughter at points. When he finally said good night, the crowd rose to its feet and he had to come back on stage to take another bow. As he did, he looked down at Shay and winked. She felt a flush cross her face.

"That man is a genius," Marty laughed, wiping the last of the tears from her eyes. "You've got lively times ahead of you, Shay, working with *him* every day!"

Shay didn't say a word, but was thinking *What am I going to do if the times get more "lively" than I can handle?*

On the way backstage, they were stopped a time or three by autograph seekers. One woman had one of Shay's books in her tote bag! "I don't like to gamble," she explained, "but I dare not leave my husband in the casino alone. So I sit somewhere close by, and read while I keep tabs on him."

By the time they were shown to Woody's dressing room, he'd already showered and greeted them in a terry bathrobe. "Hope you enjoyed the show, ladies," he said, offering them seats.

"Woody, you're sensational!" Marty said, still chuckling, remembering one of his best lines, "Even better in person than on TV!"

"Did you like the show, Shay?" he asked, looking as

though her reply mattered to him a great deal.

"Yes, I did, Woody; you were fabulous!" Shay said sincerely. "But you should have warned us about the introductions," she chided. "I almost dropped my teeth!"

He went to her, and gently grasped her chin, looking thoughtfully into her mouth, "Funny, they don't look like the removable kind to me!" Marty cracked up at that.

"Anyway," Woody added, "You had to be pleased with the reception you got. I didn't realize what a big following you have, 'Ms. Logan'."

"I *was* pleased—and stunned," Shay confessed. "I still can't believe it when people ask me for autographs."

"Better get used to it," Woody advised. "I think it's going to be a permanent part of your life from now on. You're a talented lady."

"With a hungry agent," Marty put in. "Now that you've nourished our psyche with laughter, Mr. Hollister, I believe you promised to feed us, as well."

"Sure did. And I'm starving," Wood replied. "Marty, do you know Darnell Franklin?"

"Well, of course, I know *of* him, but I've never met him; more's the pity. Why?"

"He's here for a celebrity golf tournament. I asked him to join us for dinner, if that's okay."

For once even the Unsinkable Martha Tibbs was momentarily caught speechless. But she quickly recovered. "I think I could put up with one of the finest men on earth for a least one evening," she quipped with a gleam in her eye.

Woody laughed, "Good. Let me make a quick change, and we can go up to my suite. I've arranged for dinner there, so 'Ms. Logan' won't be interrupted by her fans."

"Ms. Logan's" fans weren't the problem when they left the dressing room. There was a sizable crowd waiting for Woody outside, along with a couple of bodyguards. Woody took 15 minutes or so to sign autographs, and chat a bit with his fans before his guards extricated them and escorted them to the elevator.

Woody was in the penthouse, at the very top of the hotel. "Here we are ladies," he said as the elevator opened in the foyer of the suite. Before they could reach the door, it was opened by a tall black man in butler's livery.

"I thought I heard the elevator bell," he said in a musical Jamaican accent. "Good evening, Mr. Hollister."

"Good evening, Richmond. Shay, Marty; my butler, Richmond. Richmond, our dinner guests this evening, Miss Tibbs, and Miss Logan."

Richmond bowed, "At your service, ladies. Would anyone care for a cocktail?"

"I'd like a sloe gin fizz, please," Marty said.

"Certainly, ma'am. And for you, Miss Logan?" Richmond asked, turning to Shay.

"Nothing for me, thank you."

"Has Mr. Franklin arrived, Richmond?" Wood asked.

"Yes, sir. He's waiting in the living room."

"Ladies, shall we?" Wood prompted, directing them to a hallway to the right. "Richmond, I'll have a Remy Martin neat," he said as they walked away.

"Very good, sir."

The living room was huge and beautifully decorated in muted shades of sand, saffron, and black. Darnell Franklin, whose flawlessly handsome face on the silver screen made female hearts flutter all around the world, was flopped in an overstuffed chair in front of the TV. He had one leg thrown over the arm, drinking a beer right out of the bottle. He was watching a prizefight.

"Hey, Hollywood," Darnell called to Woody, not looking up from the screen, "you're missing it, man! Mayweather is kicking ass!"

Darnell looked up then and, abruptly realizing Wood was not alone, quickly stood, buttoning the jacket of his impeccably tailored suit. "Ooops! Pardon me, ladies. I thought Wood and I were going to pick you up at your suite."

"No, knucklehead," Woody said with exaggerated patience.   "I told you we were having dinner here, remember? Shay, Marty, may I present my absent-minded friend, Darnell Franklin? Darnell, this is Shay Logan, my newest business partner, and her agent, Marty Tibbs."

The same feeling of unreality hit Shay as when she had met Woody earlier that day.   Darnell Franklin was so handsome as to take one's breath away.   That, combined with his suave on-screen charm, made him, in Shay's opinion, the first black actor to truly become a "cross-over" sex symbol. Shay, and every other woman she knew, never missed one of his movies.

And he wasn't just a pretty face.   The man was a superb actor.   He'd been passed over for the best actor Oscar two years before. Shay thought he should have won.

"Enchante, mademoiselles!" Darnell declared. "It's an honor to spend the evening in the company of such loveliness! I..."

"Cut the matinee idol stuff, man," Wood said with a laugh, giving him a fond shove. "This ain't your fan club, you know. We can just be ourselves tonight, okay?"

"Okay," Darnell shrugged agreeably.   He turned to Shay and Marty with that devastating world famous smile, "What's happenin'?"

"Oh, I beg to differ, Woody," Marty said, turning her most seductive smile on Darnell. "I for one am a major fan of Mr. Franklin's," she purred, offering her hand to Darnell. "I wouldn't have believed it possible, but you're even more irresistible in person."

"*Well*..." Darnell replied, taking her hand, his interest obviously piqued, "it's certainly evident how a lady with your way with words—and other accouterments—became such a successful writer."

"Uh, *this* is Shay, my man," Wood told him, gesturing

to where Shay was standing, next to him.

Darnell looked crestfallen. "Here I try to put my best foot forward, and it keeps winding up in my mouth. Look, let's start all over again."

He drew his hand down in front of his face, which went completely blank, as though it had been erased. He then came back to life, smiled that dazzling smile again, and extended his hand to Shay, "Hi; I'm Darnell Franklin. Pleased to meet you, Shay."

Shay laughed, and shook his hand, "Likewise, Darnell."

"Look, man, *I'm* the comedian here." Woody put in, trying to look indignant. "And don't start moving in on my date!"

When did I become his "date"? Shay wondered.

"No problem there, my brother," Darnell came back. "Lovely as she is..." he offered his arm to Marty, "I'm busy moving in on my own!"

Darnell escorted Marty to the sofa (making a quick detour to turn off the T.V.) just as Richmond arrived and served their drinks.

"Here's to Wood, his scintillating new partner, and *'The SuperStar's Lady; The Movie'*, " Darnell lifted his glass.

"Hold it!" Woody said suddenly, "Shay doesn't have anything to toast with!"

"After the liquid part of lunch, I thought maybe I'd better pass on cocktails this evening," Shay said.

Woody walked to the alcove containing a small bar, fetched a glass, and poured a swallow of his drink into it. "This is just enough to toast with," he said, handing it to Shay. "Just to make that toast legit."

"And this will make it...friendlier," Marty said, hooking her upraised arm through Darnell's so that their arms were intertwined as they lifted their glasses.

Wood looked at Shay, and slowly put his arm through hers, their eyes locking as they drank the toast. She looked away quickly, uncomfortable under the candid homage of his gaze.

As they moved into the dining room, she covertly watched Wood. She had been totally taken by surprise by him. Not because he was different than she imagined, but because he really was *exactly* as she had imagined him to be.

Darnell was completely different than she would have expected *him* to be. Far from being aloof, coolly urbane, and possibly stuck on himself, as she had pictured him, he was instead friendly, approachable, and unpretentious. And that had been her experience with all the celebrities she'd met of late. Some were better, some worse, than their public image—but all of them were *different*.

But Woody wasn't, and it felt as though she knew him well, although they'd just met that day. She'd envisioned him a brilliant entertainer and businessman, and he was. But he was also intelligent, witty, perceptive, and...and something she couldn't yet define. There was something very special about him she couldn't quite put a name to...yet.

"Don't worry; she'll snap out of it sooner or later," Marty's words sank in.

Shay realized the three of them were staring at her. "Oh...uh, what did you say?"

"I said 'Shay'—three times; quite clearly and distinctly, I believe. What planet were *you* on?"

"I'm sorry, I didn't hear you. The jet lag getting to me, I guess."

"I was saying how much you love shrimp. I'm surprised you haven't mentioned it. These appetizers are delicious."

In truth, Shay hadn't even focused in on what she was eating. "Yes; yes they are," she hastily agreed.

In fact, as the meal progressed, it dawned on Shay that every dish served was one of her favorites; from the French onion soup to the filet mignon, to the twice baked potatoes. When collard greens and cornbread were served, she suspected something was up. *Who serves collard greens with filet mignon except me?* she mused. And when peach cobbler turned up as dessert, she was sure of it. She looked at Woody for some clue, but he was just his usual smiling, charming self, with no hint of anything out of the ordinary going on.

They moved into the living room for after-dinner drinks, and Shay allowed herself a glass of white wine.

"I've got the new Ric Weaver CD," Wood said. "It just came out two days ago. You guys like to hear it?"

"Oh, yes!" Marty declared. "He's my favorite singer! I'm going to get the CD as soon as I get home!"

"But you haven't even heard it yet," Woody chuckled as he put the CD in the player.

"Don't matter. That man could sing the alphabet song, and I'd buy it!"

Ric Weaver's sexy baritone floated around the room. The first cut was an up-tempo number, and Darnell and Marty started dancing. Wood settled next to Shay on the sofa.

"To our collaboration," he lifted his glass to Shay.

"Our collaboration," she echoed, clinking his glass with hers.

"I like Marty's way of toasting better," he said, inserting his arm through Shay's as they had done before. As they drank, his eyes never left hers.

"Speaking of our collaboration," Shay said quickly before the conversation could take another tack, "how are we going to go about this?"

She could sense Wood reorienting himself. Apparently, the project hadn't been the topic foremost on his mind at that moment. "Well, once you get out here, and we really get started, I'm sure a work pattern will establish itself.

"Our first hurdle will be conveying Michael and Alicia's backgrounds. The book starts with them meeting and gives their pasts narratively throughout the first couple chapters. We're somehow going to have to translate that narrative into dialogue."

"I...I had an idea on that, Wood," Shay said tentatively.

"Really? What?"

"Well...I don't know if this will work...but how about a montage of shots under the opening credits, showing each of them growing up? We could start with them as kids, and show brief scenes from their pasts.

"The whole basis of their relationship is having so much in common; although on the surface their lives have been so dissimilar." Shay's voice rose slightly, as she got into her idea. "We could juxtapose scenes to emphasize that; like a shot of Michael at his girlfriend's funeral, and then cut to a shot of Alicia at her husband's. That way, when the movie proper begins, we could start off right where the book does, with their meeting."

Wood just stared at her.

"Not such a hot idea?" Shay asked regretfully.

Wood shook his head, as though clearing it, "You don't talk much, but when you do, you sure have something to say. That's a dynamite idea! I'm ashamed I didn't think of it myself!"

He scrutinized Shay's face, "I think I made the best deal of my life today," he said softly. Just then the second cut of the CD came on, a slow, sultry ballad called "Hypnotized." Marty and Darnell were in a clinch, just barely swaying to the music.

Wood offered his hand, "Would you like to dance?"

Shay took his hand silently, and he led her to the center of the room. Her spine tingled as he put his arm around her, held her close, and they began to move to the music. Wood was a wonderful dancer; Shay felt as if they were floating as he gently and expertly guided her across the floor.

Weaver's voice was velvety and bewitching as he sang the enchanting lyrics. Shay was staring straight ahead, at the knot in Wood's tie. Without a word, his hand left her waist, and he put a finger under her chin, gently tipping her face to look into his eyes.

"Now. That's better," he said softly.

He replaced his hand on her waist, moving their joined hands to meet it, so that Shay stood with one arm behind her back, with both Wood's arms around her. He moved closer and bent down slightly so that their cheeks touched. And they finished the dance that way, cheek to cheek.

At the number's end, Wood said, "I need a breather after that one. Let's go on the balcony."

Wood opened the sliding glass door, and Shay preceded him out onto the balcony. Marty and Darnell had settled on a sofa across the room, too deeply in conversation to even notice as they left.

They were on the 53rd floor. The Las Vegas night spread out below them like a carnival of light. Although the night was warm, there was a slight breeze, and at that height, in the strapless dress, Shay shivered.

"It's a bit chilly. Here," Wood said, removing his jacket. He held it out for her while she slipped it on.

"Well, that will keep you warm," he grinned, "but it covered the best view in the city."

Shay laughed along with him, and thought this a good time to comment, "Dinner was wonderful, Wood."

"Glad you enjoyed it."

"I *had* to enjoy it," Shay said. "It was truly 'wonder-full', in the most literal sense of the word—'full of wonder.' Every dish was one of my favorites."

"Really?" he asked with a meaningful smile.

"Yes, really. Surely you don't expect me to think that was a coincidence."

"Well, surely you didn't expect *me* to go into a multimillion dollar project based on the work of someone I knew nothing about."

His candor caught Shay off guard. She expected him to hem and haw around, not flat out admit he'd looked into her background. "I...I fail to see how what I like to eat affects my competence as a writer."

"So do I," he chuckled, "although a talented psychologist could probably write a thesis on it."

He moved closer to her, "I always get background information on people I do business with. No illegal snooping—at least I don't *think* so. But my staff routinely checks out all available public info on any new business associate. In the course of doing that, they frequently pick up a lot of very personal stuff."

He smiled again, "You've given a lot of interviews lately, Shay. Remember telling Good Housekeeping your favorite foods?"

"Oh...Yes...Well, it was really thoughtful of you, Woody, but you shouldn't have gone to so much bother," Shay murmured shyly.

"It was my pleasure," He moved even closer. "When I got that information, it was as a director interested in a writer. But now," he moved closer still, "I'm glad I have it—as a man interested in a woman."

He reached out to her. Shay knew he was going to kiss her, and she was powerless to stop him. She didn't want to stop him.

Wood gently cupped her face with both hands, and his lips descended on hers, softly, tenderly. It was all Shay could do to keep from putting her arms around him. She felt that floating sensation again, although they were both standing quite still.

After a long delicious moment, Wood pulled back slightly, "I've been wondering all day how that would feel," he whispered.

"How *did* it feel?" Shay whispered back.

He put both arms around her, "It felt like more," he murmured. Woody pulled her close and kissed her again. This time his kiss was more urgent, and as his arms tightened around her, she couldn't resist the urge to embrace him in return, wrapping her arms around his neck.

The sound of the sliding door startled them both, and they turned quickly, to see Marty and Darnell standing in the doorway. "We just came to tell you all we're going down to the casino," Darnell said, a knowing smile on his face.

"We thought we'd join you for a breath of air first," Marty added, "but since you two have already used up all the oxygen, we'll be on our way." And they were gone.

Wood smiled at Shay, "Caught in the act."

"I guess."

Wood reached for her again, "Well, since we've already been found out..."

Shay hastily moved away, "Wood, I think you and I should talk."

"Isn't that what we *have* been doing?"

"Not most recently," Shay told him archly. "Anyway, without your jacket, now you're starting to shiver. Let's go back inside."

Once inside Wood asked, "Would you like another drink?"

"No, thanks, Wood. Look, this has been a really long day for me; I'm exhausted. I think I'd better head for my room."

"Are you angry with me, Shay?" Wood asked; a troubled look on his face.

"No, of course not, Wood. It's just that...that..."

"That you're worried about us working together after what just happened, right?"

Shay looked him in the eye, "Yes, Wood. Yes, I am."

"Look, sit down a minute...please."

Shay somewhat apprehensively sat on the sofa.

"Shay," he sat down next to her, "I'm concerned about it, too. I make a point of never getting involved with anyone I work with. I was attracted to you the first moment, but I tried to deny to myself it was happening. Well, I can't deny it anymore."

He took her hand, "I'm fascinated by you, Shay; as a person, and as a woman, and that feeling is not going to just go away." He paused, "I was afraid the feeling wasn't mutual, but now I'm hoping..."

"It's mutual," Shay whispered.

"Good." He looked deeply into her eyes. "We're both professionals, and we both know how important this project is. I don't see where our feelings for each other could be a problem, Shay. At least, not one we can't handle.

"Anyway, seems the question is moot. We're going to be working together, and since these feelings are not going away, we'll have to deal with the situation as is."

"Yes," Shay agreed. "But let's make an agreement. We'll down-pedal the relationship side of it until the screenplay is finished. Then..."

"...Then we can go for it," Wood finished for her, with a mischievous gleam in his eye.

"What a way to put it!" Shay laughed, "but you've got a deal." She stood, "Come walk me home."

At the door to her suite, Shay said, "I would ask you in but..."

"I know," Wood replied. "But can I at least kiss you good night?" He didn't wait for an answer, but immediately took her in his arms, and gave her a kiss Shay could tell was difficult for him to restrain. She understood precisely how he felt—because she felt the same.

Shay slipped through the door and was not at all surprised to find Marty wasn't there. She went into her own bedroom and started to get ready for bed.

Just as Shay was preparing to turn out the light, she heard the outer door open. "Shay? Shay, are you here?"

Marty called.

"In my room."

Marty came in and plopped down on the bed, "Whew! What a night!"

"Where's Darnell?"

"I sent him home...well, back to his hotel, anyway. Imagine me, Martha Denise Tibbs, sending *Darnell Franklin* home! But it was the only way."

"The only way to what?"

"To keep him. Darnell has women throwing their panties at him twenty-four seven. I almost had to stomp some wench downstairs. She kept getting in his face, even with me on his arm!

"The only way to keep a man like Darnell interested is to not be one of the crowd. That's why I told him no, and sent him on his way." She rolled her eyes, "And, honey, that was the hardest 'no' I ever said in my life! Well, at least I won't have to wait around wondering if I'll ever see him again."

"Did he ask you for another date?"

"Not exactly. He's the newest client of M. D. Tibbs, literary agent to the rich and famous."

"What!"

"He's been approached about writing a book about blacks in film, and his experiences. The book should be a blockbuster. And he's going to write it all himself—no ghostwriter. I think he can do it, too. The boy's not only gorgeous; he's got a head on his shoulders. He's got a Master's in literature, you know."

"No, I didn't know. And he asked you to represent him?"

"Sure did. He's got a whole staff of agents and aides and whatnot, but of course, he doesn't have a *literary* agent. So he asked me. He said, 'If you could get a sweet deal like that out of Wood, I want you in *my* corner.' "

"Marty, that's fabulous—for both of you!"

"Yep. Handling Darnell will make me one of the best-known literary agents in the country—and make me a pile of money, to boot."

Her face softened, "But that's not why it's so important to me, Shay. The main reason is...I'll get to spend time with him."

Shay had never seen that look on Marty's face before. "So *that's* the way it is, huh?"

"Yeah," Marty replied softly. "Looks like the huntress has finally been captured by the game." After a moment she said, "Speaking of which, what are *you* doing here?"

"Where else would I be?"

"Don't get coy with me, girlfriend. I caught your Romeo and Juliet balcony scene."

"Things *were* getting pretty hot and heavy there for a moment," Shay conceded. "But Wood and I talked it over. I'm attracted to him, Marty..." she looked away, "a lot. And he's attracted to me," she added in a whisper. "But we agreed to put that aspect of our relationship on hold until the screenplay is finished."

"And then...?"

"And then," Shay said with a joyful smile, "...we'll see."

They said good night, and Marty went off to her room. As Shay fell asleep, the song going around and around in her head was Ric Weaver's, but the face she saw before her was Woody's.

CHAPTER 3

THE WIZ

"Where's this one go, Miss?"

"In the study alcove, off the master bedr...Hey!" Shay ran over and righted the box just as it was about to slip off the dolly. "That's my livelihood you've got it that box. Be careful!"

The mover gave her a "yeah; sure, lady" look, and trundled her computer into the study.

Shay looked around her. She really loved this house. Aside from it being glorious, she loved it because it was hers; the first house she'd ever owned.

And who'd have ever thought when I finally bought a house, I'd be able to pay cash *for it?* she marveled.

True to his word, Wood had gotten his real estate agent, Marge Harris, to help Shay find a place to live in or near LA

"But are you sure you want a *house*?" Marge kept asking at first. Since Shay was in LA only to work on a finite project, Marge assumed she'd want a furnished luxury apartment.

Which probably made more sense, Shay had admitted. But she'd lived in apartments ever since she'd left her parent's home, and she wanted the privacy and freedom of a house. Anyway, now she could afford one.

Even after the novels began to earn enough money for her to feel confident quitting her job, Shay hadn't moved from the apartment she'd had when she was teaching. Her teacher's salary sure hadn't made her rich, but as a single woman with no one to support, she had been able to afford a nice two bedroom luxury apartment in a good neighborhood; initially going for the extra bedroom as a guest room.

When she began to write in earnest, the second

bedroom slowly evolved into an office. And although her friends didn't understand why she hadn't moved somewhere more upscale when the bucks really started rolling in, Shay was quite comfortable there.

But once she knew she'd be in LA for an extended period to work with Wood, she thought the time was right to make a move. After all, it didn't make sense to have the apartment sitting vacant for months, anyway. One of the great things about writing for a living was she could live anywhere, and take her office with her.

But now that she'd forayed into the world of screenwriting, she was hoping additional screenwriting other opportunities would come her way. She had an idea in mind for an original screenplay; and for a screenwriter, LA was the place to be. Anyway, the house was selling for an incredibly low price; low enough to make it a good investment, even in today's market. If she decided not to stay in LA, she should be able to sell it for at least what she paid for it, if not more.

So she put most of her things in storage and shipped the essentials—her clothes, her computer and writing materials, and a few other things she couldn't live without—to the coast.

Marge had difficulty finding a house that suited Shay, and then this one came along. Shay originally planned to rent a house, but the previous owner of this one wasn't interested in a rental deal; he only wanted to sell. He was moving to Italy and was anxious to liquidate his LA holdings, which was why the house was priced so reasonably. When he offered to leave most of the furnishings, which he was planning to just sell off anyway, that was the deciding factor for Shay.

"Hey, lady," a voice said, "heard you were looking for a handyman...and I'm the handiest man I know."

Oh no! Now *what?* Shay thought and turned to send this pest, the latest in the unending series of people determined to sell her some good or service, on his way. But it was Woody, standing there grinning.

"Wood! I didn't know you were in town! When did you get back?"

Woody had been in Cann at the film festival when Shay had arrived back in L. A. the previous week. He'd called to apologize for not being there to greet her. Shay felt a thrill go through her to see him again. Although she thought *He* would *have to see me again for the first time looking like this, in old worn out jeans, my hair in a ponytail, and no makeup.*

"Got in just this morning," he told her. "As you can see," he gestured to his T-shirt and jeans, "I came ready to work."

"And work you shall, sir. Moving is just marginally less painful than a root canal. I'll take all the help I can get. But let me show you the house first."

By the ritzy standards of Beverly Hills, the house was modest. It was the smallest one in the neighborhood. But all its wonderful features—the sunken living room with fireplace, the spacious ultra-modern kitchen, the attached two car garage, the basement rec room—made it a jewel of a house.

"But this is what really sold me," Shay said, leading him to her bedroom. The master bedroom was huge, with sliding glass doors that led to the deck surrounding the house on three sides. The bedroom had its own bath, with Jacuzzi; and it had an attached study.

"This is perfect for my office," Shay said, showing him the study. "It can be entered from the living room, as well, through that door," she said pointing.

"I like this entrance better," Wood replied, leaning against the other door frame, looking longingly back into her bedroom.

"Well...uh...Let's go into the kitchen. I've started some coffee," Shay said quickly.

With Wood there to keep the movers in line, things progressed speedily. At one point, when Wood was helping them unpack Shay's computer, one guy said, "Hey, man; aren't you Woody Hollister?"

Wood looked at him as though he were crazy, "Yeah, right. I'm sure Woody Hollister would be here sweating over these boxes."

The guy left to get another box, chuckling over his silly mistake.

Wood looked at Shay, and winked, "Works every time."

In no time all the stuff was in, and Shay and Woody were sitting in the living room, pausing for another cup of coffee, discussing the screenplay. They'd been in constant phone contact over the past month, while she went home to Detroit, preparing to move, and they had already worked out an approach to the work.

What Shay hadn't told Wood was that she'd already started, and had 25 pages of a screenplay already finished. She told him then and watched anxiously while he read it.

About ten pages in, he looked up, "Well, I don't know what you need *me* for."

"You like it?"

"It's good—needs a little re-write—but good; very good. You've got us off to a terrific start, Natasha."

"That's *Shay*, Mr. Hollister."

"I don't understand why you don't use your full name; it's beautiful...Natasha."

"You should talk—-*Woodrow*."

"*Would* that it was that simple—no pun intended. At least there was a President named Woodrow. My name's not Woodrow, Shay."

"It's not? Well, what is it?"

Woody looked at her self-consciously for a beat before saying softly, "It's Woodington."

"It's *what*?"

"It's 'Woodington', Shay."

Shay paused a moment before asking, "Uh...How did you wind up with a name like Woodington?"

He smiled resignedly, "Wait; it gets worse." He stood, and drew himself up to his full height, "My full legal name is Woodington James Hollister—the third. So you see how I got it. I inherited it."

Shay blinked, "Good Lord."

"Woodington was my great-grandmother's maiden name, and *her* father was born a slave. He was one of the first post-slavery blacks to get an education, and he became a teacher." Wood paused a moment, remembering.

"I'm sure you know that during slavery it was illegal for blacks to learn to read," he continued. "Anyone who taught a slave to read was severely punished. So my ancestor spent his life teaching other black people how to read. However, even though slavery had by then *technically* ended, he was caught teaching—and lost his life because of it."

Shay looked up at Woody, spellbound by this tale.

"He had no sons. Understandably, my multi-grandma, his daughter, was proud of him and didn't want his name to die with him, so she named my grandfather Woodington."

"What a sad—and beautiful—story. It's a name you should be proud to bear."

"It's a mouthful. When I was a kid, I sure got into enough fights because of it. But when I got old enough to understand... Yes, I *am* proud of it."

"You know, it's not that it's an *unattractive* name. It's just such...such..."

" 'A mouthful?' " Wood suggested.

"Yeah," Shay laughed. "But it has a ring to it. It sounds...noble. Like you should be a duke, or an earl, or something."

Wood looked at Shay and starting singing softly, "'Duke...Duke...Duke...Duke of Earl...Duke...Duke...'"

And Shay laughingly joined in, "'Duke of Earl...Duke...Duke...Duke of Earl...Duke...Duke...'"

Wood suddenly burst out with the first verse in a surprisingly good tenor. They went on with the song, Shay trying her best to sing back-up, although her voice was too definitely soprano to be truly effective on the bass line.

At the end of the song, Wood collapsed next to her on the sofa, laughing.

Over the next two weeks, they established a pattern. They'd work on the screenplay separately, and then meet to dissect what they had written. Revisions were no problem. If Wood came to her place, he'd bring what he'd written in printed format, but would also drop it to a flash drive. That way, after they'd made changes to both their contributions, they could go into Shay's study, and edit the script right then and there, on her computer, combining his stuff with hers.

Late one evening, right after Wood had left, Marty called from New York, "Hey, girl! How's it going?"

"It's going great, Marty," Shay said, curling up on the sofa. "In fact, Wood just left. We usually work here, but sometimes I go to his place, just for a change of pace. Marty, you should see it! What a spread! But the script's going fine. We mesh like clockwork working together. You were right; this was the best idea you ever had."

"Has there ever been an occasion when I *wasn't* right?" Marty asked with—for her— typical modesty.

"In business, no. But I seem to remember a night in New York when we just barely escaped going to jail because you..."

"Never mind. I saw you on the tube last night. The Academy Awards! That had to be a blast!"

"You saw *me*?"

"Yeah, I caught you a couple of times when the camera panned the audience. I mean, you *were* sitting right up front, honey."

"We had to, so Wood could slip backstage quickly when his turn came to be a presenter. And it *was* a blast! It was all I could do to keep from craning my neck to check out all those celebrities!"

"I hate to be the one to break it to you, dear, but you're a bit of a celebrity yourself, now. And that appearance on Wendy Williams sure didn't hurt. The bookstores can't keep *Superstar* on the shelves," Marty said gleefully. "Honey, you just bought me a new BMW!"

"Be that as it may, I'm sure not in the same league with those folks. Although, when Wood took me to the after party, Whitley Halston told me 'I'm one of your biggest fans'. Can you imagine Whitley Halston being *my* fan?"

"What's she like, anyway?"

"Just as nice and down to earth as you please. We're going shopping and out to lunch this weekend."

"I knew you'd make 'em stand up and take notice. But back to Wood. What about the *other* factor? "

"So far, that's going fine, too. Wood's been true to his word and kept our bargain. He hasn't even mentioned...er...Las Vegas...Still..."

"What?" Marty asked eagerly.

"Well, I make a point of us entering my study through the living room—not the bedroom—entrance," Shay told her.

"Why?"

"Just to be on the safe side. After all, he's only human—and so am I."

Wood's manner toward her had been just that of a friendly colleague, but she frequently caught a flash of smoldering fire in his eyes when he looked at her and knew it would only take a word from her to re-kindle it.

"Enough about me," Shay said changing the subject she didn't want to think about—just yet. "How did it go with Darnell last week?"

"Oh, it was wonderful," Marty sighed, using the muted

voice she used only when talking about Darnell. Darnell had gone to New York for an appearance on The Tonight Show. "I went to the show with him, and afterward we went out to dinner and...back to my place."

"So it was 'yes' this time, huh?"

"Yeah. He calls me almost every day. I think there's really something happening here, Shay." Her voice got even softer, "At least, I hope so.

"Anyway," her voice got brisk again, "he's coming back out in a month or so to sign his book contract, and he invited me out there for that party Wood's giving in a couple of weeks."

"Yes, Wood told me. I can't wait to see you!"

The following week, Wood started casting for the movie. He wanted to be ready to start shooting as soon as possible. "Even if we don't have the screenplay completely finished when we start shooting, it's no problem," he told Shay. "You're so great at this that I can leave the bulk of the writing to you, and just help out with the revision and editing. That leaves me freer to take care of the other stuff."

But it did create one problem. When, much to her surprise, Shay was invited to be a presenter at the Black Media Awards, Wood was already obligated to a trip to New York, to woo stage actress Vanessa Sweet into taking the role of Alicia. He wouldn't be there to escort Shay to the program.

"Maybe I could call her, and set up another time for the interview," he said.

"But do you think that would be a good idea?" Shay asked. "You said the lady was rather difficult to deal with as it is, and you do really want her for the part."

"Yeah, I do. The two leads have *got* to be right, or the whole movie will fall apart, and I'm having a hard enough time casting a Michael."

"Why don't you play him, Wood? I've heard you sing;

you're pretty good."

"'Pretty good' ain't gonna cut it for this role. And nobody should know that better than you, Shay. You created this character. Did you create Michael as a 'pretty good' singer?"

"Uh...no," Shay admitted sheepishly.

"Damn right you didn't. I'm thinking of casting myself in a smaller role, but I couldn't handle this one even if I wanted too. I'm wearing enough hats as it is, directing and producing this thing. Michael is a big-time demanding role.

"And anyway, I'm just not right for it. I need a Michael that's dynamite; as a singer and in the looks department. I haven't broken many mirrors lately, but I'm not the kind of man women swoon over."

"About a million of your fans would disagree with you on that point," Shay said, "and I'm one of them." She was rewarded by his lopsided grin. "Well, how about Darnell? Is he handsome enough for you?"

"Loverboy would be perfect in the looks department, but he's already working on a movie, and I wouldn't want to wait 'til he's free. Anyway, Shay, have you ever heard Darnell sing?"

"No."

"If you're lucky, you never will. I don't want to dub Michael's singing. It's too critical a part of the character. I need an actor who can really sing..." Woody paused a moment, "Or a singer who can really act. Either way, but I need that authenticity. Well, I'm working a couple of angles for Michael, but in the meantime, I really want Vanessa Sweet for Alicia."

He shook his head, "I hope I'm not making a mistake casting that hellion. By all accounts, she's a holy terror to direct. But she's a great actress, and perfect for Alicia."

"Then I think you have to go for it, Wood. And I don't think it would help to start by ticking her off, by postponing your meeting with her."

"You're right.   I'm having a hard enough time convincing Her Theater Majesty that doing a movie isn't a step down from 'the legitimate stage.' "

Wood sighed in disgust.   "The timing couldn't be worse. Gabe could take you to the awards program, but of course, he's going with me. And Darnell is still on location in Zimbabwe. Listen, you haven't met him yet, but I've got this friend, Tony, who's a film editor, and he could..."

"No, thanks. I'm nervous enough about this already without going with somebody I don't know. Don't worry about me, Wood. I'm a big girl, and I'm okay going stag. The awards committee is providing me with a limo and driver, and that's really all I need; a way to get safely there and back. I'll be fine."

But Shay wasn't so confident when the big day came, and she was standing alone backstage at the award program, feeling lost. She didn't see any of the few people she'd met in LA, and was wondering what to do next when a thin tuxedoed man with a clipboard bustled up to her. "And you are?" he asked brusquely.

"Ah...Shay Logan," she told him, wondering who the hell he was, and why he wanted to know.

"Shay Logan...Shay Logan," he repeated, checking his clipboard. "There's some Natasha Logan listed here, but no *Shay* Logan."

"Well, 'some' Natasha Logan is me," Shay replied, starting to get annoyed with this officious idiot.

"Well, why didn't you say so?" he snapped back. "Do you have any ID? Where's your backstage pass?"

He caught Shay off guard with that one, "I...I didn't know I was supposed to have one, and..."

"We get all kinds of nuts trying to get backstage at these affairs," he eyed her suspiciously. "Without a pass, how am *I* supposed to know who you are? How do I know you're really this Natasha Logan?"

"Because *I* say she's Natasha Logan," a resonant voice

came from behind Shay.

Shay turned and found herself looking right up into the eyes of Ric Weaver.

But Weaver wasn't looking at her. His eyes were boring a hole into the pompous ass that had been harassing her.

"Oh...Mr. Weaver...I didn't know...well, of course, if *you* vouch for the lady..."

"In case you weren't listening, buddy, I just did. Now, why don't you shove off, and find Miss Logan a dressing room, where she can wait for her appearance?"

"Certainly, Mr. Weaver." He looked a Shay with a new found respect, "I'll be back for you shortly, Miss Logan."

As the guy hustled off, Weaver shook his head, and smiled at Shay, "What a jerk."

"Th...Thank you," Shay stuttered. "I don't know what I would have done if you hadn't come along."

Weaver was tall and athletic, but his every movement was nonetheless elegantly graceful. His face entranced her with its smooth deep chocolate complexion, high cheek bones, and bottomless dark brown eyes fringed with heavy lashes.

Shay thought some men looked silly in tuxedos, but Ric Weaver looked like a prince. In fact, it was impossible to imagine this man not looking magnificent in *anything* he wore, or—the thought flitted through Shay's subconscious—nothing at all. *Good Lord!* she thought, *What a man! They don't call him "Dream" Weaver for nothing!*

"It would have been all right," Weaver was continuing. "He knows people sometimes don't get their passes delivered in time. He takes so much crap from some of my mega-ego colleagues that he tries to bully anybody else he thinks he can get bad with it. Well, I guess we can't expect *him* to recognize a best-selling author when he sees one.

The chump probably can't even read."

The thought that popped into Shay's head popped out her mouth before she knew it, "How in the world did *you* know I was?"

"I saw you on Wendy Williams." He gave her his slow, easy smile again as he checked her out from head to toe, "And I gotta say, great as you looked on the tube, it ain't nothin' compared to the real thing."

Shay could have echoed those words. As many times as she'd seen Ric Weaver on TV, and in videos, it didn't come close to the electric impact of his physical presence. Everything about this man was sensual, from his dazzling smile, to the warm depth of his voice, to those smoldering dark brown eyes. Shay felt herself getting lost in his eyes, and realized with a start he was waiting for her say something.

"Well...well...thank you again. I'm nervous enough already about this without that additional hassle."

"Nervous? For what?" Weaver replied. "You don't have anything to be nervous about. You're a beautiful, talented woman." He looked her over again, "And you're wearing a beautiful dress that you fill out in a *very* talented way. Don't worry about a thing; you'll be great."

"Hey, man," a voice called out. Shay looked up and saw a tall slender dude with salt and pepper hair motioning to Weaver, "Don't you know you're on next? You best to hump it on over here, or they're going to wind up introducing an empty stage."

"Okay, Book; on my way." Ric gave Shay one last smile, "Well, gotta go to work."

"Break a leg...Mr. Weaver," Shay said shyly.

"It's 'Ric' to all lovely ladies. And tradition be damned, I'm not going to wish you the same—those legs are too gorgeous to come to any harm...Shay."

He started to walk away, but turned back suddenly, "Shay..." he repeated. "I like that. It suits you. Well, catch you later."

Just as Ric started for the stage entrance, Mr. Bustle came back and deferentially escorted Shay to a dressing room. While a make-up artist was touching up Shay's hair and make-up, they watched the program on a monitor.

As well as presenting, and receiving, an award that evening, Ric was part of the entertainment. Screams came from all about the room as he was introduced, and stepped on stage.

"That man is *too* fine." the make-up girl said to Shay, her eyes glued to the monitor.

"He sure is," Shay agreed.

"And he's so sexy! He could put his shoes under *my* bed anytime. He's so fine he doesn't even need to sing, but what a voice! And he also *wrote* that song, you know."

As providence would have it, the song Ric chose to perform that night was "Hypnotized," the same dreamy ballad Shay and Wood had danced to in Las Vegas. But she wasn't thinking about Wood then. She couldn't take her eyes off the monitor as Ric sauntered across the stage, in sync with the seductive rhythm of the music.

Shay was mesmerized, unable to look away, and only she truly knew why.

When she wrote, Shay always had a model in mind for each of her characters; a friend, a family member, someone she knew or knew *of,* and tried to capture the essence of that person in her character. Unknown to anyone, the model Shay used for the character Michael was...Ric Weaver.

Shay had meant it when she'd told Wood she put a lot of herself into her novel. She always thought one reason her novels were so successful is that she unfailingly fell in love with each of her heroes as she was writing, and Michael was no exception.

And as she watched Ric smoothly maneuver the stage, she realized she'd felt such a jolt when she met him because it was as though her Michael, the perfect man born of her imagination, had come to life, and was standing before her.

As Ric's song ended, Mr. Bustle came back for Shay; it was almost time for her presentation. She'd been so absorbed in watching Ric she'd forgotten to be nervous about her own appearance. And it actually helped, as she stood in the wings waiting to be introduced.

She smoothed her skirt, the feel of the satiny fabric further calming her. Ric was right; this was a beautiful dress. The modesty of its long tight sleeves and full floor-length skirt served only to emphasize the scoop neckline, so deeply cut as to be just this side of audacious. The jet black background was covered with a pattern of widely placed tiny red stars, whose fire was echoed in the small ruby pendant and matching earrings she wore. Her five-inch Louboutin heels were also black satin, with narrow red piping around the vamp, and of course the trademark red sole.

Her name was called, and as she stepped on stage, Shay received a very reassuring round of applause. Being on stage was not new to Shay. She'd moonlighted as a singer and actress for years, even doing some local TV and radio commercials. But she was used to being on stage as a character, not as herself.

Still, as she walked to the podium, she felt confident. Suddenly, Ric was in the wings on the other side of the stage. He grinned and gave her a thumbs up. She almost stumbled, shocked at his unexpected appearance, but then felt even more assured by his support.

Shay safely reached the podium, read the prepared speech on the teleprompter, and then her function was basically over. All that remained was to applaud as the excited recipient came on stage, hand him the award with a peck on the cheek, and stand smilingly by while he made his acceptance speech, which was mercifully brief. He then offered Shay his arm and escorted her offstage.

Whew! Glad that's over, she thought.   But she felt she'd made a good showing. The program was almost at its end, and people backstage were all preparing to leave, excitedly talking about the after party for the event.

Shay found her way back to the dressing room and retrieved the tote bag she'd placed under the make-up counter.   As she approached the backstage entrance door she pulled out her cell phone.   Her driver had told her to call when she was ready to leave.

She found the mobile phone number he had given her and punched it up.   "Hi, Sylvester. This is Miss Logan. I'm ready to leave now."

"Yes, ma'am.   I'm in the parking lot, but I'm way at the back, and there's such a jam out here, it's going to take me a half-hour or so to get to the entrance."

Damn, Shay thought. *Well, I'm sure not standing around here like a dummy for half an hour.*   "Then I'll come to you," she told him.

"You'll what?"   Obviously, that wasn't an option most of his passengers would have chosen. "Then I'll walk up to the stage door to fetch you," he offered.

"Sylvester, there's a thousand people milling around out there.   I'll be perfectly safe.   Just sit tight, and I'll be there in a few minutes."

Hanging up the telephone, she looked around for somewhere to sit.   There was a stool against the wall.   She sat down and reached into her tote bag for the Nikes she'd brought with her.   *No way am I wearing five-inch heels traipsing around in that jungle of limos looking for Sylvester,* she thought.

She put on the sneakers and was picking up her bag to leave when a voice said, "Interesting fashion statement. But I think your other shoes are a bit more simpatico with that ensemble."

She knew before she looked up that it was Ric.   He stood with his arms crossed, nonchalantly leaning against the wall, gazing down at her with an amused look in his eyes.

Shay felt the shock of his presence once again *But damned if I'll let you know how shook up I am, Mr. "Dream" Weaver.*

"I agree," Shay replied, trying her best to sound nonchalant herself, "but they're not real good for limo safaris."

He blinked, "I beg your pardon?"

"I have to go hunt down my limo. My driver's stuck in a jam somewhere in the back of the parking lot. So I'm going out to meet him."

"What's he doing back there? My car is right out front."

"That, sir," Shay informed him, "is probably why mine can't get to the door. I'm afraid I'm not in your league. My car apparently didn't rate parking 'right out front.' "

"Even after you get to it, it's going to take you forever to get out of the parking lot. You'll be late getting to the party."

"Oh, I'm not going to the party, anyway."

A look of concern crossed his handsome face, "You aren't? Why not?"

"Well, I don't know many of the people that will be there, and..."

"Where's your escort?" Ric suddenly asked, as though that thought had just occurred to him.

"Don't have one, other than Sylvester."

"Sylvester? Who's he?"

"My driver."

"Well, tell you what," Ric said, stepping toward her, "I've got a limo, too. And I'm dateless, too. So instead of having the devastating Sylvester drive you home, why don't you go to the party with me?" He was right in front of her now, "But you gotta change those shoes," he finished with a grin.

Shay was caught speechless, "Well, ah...I..."

"Oh, come on," Ric urged. "Whatever you might have heard about me, I don't bite, at least..." he said with a wicked ambiance, "not unless I'm *asked* to. And the party's going to be a blast."

When Shay continued to hesitate, he added, "Look, Shay, all kidding aside, the party really will be a lot of fun. It's a great place to network, too. And I promise to be on my best behavior."

Shay had to smile at that one, "No offense, Ric, but from what I've read, even your *best* behavior isn't very...uh...commendable."

"Au contraire," Ric leaned forward to whisper, fixing her with a suggestive look, "I've been commended for it often."

Although the prudent side of her brain still had reservations, the other side said *Girl, are you nuts? Are you going to turn down a chance to go out with* Ric Weaver? But it wasn't his star status that finally made up her mind, it was the man himself. His eyes were compelling, inviting. She found it difficult to look away. And she felt as though she knew him. He was so intertwined with Michael in her mind she had difficulty separating this real man from her imaginary one.

"But what'll I do about Sylvester?" Shay finally said aloud.

"He's a big boy. I'm sure he can find his way home all by himself. You can call him when we get to my limo," Ric said, taking her hand, leading her away. A lightning bolt flashed down her spine at his touch; she was powerless to resist.

The crowd out front still hadn't thinned much by the time they reached the front exit. Just before they got there, Ric said, "Better change those shoes now, honey; there are a lot of cameras out there. They'd zoom right in on *those*," he pointed to the Nikes.

There was nowhere nearby to sit, so Shay held on to Ric's arm as she bent to change shoes. She caught her breath when he instead slid his arm around her waist to support her. After she put her Nikes back into the tote bag, Shay quickly called Sylvester with the change in plans.

Then Shay and Ric exited the building. The instant they stepped out the door, women in the crowd surrounding the entrance started to scream. Photo flashes were going off like crazy, along with the steady, blinding lights of video cameras. Microphones sprouted up like weeds, all stuck in Ric's face—and hers—as they made their way to the curb.

But none of this seemed to faze Ric in the slightest. He stopped to wave at the crowd, and the screams increased in intensity. Reporters were calling out to him, "Any comments about your award, Ric? Look this way, Ric. Who's the lady, Ric?"

At that question, a woman reporter turned the male colleague who had asked, "You big dummy," she told him. "That's Natasha Logan, the romance novelist."

Then some of the reporters switched their questions to, "How long have you been seeing Ric, Natasha? How did you two meet, Miss Logan?"

Following Ric's lead, Shay said nothing in reply and just smiled as Ric took her arm, and led her to his black stretch limo. As they approached it, his driver opened the rear door, and Ric motioned her in.

In the back of the car was the man that had hustled Ric on stage. He seemed surprised to see Shay. Ric hopped in after her, and said, "Shay, this is my manager, Booker Madison. Booker, Miss Shay Logan, the novelist."

"Pleased to meet you, Miss Logan," Booker said. But I thought your first name was 'Natasha.' "

Now, how did he know that? Shay wondered, but said, "Pleased to meet you, too, Mr. Madison. Natasha *is* my real name, but I prefer Shay."

"And speaking of names," Ric interjected, "why don't you make like *your* name, man—and book.   You too, Andre," Ric called to a burly guy sitting up front with the driver. "Miss Logan and I want a little privacy. Why don't you gentlemen move to the other car?"

Booker turned an inscrutable look on Shay but just said, "Nice to have met you," as he opened the door, and left.

As soon as the guy in the front followed suit, Ric called to the driver, "To the party, Jose," and pushed a button that raised a privacy screen, sealing off the back of the car, as it pulled away from the curb.

"You didn't have to send them away," Shay said. "I would have enjoyed talking with your manager."

"I thought we could get to know each other better one on one," Ric replied, sliding closer to her.

"And what 'other' car?" Shay asked, not that she really wanted to know; it just seemed a safer subject for discussion than whatever Ric had in mind.

"I have to bring a security crew with me to things like this," he said. "There's another car behind us with my bodyguards."

"Do you have to use bodyguards everywhere you go?"

"Just about—public functions, at least." He moved even closer to Shay and put his arm around her shoulders. "And who's guarding *your* body these days?" he said with an impish grin, looking down the neckline of her evening gown.

Shay had no intention of spending the evening fending off Ric's advances and thought she'd better let him know where she stood right from jump street. She removed the hand that was resting on her shoulder and placed it on his knee.

"Look, Ric; maybe we better get something straight. I don't play that."

"Play what?" he asked. Suddenly he was boyishly

innocent, with a completely guileless look in those enormous brown eyes.

"I'm new around here," Shay said, "but I've read..."

"A lot of stuff about me?" Ric finished for her. "Stuff like how I always have a woman on each arm, another one in my bed, and two or three spares tucked under the mattress? If that were true, Shay, why wouldn't I have a date tonight?"

"Oh, come on, Ric. It's not like you *couldn't* have had a date. I sure there are a couple of million women who would have gladly accepted your invitation."

"Then doesn't the fact that I don't have a date tell you something?" he probed.

Shay didn't have an answer to that one.

"Shay, you can't believe everything you read. I'm a young, single, relatively attractive man who sings love songs."

That's the understatement of the year! Shay thought.

"I make good copy for the media," Ric went on. "And to be frank, sometimes I encourage it. It helps sell CDs.

"But I think everyone deserves a chance to be judged on who they are, not on who people *say* they are..." he looked deeply into her eyes, "don't you?"

Shay felt suddenly ashamed, and it made her defensive, "Yes, I do, but you were starting to get..."

"Hell, woman, all I did was put my arm around you!" Ric laughed. "If it's a crime for a man to put his arm around a beautiful woman he's taking to a party," he smiled at her, "I'm guilty as charged."

Shay's heart melted. He was right. He hadn't done anything she would have found objectionable from another man. She was being influenced by who he was, and his so called reputation. And also, she reluctantly admitted to herself, apprehensive about the strong, almost irresistible attraction she felt for him.

"Ric," she looked up at him penitently, "I...I guess I did

jump to a lot of unwarranted conclusions about you. I'm sorry."

"No apology required. But since we're on the subject of reputation and rumor; one even hears rumors about *novelists* from time to time..."

Shay arched one eyebrow, "Such as?"

"Such as one being seen out with a certain multi-talented dude in the film industry. Such as a budding romance going on there. Any truth to *that* rumor?"

"Well...Uh...No," Shay said simply, feeling uncomfortable about her answer. *But how could I say otherwise? So far, nothing really has gone on between me and Wood, except one moonlight kiss.*

Ric gave her his slow, lazy smile once more, and gently took one of her hands into both of his as he gazed provocatively into her eyes, "I'm glad."

CHAPTER 4

IT HAPPENED ONE NIGHT

Shay was used to being stared at. She'd been out publicly with Wood on several occasions, and she was beginning to get used to being recognized in her own right, as well.

But she wasn't used to the intensity of the attention Ric attracted. Wood's fans tended to approach him as a friend, a buddy, and although he did, of course, have adoring female fans, a lot of older women came on to Wood with an almost motherly approach.

No so with Ric. Men tended to defer to him like he was some sort of guru, and women—of all ages—fell all over themselves to get his notice or favor. People were drawn to him like a magnet. Even in this room full of people frequently sought out by fans themselves, he was at the center of attention.

This gala had a different universe of celebrities than the Academy Awards party. Since this was a cross-media event, Shay found herself meeting network newscasters, talk show hosts, newspaper columnists, magazine owners, and megawatt radio station disc jockeys; although there was a significant representation of those the music and film industries as well.

She and Ric had settled at a big round table that also boasted a well-known CNN newscaster and wife, and an MTV executive, who was apparently a buddy of Ric's, although his date seemed to be more interested in Ric than in her escort. Rounding out the table was, with her companion, the female publisher of a major magazine, and Ian Trevor Howard, the British actor.

The publisher had been rudely leaning across Shay; talking past her for the last several minutes, trying to cajole Ric into an interview with her magazine. "Ric, eighty percent of my readers are women, you know. We'd give you the cover story. This could be great publicity for you."

Wouldn't do your sales any harm, either, Shay thought, knowing Ric's face on the cover alone would guarantee a sell-out issue.

"Let me think about it, Marsha," Ric replied for the second time. "Anyway, the guy you should really be talking to is my manager, Booker. But Shay here would be a wonderful interview subject for your magazine, since most of her readers are women, too."

"Yes; one of my staff writers has already suggested an interview with Miss Logan," Marsha sniffed dismissively, talking as though Shay weren't even present, "and I'm sure one of my people will be getting in touch with her agent eventually. But an interview with *you* would be special..." the clear implication being that an interview with Shay was not.

Oh, honey—now *you've done it* Shay thought. *That magazine of yours will turn to dust before you get an interview out of* me.

"Marsha," Shay said aloud, "I'm honored your staff would consider me. But I'm not sure I'm right for your readers. Aren't they mostly elderly ladies..." Shay smiled sweetly, "like yourself?"

Shay was well aware that the well preserved fifty-something Marsha was hardly elderly, nor were her readers, but Shay's comment had the desired effect. It shut Marsha up. Marsha turned dark as the CNN guy had a sudden coughing fit, hiding his mouth with his hand. Ian Trevor Howard didn't even try to hide it, laughing out loud.

"Come, on, baby," Ric said with a sly grin, standing and taking Shay's hand, "They're playing our song."

Out on the dance floor, Ric threw his head back and laughed as he embraced Shay, "Girl, you are a pistol! Talk about the iron hand in the velvet glove! You sure put Marsha in her place. But you can forget a decent book review from *that* magazine for the next millennium!"

"Who cares? I was tired of that second rate Fanny Hearst breathing in my face."

"Don't think you have to worry about that anymore," Ric nodded toward their table. Marsha was busily gathering up her purse, evening wrap, and escort, and cast one last baleful look toward the dance floor before beating a huffy exit.

"Well, tough," Shay told him. "If she couldn't stand the heat, she should have kept her butt out of the kitchen."

"You are an amazing woman," Ric said, looking into Shay's face, totally enthralled. "You looked so defenseless backstage when that fool was giving you a hard time. I thought I was rescuing you, but now it looks like I was rescuing *him*."

He held her closer, "Beautiful, brainy, *and* sassy, all in one package. That's a rare combination..." he looked into her eyes, "and a very enticing one."

Shay didn't respond. Her anger with the dearly departed Marsha quickly faded as it suddenly hit her that she was in Ric's arms. She could feel the power of his body as he held her close. She was fiercely aware of his nearness; his cologne, his breathing, even the beat of his heart.

The song ended, and they returned to the table. "What happened to Marsha?" Ric asked with a mischievously knowing grin.

"*Said* she had a headache," Ian Trevor Howard responded in his lilting British accent. He turned to Shay with a straight face, "Happens sometimes with *elderly ladies*, I understand."

The CNN guy snorted, as his wife smilingly told him to cut it out. Everybody started dancing then. The MTV guy asked Shay for her telephone number, for a possible future interview—he said. The CNN guy's wife looked giddy, returning to the table after a dance with Ric. The

CNN guy looked pissed after his wife returned to the table looking giddy after a dance with Ric.

Later in the evening, Ian said he wasn't going to stay much longer, then added, "But I can't leave without a dance with our authoress." He turned to Ric, "May I?"

"Just don't try to slip out the door with her, my brother," Ric told him.

"Wouldn't dream of it, old man..." Ian smoothly replied as he held out Shay's chair, "unless you happened to leave the room."

"It's fascinating to meet you, Miss Logan...Natasha," Ian said out on the dance floor. "Romance novels aren't usually my cup of tea, but I enjoyed yours immensely."

"*You've* read my books?"

"I've read *The SuperStar's Lady*. It's delightful; as well as being romantic as all get out it's funny, imaginative, and even suspenseful. Gabriel Lamont contacted my manager about me playing the lead in the movie."

"*You*?" Shay asked.

"Your incredulity is not flattering, my dear," Ian said with a smile. "I *do* sing, you know."

Of course, Shay knew. Ian was the biggest star to hit the musical stage in ages. And God knew he was certainly handsome enough to play Michael, but...

"But," Shay put her thoughts into words, "Michael's American, and charming as it is your accent..."

"Hey, don't worry about *that*, baby," Ian replied, suddenly shifting gears and sounding like he could have been born in Detroit. "I'm an actor—a good one. I can get down with the 411 twenty-four seven if I feel like it."

Shay laughed, "So I see."

"Speaking of *The Superstar's Lady*," Ian continued in his own voice, "well, I don't wish to pry...but I will anyway. Are you and Ric a case of life imitating fiction?"

Shay started to politely tell him that it was none of his business, but she looked into his face and saw there not nosiness, but concern. "I...we just met earlier this evening," she told him.

"I see," Ian said solemnly.

They danced silently for the next several moments.

"Why?" Shay suddenly asked.

"I beg your pardon?"

"Why? Why did you ask about Ric and me?"

"Oh, no reason."

Shay looked into his eyes, "You don't strike me as a man who does things for 'no reason,' Ian."

He didn't reply.

"I know Ric has something of a reputation," Shay said, for some reason she didn't comprehend feeling compelled to offer this explanation, "but he's been a perfect gentleman with me this evening."

The song ended then, and Ian took her elbow as they walked back to the table. Just before they got there, he leaned over and whispered, "It might be wise to remember, dear Natasha, that where there's smoke, there's usually fire. Watch your step."

The CNN guy and his wife had left. Ric turned to Shay, "Looks like this thing is winding down; ready to leave?"

"Yes. I've had a ball, but it's been a long day."

"Think I'll be shoving along, as well," Ian chimed in. "May I walk out with you?"

After saying goodbye to Mr. MTV and his lady, the three of them made for the exit. Ian's car arrived first. He shook Ric's hand, "Good to see you again, Ric."

"Likewise, man. Take it slow."

Ian took Shay's hand, "And it was a great pleasure to meet you, Shay." He bent to kiss her hand, looking up at her with even more concern than before. "Hope the reviews are favorable."

Their eyes locked in understanding, "I'm sure they will be," Shay whispered, "but thank you, Ian."

As his car pulled away, and Ric's limo moved forward for them, Ric turned to Shay, "What reviews?"

"Oh, we were talking about the release of my next book," Shay fibbed.

Once in the limo, Ric wouldn't drop the subject, "So that's what you two were all huddled up about on the dance floor?" he pointedly asked.

"We were hardly 'huddled up,' Ric. We were just dancing." Shay looked away, "And Ian is a very nice and...uh, thought-provoking man."

Ric moved closer to her, "Hope he hasn't made you forget the nice man you're with."

"Of course not. In fact, I was just wondering how the nice man I'm with is going to take me home when he hasn't asked where I live."

Ric took her hand, "Well, actually, Shay, I was thinking we'd maybe go by my place first, and..."

Shay pulled her hand from his and just looked at him.

"Not a good idea, huh?" Ric asked.

"Uh-uh," Shay replied.

"All right, then. Where *do* you live, Miss Logan?"

Shay told him, and he passed the information along to his driver. On the way there, Ric was 'a perfect gentleman,' as Shay had told Ian; just making small talk about their evening and the people they'd encountered.

When they arrived at Shay's house, the driver opened the door for Shay, and Ric slid out after her. Ric walked with her to the door.

"I really had a great evening, Ric. Thanks for rescuing me," and Shay offered her hand...which Ric ignored.

"Nice house," he remarked, looking about him.

"Thanks. I like it."

"How many rooms you got here?"

"Nine."

"Nine? Really? Must be an ingenious design; doesn't look that big from the *outside*," he looked at her suggestively.

"I'd invite you in, Ric, but..."

"Thought you'd never ask," he said, opening the door she'd already unlocked and going inside.

Shay hadn't planned on inviting him in, but shrugged, *Well, what's he gonna do—rape me? With two cars and four or five men waiting just outside?*

As they went into the house, and Ric started walking around, looking into the kitchen, out onto the deck, "Nice," he pronounced.

"It's perfect for me," Shay allowed, "but I'm sure it's a lot smaller than what you're used to."

"It's all about quality, honey; not quantity. And this is choice digs. Where do you write?"

Shay showed him her study, in its usual state of controlled chaos, with papers, books, and records strewn about in a filing system only she understood.

"What's in there?" he pointed to the other door.

"My bedroom," Shay hesitantly answered.

"Oh, really?" His eyes lit up. "I'd definitely like to see that," he replied, heading for the door.

"Uh...I don't think so," Shay took his arm, and steered him toward the other exit. "It's not included in the Grand Tour itinerary."

Back in the living room, Ric rubbed his hands together, "Well, guess I better be getting on my way." Shay experienced the curious feeling of being both relieved and disappointed at the same time. "But before I do," he continued, "how about a nightcap?"

"I...I don't drink much, and I haven't really entertained since I've been here..." Shay replied. As a hostess she was somewhat embarrassed, "and I don't think I have much of anything..."

"No problem at all—allow me," Ric quickly responded, heading for the door. "I'll be right back."

Where's he going? Shay wondered. *I don't think they*

have all-night corner liqueur stores in this neighborhood.

But Ric was back in a matter of moments, carrying a huge bottle of champagne. He headed for the kitchen, "Where are your wine glasses?"

"In the cupboard over the dishwasher", Shay told him, feeling this was getting a little out of hand. "Uh...Where'd you get the champagne?"

"From the limo, of course," Ric replied, coming into the room with the champagne and two glasses, "I never leave home without it." He sat the glasses and the bottle down on the coffee table and went over to her sound system. "Got these, too," he said, reaching into his pocket, and pulling out two or three CDs.

Shay crossed her arms, "I hope you don't think you're going to be here long enough to listen to all of those," she said firmly.

By this time Ric had put on one of the CDs; his own, as it turned out. "Hope you don't think it's nervy of me to play my own stuff," he said as the sensual sound started to fill the room.

"Ric, is there anything about you that *isn't* nervy?" Shay asked with a resigned smile.

Ric had picked up the champagne bottle, was starting to open it. "Not much," he admitted with that heart-breaking unabashed grin, just as the cork popped. He then proceeded to fill their glasses.

"Ric, I don't think you understand that I..."

"I understand perfectly," he said handing her a glass. "One glass of champagne and I'm outta here."

"But..."

"To a wonderful evening," he said, touching his glass to hers. "It really was a wonderful evening, Shay. The best one I've had in a long time," those magnetic dark eyes were looking deeply into hers, "...because I spent it with you," he finished softly.

Shay was transfixed for a moment, then hastily took a

sip of her wine to escape his gaze.

"You think we could sit down to drink this?" Ric asked, looking at the sofa. "I don't know about you, but my feet hurt."

Shay laughed, as she sat on the sofa, "Well, imagine how mine must feel. At least you don't wear shoes like *these*," she held out one foot, showing him the five-inch heeled torture chamber.

"Maybe I can help," he said, sitting beside her. He put his glass on the table and bent down, picking up her foot and placing it on his lap.

Shay almost spilled her champagne, "Ric! What are you...?"

"I give the best foot massage in town," he said, flipping off her shoe, and tossing it over his shoulder to the floor. He began to rub her foot, and it felt wonderful.

"Well? Madam is pleased?" he said after a few moments of silence.

"Madam is very pleased," Shay admitted softly. A warm glow was starting to spread through her body, and she closed her eyes. It was as though each of her senses was being assailed with pleasure: The exquisite touch of his hands, the piquant taste of the wine, the compelling beat of the music, the pungency of his cologne, and of course, the incomparable sight of his handsome face.

"Here; you need a refill," Ric's voice brought her out of her revelry as he again filled her glass.

"Ric, I don't want..."

"Well, you might as well. I gotta do the other foot," he said logically. He put her other foot in his lap and began to massage it as well.

The CD had reached the second cut now, "Hypnotized". As his definitive baritone continued to fill the room, Shay was enthralled. "Did you write that song?" she asked somewhat unsteadily.

"Yes. Do you like it?"

"It's mesmerizing," Shay whispered.

He started to sing along with the recording, his authoritative voice coming at her in a double dose, sounding even more dynamic in person. Shay hardly noticed as he filled her glass yet again.

Ric's hands slowly left her foot and began to travel up her leg, sensuously creeping under the delicate fabric of her evening gown. Shay sat up suddenly, the abruptness of the movement causing her to feel a little light-headed, "Ric, I...I think maybe we should call it a night," she said with a quiver in her voice.

Ric quickly moved closer, his face mere inches from hers. "So do I," he whispered hoarsely and cupped her face in his hands as he bent to kiss her.

His lips were soft; his kiss both tender and intense at the same time. Before she could pull away from him, he stopped, his eyes searching hers, "Shay, I'm intrigued by you; drawn to you. I haven't felt this way about a woman in a long, long time. You're so sweet, so special," he took her in his arms, "...so womanly."

Ric's arms tightened around her, and he kissed her again; this time his kiss was more demanding, more possessive—this time, he meant business.

With some difficulty, Shay pulled away from him briefly. "Shay, why do you think I wasn't with a date tonight?" he told her urgently. "Sure, I could have all kinds of women, and I don't deny that in the past—I have. But I've reached the point where I don't want to be with a woman just because she's there. I've reached the point where I want someone I can feel something with; someone I can feel something *for*." His eyes bored into hers, "And I feel something very insistent—for you."

He leaned forward, and nuzzled her neck, "I want you, Shay. I want you more than I've ever wanted a woman. I'll leave if you tell me to...but I don't want to." He looked into her eyes, his hands tenderly caressing her back, "And you don't want me to; do you, honey?"

He kissed her again, and this time Shay couldn't resist the hunger that coursed through her body. Involuntarily, her arms wrapped around him, as they sank down prone on the sofa.

The next time they broke apart, Shay found that Ric's wandering hands had totally unzipped her dress, and it had slipped down over one shoulder, partially exposing her delicate black lace bra. With one deft movement, he popped the slender clasp at the back.

"Ric...please...don't...I..." she murmured.

"Don't be afraid, baby; don't be afraid. This is right, and you know it."

He slipped the dress and the bra straps down past her slender shoulders, and as her full, round breasts burst into view, he sharply inhaled. "My God, you're even more beautiful than I imagined," he breathed in an awed whisper as he bent to take one quivering, already puckered nipple into his mouth.

Shay felt a river of fire flow through her, unlike anything she'd ever felt before, as he continued to gently caress her back, while he licked her nipple with his tongue. His hands had continued to draw her dress even further down, until now it was around her waist, the silky fabric of the full skirt billowing around them both, enveloping them in a wave of black satin.

"Ric...Ric, we can't do this."

"Yes, we can, sweetheart," he murmured, moving his mouth to her other nipple.

Shay was totally overwhelmed by the feelings he aroused in her; totally out of control of the situation. But maybe he was right. Maybe this was right. It felt right; it felt as though this was the way things should be, as though being in his arms was where she belonged. She ran her fingers through the thick, softness of his hair, as he began to gently bite and suck her nipples, alternating from one to the other.

Somehow he'd managed to remove his jacket, and lay it on the coffee table. He snatched his bow tie open and pulled apart his shirt, the buttons flying all about the room. He wore nothing beneath, and the strong contours of his muscular chest came into view.

"Ric," she pleaded with him once more, "Ric, please; please stop. I feel so...so self-conscious with all those guys outside, wondering—*knowing*—what we're doing in here."

"There ain't nobody outside, baby," he whispered against her neck, as his hands slid under her skirt, and began to stroke her thighs.

"What...what do you mean?"

"I sent them all home. They left the backup car for me, and they all climbed into the limo and took off. So there ain't nobody outside; there ain't nobody to wonder about what we're doing. It's nobody's business, anyway—but yours and mine," he said, standing.

He quickly stripped off his shirt, and stood there before her, the muscles in his powerful arms and shoulders rippling as in one swift movement he pulled her dress downward past her feet and tossed it to the floor. Then he swept down and lifted her in his arms, her arms instinctively circling his neck as he kissed her yet again, and began to slowly walk toward her bedroom.

He placed her on the bed gently and slipped off his pants so that he stood before her with only his briefs concealing the manliness that was by then so visibly evident.

He sat on the bed beside her, and reached for her waist, slowly peeling her pantyhose down over her legs, following its movement with his lips; kissing her thighs, her knees, her legs, her ankles, her feet, her toes, until she lay there before him, completely naked, trembling, and helpless.

He spanned over her, and kissed her yet again, "Shay," he whispered, "this is too important to me—*you're* too important to me—for things to start off wrong between us. So before this goes any further, I want you to tell me you're sure this is what you really want. Because if you're not, I'll stop; even now, I'll stop, if that's what you want."

Ric kissed her again, his tongue languidly exploring her mouth, as his hands cupped her breasts, squeezing each nipple. The universe seemly filled with his eyes as they drilled into hers, and whispered, "Do you want me to stop, baby?"

And she could withstand the feelings that had overcome her no longer. "No," she whispered as she reached up to embrace him.

A long time afterward, she lay there in Ric's arms, feeling the beat of his heart against hers. He leaned forward, brushed back her hair, and kissed her temple, "This ain't no one-night stand, baby. You understand that?"

"Yes, honey."

"I really care for you, Shay—deeply. I want you in my life. This is just the beginning for you and me."

He started to kiss her once again, slowly climbing on top of her as he kissed her eyes, her nose, her lips, sliding his lips down her slender throat to her breasts, which he began to nuzzle and kiss once again.

Shay embraced him, "Oh, Michael," she moaned, not realizing what she was saying.

Ric abruptly stopped, "What?"

"What's the matter?" Shay asked shakily.

"You called me 'Michael'."

"No, I didn't."

"Yes, you did!" He was furious. "You most distinctly said 'Michael'. Who's this Michael? I'm not in the habit of having a woman I make love to call out another man's name!" He violently threw back the covers, and got up, striding over to the balcony doors.

Oh, boy; I've really done it, Shay thought. She realized the only way out was to come clean.

Shay went over to him; he didn't turn around as she approached, "Ric?"

He didn't answer.

"Ric...Michael is the hero in my last book."

He slowly turned around, "What?" He was searching her face, trying to decide if she was making this up.

"I said Michael is the hero in my last book...well, my last published book. The one Woody Hollister is making into a movie."

That didn't help much. His eyes still snapped with anger, "And you're telling me you were lying there thinking about some *book* while I was making love to you?"

"Yes...Well, not exactly...you see...you see...well..." Shay stammered, ashamed to admit this to him, but seeing no other way of letting him know it *was* him she was thinking of—in a manner of speaking.

"No, I *don't* see. What are you trying to say?"

"When...when I write, I always have someone in mind as a pattern for the personality of each of my characters, and the person I had in mind for Michael, the whole time I was writing the book," she looked up at him beseechingly, "...was you."

He was still scrutinizing her face. Finally, he said, "Are you bullshitting me?"

She shook her head, embarrassed, "No, Ric, I'm not. It's the truth."

When he didn't respond, she asked softly, "Are you still upset about this, Ric?"

But she knew the answer before he spoke. The anger had left his eyes, and she saw there a kind of pleased wide-eyed wonder.

Then he surprised her by laughing, "No, baby. No, I'm not upset with you. You've just handed me the biggest compliment I've ever gotten in my life. So your hero is really me, huh?"

She could tell from the way he said it he was getting a

tremendous kick from the whole thing. "Well, he's not *you*," Shay stammered, "but you were the...the blueprint. I...I know this must sound silly to you, Ric, but I think I almost fell in love with him. Especially when I was writing the book, I thought about him all the time. I even dreamed about him sometimes. And when I did, the face I saw in my mind—was yours."

He grinned, "You must have had some big-time crush on me, huh?"

"Yeah...I did," Shay admitted, mortified. "But meeting a woman with a 'big-time crush' couldn't be a rare occurrence for you."

"No, it's not," he replied softly, "but me having one in return *is*."

Ric came slowly toward her, his eyes glowing as he put his arms around her waist. "Baby, from now on you're not going to dream about no imaginary man. You got a real man now—one who's going to take care of your every need." He laughed again, impishly, "They *do* call me 'Dream' Weaver, you know."

Shay laughed with him, "So I've heard."

Ric's face got serious as he took her hand, and led her toward the bed, "Well, then, come on over here, sweet thing—and I'll show you why."

CHAPTER 5

THE BIG CHILL

The sun shone brilliantly through the sliding glass doors. Shay drifted to consciousness slowly, feeling warm...and achy, but pleasantly achy. She rolled to her side, to wake Ric with a kiss, but was amazed to find herself in bed alone.

My sweet baby, he didn't want to wake me, she thought; *he wanted to let me sleep.*

She didn't hear any sounds of water or movement from the bathroom, but she crept to the door anyway and peeped inside. Nope; he wasn't there.

I bet he's gone into the kitchen; he's probably hungry, poor thing. What kind of woman am I to let a man fix breakfast for her, she giggled, *...well, at least not after their first night together.*

She looked over at the bedside clock and saw to her surprise it was almost 11:00. *Ooops! Guess maybe that should be brunch! Let me get out here, and show this man cooking is one of my talents he* doesn't *know about.*

Shay snatched her robe from the closet and, belting it around her, went out through the silent house into the kitchen. She stopped short—he wasn't there, either. Quickly turning, she ran into the living room. All his clothes were gone. In fact, every trace of him was gone. All that remained to manifest last night was not a dream was the aching in her muscles, *her* clothes crumpled in a heap on the floor, and the almost empty champagne bottle, lying on its side on the coffee table.

She ran to the front door. No car out front; limo, backup car, or otherwise. *He can't be* gone, she thought. *He wouldn't have left without waking me to let me know; without saying something.*

Shay went slowly back into the living room and

noticed the two CDs, still lying on the entertainment center, next to the sound system. Still not believing he could have left without leaving her some word, she went back into the bedroom, searching the bedside table, the bathroom, her dresser, for a note he might have left behind. Nothing. No word at all.

Well, she reasoned then, *he probably had an appointment. Maybe he had an early morning recording session or something and didn't want to wake me. And he sure couldn't have gone anywhere in a rumpled tuxedo and a button-less shirt. He got up extra early to go home and change first.*

That's got to be it. That's certainly understandable. I'll just wait until I hear from him. He'll call as soon as he's free.

Shay busily started tidying up the living room; picking up her clothes, putting the wine glasses in the dishwasher. She went into the bedroom and taking the condom wrappers from the bedside table tossed them in the trashcan. She made up the bed—but not before burying her face in the pillow where he slept; the faint spicy tang of his cologne still lingering. *I'm going to change the linens, she thought—but not today. And I'm* never *going to wash this pillow case.*

Shay took a shower and dressed in an old, comfortable sweatsuit. She didn't feel like eating, so she went into her study, and started to work on the screenplay. They were three-fourths finished, and as soon as Wood got back in town, probably sometime today or tomorrow, they could get together, and compare notes once again.

Wood. Shay didn't know what to do about him. She dreaded telling him, knowing he would be hurt. And somehow the thought of hurting Wood made her strangely melancholy. *I'll just have to cross that bridge when I come to it.*

Wood had already cast most of the secondary players

and had lined up the world famous Quinton James as his musical arranger and director. He'd plotted and secured the locations, and hired the technical, make-up, and costume people. All that basically remained before he could start shooting was to cast his leads.

As she sat at her computer, Shay couldn't concentrate. Every time she worked on a scene that contained or referred to Michael—which was most of them—she kept seeing Ric's face; she kept hearing the sound of his voice.

Without consciously deciding to, she left the study and drifted into the living room. She wandered over to the sound system and put Ric's new CD on again. There were still a few swallows of champagne left in the bottle. She sat on the sofa, curling her legs under her and, not bothering to go into the kitchen for a glass, just put the bottle to her lips, sipping slowly.

She closed her eyes and let herself get lost in Ric's music. *I can't believe it. This wonderful, fabulous man cares for me; wants me to be a part of his life.* She shivered from just thinking about being with him again.

Her mind began to wander, anticipating all the things they'd do: evenings together, *nights* together, being backstage at his concerts, the first time she'd visit his house. As Marty had so accurately pointed out, a vivid imagination was Shay's strong suit, and as she rested her head against the sofa cushions, she let her daydream run wild, even to the point of contemplating white lace, thrown bouquets, and golden rings.

Just when she was deepest into her fantasy world, the telephone rang. Shay stubbed her toe leaping up from the sofa to answer it. "Hello?" she said breathlessly.

"Hi, Shay, I'm back, and I've got great news." Wood's voice was bubbling over with excitement. "Miss Vanessa Sweet, star of the Broadway stage, has condescended to be our Alicia!"

"Oh, Wood! That *is* wonderful news." As truly

pleased as she was about this development, for Wood's sake, and the sake of the movie, Shay couldn't hide her disappointment that it wasn't Ric at the other end of the line.

"Shay, are you all right?" Wood asked with obvious concern in his voice.

"Yes, Wood. I'm fine; even better than fine, I'm sensational!"

"Well, you don't sound sensational; you sound...strange. Are you feeling all right?"

"I feel marvelous." *I couldn't feel any other way; I'm falling in love.*

"Well, if you say so," Wood said dubiously. "But anyway, with Vanessa on board, there's only one last hurdle: finding a Michael."

"I'm sure the right person will turn up, Wood."

"I got a couple of irons in that fire already."

"Yes; I met one of them at the party following the award program last night."

"You did? Who?"

"Ian Trevor Howard."

"Quite a guy, isn't he?" Wood said with a smile in his voice.

"Yes," Shay thought back on the warning Ian had given her. "Yes," she repeated, her voice not quite as buoyant as she remembered, "...he is."

"I don't know him very well," Wood said. "I was kind of thrown for a loop at first by that accent and that oh so veddy British manner, but from the few times I've run into the guy, he seems like a straight up dude."

"Yes, he is," Shay repeated. "I liked him very much."

"You didn't like him *too* much, did you, Shay?"

"Huh?" Shay had still been dwelling on Ian's warning and hadn't really been listening.

"I said...oh, never mind. I was just teasing, anyway...Are you sure you're all right?"

"Wood, I told you, I'm fine," she replied a bit testily.

"Hey, Okay! Don't bite my head off! I'm just concerned about you, lady; a man has to be concerned about his *partner*." The emphasis made it clear he considered her his partner in more than just writing a script.

"Anyhow," Wood went on, "I'm really considering Ian quite seriously. The accent took me back at first, but I rapidly found out when we talked with him and his manager, the guy can change *that* like putting on a coat."

That got a bit of a laugh from Shay, "Yes, I know. He showed me a little bit of his performance virtuosity last night."

"This role is completely different from the types of roles Ian is used to. I mean, this ain't no Phantom of the Opera. But I'm confident enough in Ian's ability as an actor to believe he could pull it off. And the man *can* sing.

"I'd almost made up my mind to offer him the role, but another option has popped up. By one means or another, we'll have a Michael to introduce at my party next weekend.

"But that's enough about business. Have you had lunch yet? Let's go out for a bite to eat." His voice softened, "It's only been a few days, but I really missed you, Shay. I can't wait to see you."

Shay's feeling was just the opposite. She'd missed Woody, too, but she wasn't ready to see him—not just yet. Now that she had to face the reality of telling him about Ric, Shay realized just how much she really *did* care about Wood, because she didn't want to hurt him.

"Woody, no, I haven't eaten yet, but I guess I am not feeling quite myself today. Can I get a rain check?"

Woody was immediately concerned," I knew something was up with you, Shay. What's the matter?"

"Nothing...nothing, really. It's just that I woke up with a headache this morning, and I was thinking of taking a couple of aspirin and lying down for a while."

"I thought you said you felt 'sensational'."

"I...I just didn't want you to get worried about me...like you're doing now."

"Well, look...uh...do you think you need to see a doctor?"

"No, Woody," Shay laughed, "I just have a headache."

"All right," he said. "Still, I'll call you later this evening to make sure you're all right."

After they hung up, Shay found she really was sleepy. After all, she hadn't gotten much sleep the night before, and those few sips of flat champagne on an empty stomach had about finished her off.

She went into her bedroom, and lay down, first pulling the telephone close to the edge of the bedside table, where she could reach it quickly when Ric called. She even lifted the receiver to listen to the dial tone to make sure it was working, then laughed at herself. *You must be bitten by the love bug, girl. You haven't pulled that particular stunt since high school.*

Shay lay back down, then sat up again to pull over the pillow Ric had slept on. She lay back on it and closed her eyes. With the smell of him taking her back, she unleased her imagination once again and, remembering the night before, and savoring the expectation of all the days to come, drifted off to sleep.

Shay woke with a start. The room was completely dark, the only light the glow from the bedside clock. *Good Lord! It's 9:30! I slept all day.* She snapped on the light and looked at her answering machine. The red light was steady—no messages. *What on earth could have happened to Ric? I hope he's all right.*

That's when it dawned on Shay that she didn't have any way to reach *him.* She didn't know his cell phone number, the telephone number at his home, or his office...or his limo, for that matter. *And something tells me he's not listed,* she mused. She didn't have any way at all to get in touch with him.

Maybe he'll just come by. She looked in the mirror at her mussed hair and baggy sweat suit. This would never do. She took another shower, did her hair, put on a little makeup, and changed into a white lace at-home outfit. She put on one of Ric's CDs and was just starting to listen to it for the second time when the telephone rang. *Finally!* she thought with relief.

She didn't want him to think she'd been waiting all day for his call—although she had—so she was carefully nonchalant when she answered, "Hello?"

"Now, *that* sounds more like the woman I'm used to," Wood said cheerfully. Feeling better?"

Although she was once again disappointed it wasn't Ric, it was good to hear Wood's voice. "Yes, much better, Woody."

"Good. I've got a million ideas to go over with you about the script, and—who am I fooling—I just want to see you. Is it too late for me to come over?"

"Well, I'm not looking fit for human eye consumption just now, Wood," Shay fibbed.

"All right, then let's go out to breakfast."

"Make it lunch, and you've got a deal." She couldn't avoid him forever; didn't want to, really. She liked Woody, very much. She just didn't know how to tell him about Ric—or how he'd take it.

Lunch was the best plan. That way, if Ric came over in the morning, or still tonight, she'd have time to call Woody and cancel. God forbid they should wind up there at the same time!

"Great! I'll call you about noon. Get a good night's sleep."

I just did—all day. "Okay, Wood. See you tomorrow."

Shay ran a reality check after she hung up the phone. *Time to get a grip. Ric's a busy man, and you're a big girl now. He told you how much he cares for you—isn't that enough? One of the things Ric admires most about you is your independence, and here you are acting like* Tammy In Love. *You've got work to do.   You'll hear from him tomorrow.*

She felt better about the whole thing then, although a small voice from deep inside somewhere popped up to say *But why haven't you heard from him* today?

But she ignored it and went into the kitchen to fix herself a sandwich and some fruit, taking them with her into the study. She worked on the script until three o'clock and went to bed.

The telephone's ringing woke her the next morning. *I knew he'd call early today!* she thought triumphantly. "Hello!"

"Well, hello to you, too! When did *you* start being so chipper in the morning?" Marty asked. "You sound like Mary Poppins...or Poppin' Fresh, take your pick."

"Oh. Hi, Marty."

"Damn; I've gotten warmer welcomes from a tax auditor. Hmmm...she picks up the phone happy as a lark, only to be disappointed when it's just little ole me. I deduce there's a man in the equation. Who is it?"

"Oh, Marty."

"Come on; come clean. Tell Auntie Martha all about it."

"I thought you'd promoted yourself to 'Mama' status."

"Whatever. Come on, Shay, who is it? Have things finally gotten tight with Wood?"

"No; no, it's not Woody. It's...it's Ric Weaver."

"Ric Weav...*Ric Weaver*! Ric Weaver? You mean *the* Ric Weaver?"

"Yes, Marty; *the* Ric Weaver."

"No wonder you're acting like a crazy woman! You must have died and gone to heaven—and back. Where'd you meet him? What's he like? Hold on a second." Shay could hear Marty telling her secretary to hold all her calls. "All right, I'm back. Now start at the beginning, and don't leave *anything* out!"

So Shay started with meeting Ric at the award program. "You mean when you woke up yesterday he was just *gone*?" Marty asked when Shay got to that part.

"Well...yes, Marty; but I'm sure he had an appointment or something."

"What do you mean, you're 'sure he had an appointment or something'? Didn't you *ask* him why he left so suddenly?"

"I...I haven't spoken to him since then. He hasn't called me yet."

"He didn't call you all day yesterday?"

"No...he didn't. That's why I was so sure it was him when I answered the phone just now."

Marty was uncharacteristically silent. The doubt that had started as just a small voice in Shay's mind got louder. Shay suddenly remembered what Marty had said in Las Vegas: *"The only way to hold a man like Darnell's interest is to not be one of the crowd. That's why I told him no, and sent him on his way."*

"You think I've been had...don't you, Marty?" Shay asked softly.

"No...no, Shay...it doesn't necessarily have to mean that...I mean...well as you said, he could have had an appointment...or..."

Hearing the usually glib Marty stutter over the rationalizations she'd been making to herself made Shay see them for the lame excuses they really were. There could be only one reason Ric hadn't called by now—he didn't want to.

"Shay? Shay, are you still there, honey?" Marty's voice called her back.

"Yes, I'm still here. Look, girl, I'm going out to lunch with Woody; I'd better get up and get dressed."

"Are you all right, Shay? I'm coming out next week for the party, but I could come a couple of days earlier if you want me to."

"No, Marty. Thanks anyway, but I'm all right, really."

"Maybe it's not that way, Shay. Maybe you'll hear from him soon, and..."

"Maybe. In either case, I'm not going to sit around here waiting for the phone to ring. I've got things to do and people to see."

"That's my girl! Hang in there, honey, and I'll see you next weekend."

Shay looked at the pillow she'd been sleeping on. It still faintly held Ric's scent. Then she viciously punched it once, threw it under the bed, and got up to get dressed.

Shay had a wonderful day with Woody. Determined to put Ric out of her mind, she concentrated on Wood and found herself once again relishing his company at lunch, and at his house, where they went to go over their most recent additions to the script, finishing with a relaxing dip in his pool.

When Wood suggested going out to dinner with Gabe and his wife, Shay said, "Sure, I'd love it."

They made a quick stop by her place for Shay to change, and after dinner, the four of them finished off the evening laughing at Gabe's show biz war stories; dancing until the maitre 'd started looking at his watch, and the supper club orchestra began packing up their instruments.

Back at her house, as Shay unlocked the door, Woody said, "It's been a wonderful day."

"Yes, it has, Woody. Thank you."

He took her hand, "Shay, I missed you so much while I was in New York. I think I realized then just how much..." He licked his lips before he went on, "... just how much you've come to mean to me..." He moved closer.

"Woody, we agreed to..."

"The screenplay's almost finished now, Shay," he

whispered as he took her in his arms, "...and I, for one—can hardly wait." He kissed her, for the first time since Las Vegas.

Shay stiffened at first, then began to relax as she once again experienced the mellow warmth of his embrace. Wood's kiss was different from Ric's; more tender, more substantial. Where Ric was all fireworks and fury, Wood was tenderness and warmth.

Shay felt wanted, needed, cared for in his arms, and just as she started to embrace him in return, the telephone rang.

"Oh...I'd better go answer that," Shay said breathlessly—it might be someone from home."

"Sure, Shay. Well, talk to you tomorrow."

"Good night, Woody."

"Good night," he smiled, gazing devotedly into her eyes, "...Natasha."

As Shay entered the house, she could hear her answering machine message start, but before she could pick up the line, the caller hung up.

Damn! Well, it couldn't have been him, anyway. Why would he hang up on my answering machine? Why wouldn't he leave a message? She flopped down on the sofa in defeat. *Time to face it, honey. He's not going to call.*

She looked over to the entertainment center. The two CDs Ric had left were still there. She went over and picked them up. *At least leaving these was slightly less tacky than tossing a twenty dollar bill on my dresser. But why did you have to say all those things?* That's *what I'll never forgive you for. Lying to me that way; telling me you really cared, when all you were after was a roll in the hay.*

Shay laughed bitterly. *You even used the old 'liqueur is quicker' shuffle on me—and I fell for it! How could I have been so stupid! Well, congratulations, "Dream" Weaver; you've got another notch in your belt, but* you're *the loser here, friend; not me.*

Shay put the CDs away in a drawer, went into her room, and got ready for bed. She turned off the light, but after a few minutes, reached under the bed, and got Ric's pillow. As she laid her head down on it, the tears started.

One night. I'll allow myself just this one night to cry; to mourn what might have been. Then in the morning, I'll burn *this damn pillow case, and that will be the end of* that. She buried her face deeper into the pillow, where the last trace of Ric's cologne was washed away by her tears.

Over the next few days, Wood and Shay finished all but the last few scenes of the script. "We'll probably be making revisions all through the filming," Woody told her, "but we're got a great foundation here. The actors may give it a look and a voice, but the script is the heart of a movie."

They were sitting out on Shay's deck, overlooking her pool and the lush landscaping surrounding her house. "You know, Shay," Wood continued, "it's a major tribute to you—and to me—that I was able to cast this thing without a finished script to tempt the actors. They accepted their roles on just the strength of your book alone—and my reputation. Although Madame de la Vanessa..." he rolled his eyes, "*did* insist on seeing the rough draft."

So far, Shay had been successful at keeping things semi-platonic, but she knew Woody was not going to wait much longer before becoming more insistent. After all, their deal was to cool it until the script was finished. Now it was close to being just that.

It wasn't that Shay was not still strongly attracted to Wood. She was; perhaps even more so as she had come to know him, and discovered what a truly special person he was. And she appreciated his style of wooing—respectful, affectionate, tender—even more after Ric's heartless double dealing.

Still sometimes, in spite of herself, especially late at night, Shay found herself thinking about Ric; wondering where he was, what he was doing, who he was with.

And since Ric was *who* he was, sometimes she didn't have to wonder. There he was on TV, or on the cover of a tabloid. That was worse than the wondering. Shay had stopped listening to the radio in her car since the time one of his songs was unexpected played, and she'd almost run a red light. Philosophically, Shay realized Ric wasn't worth a second thought. In actuality, though, she just couldn't help it.

So she held Woody at bay; skillfully maneuvering around occasions when he tried to deepen their relationship. Shay sensed Wood's confusion at her reserve; sure he had to be wondering if she'd stopped caring. She hadn't. She just wanted him to wait. He wisely seemed to sense this, and did, however reluctantly.

You're a fool, girl, she finally told herself. *A man like Wood is not going to wait around forever. He's waited for weeks already. That in itself is testimony to how very unlike Ric he is. Wood's the kind of man a woman can build a lifetime with. So you best to put your little girl fantasies aside, and choose up on this man before some other woman trips him up.*

Shay decided to stop running. The next time Wood made a move, she'd move with him.

The next day, Wood came by unexpectedly. He'd never done that before; in the past, he'd always called first.

"Woody! What a surprise! I didn't know you were coming by."

"I was in the neighborhood. Are you busy? May I come in?" He seemed rather tense. He looked strange without the smile that usually adorned his face when he was with her.

"Of course! I was just having some lunch, going over

my publicity itinerary for *Challenges* after its release next month. Want some?" Shay asked, preceding him into the kitchen.

"No, thanks. I'm not hungry." He turned a chair around, and sat on it backward, facing Shay. "You know, I might need your participation in some publicity stuff for the movie if you're game."

"Sure, Wood, just say the word," Shay replied, biting into a sandwich.

"I'm sure you'll be great at it. I heard what a fabulous job you did at the award ceremony last week."

Shay waved her hand. "Piece of cake. Walk up to the podium, read the speech; that was all it took. Although I gotta tell you, I was nervous as all hell beforehand."

"Well, I heard you did a wonderful job, and looked dazzling, to boot." He moved his chair a little closer, "Heard you looked good at the *after party*, too."

Shay's antenna went up. *Uh-oh; what's this all about?*

"It was a great party," Shay said softly.

"And didn't you say you met Ian Trevor Howard there?"

"Yes, I met Ian at the party. I told you that, Woody, remember?" Shay said cautiously.

"Yes; now that you mention it, I do." He paused a beat, "Ric Weaver was at that party too, I hear," Wood added, watching Shay closely.

That caught Shay off guard, "Yes, Wood. Yes, he was," she replied warily.

"Hollywood's just a big small town when it comes to gossip, Shay, and rumor has it Ric Weaver was at that party—with you."

"Well, I...I wouldn't exactly say he was *with* me. I mean, it's not like he was my date or anything. We just met that night."

"Did you have a good time?"

"Of course I had a good time," Shay said a bit too

forcefully. "I already told you about meeting the CNN guy, and the MTV guy, and Ian, and..."

"What about Weaver?"

"What *about* Weaver? What is this, Wood? You're a few centuries late for the Spanish Inquisition."

"Why are you so touchy about this, Shay? And why didn't you tell me you met him? What happened that night?" Wood leaned forward, a wild look in his eyes, "Did he hurt you, Shay?"

"Did he *hurt* me? What do you mean?

"Just what I said. Did he...do something to you?"

"Wood," Shay attempted to laugh, "what are you asking me? Are you asking if he *raped* me, or something?"

Wood didn't crack a smile, "Well...*did* he?"

"Woody, I don't *believe* this! How could you even think such a thing?"

"I'll tell you how. Ric Weaver is the biggest player in town—and in a town like LA, that's quite an accomplishment.

"Look, Shay, I've been with you almost every day for the past few weeks, and I've gotten to know you pretty well. Ever since I got back from New York—right after that party—something's been different about you. And I can tell from the way you're fidgeting right now the 'something' had to do with *him*."

"Well, to answer your question, Wood; no, the man did not rape me." *It's not rape if the victim is a fully cooperative accomplice,* she thought ruefully.

"So what *did* happen?"

"Nothing happened, Wood. I met him at the program, I went with him to the party, and he brought me home, okay?" *All of which is true.*

"And he didn't try anything?"

Thinking fast, and realizing Wood wouldn't believe a negative answer anyway, Shay replied, "Well, of *course,* he tried something. A man like Ric would *try* something with my grandmother. He brought me home, and he hit on me."

"And?..."

"And nothing. He brought me home, he hit on me, and then he went on his merry way." *And that's all true...I just left out a few hours.*

"And that's all that happened?"

"Yes, Wood. He didn't force me to do anything." *He didn't have to.*

"Why didn't you tell me?"

"I'm a grown woman, Mr. Hollister; and I know how to handle a man's unwanted attentions without enlisting a male benefactor to go beat him up." *And I do know how, even though I didn't do a very good job of it with Ric.* "And that's what you *would* have done if I had told you, isn't it?"

"Well..." Wood had to smile in spite of himself, "I would have felt like it."

Good job, girlfriend! Whew! Dodged a bullet!

Wood searched her face carefully, "All right; that's what I needed to know. I don't blame the guy for putting a move on you, Shay. Any man that wasn't halt or lame would *want* to. I just wanted to make sure old 'Dream' boy didn't get out of line with you."

"Oh, Woody, you don't have to act like it's the end of the world because a man makes a pass at me."

"Maybe not the end of the world, but if he *had* gone too far—beside it being cause for me bust his head open—it could have been a tad awkward. You don't know what a load it is off my mind to hear you say there was no problem with him."

Wood paused a moment, "And it would have cast a shadow over the big news I've come to tell you. Shay, I've finally signed our Michael."

"You have? Oh, Wood that's wonderful! I'm surprised you're not grinning from ear to ear! Did you go for Ian Howard? Or did you finally find a newcomer who fit the part?"

"No; he's hardly a newcomer," Wood said slyly.

"Who is he? Anyone I'd recognize?"

Wood gave her a smile, "Oh, you'd recognize him, all right. Shay, what do you think this third degree I've been giving you was all about? Can't you guess who it is?"

Shay was sure she hadn't heard him correctly, "Excuse me?"

Woody beamed, "We've got our Michael! It's Ric Weaver."

Shay's heart sank to her shoes, but Woody was so excited now, he didn't notice.

"Ric's our Michael, Shay!" He laughed, "Even if he wasn't a good actor—which he is—all he'd have to do is be himself. He's absolutely perfect for the part. You could have written it for him!"

Could *have written it for him? If you only knew!*

"He was my first choice," Wood enthusiastically went on, "but when I first approached his manager, Ric said 'no way,' wouldn't even discuss it with me, or read the book. But I guess he had a change of heart, and last week, his manager called Gabe."

"That's...that's fabulous, Wood," Shay murmured.

"Even though you won't be on the set much, once shooting begins, I'll need you there from time to time. That's why I wanted to make sure nothing that would make you uncomfortable about it happened between you and Ric.

"So now that everything is in place, and I can have my launch party introducing the cast this Saturday as planned."

I can hardly wait, Shay thought with a shiver.

CHAPTER 6

CLEAR AND PRESENT DANGER

Shay approached Woody's house slowly. For one thing, she drove everywhere slowly in her new Mercedes. Shay was still not used to her new tax bracket, and the car's price tag kept flashing before her eyes every time another driver got too close.

But the main reason Shay approached Woody's house slowly was that she was in no hurry to see Ric again face to face. Wood had offered to send his car to pick Shay up, but she'd declined, telling him she'd rather drive herself. She, of course, knew the way to Wood's house, having been there several times. It was one of the few places she *could* drive to in metropolitan LA without getting lost.

Shay didn't tell Wood, but she wanted her own car there so she could slip away from the party unnoticed if the situation proved to be too uncomfortable. Still, she was determined to tough it out, come hell or high water.

I'll show him, she thought. *I'll just treat him like a casual acquaintance; as though that night between us never happened. I'll be damned if I give him the satisfaction of thinking it meant anything more to me than it meant to him—just a tumble in the sack.*

Shay purposely arrived late, to eliminate standing around nervously waiting for Ric to show up. The guards at the gate recognized her, and greeted her by name, not needing to see the invitation she had in her purse. One of them gave Shay an especially long look, and in the rearview mirror, she could see his appreciative gaze following the car as she drove toward the house.

That gaze gave Shay another little boost of confidence. She'd been extra meticulous about her appearance tonight, wanting to both show Ric she hadn't been moping around because of him and taunt him with what he'd be missing.

Her red silk dress fluttered freely; her one bared shoulder feeling the kiss of the warm summer breeze from the open window. The dress had a wide waistband that emphasized the tininess of her waist and the fullness of her breasts. The skirt was full, but hung straight when she was standing, due to the soft pliancy of the fabric, and moved fluidly three inches above her knees when she walked. "You look like you're floating," the saleswoman had gushed when Shay had tried on the dress.

As Shay approached the house, she could see several red-coated valets standing around, two of which were helping other guests out of their cars. She came around the circular drive to the front of the house and put the car in park as a valet opened her door.

"Good evening," the valet said, looking Shay over with a huge grin.

"Good evening," Shay responded, noting how his eyes pivoted to her legs as she swung them around to get out of the car, the dress rising slightly more above her knees. The valet offered his hand to help Shay from the car, and it seemed to her he held it a beat longer than necessary.

"I may be leaving rather early," Shay told him. "Could you park my car where it can be accessed easily?"

"Yes, ma'am," he energetically replied. "I'll fetch it for you *personally* whenever you're ready."

Shay looked around her. She loved Wood's house, tucked cozily into a niche surrounded by trees and shrubbery, although she guessed "cozy" may not have been the best term to describe a 20 room mansion. Still, despite its size, the house had an air of warmth; *just like Woody,* she mused, as she climbed the few steps to the front entrance.

Shay was surprised when Woody himself answered the door. "Shay! Well, this is the big day!" He stepped back to look over her outfit, "Lady, you look fabulous!"

"So do you, Mr. Director," Shay laughed. Wood

looked sharp in a crisp white dinner jacket, with black pants, and red bow tie and vest. "But you're opening the door yourself? Where's Richmond?"

"Oh...well, I just happened to be near the door when I saw you coming up the steps." Wood wasn't a very good liar; Shay knew he had been waiting for her.

"The party's outside, Shay," Wood gave her a sly look, "and there's somebody there who's eagerly looking for you."

Shay's heart skipped a beat until she realized he was talking about Marty.

Richmond came walking by with a tray of hors-d'oeuvres, "I'll cart these outside, Richmond," Wood told him, taking it. "You can take over at the door now."

"Very good, Mr. Hollister. Good evening, Miss Logan."

"Good evening, Richmond...mmm, these are delicious," Shay said, sampling one of the hors-d'oeuvres.

"Thank you, ma'am."

Shay walked with Wood through the library out onto the terrace. There were ten or twelve round tables set up all along the terrace, and a wet bar set up on the side. Out in the yard, a huge tent had been set up housing more tables and a band.

Brightly colored lights had been strung all around the entire area, especially around the pool, where several guests in swimwear were taking a dip, or just strutting their stuff.

Wood took her over to a man whose face Shay knew well, although they'd never met, "Shay, do you know Quinton James?"

"No; although I've been a big fan of yours for many years, Mr. James," Shay offered her hand.

"Who's Mr. James? No formalities allowed around here...Shay," Quinton bent to kiss her cheek. "We're all going to be just one big happy family for the next several months. Just call me Five, honey."

"Uh…'Five'?"

"From 'Quint,' Shay," Woody clued her in.

"That was some story you wrote, Shay," Five was continuing, "One that's going to make us all a lot of money unless I'm grossly mistaken. And Ric and I have already started working on a score to go with it. We see eye musically; we've worked together a hundred times before."

Shay tried not to cringe at the mention of Ric's name. She already knew of their past collaborations. Quinton James had produced several of Ric's recordings.

The three of them chatted on for the next few moments, but all the while, Shay's eyes darted around the veranda, and every time someone new entered, she flinched. Ric apparently hadn't yet arrived; at least, Shay hadn't yet seen him. Shay was determined to be cool whenever she did, but she didn't want to be caught by surprise.

Quinton excused himself to go across the way to speak to Vanessa Sweet. Shay was still standing there looking around when she realized Wood was looking at *her*. She turned slowly to see the confusion in his eyes.

"What's the matter, Shay?" Wood asked softly.

"The matter? Why…why nothing, Woody. Nothing at all," Shay said, knowing she wasn't fooling anybody. Somehow Wood sensed her uneasiness.

"Then why are you looking around so…apprehensively?" Wood asked even softer, still watching her face.

"Woody," Shay tried a rather unsuccessful attempt to laugh, "I'm not *apprehensive*. Why would you think that? And who would I be looking for except…"

"Well, it's about time you showed up, honey chile," a voice burst in. It was Marty. She came up to Shay and gave her a big hug. "Hmmm…looks like the Hollywood life agrees with you," she added, giving Shay a comprehensive once-over. "What do you think, honey?"

Marty turned with a smile to Darnell, who was coming up behind her.

So it's "honey", now, huh? Shay noted with satisfaction.

"I most definitely agree," Darnel leaned forward to kiss Shay's cheek.

Darnell's smile was merely one of friendly greeting, but despite her words, Shay saw the guarded concern behind Marty's. Marty was the only other person who knew what really happened that night between Shay and Ric. Marty had called two nights ago, the night before she left New York, and Shay had brought her up to date on developments with Ric; namely, that there were none.

Marty also knew of Shay's resolve to face Ric down today, and she knew how difficult it was for her. Marty shook her head almost imperceptibly now, to tell Shay, no, Ric wasn't there as yet. And behind Marty's smile, Shay gratefully saw a look of firm support that said *Don't worry, girlfriend, I've got your back.*

"So how was Zimbabwe, Darnell?" Shay asked, as though a major unspoken conversation had not just occurred between her and Marty.

"Hot. And lonely," he looked lovingly over at Marty. "I'm glad to be back to both my air conditioner...and my lady."

"Look, man; I can see the ladies want to do a little catching up." Wood said perceptively. "Let's you and me go over and get us all something to drink."

Shay and Marty settled at a nearby table. "When did you get in?" Shay asked her.

"On the red eye, last night about midnight, your time."

"I feel guilty about not being there to meet your flight."

"But I told you Darnell was picking me up at the airport."

"It wasn't that late; I could have easily come with him."

"No offense, girl, but I kind of *preferred* it that way, if you know what I mean. I stayed at Darnell's house; it's fabulous..." she looked over to where Darnell was standing, talking with Wood, "...and so is he."

Shay smiled, "Things are moving right along, I see."

"Yes, better than I ever dreamed. I think this is it, Shay. And I think Darnell feels the same."

Shay took her hand, "I'm so happy for you, Marty. Darnell's terrific."

"So is *Wood*," Marty said pointedly. "How are things going on that front?"

"He still cares; I think even more as time has gone on. And I care for him, too. He's one in a million, Marty, but..."

"But the shadow of Mr. Excitement has come between you?" Marty finished for her.

"Well...yes...sort of. Word got back to Wood I was at that awards party with Ric. I tried to explain it away; told him nothing happened, but I'm not sure he believed me. I'm a good actress, Marty, but not when it comes to playing myself."

"Then why don't you just tell Woody the truth? He'd understand. You don't want that scumbag Weaver *back*, do you?"

"God, no!" Shay shivered. "But I'm ashamed to tell Wood. I don't want him to think I'm the kind of woman who goes to bed with men she's just met. I've never done that before in my entire life." Shay shook her head in puzzlement, "I don't understand why I did that time."

"Honey, you were manipulated by one of the best. That man's got a list of conquests as long as *both* our arms. He's got seduction down to a science. The dog!"

"So...he's not here?" Shay asked softly.

"I haven't seen him yet, Shay."

"I don't know what I'm so nervous about," Shay said, wringing her hands. "Ric's such a playboy he probably won't even remember *me*."

"Don't count on *that*, girlfriend. That kind of man always returns to the scene of the crime, wanting seconds. But don't worry; if he starts anything, I'll get you out of it in a hurry! And I'll get Darnell to smack him around a little if need be."

"No, Marty; you promised! I don't want Darnell to know anything about this. I don't want to cause a scene, and anyway, he might tell Woody. Please, Marty!"

"Okay, okay! I won't tell Darnell. But if Weaver gets out of line, I just might smack him around myself!"

Woody and Darnell came back with the drinks then; lemonade for Shay. She was taking no chances. She had to be fully in control.

Woody took Shay down the steps leading to the lawn and the party tent to meet the members of the cast. Holly Benson was first, who'd been cast in the role of Barbara, Alicia's best friend.

"So you're Nashasta Logan," Holly slurred. "That's a hell of a book you wrote, honey," she added, familiarly putting her arm around Shay's shoulders.

"I tried to talk Woodsie into giving me the lead, but I'll take Barbara. At least I'll be around *him* every day." Holly walked over to Woody and put her arm through his, looking up at him in what Shay assumed she thought was a seductive manner. "'Holly Hollister'—has a nice ring to it, don't you think, honey?"

She's a beautiful woman, Shay thought, *but it's awful hard to look seductive when you're three sheets to the wind.*

"Uh... Well, it's alliterative, all right," Shay replied aloud with an almost concealed smile.

"All-litter-*what*-tive?" Holly asked, trying to focus on Shay, clearly not sure if this was a compliment or not.

"Look, Holly, I'm going to be introducing the cast soon. Why don't you just take it easy over here for a while," Wood suggested, beckoning for Johnny Marlon, his

PR guy, to join them. Johnny came over and sat Holly down, attempting to sober her up a little with some coffee.

"One of your many admirers, Woody?" Shay teased as they walked away.

"She does that every time I run into her," Wood said in dismay.

"What? Get plastered—or hit on you?"

"Both. And I hope neither is going to be a problem during the shoot. Holly's pretty, and a fantastic actress. Too bad she's as deeply into the bottle as she is into the performance."

Wood took Shay around to meet the other members of the cast and crew. Vanessa Sweet looked disdainfully down her nose when Wood took Shay over to meet her. "So this is our little author," she sniffed. "You don't look much like a writer to me. Did somebody have to write that book *for* you?" she asked with a mean little smile.

"No," Shay answered just as sweetly. "Did somebody have to *read* it to *you*?"

"Uh...Let's dance, Shay," Wood said quickly as Vanessa started to sputter, but Shay caught the grin on his face.

"Jeez! What brought *that* on?" Shay asked as they started to dance. "I've never met the woman before in my life. Why would she attack me that way?"

"Two reasons. One, girlfriend has a Snow White-Evil Queen complex. She wants to be the 'fairest in the land', and she doesn't appreciate *any* woman who is prettier than her."

"Are you kidding? However bitchy, she's *gorgeous*. I'm not prettier than her."

Woody smiled, "Yes you are, Shay. Secondly, she's used to getting very *friendly* with her male directors and co-stars. Seems she uses her looks and her...ah, feminine charms to manipulate men into giving her what she wants professionally; a bigger dressing room, more publicity, you name it.

"She tried that with me, and I nipped in right in the bud. I think she's already deduced *you* were one big reason why." Wood held Shay a little closer, "And she's right," he whispered.

"That's some cast you've got there, Woody," Shay commented quickly changing the subject. "You're going to have your hands full."

"Don't I know it! I've already laid in a six month supply of Prozac! It's an unfortunate fact of life that a lot of creative people are also rather...uh...dysfunctional people as well. But everybody in this cast is brilliant at what they do, and if all goes well, we'll wind up with a dynamite movie—if we don't all kill each other before it's finished!"

Wood's arm tightened around Shay's waist, "Speaking of things being finished; the script's finished now, Shay." He looked meaningfully into her eyes.

"Yes, Wood; I know," Shay answered softly, avoiding his gaze.

"What's the matter, baby? You know how I feel about you, girl." He held her even closer, looking at her intently, "Shay..."

Just then there was an excited hubbub from the terrace entrance. People started gravitating in that direction, necks craning to see what was going on.

"Sounds like the Ring Master of this circus has arrived," Wood said dryly. He looked at his watch, "And only an hour late! How magnanimous of him." Wood put his arm around Shay and led her off the dance floor. "Well, at least now we can get this show on the road, now that Mr. Weaver has seen fit to join us!"

As they walked toward the terrace, Ric appeared at the top of the steps. He was wearing a black pin-striped suit, with a black shirt, white silk tie, and black and white spectator shoes. The man looked incredibly sharp—and he knew it.   Several guys were with him, including Booker Madison, whom Shay had met the night of the party.

The same phenomenon happened as had at the awards party. Although this gathering also encompassed some of the biggest names in show business, Ric immediately commanded attention.   Being too sophisticated to stare, many tried to act as though his presence was no big deal, but their constant veiled glances in his direction gave them away.

Shay tensed as Wood steered her toward where Ric was descending the stairs. And although she resisted it, she felt a bolt of fire go down her spine as Ric drew near. Woody apparently felt her unrest, as he gave her a perplexed glance, but said nothing.

Ric was descending the stairs with his characteristic light and graceful stride when he glanced down to see Shay and Wood coming to meet him. It seemed to Shay his step faltered an instant, but then decided it was just her imagination, as he held out his hand to Wood with his usual unshakable self-assurance.

"Hey, Woody! What's happenin'? Nice shindig, man! You pulled out all the stops for this one!"

"Glad you could join us," Wood said, coolly shaking his hand. He looked over at Shay, "I believe you already know Shay Logan?"   Shay wasn't sure, but she thought Woody's arm, which was still around her waist, tightened slightly.

Ric hadn't looked directly at Shay until that point. As he shifted his gaze to include her, she thought she saw just a flash, a flicker, of...something.

But Ric smoothly reached forward, and took Shay's hand, "I certainly do," said, leaning forward to kiss the back of her hand. "How are you, Shay? As beautiful as ever, I see." He looked up as he kissed her hand, and Shay thought she again saw that momentary cryptic glimmer.

The nerve of him! Shay thought. *But that's all right,*

buddy—two can play that *game!*

"And you're just as *care-free* as I remember *you*, Ric," Shay smiled, without missing a beat.

She sensed a fleeting uncertainty in Ric, but then he grinned at Wood, "Well, man, when are we going to get to the formalities?" Ric said, rubbing his hands together. "Let's get that stuff over with so we can party!" But Shay noticed Ric's eyes almost involuntarily going to Wood's arm, still encircling her waist.

"Now that you're here we can," Wood said shortly.

Woody led the way under the tarpaulin, taking care to leave Shay with Marty and Darnell. Ric wandered over to where Booker and some other members of his entourage were standing. They were immediately joined by a number of women guests, who were in absolute heaven having Woody Hollister, Darnell Franklin, *and* Ric Weaver all in the same place at the same time.

Wood stepped up onto the small stage where the band was playing and spoke briefly to the leader. The guy cut off the number the band was playing, and they gave out a musical flourish.

Wood was at the microphone, "Ladies and gentlemen: may I have your attention, please?"

As the guests turned to the stage, Wood waited a few moments for those who had been up on the terrace and wandering around the grounds to gather under the tent.

"As you know," Wood began once it quieted down, "I've invited you all here tonight to celebrate the initiation of a major motion picture I'm privileged to be producing and directing. I'm extremely excited about this project, and want to introduce all the participants to each other, and to the press."

Wood gestured then to a cadre of reporters and photographers, who had been admitted for just this portion of the party. They'd be allowed there for Wood's presentation and a brief while afterward, too, as a group, have short interviews with the principals.

"The project I'm referring to is, of course, *The SuperStar's Lady: The Movie.*" There was a spirited round of applause, cheers, and whistles.

"First, I'd like to introduce our musical director; Oscar, Grammy, and Emmy winner—Quinton James."

Five stood to a lively ovation, making a heavy-weight champ-like clasped hands wave to the assembled guests. Wood went on to introduce the heads of the various technical departments: cameras, lighting, costume, make-up, sound.

"And now..," Wood continued, "our cast." He started with Milo Webster, the young actress playing Alicia's daughter.

And after introducing the supporting players, Wood said, "Now, as you know, *SuperStar* is a romance, and I'm particularly delighted to introduce our leads. First, as our Alicia, I'm thrilled to present Tony winner, the ravishingly beautiful Miss Vanessa Sweet!"

Vanessa stood to the ovation. Although she was certainly most ravishingly beautiful, she didn't look very "sweet." She looked mad. She was, in fact, seething; planning to tell Wood off at her earliest opportunity for not introducing her *after* Ric. *She*, after all, was the *star* of the movie.

"And as our 'SuperStar', Michael—and I want you to know this is blatant typecasting..." there was a ripple of laughter, "Mr. Ric "Dream" Weaver." The round of applause was tumultuous as Ric stood and waved. Even in this illustrious meeting of the rich and famous, past, present, and future, there were a few female squeals.

"Thank you all for coming," Wood went on, "but before I shut up and sit down..."

Oh, no! He's doing it again! Shay knew right away.

"I'd be remiss to not introduce the woman without whose vibrant imagination none of this would have been possible; the author of *The SuperStar's Lady*, the novel— Miss Natasha Logan!" This time Shay managed to stand quickly enough to avoid Marty's poke in the ribs to prompt her.

"Shay, come on up here!" Wood motioned. The applause increased.

I'm going to kill *you, Woodington James Hollister, III,* Shay thought as she made her way to the stage, trying to look gracious.

"As some of you may not yet know," Wood went on, after taking Shay's hand to help her on stage, "Shay not only wrote the original story but has been my collaborator on the screenplay, as well. In fact, she could probably sue *me* for claiming co-credit."

There was a burst of laughter. Looking around the room, Shay's eyes reflexively zeroed in on Ric. He wasn't laughing. He was just staring at her with the strangest expression on his face. His eyes traveled down to where her hand was still joined with Wood's, then traveled back to her face again, in the same enigmatic manner.

"Anyway, with a great story, a wonderful script, a fabulous crew, and a magnificent cast, even *I* won't be able to blow this one! We've got a lot of hard work ahead of us, but for tonight—let's party! Thanks again for coming."

The band started up again as Shay and Wood left the stage to a huge round of applause. They joined Marty, Darnell, and Gabe at their table.

"The press group is going to want to talk with us a bit in a little while, Shay. Is that all right?" Wood asked her.

"Sure, Woody," Shay replied, looking over to where Vanessa was obviously in her element, holding court in the center of the group of reporters, talking about her favorite subject—herself. "If they have any lead left in their pencils after talking to your leading lady."

Wood put his arm around the back of Shay's chair, and looked devotedly into her eyes, "*You're* my leading lady...Natasha," he answered softly.

Now's the time, girl! Let him know you still care for him, too. Shay opened her mouth to reply, then over Wood's shoulder noticed Ric staring at her again. And he didn't even try to hide it. He just kept staring, even after he had to know she'd caught him at it.

Shay quickly looked down to where her hands were clasped in her lap. *Why won't he leave me alone! Does he think this is funny? I'm willing to pretend the whole thing never happened; why won't he?*

"Cat got your tongue, Shay?" Wood brought her back to earth.

"I believe the lady told you the day you met, Hollywood, that she can talk just fine—whenever you stop long enough," Gabe put in.

Marty and Darnell cracked up at that. "Come on, 'Hollywood,' " Marty said, taking Wood's hand. "You and I better get a dance in now, before you put your *other* foot in your mouth—again."

"Sounds like a good idea to me," Darnell pitched in, taking Shay's hand, and leading her to the dance floor as well.

"So, what have you and my movie struck buddy been up to while I was off in Zimbabwe improving my tan?" Darnell asked Shay with a smile, smoothly leading her into the rhythm of the music.

It *would* have to be Ric's "Hypnotized". Shay wouldn't have minded if she never heard the damn thing again, but it was hard to avoid, being number one on the charts ever since the single was released.

"Just working our tails off to finish the script so Woody could start shooting on time."

"Is that *all*?" Darnell asked pointedly, with a smile.

Shay laughed, "Look, you. You're as bad as Marty with this match-maker stuff."

"Well, since you and Wood were so instrumental in

bringing Marty and me together..." Darnell looked over fondly to where Woody and Marty were dancing, laughing their fool heads off about something or the other, "I feel the least I could do is to return the favor."

Just then, a voice that Shay knew only too well, interrupted with, "Hey, man, can I cut in?" as a hand tapped Darnell on the shoulder.

Darnell turned to look at Ric incredulously, "'Cut in'? Man, are you kidding? What do you think this is—the Waldorf? I thought 'cutting in' went out with the big band era."

"Be that as it may, my brother," Ric said, stepping in front of Darnell, looking at Shay intently, "I'd like to discuss my character's motivation with my screenwriter, if you don't mind."

Shay deeply regretted then not letting Marty give Darnell the 411 on Ric. Shay knew Darnell would have shielded her from Ric, had he known; if necessary even giving Ric that "smacking around" Marty had referenced earlier.

But, since Darnell *didn't* know, he just shrugged, taking it as Ric's typical behavior; moving in on every pretty woman he met. He could only assume Ric and Shay had just met that evening. He hadn't been in town to hear whatever gossip had reached Wood's ears about the two of them at the party, and it was obvious Wood hadn't mentioned it to him.

"Okay, man. But you sure picked a bizarre time to seek artistic enlightenment. And just make sure that's *all* you're seeking," he added in loyalty to Woody, giving Ric a warning look. He turned to Shay, "You want to dance with this character?"

Shay knew if she objected Darnell would get Ric away from her, by one means or another, but of course, a lot of people were looking at them. And anyway, Shay wasn't about to run.

"Sure, why not?" Shay boldly replied. She returned Ric's stare head-on. "I enjoy a challenge."

Just then Johnny Marlon came up to them, "Ric! The reporters are waiting to talk to you now."

"Not now, man. Can't you see I'm busy?" Ric said testily, his eyes never leaving Shay's.

"And can't *you* see Vanessa's trying to monopolize the whole evening? But they'll drop her like a hot potato if *you* step over there. This is an emergency; come on!" He grabbed Ric's arm, and Ric reluctantly let himself be led away, giving Shay one last lingering look.

"Boy, you better watch out for that one, Shay," Darnell said as he put his arm around her again to resume their dance. "Looks like he's on the prowl yet again, and I think he's got *you* staked out. But don't worry about it. Woody will cool his jets in a hurry."

But it didn't look like Woody had even seen the encounter. By now he and Marty were way on the other side of the dance floor, and there was a throng of people between them. Shay was glad. She knew even better than Darnell just how much Woody wouldn't like it, and she didn't want anything to get started.

"Is Ric Weaver as bad as they say?" Shay asked Darnell in what she hoped was an only conversational tone.

Darnell snorted, "Huh—worse. Take everything you've heard about Ric, and multiply it by ten. Most of the pranks he pulls never get in the press. A lot of guys in our position go through a stage at the beginning where they play fast and loose with women. I know I did," he confessed, shaking his head regretfully. "But most realize after a while that's no way to live, and get past it. Ric never has."

The song ended, and the band started to beat out a torrid up-tempo number. "Game for one more?" Darnell asked. "You know how to do the 'Turbo Boost'?"

"Know it? I *invented* it!" Shay teased, busting a move.

"Pick up on *this*!"

When they finished the dance and got back to the table, Marty and Gabe were there alone, talking.

"Where's Woody?" Shay asked breathlessly.

"Over with the reporters," Marty said. "They want to talk to you, too; Shay. Wood said he'd let you know when. So how's it going?" she asked meaningfully, although only she and Shay knew the true question behind her words.

That told Shay what she needed to know. Wood and Marty *hadn't* noticed the business with Ric on the dance floor.

"Just fine," Shay replied with a smile, still gasping a bit from the last dance. "Just keep this wild man away from me in the future," Shay nodded to Darnell. "I thought I could dance, but it was all I could do to keep up with him."

"He *is* a bit of a handful..." Marty replied, reaching over to take Darnell's hand, "but I'm not complaining." Darnell grinned at her in return and put his arm around the back of her chair.

"Now don't start *that* stuff again," Gabe needled them. "Every tabloid in the country is going to print that you two are in the midst of the most torrid love affair of the century if you don't cut it out."

"Let 'em," Darnell said, his eyes never leaving Marty's. "For once..." he squeezed her hand, "they'd be right."

Woody and Johnny came back to the table, "Ready to meet the press, Shay? They're waiting for you," Woody told her.

"Sure, Woody."

"Come on; I'll go with you."

"No, you can't, Wood," Johnny put in. "You promised Entertainment Tonight a private interview, remember? They're waiting for *you* in the house. I'll go with Shay."

"My goodness," Shay said in mock exasperation. "You fellas act like I've never been interviewed before."

"These people aren't the polite book reviewers you're used to Shay. They can get pretty ruthless at times," Woody said worriedly.

"I'll be fine. And I'll have Johnny there to bail me out if things get a little rough. Go on and do your interview, Woody."

"Well...all right," Wood said reluctantly. He turned to Johnny, "Stay nearby in case she needs you, man."

"Will do, chief. Now, you better get going. They're already testy about waiting *this* long. No need to start the interview off on the wrong foot."

"On my way. " Wood looked at Shay, "This won't take long. See you back out here in a little while." He turned and started toward the house.

Shay went with Johnny over to the area that had been reserved for the press. "Miss Logan will be happy to answer your questions now," he told them.

The interview started off tamely enough. Shay had been asked questions like "Where do you get the ideas for your books?" and "How do you deal with writer's block?" so often she could handle them in her sleep. But then things took an unexpected turn.

"Miss Logan," one woman reporter said. "It's been reported Ric Weaver escorted you to the Black Media Awards after party. Is that true?"

Keep your head, Natasha, Shay warned herself. "Yes. I'd just met Ric that night, at the award ceremony. He was nice enough to see me to the party," Shay replied in what she hoped was a matter-of-fact tone.

"Then it's true; the two of you *are* seeing each other?" The reporter persisted.

"No, we're not. In fact, since that night, I hadn't even talked to Ric until an hour or so ago."

"I see," the reporter replied skeptically.

"You've been seen with Woody Hollister frequently of late," another reporter chimed in. "Any truth to a romantic involvement there?"

"As he just told you, Woody and I have been collaborating on the movie's screenplay," Shay replied, starting to get more than a little perturbed with this whole line of questioning. "Is it so surprising we should be spending a lot of time together?"

"But didn't you go to Las Vegas with him a few months ago?" yet a third reporter countered.

"My agent and I *both* went to Las Vegas as Woody's guests, to celebrate our deal on the movie rights for my book."

"But didn't you..."

"Look, folks, I think we're pretty much covered Miss Logan's comments about the movie," Johnny blessedly cut in. "Why don't we let her get back to the party now." He smoothly took Shay's arm, and headed back to the party tent, although some of the press group clearly had more questions.

"Thanks, Johnny," Shay whispered as they walked away. "That was getting intense."

"My pleasure, Shay. They can turn into piranhas if they think they're onto a hot story...Oh, damn! Holly's headed over that way, and she's still drunk as a skunk! Excuse me, Shay."

As Johnny hustled over to try to keep Holly from making a fool of herself, Shay just stood there a moment, trying to calm down. She'd presented an unruffled veneer for the interview, and she was proud of how she'd handled it, but inside she was quaking. At that moment she wasn't ready to deal with Ric, or Woody, or even Marty. She just needed a few minutes alone to collect herself.

Woody's large estate bordered a small lake, and Shay thought a walk on the beach would be just the ticket to help her gather her composure. She looked toward the tent. Ric and Woody were nowhere in sight. Marty and Darnell were dancing, at that moment oblivious to everyone on earth but each other. Shay smiled, touched by their happiness. This would be a good moment to slip away unnoticed.

She started down the walkway alongside the end of the terrace that led to the lake. Just as she turned the corner, she looked up and silently gasped. Ric and one of his boys were sitting on the ledge of the terrace, talking. It took her a moment to realize they couldn't see her there on the path below them.

Thank God! Another confrontation with Ric is about the last thing I need right now! She was just about to continue down the pathway, when Woody came out of the house, toward Ric and his companion. "Yo, Ric," Wood called to him. "Can I get a word with you?"

What about? Shay wondered.

"Most certainly, my directorial brother," Ric gave his companion some skin as the dude moved on toward the food and the dance floor. Ric turned back to Wood, "What's on your mind?"

"*Mr.* Weaver," Wood said, enunciating each syllable, "it may interest you to know you arrived at this party one hour and seven minutes later than I'd asked you to."

"Well, hey, man; you know how it goes. I got busy doing this and that, and I had to spruce up..." Ric pulled at the lapels of his jacket. "You didn't want me to walk in here looking just *any* way, did you? And..."

"And the only thing it produced today, besides a demonstration of incredible rudeness..." Woody was continuing as through Ric hadn't spoken, "was causing my guests to wait later than I'd planned for the presentation. But if it happens on the set, it's going to cost money—*my* money. That's not acceptable, Ric."

Ric backed up, his arms spread wide, "Well, excuse *me*. I thought this was a party. I didn't know I was supposed to be *working*. After all, you're not *paying* me for this."

Wood sighed, "Look, Ric; I don't want to start off on the wrong foot with you. That's why I'm saying something to you now. Today is cool. I get behind schedule sometimes, too. I'm unfortunately known to be frequently late for appointments. But not for performances.

"You're a professional in this business. You know you can't *afford* to be late for a performance. I just want to be sure you understand when you're making a movie, every time you step before the camera... Correction: every time you're *scheduled* to step before the camera is a performance. You dig?"

Ric started to glower, then just shrugged and laughed, "Okay, okay, my man; you win. I dig where you're coming from. And from now on I'll make sure I have my professional ass where it's supposed to be—on time." Ric offered Wood his hand, "It won't happen again—Boss."

Wood took his hand, looking stern at first, then he laughed too as they shook hands.

Good. Shay thought. *Maybe Woody has gotten over his misgivings about me and Ric. I sure hope so, for all our sakes.*

She continued on through the trees and shrubbery along the moonlit pathway to the lake. When she reached the sandy area, she took off her shoes, and continued on her bare feet, enjoying the warm pliancy of the sand. At the edge of the water were a few large boulders. Shay sat down on one. The liquid beauty of the moon reflecting on the water and its gentle motion were somehow soothing.

She heard a slight rustle behind her, but he spoke before she could turn around.

"Hello, Shay." Ric's voice was muted.

Shay's spine stiffened. What colossal nerve for him to seek her out! *Now, hold on, girl,* she told herself. *You've handled it just fine so far. Just stay cool.*

She turned her head slightly and smiled, "Oh... Hi, Ric." Good; just the right touch of indifference in her voice.

His footsteps crunched the sand as he walked up behind her, "How have you been?" he asked in the same subdued tone.

As if you *gave a damn!* But she replied, "Just great. Busy as all hell putting the finishing touches on the script, but otherwise, right as rain. And you?" she added in an off-hand manner, as though she couldn't care less.

He was standing right next to her now, "Not too good."

"Oh, really? That's too bad." Her tone was one of polite distant concern. "What seems to be the problem?"

Ric moved around to stand directly in front of her, "You." He said, looking down into her eyes. "You," he repeated; "*you're* the problem."

Shay was thrown off stride. That was the *last* thing she expected him to say. She struggled to hold on to her indifferent pose.

"*Me?* I can't see where *I* could have caused you any problems. I haven't even seen you or *heard* from you..." she couldn't keep the bitterness out of her voice, "in weeks."

"That's the problem." Ric moved closer. "That I haven't seen you in weeks."

"Well, you know, Ric," Shay shot back, "it's not like I've been in Tibet. Most of those 'weeks' I've been right where you *last* saw me."

He continued to study her face, "I can't stop thinking about you, Shay," he said softly. "I can't get you out of my mind." He reached for her, "I think about you all the time."

Shay quickly stood, and walked away from him, looking out over the lake, "You expect me to believe that?" she asked with a caustic laugh.

Ric walked up behind her. He didn't touch her but was so close she could smell his cologne. "No, I don't expect you to believe me. But it's the truth."

At that, Shay became so infuriated her cool facade

flew out the window. She turned to face him, eyes flashing fire.

"The *truth*? You wouldn't know 'truth' if it slapped you across the face, which is what I should do! You've got more nerve than a toothache! I'm not one of your bimbos, Ric. Your smooth talking got you in the door once, but I don't make the same mistakes twice!"

She turned to walk back to the house, but he grasped her arm, so tightly it hurt, and held her there, "Shay, I don't blame you for feeling the way you do, but let me explain! Just give me a chance!"

"A chance? I *gave* you a chance! That's how I got into this mess to begin with! Take your hands off me!" Shay snatched her arm back from him.

"You know the most pathetic part of it, Ric? You didn't need to lay that load of crap on me, about how deeply you cared, how much I meant to you. You already had what you wanted. Adding that double-talk was just overkill, and unworthy of even *you*!" Shay turned again, heading for the house.

"I meant everything I said to you that night, Shay," Ric said softly from behind her. "That's why I didn't call you."

Shay stopped short and whipped around, "*What*? Now that's a new twist. I gotta at least hand you the prize for originality if nothing else. You didn't call me *because* you care for me? I've *got* to hear the explanation for that one."

Ric didn't answer; he just stood there looking at her.

"Can't come up with anything on such short notice, huh?" Shay said, turning once again. "I thought as much. Well, let me know if you need a good scriptwriter," she threw over her shoulder. "I'm in the business now, you know."

Ric ran a couple of steps toward her, "No, Shay! Wait!"

Shay turned yet again, and this time just stood looking at him, her arms crossed.

"Shay, that night at your place...   After you went to sleep, I couldn't. I couldn't go to sleep," Ric said urgently. "I just lay there looking at you. I didn't feel in control anymore. I felt something I'd never felt before, and it...it shook me up.

"I've given women the same old lines more times than I can remember, but what spooked me was I suddenly realized that for the first time, I actually *meant* them. I didn't know how to handle it. I didn't know what to do. So I split.

"I told myself you were just another woman, that I'd forget all about you in a day or two. But I didn't. I can't." He took another step toward her, "And I don't want to," he whispered.

All of Ric's bravado of earlier was gone. He just stood there, arms at his sides, looking at Shay, beseeching her with his eyes. Those eyes. Shay felt herself becoming lost in their smoky depths once again. She struggled to retain her composure.

"What do you want from me, Ric?" she asked him bluntly. "Haven't you hurt me enough? You could have any woman you want. Why won't you leave me alone?"

"Because *you're* the woman I want, Shay. The only woman I want. And all I want from you is just for you to forgive me, and give me another chance. That's all, baby; just another chance."

Shay bristled, "Another chance? For what? For you to use me? For you to hurt me?"

Ric took another step forward; now he was so close Shay had to look up to look into his eyes, but he didn't try to touch her.   "No, Shay," he whispered. "Another chance...for me to love you."

The man before her wasn't the Ric Weaver she knew; the supremely confident, glamorous, suave man she'd experienced, both on stage and at their previous encounter. Not even the man she'd met earlier that evening. *This* man was...humble; a word Shay never thought would be associated with Ric. Humble and pleading. And despite her better judgment, Shay was moved.

Ric stood there waiting for her response, looking at her as though his very existence depended upon her reply.

What's going on here? Shay's mind was reeling with bewilderment. *Does he mean this? If he's faking, the man truly* is *a great actor. I don't know how to take this. I don't know what to say.*

Shay *had* no response for Ric, so rather than even attempting one, she solved the dilemma the only way she could. She fled. Quickly turning, she started once again toward the house; praying that he didn't follow her; try to stop her.

He didn't. Ric stayed where he was, but called out as she left, "Just think about it, Shay; all right? Please. I know I don't deserve it, but just give it some thought. That's all I'm asking for now."

Once she left the beach, Shay paused just long enough to brush the sand from her feet and put her shoes back on. She continued on back toward the lawn and the party tent.

Just as she rounded the corner of the terrace, she saw Woody, walking around as though lost, constantly looking about him. He spotted her as she approached, and quickly came to meet her.

"Shay, where in the world have you been?" he asked anxiously. "I've been looking everywhere for you. Johnny told me they were pretty rough on you at that press conference. Are you all right?"

Shay was no fool, and she knew Wood wasn't either. He had to have noticed Ric disappeared the same time she did. Shay was certain *that* factor added to Woody's anxiety even more than the grilling she'd taken at the hands of the reporters. But, thank God, he didn't mention it.

"Yeah, Wood; I'm fine. But it *was* kind of overwhelming. I just needed to get away for a few minutes, that's all."

"Come on back over here, honey," Wood said, putting his arm around her protectively. "Let's go join Marty and Darnell, and just enjoy the rest of the evening." He looked at her meaningfully, "And then you and I can enjoy the rest of the night."

Shay looked him in the eye, "Woody, I know you've been patient—probably more patient than I could reasonably expect. But I'm just not ready for that yet; not tonight. Please understand."

Wood looked at Shay a long moment before replying, "I understand, honey. I'm disappointed, but I understand. There'll be other nights. But for now, we've got one difficult project—the script—behind us. So let's just relax, and enjoy each other's company, before we start to tackle the difficult project ahead."

Woody led Shay back to the table, where the others were waiting for them. Just as they were taking their seats, Shay saw Ric coming around the path, back onto the lawn.

Gabe was making a toast. "Well, folks, we've finally got this thing launched. Here's to you, Hollywood; and you, Shay, and everybody else connected with this venture. It promises to be a very lively next few months."

Shay shivered as little as she thought *Truer words were never spoken.*

CHAPTER 7

THE GOOD, THE BAD, AND THE UGLY

"Good afternoon, Miss Logan," the guard said respectfully as Shay's car pulled up to the studio entrance. "Mr. Hollister left word we should expect you. How are you today, ma'am?"

"Fine, thank you."

"Look," he said, glancing around quickly, "we're not supposed to do this with the actors and all, but since you're a writer, maybe it would be all right..." He pulled out a pen and a pad of paper.

"My wife just loves your books. She's reading the one that just came out—for the second time now. I wonder if..."

Shay smiled. "It would be my pleasure," she said, taking the offered items.

"Her name's Ethel," he added, looking over Shay's shoulder as she signed the autograph. "Thank you; Ethel will be tickled to death." He said, tucking the pad and pen back into a pocket.

"Mr. Hollister is shooting on sound stage D, Miss Logan. To get there, you go straight ahead past the parking lots for the business offices until you reach a fork in the lane. Go right. That will lead you to another guard station. That guard will direct you from there. Have a good day, ma'am," he told Shay, touching his cap.

Although the movie was in the third week of shooting, this was Shay's first visit to the set. She thought the timing that caused her to go to New York for two weeks right after Wood's party was heaven sent. The launch her new book, *Challenges,* gave her the perfect way to avoid having to deal with either Woody *or* Ric for a while.

Well, not *totally* avoid them. There was a huge bouquet of flowers from Woody waiting when she checked into her hotel in New York. And he called every day, somehow squeezing in the time to do so, even though now that the actual shooting of the movie had begun, he was so busy he barely had time to sleep.

And unknown to everyone but Marty, Ric called, too. Shay ignored his frequent messages, left at the hotel, and at her publisher's; but twice she had picked up the phone and he'd caught her in. She quickly terminated both conversations, the second time flat out asking him not to call her anymore, since he apparently didn't get the hint the first time. He honored her wishes on that but then started to send a barrage of flowers and gifts. She sent the flowers to a nearby children's hospital but returned every one of the scandalously expensive gifts to him.

She'd been out to dinner twice with Woody since her return to LA She sensed he was hurt she hadn't visited the set by then, but he was so overloaded with work, the few times she had seen him he'd been too exhausted to put up much of a complaint.

She shivered as she remembered a few days before when her doorbell rang, and she'd looked out the peephole to see Ric, all alone, standing there. She'd gone back into the living room, and just sat on the sofa, staring at the door as he continued to ring the bell, and when there was no answer, even started pounding on the door. Thank God, her car had been in the garage, and he eventually went away, probably assuming she wasn't home.

Now, in now time at all, Shay found herself on the sound stage, approaching the area where Wood was deep into setting up a scene between Ric and Vanessa. Like most movies, *SuperStar's* scenes were not being shot sequentially, in the order they'd finally be shown on the screen. Woody had told her he was having trouble with Vanessa about this.

"Being a stage actress, Vanessa is of course used to performing her scenes in sequence, Shay," Woody had told her. "She complains incessantly, asking how I could possibly expect her to be 'emotionally prepared' for a scene when she hasn't yet done the scenes leading up to it."

"That's a tricky question, Wood. How do you deal with it?" Shay had asked.

"I've learned the only way to deal with 'The Diva'—as she has lovingly come to be called by the crew—is to be tough with her. Vanessa is world class pushy, and the only thing she understands or defers to is somebody who pushes back.

"So when she starts that junk, I just tell her, 'I expect you to *act*. You're supposed to be an actress—prove it'. And it works. She really is a phenomenal actress, Shay. I couldn't be more pleased with her work on the film, but God knows it's like pulling teeth getting it there!"

As she stood back watching, Shay saw what Woody meant. They were shooting a love scene, and Vanessa's attitude toward Ric, Wood, and everybody else was hardly loving. There was an enormous frown distorting her beautiful face as she stood listening to Wood's instruction, one hand on her hip. Ric just looked bored. Shay was glad neither Wood nor Ric could see her, standing where she was, partially hidden by a piece of scenery.

"Hi," a voice came from behind her.

Shay turned and saw a rather plump young woman with short curly dreadlocks in a white lab coat type jacket coming up behind her. The jacket was splattered in spots with what looked to be make-up.

"Looks like the Diva's doing it again. Lunch was supposed to be an hour ago, but Woody's determined to get this scene in the can first. At this rate, it might run into dinner!"

She looked Shay up and down, "I don't remember seeing *you* before. Hope you're not La Belle Vanessa's sister or something," she added but looking like she wasn't about to retract her remarks, even if Shay was.

"God forbid! I have a few relatives who are rather obnoxious people, but none *that* bad, thank goodness! I'm Shay Logan," she told the woman, offering her hand.

"Shay Logan...*Natasha* Logan? The woman who *wrote* this thing?"

"Guilty," Shay said with a smile.

"Oh, my God! I'm so happy to meet you, Miss Logan!" she said, pumping Shay's hand. "Your books are fabulous! I just read *Challenges*, and I can't wait for the next one! And *SuperStar* is going to make a spectacular movie. I'm Simone Harris, Ric's make-up artist."

Shay involuntarily recoiled internally at that disclosure. Then she silently rebuked herself. Ric would have hardly told his make-up artist anything about the two of them. And this pleasant, likable woman was not at fault in her boss being a degenerate.

"Pleased to meet you, too, Simone," Shay replied. "And I'm 'Shay', not 'Miss Logan' to all fellow sufferers of Vanessa's proximity. So, what's going on up there now?" Shay asked, inclining her head toward the set.

"They're doing the scene where Alicia and Michael first realize they're falling in love, and Vanessa keeps blowing her lines. They've run through it at least three times already. Poor Ric," Simone added feelingly. "How could any woman in her right mind have difficulty doing a love scene with *him*?"

I *sure as hell would,* Shay reflected silently. But she too was surprised that Vanessa would. *I'd have thought Vanessa would eat it up, relishing it as a chance to move in on Ric in real life. And from that starry look in Simone's eyes, I wonder just how closely* she *works with her employer.*

While they were talking, Shay and Simone had moved a little closer to the set. Woody looked around, perhaps hearing the whispered conversation, and saw Shay. His face broke out in that beaming lopsided grin as he waved to her. Seeing the gesture, Ric followed Wood's gaze. He didn't wave at Shay but didn't take his eyes off her. Despite herself, Shay felt her face flush under his gaze. As he slowly nodded a greeting, the look in his eyes could only be described as...yearning. It was so obvious, it caused Simone to turn and look at Shay in a new light.

"Do *you* know Ric?" Simone asked in confusion.

"Not really," Shay lied. "We met at an awards thing a couple of months ago," Shay said this as offhand as she could manage, but was aware of Simone continuing to give her sidelong question-filled glances.

Shay waved back to Woody, who then held up one finger, to indicate he'd be free shortly.

It sure didn't look like it. They went through the scene once again. Vanessa hit all her lines this time, but nobody could believe she meant any of them. Her facial expression and body language would lead the viewer more to a conclusion Alicia hated Michael than that she was falling in love with him.

But Wood was apparently satisfied with the rehearsal. He called out, "Okay; we're going for a take this time. Quiet on the set! Camera! Speed!" A technician stepped forward and slapped a clapboard in front of the camera. As soon as the guy was out of the way, Wood called out, "Action!"

As Ric and Vanessa started the scene, Shay was staggered at the transformation in them both. The stony demeanor left Vanessa as she looked at Ric with the totally beguiled gaze of a woman who's just realized she's falling in love. Her every movement betrayed the deep feelings, Alicia, the woman executive, had come to have for the man standing before her.

And Ric! The bored glaze left his eyes as he looked in wonder at Vanessa cum Alicia; the woman Michael suddenly realizes is the love he never thought he'd find.

Shay knew Ric could act. Although he was primarily

famous for his mastery as a singer/songwriter, this wasn't the first dramatic role he'd ever done; although it was the most complex. Ric was magnificent. All his real-life swagger melted away, and before the camera was the Michael Shay had envisioned as she wrote the book—a sweet man of great gentleness and affection, whose lonely position at the pinnacle of the entertainment world had made him despair of ever finding someone who'd love him for himself.

Shay looked around her. Everyone on the set was just as enthralled as she; their eyes riveted to the pair in the poignant scene. Shay lifted her head in pride. *This* was her Michael and Alicia as she had visualized them; two people of great professional success, but resigned to empty hearts, until the miracle of love found them from the most unexpected quarter.

Wood had leaned back in his director's chair. His eyes never left his actors, but there was a small smile of satisfaction on his face. Shay's respect for Wood's talent went up a notch as well. Wood was right—these two were absolutely perfect for these roles. And Woody had brought them together with direction that made the most of their already considerable talents.

And although Wood belittled his contribution to the screenplay, Shay did not. She alone knew just how truly their work had been a collaboration, with his input to the finished product just as invaluable as her own.

But the scene was right in the middle of one of Ric's most tender lines when Vanessa closed one eye, held a hand up in front of her, and said petulantly, "That damn light is shining right in my face!"

"Cut!" Wood shouted with weary patience. He jumped down from his chair, and slowly walked into the set, and up to Vanessa. "Vanessa, my love," he said, looking down at the floor, "did you not realize that light was in your eyes *before* we started shooting?"

"Yes, I did," she replied defiantly.

Wood looked up then, directly at her, "Then could you tell me why you didn't mention it *before* I said 'Action?'" Wood maintained an exaggerated patience, as though he were talking to a two-year-old, which Shay thought extremely apropos to the situation.

"Well, I thought I could put up with it, but when Ric moved forward..." she glared at Ric accusingly, as though the whole thing were his fault, "I caught the full strength of it right in my eyes. You can't expect me to maintain a scene that way!"

Wood didn't bother to mention the movement was the way he had blocked the scene, and that Ric had made exactly the same step forward at the same point in each of the run-throughs—with the light being in exactly the same position, as well.

"All right, everybody," Wood said resignedly. "I think we could all do with some food. Let's take an hour lunch break, and try it again when we come back."

Vanessa gave Wood, then Ric, a cutting glance, and flounced off to where her personal maid was waiting to serve Vanessa's lunch privately in her trailer.

Ric just stood looking lost for a moment. He looked over to where Shay was standing, and took a couple of steps in that direction, but stopped as he saw Woody rapidly heading that way. He finally wandered off to join Booker, standing over on the other side of the sound stage.

"Well, I gotta go now. With these hot lights, I'm going to have to totally redo Ric's make-up before he gets back on the set. It sure was a pleasure to meet you, Shay." Simone said, the same puzzled look in her eyes. Shay knew she hadn't missed Ric's movement in their direction—and had the definite feeling Simone didn't think Ric had been coming over to *her*.

"It was nice to meet you, too, Simone. Hope to see you again later."

"Oh...you're going to be on the set more, now?" Simone asked, with a cryptic expression.

"Probably," Shay said carefully. "I'm going to be doing some re-writes on the script and working with Quinton and...Ric on the lyrics for a few of the songs."

"Oh..." Simone said. "Well, then, I guess I'll see you later." She hustled off in the direction Ric and Booker had headed but turned to give Shay one last troubled look as she left.

Wood reached Shay's side just as Simone walked off, "Shay!" he beamed. "You're finally here! Welcome to the world of the *SuperStar* and his *Lady*. What do you think?"

"I think it's fabulous! I didn't get to see much, but what little I *did* see was spectacular! Woodington, you are a genius!"

Woody gave her a bow, "Thank you, ma'am," he grinned. "And may I say that you have incredibly discerning taste!"

Shay laughed at his tomfoolery, then said seriously, "But what in the world is going on between Vanessa and Ric? Off camera, she acts as though she absolutely hates the man."

Wood took Shay's elbow and steered her toward one side of the sound stage. "She does. She hates any man who doesn't have the insight to realize she's the most wonderful woman in the world. You know the saying 'Hell hath no fury like a woman scorned'? Well, girlfriend takes that to new heights."

"Oh, really?"

"Right. She tried her best to run her stuff on me, but there was no way. I wouldn't make love to Vanessa through a straw. Sure, she's foxy, but she's also mean as a pit bull. Or maybe in her case, a pit *viper* would come closer to the mark. So she started to treat me like dirt when I wouldn't go for it."

"That sure couldn't help, when you're trying to direct

the woman."

"Oh, she got over *that*. It didn't take her long to realize that being snotty to the man who decided what close-ups she got and which of her scenes got cut wasn't in her best interest. But then she set her sights on Ric, and—to my absolute astonishment—he apparently turned her down flat."

"He did?" Shay asked softly, looking away.

"He sure did. I'm kind of disappointed with that development."

"You are? Why?"

"I thought it a sure bet those two overworked libidos would be getting it on *off* camera, which certainly couldn't hurt their love scenes on screen. But, alas, it was not to be."

"Woody! You're terrible!" Shay laughed.

Woody just shrugged, "Well, that's life in the big Hollywood city, Shay. I'd never encourage two of my actors to have an affair, but with Vanessa and Ric, I thought it was a lock. Ric makes a move on almost every woman he meets," Woody looked at Shay meaningfully. She glanced away. "Hell," Wood added, "he's even had an affair with his own make-up artist."

"He *has*?" Shay looked up in surprise.

"Yeah. Simone; the woman you were talking to. Everybody knows about it. And she's still with him. Well, I guess the job pays well, and then there's the travel and the glamor, and all that, too."

Shay didn't think it was the pay, or 'the travel, and the glamor, and all that, too' that kept Simone in Ric's entourage. *Now I understand why she looked so strange when Ric kept staring at me. She's still in love with him.*

By this time they'd reached Wood's office, a large messy room with a desk overflowing with papers and reels of tape. But there was a relatively clear area with a large table and several chairs over to the side. Wood steered

Shay to that section of the room, "Why don't you have a seat here, Shay. That way I won't lose you under a pile of paper. I'll call over to the commissary to bring us some lunch. Have you eaten yet?"

"No, Woody, I haven't," Shay replied, sitting in the chair he was holding out for her.

Woody went over to the desk, and after searching around for it under some documents, found the telephone, "What would you like?" he asked.

"Oh, something light. Maybe a chef salad and iced tea."

"Coming right up." He punched out some numbers and placed their orders, then came back over to the table, and took a seat. "It'll only take a few minutes."

Woody reached over and took Shay's hand, "I thought I'd never get you here. What with the way I've been running around like a crazy man lately, and your trip to New York, I've hardly seen you in weeks." He squeezed her hand, and moved a little closer, "And that just won't do," he whispered.

"So...so we need to do a few re-writes?" Shay asked quickly to change the subject.

"Right." Wood released her hand and went to the desk, where he somehow found the master copy of the script, bringing it over to the table. "I've marked the sections that need changes and a brief description of what's needed. I'm afraid I'm going to have to dump this totally in your lap, Shay. Now that we're in production, I barely have time to catch my breath, let alone write. I know the timing's not good for you, with the publicity for your new book coming up."

"No, it's fine, Woody. I've decided this time around I'm not going to travel for months at a time. From here on out, none of my trips are for more than a week, with plenty of downtime in between. I *wanted* to be available while the movie's in production, and anyway, all that travel is just too hard on me. Maybe I can relax a little, now that I've established myself somewhat."

"'*Somewhat*'? The woman calls three best-sellers in a row establishing herself 'somewhat'! Congratulations, honey; I heard sales for *Challenges* are even out-striping the first two!"

"Yes, Wood, they are; and I'm absolutely thrilled. I guess three *is* a charmed number. Now I feel like a real writer, not just some incredibly lucky imposter."

"You *are* a 'real writer'—and nobody knows that better than me. This is the best script I've ever worked with...and it's your contribution that gives it that special...panache," he said, with a flourish of his hand.

Shay laughed, "Somehow I don't think that's a purely objective and dispassionate opinion, sir."

"You're half right. It's objective; your work *is* great. But I guess I can't claim it's dispassionate..." he took her hand again,"... not when I'm trying to get *passionate* as fast as I can."

There was a knock at the door just then; their lunch arriving. They discussed the changes to the script as they ate. Shay gave Wood a couple ideas on the spot that she thought would create the effects he was seeking. He agreed, and Shay was to start working on the changes immediately.

"And I need to arrange a meeting between you, Five and...and Ric as soon as possible," he said cautiously, watching her reaction.

SuperStar was a musical. In the book, Shay cited, by title, nine songs Michael had written, and his performing five of them were part of the novel, and part of the movie script. Originally, Quinton was going to write all the original music needed for the movie, but when out turned out to be Ric— one of the world's most successful song-writers—who'd been cast as Michael, it was decided he and Quinton would both write the music.

One pivotal part of the plot occurred when Michael composes and performs the song "I Need You Near Me" for Alicia. This was the one song whose lyrics Shay had actually written, and were a part of the novel. Now Five was writing music for those lyrics, and, although they had at least rough drafts of most of the music already, he and Ric wanted to talk to Shay on her concept of it, and the other songs as well, before completing their final scores.

"I'm ready whenever you say, Woody," Shay replied as casually as she could manage. "I don't have another publicity tour for two weeks."

"All right; I'll set things up with Five and Ric. Is tomorrow too soon?"

"No, that's fine."

He leaned closer, "And is tonight too soon for us to have dinner together again?"

Shay smiled at him, "No, Woody; that's fine, too."

"I'm tired of restaurants, and it would be great if we could just have some time alone for a change." He looked deeply into her eyes, "How about if I have my cook fix something—and we eat at my place?"

Shay knew what he was asking. *I can't keep him waiting forever,* Shay thought. *And I really do care for this man. Maybe this step is what I need to get Ric of out my head—and out of my dreams—once and for all.*

"All right, Wood," she replied quietly.

"*Really?* You're sure?" He scrutinized her face, wanting to be sure she understood what he was asking.

Shay placed her hand over his, "Yes, Woody; I'm sure."

He didn't speak. He just picked up her hand, and kissed it, looking into her eyes.

There was a loud knock at the door, and Sherry Balboa, Wood's assistant director, burst into the room. "Hey, Wood; you've got a set full of antsy people out here waiting for you, and...Oh, I'm sorry! I thought you were alone."

"No problem. Come on in, Sherry." Wood introduced Sherry to Shay, as the three of them walked back out to the set. "Are you going to stick around a while and watch, Shay?" he asked.

"Yes, Wood. I think I will," Shay replied. He beamed. Shay knew he wanted her to, and anyway *she* wanted to. She found the process of seeing her work captured on film fascinating.

Shay went to the back of the sound stage and found a stool to sit on, while Woody rejoined the cast and crew. The errant light that had caused the problem before the break had been realigned. Ric and Vanessa, having been re-beautified by their hair and make-up artists, were ready to go. Shay saw Ric look around the set, and could sense him zeroing in on where she was sitting. She looked around, too; but Simone was nowhere in sight.

They started the scene again. Although she was seeing it for the second time now, Shay was just as entranced as before. There was dead silence on the sound stage as Ric and Vanessa became Michael and Alicia. This time there was no peevish interruption. Vanessa had apparently taken to heart whatever it was Wood had taken her aside to say privately just before they began. Shay found herself forgetting who these people really were. Even the maelstrom she felt about Ric faded away as she watched. When Wood finally called "Cut!" the return to reality came as an intrusion.

"Great!" Wood shouted, leaping up from his seat. "That's a print!" There was resounding applause from the onlookers and crew. Ric grinned and took a flourish-y bow. Vanessa nodded curtly and looked haughtily about her, as if to say, "Well, of course...what did you expect?"

"Okay; now let's set up for the Sunday dinner scene," Woody said. "You two can go make your costume changes," he told his actors.

Ric and Vanessa walked off toward their respective trailers, Ric giving one last look in Shay's direction as he went. Wood turned to Sherry, saying "Go tell Milo, Jake, and Danny we're ready for them now," as a host of technical people descended on him with questions.

"Well. Good to see you again," a deep male voice said near Shay's ear.

It was Booker Madison, Ric's manager. "Oh, hi," Shay replied. "I didn't see you standing there. Good to see you again, too. How have you been?"

"Oh, fine. I'm just glad Ric finally decided to do this thing. When Woody first contacted me I told Ric this role was perfect for him and could add a whole new dimension to his career. But he didn't want any part of it. I couldn't change his mind no matter what I said." He gave Shay a bawdy glance, "But then, I don't have the same type of persuasive...uh, endowments *you* used on him, Shay."

Shay turned on him, "*I* used on him? What do you mean? I didn't talk Ric into this. I didn't even know Wood was considering him for the part until it was a done deal."

Booker smiled lewdly, "Okay, honey. Have it your way."

Shay didn't care for his tone or his insinuation. "It's not *my* way, Booker. That's the way it was." Shay had no intention of getting into a squabble with this man. Let him think whatever smutty thoughts he wanted. "Look, I have to be going," she told him.

"I understand. But with your looks, Shay, it really *was* a pleasure to see you again. I sure can't blame Ric," Booker said with a smirk. "Hey, look, before you go, there's something I want to ask you. I know it's none of my business, but I'm dying of curiosity here. What's the matter with you, sweetie? Don't you *like* diamonds?"

Shay gave Booker a wintry look, "I beg your pardon?"

"Oh, come on, honey." He leaned against the wall, "I know almost more about Ric's business than *he* does.

Those were some pretty fancy baubles he sent your way in New York. You kept the flowers but returned every last one of the gifts. That stuff wasn't cubic zirconium, you know.

"And I'm sick and tired of Ric walking around so restless. For the last month or so, he's been jumpy as a one-legged man at an ass-kicking contest. You didn't seem to have a problem seeing things his way the night you met. So, excuse me, honey; I'd just like to know—what *does* it take? The rocks weren't *big* enough for you, or what?"

Shay drew herself up to her full height, "Tell you what, *Mr*. Madison," Shay looked him dead in the eye. "Maybe I can best explain my viewpoint on *that* by telling you a story.

"A man once asked a woman if she'd go to bed with him for a million dollars. She said 'Sure'. He then asked if she'd go to bed with him for dinner and a movie. The woman got extremely angry, and asked him, 'What do you think I am, a whore?' The man replied, 'We've already established what you *are*; now we're just negotiating the price'."

Booker looked taken aback, and suddenly stood up straight.

Shay took a step closer to Booker, "You seem to have made a lot of bogus assumptions, but you're right about one thing at least. It *is* none of your business. Whatever happened between Ric and me happened because I allowed it to. Period.

"So, in case the point of my little story went clean over your head, let me break in down in terms even *you* can understand. What's my price?" Shay looked Booker up and down, "Ric ain't *got* that much money. And neither does anybody else."

Shay turned on her heel and started to walk away, but abruptly turned back, "Oh, and incidentally, I didn't keep the flowers. I donated them to a hospital; but then, *that's* none of your business, either." Shay turned and once again started to walk away with more than a little bit of stomp in her step.

"Shay, wait! Hold up!" Booker called after her. Shay turned and waited.

"Look, Shay, I'm...I'm sorry. I was way out of line just now. I made a lot of presumptions about you I see now were unjustified. I guess I thought..." he smiled sheepishly, "well, you *know* what I thought. I was wrong. Please..." he offered his hand, "forgive me."

After a moment's hesitation, Shay wordlessly shook hands with him, then turned and walked away. *I need to get away from here,* her thoughts raced. *I'm just not ready to deal with all this yet.*

She went up to Woody, who excused himself from the lighting technician he was talking to. "Wood," Shay told him, " it was wonderful, but I think I'll head on home now."

"Why, Shay?" Woody was obviously disappointed. "I hoped you'd stick around a little longer today."

"Well, the sooner I get started on the revisions, the better."

"You can work in my office. There's a computer in there, somewhere under all the mess, and it's already got the entire script on the hard drive."

"Maybe I'll do that in the future, Woody, but I'm still not quite recovered from my trip. I think today I'd be better off working at home."

"All right, Shay; whatever you think best," Wood replied, clearly still not understanding why. "I'll pick you up about eight, all right?"

"Fine, Woody; I'll be ready."

He bent forward and kissed her cheek, "So will I," he whispered. "I'll walk you to your car."

"Are you kidding?" Shay looked over to the legion of techs waiting to discuss some aspect of the next scene with Woody. "I wouldn't dream of taking a general away from his troops," she said with a smile. "I can find my way out just fine. See you tonight."

Woody smiled, "Okay, honey."

As Shay left, he was quickly surrounded by the technicians but stopped long enough to look back, smile, and wave before she got out of sight.

Shay was out in the parking lot, halfway to her car, when a voice called after her, "Shay! Shay, wait up!"

Her first impulse was to run the other way, to sprint for the car, and drive off before he could catch up with her. But then her self-respect override cut in. *Why should I run? I haven't done anything wrong*—stupid, *maybe*—but *not wrong.* He's *the bad guy here, why should* I *run from* him? *If he thinks I'm going to run and hide, or turn into some quivering mass of jelly at his feet, he's got another think coming! You want a showdown, pal? You got one!*

Shay turned and stood her ground, watching as Ric ran up to her.

"Shay," Ric panted as he reached her side, "I've...I've been looking for an opportunity to get in a word with you ever since you got here."

"Oh, really?" Shay coolly replied. "Is that why you sicced Booker on me?"

"Booker? What's he got to do with this? What are you talking about?"

Shay was willing to take his reply at face value on that one. It wasn't important anyway. "Never mind. What do you want, Ric?"

He moved a little closer to her, "I think you already know what I want, Shay."

Shay stiffened, "Well, you've already had *that*," she said, turning again. "And I sure hope you enjoyed it— because there won't be a *repeat* performance."

He touched her arm, "You know that's not what I'm talking about, Shay." His eyes were pleading, "I'm talking about what I told you at the party. I just want us to start over again; to give it a try for a *real* relationship between us."

Shay crossed her arms, "Ric, at this point the jury's still out on whether you even know what a real relationship *is*."

Ric looked chagrinned, "When they come in, I'm sure the verdict will be 'guilty'. But I'm willing to try to learn—with you."

He looked at her so intently Shay felt almost scorched under his gaze. Once again Shay saw another side to Ric; a man that wasn't all powerful and in control. A man not too proud to plead.

"Look, Shay, I just want us to get to know each other; to spend some time together, that's all. I know things can't start back up where they left off before...before I blew it."

"*That's* for damn sure," Shay said emphatically.

"So why don't we just start off slow. Let me take you to dinner tonight."

Shay lifted her chin, "I already have plans for tonight."

"With Woody?" Ric asked softly.

Shay just looked at him, not dignifying his question with an answer.

"All right, Shay," he finally said. "Tonight's out; but what about tomorrow—or the next day—or...or any time you say?" He touched her arm again lightly, "Will you at least *think* about it, Shay?"

Shay shook her head, "Ric, I don't understand you. What's behind all this? *You* certainly couldn't be hurting for a woman. Why won't you leave me alone? Is this some sort of macho challenge for you, getting me back? Surely it couldn't be worth this much trouble, just to prove a point."

"I think you just answered your own question, Shay," he whispered. "I *wouldn't* go to this much trouble just to prove a point." He moved even closer, "Which leads to only one other conclusion," he added, as he took her hand.

Shay pulled her hand back quickly, suddenly confused, "I...I have to go." She started again for her car.

"Shay! At least consider it, all right?" he called after her. "At least give it some thought! Will you at least do that?"

Shay stopped cold. She could no longer pretend, not even to herself, that she wasn't touched by his persistence and the apparent sincerity of his plea. She turned slowly. He stood with his arms slightly outward, as though reaching toward her.

"All right, Ric," she said slowly. "I will *think* about it," she replied unsteadily.

His face broke into a smile as brilliant as the sun. She tentatively gave him a shaky smile in return, before turning once again, and heading for her car.

CHAPTER 8

STAR WARS

Shay slowly drove home, more unsettled than ever. Why had she told Ric she'd think about it? She didn't need to think about it. She should have told him to leave her alone. She should have told him to go to hell. She should have threatened to tell Woody. She should have told him *anything* but that she'd think about it.

Shay entered her house, intent upon starting the revisions for the script, but her whirling thoughts wouldn't let her concentrate. Seeing Ric portray Michael had entwined the two of them in her mind more than ever. Suppose he wasn't just playing a role? Suppose that really *was* the man he was inside? Suppose he really did mean what he was saying to her now? She kept seeing Ric standing there, his very posture beseeching her, reaching out to her.

Shay tried to suppress it, but thoughts of their night together surfaced. She wandered into the bedroom, and sat on the bed, stroking the bedspread, letting memory take her back Once again she recalled the magic of Ric's kiss; the wonder of his embrace. Would it feel that way again, or was that torrent of passion just a figment of her imagination?

Shay laughed bitterly. How many women would give everything they owned to be in her shoes; having to choose between Woody Hollister and Ric Weaver? Shay knew there was a time, not too very long ago, when she herself would have though such a thing was a dream come true. But this was no dream. It was a nightmare; *worse* than a nightmare. There was no waking up and finding everything all right here. Shay felt like her mind and her heart were being torn apart.

Woody. Didn't she care for him? Of course, she did.

She knew she did. She felt a special warmth with him she'd never felt with anyone else, not even Ric. Woody was sweet, and funny, and thoughtful, and caring, and he treated her with more gentleness, consideration, and outright respect than any man she'd ever known. And there was something else, something undefinable she'd felt for Woody right from the start. And whatever that something was, it sure wasn't sisterly.

She remembered when they met, how attracted she'd been to him, right from the beginning. *I've never really even given him a chance* she suddenly realized. Instead of giving *Ric* another chance, shouldn't she at least try; really *try* with Woody? *He* deserved it. Ric didn't.

Shay found herself genuinely looking forward to the evening with Wood. *I always enjoy myself when I'm with Woody, no matter what we're doing. And I don't have to wonder if he means what he says. I know he does. He's proven it a hundred times over already, even with me resisting him at every turn.*

Shay stood quickly, her mind made up. The hell with Ric; he'd *had* his shot, and had, as he so accurately put it himself, blown it.

This is going to be a one-of-a-kind evening for me and Woody, and I'm going to give it everything I've got. I'm going to put old 'dream-boy' clean out of my head and just concentrate on Wood. I don't know where it's going to lead, but I know he's already one of the most indispensable people in my life. That's one hell of a good start.

Shay went into the bathroom and started a tub, adding her finest bath salts and body oils. After a long relaxing hot soak, she washed her hair. She gave herself a pedicure and manicure while her hair was drying, and then styled it, the full, heavy black curls making a frame around her face, falling softly onto her back and shoulders.

Shay went to her closet and looked over her wardrobe with an analytical eye. For a quiet at-home dinner, she could have just kept on the jeans and silk blouse she wore to the studio. But this was going to be a special night, and she wanted something special to wear. She wanted Woody to know from the moment he saw her that tonight was different. Tonight she was sure. Tonight he was going to have her total, complete, and undivided attention—and more.

After much internal debate, she finally decided on a two piece white dress of creamy soft leather. The top was really not much more than a vest, sleeveless with a discreetly plunging neckline. The skirt was straight and ended about three inches above Shay's knees. She selected sheer white pantyhose to go with it.

Shay was especially careful in choosing her underwear, picking a matching white lace bra and panty set. She wondered how Woody would like them, and to her surprise, found herself blushing at the thought.

Shay then went to her vanity table and took her time applying make-up. She never wore a lot of make-up, but knew that just the right amount, applied with a sparing hand, could bring out the best of one's features. She paid special attention to her eyes, applying her eyeliner and mascara to enhance their slightly Oriental cast, and finished off with a deep rose lipstick that matched the polish on her fingers and toes.

Satisfied with the face in the mirror, she quickly dressed, pulling on the high heeled white ankle boots that went with the dress. She added a pair of earrings that were just two-inch strands of gold with one small pearl at each end.

She turned and examined herself in the full-size mirror. Not bad. But something was missing. She wanted a little color. Snapping her fingers, she ran outside into her garden and cut a red rose from the bush near her bedroom door. Back in the bedroom, she pulled her hair back from her ear on one side, and secured her hair with a bobby pin, holding it and the rose in place.

She checked the mirror again. Perfect. The outfit produced just the effect she wanted; sexy and alluring but in a subtle, romantic way. Maybe a tad over-dressed for a quiet evening in, but she didn't think Woody would mind. *No sir,* she thought, twirling in front of the mirror again, *somehow, I don't think he's going to mind one bit.*

It was a quarter to eight. Woody would be here any minute now. Shay giggled, thinking of the look on his face when she opened the door. Since she had dressed up, maybe she should have called and given him a delicate hint that a sport jacket was the ticket for tonight. But if she knew Woody, that wouldn't be necessary. He knew tonight was special. He wouldn't show up in a T-shirt and jeans.

By quarter to nine Shay was worried. Woody could sometimes be late, but she couldn't imagine him being late *tonight.* Just as she was thinking of calling his house, the telephone rang.

"Hello?"

"Hi, baby; it's me."

"Woody! I was starting to worry. Are you all right?"

"In a word—no."

"What's wrong?" Shay asked in alarm. "Were you in an accident or something?"

"No, honey; nothing like that. I'm fine physically, but I think I've finally lost my mind. I'm still at the studio."

"At the studio? Wood, it's almost nine o'clock! Why are you there so late?"

Wood sighed, "Shay, all hell has broken loose down here. Holly went and got herself arrested on some drug charges—in Mexico."

"What!"

"Yep," Wood replied in disgust. "I knew she was into the booze, but I *didn't* know about the weed and the cocaine. Wait—it gets worse. They're not just charging her with possession. She had so much on her, they're charging her with *dealing*, as well."

Shay sank down to the sofa to absorb all this, "Woody, I can't believe it!"

"Neither could I. What a mess! Just as I was getting ready to leave for the day, her manager called all in a panic, right after Holly's sister called him. And in spite of all the money Holly's made from movies and endorsements, seems she's flat broke. I guess it's obvious now why. Nose candy is expensive.

"She can't afford attorneys. For the last three hours I've been on the phone with *my* attorneys, and the LAPD, and the Mexican police, and the American Embassy, and her manager, and her crying Mama down in Soso, Mississippi!"

"Oh, Woody...Is there anything I can do to help?"

"No, Shay, but thanks for the offer. God knows Holly probably deserves to have them lock her up and throw away the key, but I can't just abandon her. After all, I *am* her employer. And there's nobody else to help. I might even have to fly down there tonight. I'm sorry, Shay."

Shay was disappointed; deeply disappointed. But she was proud of Wood. A lot of people in his position would have let Holly rot where she was, but Shay knew Woody's conscience—and his kindness—wouldn't let him just walk away.

"I understand, Woody. And it's wonderful of you to try so hard to help."

"I feel so bad about this, Shay. Tonight of all nights, when we'd planned..."

"It's okay, Wood; there's always tomorrow."

"Well, my name ain't 'Annie.' *Tomorrow* is definitely not my theme song, especially when it comes to you."

"Oh, Woody," Shay laughed, "how can you make bad jokes at a time like this?"

"I'm laughing to keep from crying, honey, and anyway..." a mischievous lilt came into his voice, "I thought it was pretty good." Woody lowered his voice, "Can I get a rain-check, lady?"

"Redeemable at any time, sir," Shay whispered back.

"Look, if it's not too late, I'll call you when this whole thing shakes out, all right? If not tonight, tomorrow morning."

"All right, Wood. Talk to you then."

Well, I might as well get out of these glad rags Shay thought dejectedly *and fix myself a hamburger or something for dinner.* She went into the kitchen, took some ground round out of the freezer and put it in the microwave to thaw. She was scrounging around in her nearly empty cabinets for something to go with it when the telephone rang again. Woody calling back so soon?

No, it was Marty. They talked for an hour, catching up on the latest in each other's lives, including this latest development with Holly. Marty knew how to keep her mouth shut, and anyway; Shay knew there was virtually no way a scandal *this* big wouldn't eventually leak to the press.

When they finally hung up, Shay went into her bedroom to change. It wouldn't do to spill anything on this outfit. Just then the doorbell rang.

Woody! He must have decided to just drop by, rather than calling. Maybe the evening won't be a wash after all! She quickly checked her hair and makeup and ran to the door. She was so sure it was Wood she flung the door open without even looking out.

But it wasn't Woody. It was Ric.

Shay just stood there, stunned.

Ric had gasped when she opened the door, and now was just staring at her wide-eyed. "Shay," he finally whispered, "there are no words to tell you how beautiful you look."

Shay finally found her voice, "Ric! Ric what are *you* doing here?"

"I thought if I called first, you'd hang up on me."

Shay crossed her arms, "You were right."

"Why are you so dolled up? You going out?"

"How did you know I was home?"

"Well, your car's in the driveway, and..."

"But I told you earlier I had plans for the evening." Shay's eyes suddenly narrowed, "You found out Woody's stuck at the studio, didn't you?"

"Yes, Shay, but..."

"And you decided to scoot on over here, and try to take advantage of that fact," Shay continued, ignoring his interruption. "Ric, if I thought you were capable of understanding what I was talking about, I'd tell you that you should be ashamed of yourself. But under the circumstances, all I have to say to you is...good night."

Shay started to close the door, but Ric stopped her. "Shay...can't I come in for a minute?"

"Not on your previous existence. Not after what happened the *last* time you were here. And the way you left."

He looked anguished, "I've already explained why I left the way I did, Shay. Don't you believe me?" He moved a little closer. "This afternoon I *thought* you did." She could see the torment in his eyes, "You said you'd think things over, Shay."

"I...I know I did, Ric...but..."

"Listen, if I can't come in, come out with me for a little while. We could go for a bite to eat. Have you had dinner yet?"

"No, I haven't, but..."

"I haven't either. And you're all dressed to go out. Just for a little while. I'm all by myself; no Booker, no bodyguards; just me."

Shay couldn't suppress a little smile, "It's the 'just you' that I'm worried about, Ric."

"Look," he said, "I promise—no funny business." He suddenly reached up to his neck, loosened his tie, and snatched it off. He wrapped the tie around both his hands, "If you're worried about me getting too cozy, I'll keep this on the whole time."

Shay had to laugh at that one. "Going to be pretty hard driving that way."

"You can drive."

"I think I'd feel safer with *you* driving, at least that way your hands would be on the steering wheel."

"Then you'll go?"

The hopefulness in his eyes could not be mistaken. Nobody was *that* good an actor. Which reminded Shay of Ric playing Michael in the ethereal scene earlier that day. How would he even have a reference for the tenderness that scene required unless he possessed that quality in some degree himself?

As roguish as Ric was, Shay didn't think he'd try to force himself on her. Ric was a womanizer, but he wasn't a rapist. And he looked so lost, so...needy. Seeing a proud man beg was a moving thing. What harm could dinner do? She *was* hungry, and she was all ready to go out.

"All right," Shay finally made up her mind. "But just for dinner," she added sternly, "and I expect to be brought home directly afterward—without a wrestling match."

He didn't speak, but his face broke into a beaming, thankful smile, as though she'd given him the Nobel prize.

"I have to close up the house and get my bag. No, you wait for me here," Shay commanded when he tried to follow her into the house.

Shay quickly grabbed her purse, and turned on the alarm system, then joined him back outside. "Okay; I'm ready."

Ric led her to a twelve- or fifteen-year-old Toyota Celica sports car. The car was clean and shining and seemed to be in mint condition, but Shay was surprised. The car was hardly what she'd expect a multi-millionaire to drive.

Ric read her look, "I bought this car right after my career started to take off. It's what I drive on the rare occasions I *don't* want to be recognized," he added with a self-deprecating grin. "It was the first car I ever paid cash for, and it means more to me than my limo or the flashier stuff I drive when I want to impress."

"Oh, so you're not interested in impressing *me*, huh?" Shay teased as he held the passenger door open for her.

"I'm *very* interested impressing you, Shay," he replied as she got into the car. Shay noticed that his eyes almost involuntarily went to her legs. But then he looked into her face, and smiled, "But I want to impress you with Eric Tyrone Weaver, not his car."

He got in, and as he pulled out of her driveway, Shay asked, "Where are we going?"

"A quiet little place I know not far from here." The car didn't have a CD player, but it did have a cassette deck. He popped in a tape by Earth, Wind, and Fire.

"Oh, you like them, too?" Shay asked.

Ric grinned widely, "Are you kidding? Those dudes were seriously bad. Hell, they still are. I opened for them on a concert tour once, when I was starting out."

They listened to the music silently for a few minutes, then Shay asked, "Eric? You use your real name?"

"Uh-huh."

" E.T., huh?"

Ric laughed, "Yeah. Trust a writer to pick up on that. Folks who know me from back in the day still call me E.T. from time to time; 'phone home', and all that stuff."

"Eric... I think of 'Ric' as a nickname for Richard, not Eric."

"No, it's Eric." He paused a moment. "I was named after my father," he added with unmistakable bitterness.

"Oh, so then you're a junior?" Shay asked, confused by his tone.

"No. You're only a junior if you have your father's

entire name. I just have his first and middle names." Ric turned to look at Shay, "To tell you the truth, I don't even know what his last name *was*. Weaver was my mother's maiden name. The name she died with."

"Oh..." Shay was embarrassed her innocent question had brought up what were obviously very painful associations. "I...I'm sorry, Ric. I shouldn't have been so nosy..."

"You weren't being nosy, Shay. It's all right." He reached over and squeezed her hand. "I'm sorry I barked at you like that, it's just that... Well, as you can see, thinking about it brings back a lot of things I wish I could forget."

Shay tried to think of some way to smoothly change the subject when Ric suddenly started talking a mile a minute.

"My mother was one of the most beautiful women to ever walk this earth. She caused accidents sometimes just walking down the street. No kidding. I was there a couple of times it happened.

"Her beauty would have made her a natural to be a model or an actress. Mama didn't have the talent or inclination for either, but could she sing. She had a voice like an angel. With her voice and her looks, she could have beat the odds, and become a major singing star..." his face turned stony, "if she hadn't run into my father.

"He told her he knew Berry Gordy and could get her an audition. Of course, he no more knew Berry Gordy than I know the Pope. But by the time she found that out, she was in love with the bastard—and pregnant with me.

"He had conveniently forgotten to tell her he was married. He was some big-time lawyer and could afford to keep Mama and me in style in an apartment on the side until I was about four. And then his wife found out. She threatened to ruin him and take every dime he had unless he never saw us again. He left me and Mama flat—and flat broke.

"Mama floundered for a while, and times got pretty hard for a year or two, and then things got better again. We had money, a nice apartment, a nice car. I was slow; it took me until I was about twelve to figure out our financial turn-about was directly tied to the series of 'Uncles' that came and went.

"Things stayed that way until I was 15. Then one of the 'Uncles' decided he was jealous and beat Mama almost to death. That not only ended her beauty—which also meant the end of the "Uncle' business—it also finished off what was left of her spirit." He finally paused, stopping to take a deep breath. "She died a year later."

Shay didn't know what to say. Finally, she just reached over, and touched his arm, "It must have been very unhappy for you, growing up."

Ric gave Shay a fragile smile, "No; actually, it wasn't. After all, when I was a little kid, I didn't know what was going on, anyway. After my father left, I think I was the only thing Mama cared about in this world. She was a wonderful mother; looking after my homework, taking me to the zoo and the movies, reading me stories at night. I was usually in bed asleep before the 'Uncles' arrived.

"After she died, I lived with an aunt until I turned 18. That's how I found out the little I do know about my father; my aunt told me. Mama had told me he was a soldier who died fighting in the Middle East."

"Have you ever thought about trying to find your father now?" Shay inquired cautiously.

"Yeah, I have. I don't know much about him: first and middle names, his birth date, that he was an attorney in Chicago, a vague description. But I can afford the fanciest investigators in the world. They could probably root him out, even from that."

Ric smiled evilly, with an expression that was frightening to see, "But somehow it gives me immense pleasure to think of the bastard looking at me on T.V. or buying my CDs, not even knowing that I'm his son."

Once again, Shay was caught speechless. She looked over at Ric, a muscle working in his jaw. *God, what a hell of a way to grow up!*

Ric interrupted her thoughts, "Look, I didn't mean to lay all that on you, Shay. Not much of a way to impress a woman, telling her all about your sordid past. Only Booker and a few others know my *real* background. This stuff sure isn't what's in my official bio. But you're just so easy to talk to..." he looked over at Shay, "so different from most of the women I've...I've been with that I..."

"It's all right, Ric." Shay touched his arm again, "I'm honored you trusted me enough to tell me."

By this time they'd arrived at the restaurant. The valet said, "Good evening Mr. Weaver...Miss," and took the old car without batting an eyelash. The maitre'd greeted Ric by name as well, and they were immediately seated in a cozy out of the way table right next to a glass wall, where they could look out on a huge pond. There were several graceful swans swimming there, as if in rhythm with the soft classical music from the sound system.

As they'd been ushered to their booth, Shay saw a number of big names scattered liberally around the room. Several of the celebrities nodded or waved to Ric, and he greeted them in return, but that was it.

After the waiter left them to look over their menus, Shay gave Ric a playful glance, "*This* is your idea of a quiet little place? I'm new to the 'good life', Ric, but even *I* know what it means when the menus don't have prices."

Ric gave her his slow, lazy grin, "Well, honey, it *is* quiet, and it's not all that big. I didn't say it was *cheap*. And this sort of restaurant is the only kind I could take you to where we could eat in peace."

The meal was wonderful. The food was delightful and, to Shay's surprise, so was the company. Ric seemed to have checked all his swagger and image at the door, and she found herself in the company of an intelligent, companionable, fascinating man.

If only he could be this way all *the time,* Shay found herself thinking.

Over coffee and dessert, Ric removed a long stemmed red rose from the vase on their table and handed it to Shay. "This is to go with the one in your hair," he told her with his heart in his eyes. When she took the rose, he placed his hand over hers. Shay didn't move it away.

True to his word, when they left the restaurant, Ric took Shay directly home, without any dissembling or argument. At the door, Shay told him, "I had a wonderful evening, Ric," sincerely meaning it.

"So did I. Shay...do you think maybe we can do this again?"

Shay looked into his eyes and saw not the smooth operator who'd hurt her so many weeks before, but the sweet, sad man she had just met that evening. "Maybe...maybe we can, Ric. I..I just don't know," she whispered softly.

"Don't guess I could come in for a while, huh?"

"No, I don't think that would be such a good idea."

"Okay," he said, agreeably enough. "Well...could I at least kiss you good night?"

Shay felt consumed by those eyes, especially now, when she knew something of the pain behind them. She felt suddenly shy, "All right," she replied almost inaudibly.

Ric came one step closer and cupped her face in his hands. His lips descended on hers softly, gently. He pulled away from her and they just stood looking at each other a moment, and then he kissed her again. This time Shay was in his arms, returning the kiss just as eagerly he gave it. The remembered bolt of fire ran down her spine, and Shay felt herself melt inside at his touch.

Oh, God, it's happening again! Be strong Shay; it's not going to be easy, but you've got to tell him no, although

Lord knows just how much you want to say yes.

But when Ric reluctantly released her, he just whispered, "Good night, sweet lady." Then he turned and just walked away. He looked back just as he got to the car, and waved. Shay waved back, standing in the open doorway, watching as he drove off.

Shay closed the door, and just stood there for a moment, smelling the rose. She felt light-headed as she reached down to remove her boots.

I'm not going to think about this now. There's just too much happening here to digest at one time. I'll do a Scarlett O'Hara, and think about it tomorrow.

Just as she was turning out the lights in the living room, preparing to go to bed, the doorbell rang.

*Uh-*Huh*! I* knew *it was too good to be true. Well, you're not going to pull that Columbo come-back-for-one-last-question routine on* me, *Mr. Weaver. You're not setting foot beyond that threshold.*

Shay marched to the door, and without looking through the peephole, flung it open wide, taking a deep breath in preparation for holding Ric at bay.

But it wasn't Ric. It was Woody.

"Woody! What a surprise!"

Woody barged past her into the house, "Just thought I'd pop over to see if you were still up. I'm not *interrupting* anything, am I?"

This was a Woody Shay had never seen. His easy going manner was gone as he paced the living room like a caged tiger; his eyes snapping with anger; his face contorted into a rebuking grimace.

"Of course you're not interrupting anything. I was just about to get ready for bed."

"Yeah, I just *bet* you were! Are you sure I'm not *intruding* on anything? I mean three's a crowd, and all that." He looked her up and down, "Hot outfit," he remarked sarcastically.

Shay crossed her arms, "I don't have the slightest idea where you're coming from, Woody."

"Well, that puts me one step ahead of you, Shay. I *do* know where you're coming from. At least, I know who you came *with*."

It was all starting to make sense now, but Shay asked anyway, "You want to stop talking in circles, and get to what's really on your mind here?"

"All right, I'll tell you what's on my mind. Wondering what's on yours—or if you indeed *have* a mind at all. Shay, what were you doing with that dirtbag Weaver?"

Shay felt herself getting angrier by the second. "Since you obviously saw it, what did it *look* like I was doing?" Wood was still rambling around like a man possessed. "And if you're trying to provoke him out to face you, you can stop now. He's not here."

"I know he's not here. I saw the chump leave. I guess you were too *busy* to see me. I was waiting for you in my car, down the street."

Shay stopped short, "Are you telling me you had this house staked out, *spying* on me? Waiting for me to come home?"

"You damn right I did. And that bastard better be glad he left you at the door."

"*You're* the one who better be glad!" Shay erupted. "You're lucky I chose to come home at all. Otherwise, you might have been sitting out there in your car like a jerk all night! Who the hell do you think you are, sitting outside my house, watching who comes and goes?"

"Apparently a person with better judgment than you have. How could you go out with him? Don't you know how he is? Don't you know the things he's done?"

"We're not talking about Ric now, Woody. We're talking about you and me."

"All right, then; let's *talk* about you and me. What is this crap? I thought we had something going. I thought we cared about each other. And here you up and sport yourself around town with the likes of Ric Weaver!"

"I wasn't *sporting* anywhere with him," Shay said between clenched teeth. "I just had dinner with him, Wood, okay?"

"No, it's *not* okay!" Wood exploded. "Here like a fool I've been playing it slow with you for months. You weren't sure—I waited. You weren't ready—I waited. You just plain wanted to wait—I waited. Only to find you've been running around behind my back with *him*!"

Shay's temper had reached fever pitch by now, and as usual for her, anger made her calm. "Let's get a few things straight here, *Woodington*. First of all, not that I have to tell you a damn thing, but I *haven't* been 'running around' with Ric. He came by, he asked me to dinner—and I went."

Wood's eyes flashed fire, "And what *else* have you done that he's asked you to do?"

"None of your damn business!" Shay shot back.

"None of my business! How can you say that when we have..."

"We have a friendship, Wood. And if you want to keep it, I suggest you listen to me very carefully right about now. What did you think? That no other man in this city could find me attractive? That you had a claim staked on me? That I was your *property*?"

That took a little wind out of his sails, "No, Shay, of course, I didn't think any of that, but..."

"Then you need to understand something. I like you, Woody, and I *do* care for you. You know I do. But I go where I like, when I like, with whomever I like, and I don't need *your* permission to do it!"

Woody saw he'd made a major tactical error. Now that he had calmed down a bit, he could see that Shay was seething. "Shay, look, I didn't mean..."

"Is a little competition too much for you, Wood? Well,

if you can't stand the heat, you better get out of the kitchen. Mrs. Logan's baby girl don't play that 'I own you' crap. I already *got* a Daddy, but he's back in Detroit. And even *he* stopped trying to tell me who I couldn't go out with when I graduated from high school!"

"Look, Shay," Wood said slowly, running a hand through his hair, "I'm...I'm sorry. I didn't mean to barge in here like a crazy man.

"We finally got the Holly debacle straightened out. She's on her way back to LA So I rushed over here to see if we could salvage what was left of the evening. When there was no answer at your door with your car still in the driveway, I got worried. I was just sitting in my car getting ready to call your cell phone when you drove up with *him*." Woody spat the word out like it was slime.

"It was all I could do to keep from running up and punching that punk when he kissed you. I...I just lost it. I never felt so jealous of anything or anyone in my life. But I had no right to come on to you like that. Forgive me, Shay."

Shay gave a deep sigh. "I forgive you, Woody. I know you too well and think too much of you not to forgive you. And I can understand how it must have looked, and how you felt. But please—don't ever run any junk like that on me again. I don't like it."

"I won't, Shay; I promise. But look..." he took her hand, "we had a very special evening planned. Don't you think we could still try to save what's left of it? Richmond has kept dinner waiting at home, and..."

"I've already eaten, Woody. And I've got the headache of the century right now. I'm not in the mood."

"It's...*him*, isn't it?" Wood asked slowly, clearly dreading the answer.

Shay looked him in the eye, "Yes, Wood; it *is* him; at least partially. I can't deny any longer, not even to myself, that I have feelings for Ric. But, as you can see, I sent *him* home, too. I don't know *what* to do right now. All I know is that I need some time alone—to think."

"All right, honey," Wood kissed the hand he was still holding. "I've waited for you this long." He touched Shay's face, and looked deeply into her eyes, "I'd wait for you 'til the end of time if I had to. You know that now, don't you, baby?"

Shay looked away from him and just nodded.

They walked together to the door. "Well...could I at least kiss you good night?" Wood whispered.

Shay nodded, with the weirdest sense of deja vu.

Wood wrapped her up in his arms and held her close as if he never wanted to let her go. He kissed her passionately, but not with a passion born of lust. It was a passion born—she now knew—of love.

When they broke the kiss, Wood didn't let her go. As he looked into her face a hundred different emotions crossed his face like a mosaic. "I don't want to lose you, Natasha," he said softly. "I can't lose you. There are a lot of things I want you to do. Like bounce our grandchildren on your knee someday." He kissed her forehead, and slowly let her go, walking out the door without another word.

CHAPTER 9

RAINMAN

Wood called early the next day, "Morning, Shay. Did I wake you?"

"No, Woody, I've been up a while. I didn't sleep very well last night."

"Neither did I. Shay...about last night. I don't know what got into me... Yes, I *do* know what got into me—the green-eyed monster. But Shay, I..."

"It's all right, Woody. Last night was last night; this is today."

"You're not angry with me?"

"No, Wood, I'm not angry. Confused, yes; but angry, no."

"I'm at the studio already. Why don't you come down, and I'll call an early break so we can have breakfast."

"No, Woody; thanks, but I think I'll just work on the script at home this morning. I've got a lot of business calls to return. How are things going with Holly?"

"My attorneys got the charges dropped. I'm not exactly sure how, and I'm not going to ask. I might not want to know. Holly got back into town earlier this morning. I'm going to meet with her and her manager later today."

"Wood, I have to ask you this. You're working with...with Ric every day. Is that going to be a problem?"

There was a long pause, then Wood replied, "Shay, Ric is about my least favorite person in the world right now. But this movie is important to us all. I know that, and he knows it, too. Much as I hate to hand the man *any* compliment, Ric's too professional to let this affect his work—and so am I. It won't be easy, but we'll be all right.

"Ric is, in fact, indirectly one reason I'm calling. He's not in any scenes this afternoon, and Quint wants to meet with the two of you to discuss the score. Are you free?"

"Yes, Woody. This afternoon's good for me. When and where?"

"Ric's recording studio, Sugarland Sounds, at four o'clock. Do you know where it is?"

"I can find my way."

"Shay, you don't know how it kills me, setting up a meeting between the two of you. If I had my way, I'd kick his butt right off the face of the planet, instead of setting up a meeting for him with my girl."

"You wouldn't have much of a movie, with your leading man floating around in space," Shay weakly tried to kid him out of his animosity.

"It would almost be worth it," Wood stiffly replied.

"But Woody, you just said..."

"I know, I know. Business is business. But I don't have to *like* it. Anyway, I'll call you this evening."

"All right, Wood. Talk to you later."

"Shay..." Wood's voice got very soft, "last night didn't work out, but I thought maybe tonight we could..."

"I don't know, Woody. We'll see, okay?"

"Okay, honey." Wood said uneasily. He had obviously concluded it would not be wise to pressure her. "Talk to you then."

Shay went into the kitchen to fix herself some breakfast when the phone rang again.

"Hi, baby, how you doin'?" It was Ric. Some of the magic of last night—before all hell broke loose—came back to Shay.

"Hi, Ric; I'm fine," Shay said warmly. "How are you?"

"Better this morning than I've been in many a day; because of last night." Shay blushed in spite of herself, remembering their good night kiss the night before.

"I'm in my car, on the way to the studio," he went on. Do you know we're set up for a meeting with Five this afternoon?"

At first, Shay thought he said, "*at* five," until she remembered "Five" was what people who knew Quinton well called him.

"Yes, Wood just called to tell me."

"Woody. I know how he feels about you, Shay. It would be obvious to a blind man. Hell, I can't blame him. He's not going to be happy about last night. Did you tell him?"

Shay debated for a second whether to tell Ric the truth, then decided she was sick and tired of pretense. "I didn't have to. He had come by and was outside in his car when you brought me home. And 'not happy' is an understatement of epic proportions."

"Well, I'm sorry he had to find out about us that way; but so be it. He might as well get used to it now."

"Ric, there isn't any 'us.' We had dinner last night, that's all. And I have to tell you up front: the affection between me and Wood is no a one-way street. I care for him, too, Ric; very much."

"I know, Shay—that's obvious, too," Ric replied softly. "But I'll take my chances. I'm not asking for any iron-clad guarantees, honey.

"Ric, this isn't going to interfere with your working with Woody, is it?"

"Hell, no; at least not on *my* part. I have nothing against Wood. Like I said, I couldn't blame any man for wanting you, Shay." His voice lowered again, "I know what that's like.

"And I've always respected Wood; a lot. Much as I hate to compliment the competition, he's all right and talented as hell. It takes an extraordinary person to drag a performance out of Vanessa—without strangling her in the process. If he doesn't start anything with me, I'm damn sure not going to start anything with him."

Shay was overwhelmingly relieved to hear that. As Wood had said, the movie was crucial for all their careers, and a stand-off between the director and the leading man would help no one.

"So, I'll see you at four?" Ric was continuing.

"Yep; I'll be there."

"I can hardly wait. But," he teased, "don't wear that outfit you had on last night, baby. I need to concentrate today."

They said their goodbyes, and Shay again started breakfast. She was just sitting down for her first cup of coffee when the phone rang again. *Damn! What is this— Phone Fest 2012?*

This time it was Marty, wanting to know the outcome of the Holly impasse. Shay filled her in on that, then went on to cover the night's other festivities.

"Shay, you can't keep on this way," Marty advised. "I have to admit, I can't be objective where Woody is concerned. After all, he *is* Darnell's best friend. But I'd pull for Woody even if he wasn't. He's already proven he's for real. Honey, Ric's hurt you once already. With that reputation of his—which I understand is most royally deserved—how can you trust him?"

"Marty, if you could have seen him the way he was last night... Believe it or not, there is a real man—with a real heart—under all that hype. Ric's been hurt, too, Marty."

Shay had told Marty everything about the evening except Ric's revelations about his background. Ric had trusted her; telling her those things in confidence. Shay didn't feel right divulging it, not even to Marty, although she knew Marty wouldn't tell a soul if Shay asked her not to.

Marty just snorted. "Mr. Heartbreaker 'hurt'? *That's* sure hard to believe."

"Trust me, Marty; it's true. And I'm sure his feelings for me are genuine."

"Well, Shay, you know my opinion. But it's your decision. Either way, honey, it's time to make up your mind."

"Marty, I've tried. Maybe the problem is I'm in love with both of them."

"No, that *couldn't* be, Shay," Marty said firmly. "Real love rules that out by definition. Real love means wanting to be with one person; just that one person..." her voice became quite soft, "above all others."

"The way you feel about Darnell?" Shay asked gently.

There was a long silence, then Marty simply replied, "Yes."

"How does he feel?"

"I think he feels the same, but he's never exactly come out and said so. But he'll let me know where he's coming from pretty soon, one way or the other. Our relationship is like a growing plant whose pot has become too small for its roots. You either upgrade it to a bigger pot where it can flourish—or it dies. I know what I want, but I'm not sure how big of a commitment Darnell's willing to make."

"Marty, Darnell's crazy about you."

"Crazy love is one thing. Real love is another. We'll see which it is in time."

Shay spent the balance of the morning and the early afternoon working on the script, and her own private business affairs. She both welcomed and dreaded seeing Ric again; not knowing what to expect of him—or herself.

True to form, despite her GPS, Shay got lost trying to find the studio. The gentle, but steady rain sure didn't help. The sky was so dark she had to turn her headlights on. She wound up getting to the studio twenty-five minutes late.

Ric and Quinton were waiting for her. Ric lit up like a Christmas tree when she was shown into the studio. Quinton noticed, and looked at Shay with a puzzled expression, but was too sophisticated, and too polite, to comment.

"Shay! What happened to you, honey?" Ric asked as he and Quinton both stood. "I was about to send the cops out to find you. Is it raining?" Ric had noticed the droplets of water in her hair and on her shoulders.

"Just a light sprinkle," Shay told him, "but I didn't know that until I pulled out of my garage, and then I didn't want to go back for an umbrella. I thought the songs say 'it never rains in Southern California'."

"Well, that's poetic license, my dear," Quinton said with a chuckle, holding out a chair for Shay. "Something I'm sure you well understand since you're a lyricist yourself now."

Shay started to protest, until she remembered that now she really *was,* and officially. The words she'd written for the song "I Need You Near Me" for the novel were going to be put to music. That was a big part of why they were meeting that day.

Wood's concept for the movie's music was ingenious. Quinton and Ric were providing original music; five songs mentioned in the novel, plus instrumentals as background for scenes.

Additionally, Wood had secured the rights to several previously released hit songs by various artists; to be heard in as background, or as bridges tying scenes together. The compilation would result in a double album CD of the movie's soundtrack, to be released shortly before the movie itself. Thus the soundtrack would enhance interest in the movie, and vice versa; a formula that had worked magnificently for many such joint efforts in the past.

Ric's latest CD was still number one in the charts, even now, several weeks after its release. So the situation couldn't be better for the movie CD, with Ric performing five original songs.

Quint had already written most of the instrumental music, but he and Ric wanted to discuss with Shay her original concept of how each of the five songs she presented in the novel should sound before finishing those.

They both listened carefully as Shay described each

one, saying her perception of this one was as a scorching dance number; this one as a dreamy ballad, and so on. The songs would be titled as she had titled them in the novel, and Shay was going to receive mention—and payment—for the album, with all but one of the songs five songs showing the credit, "Based on a Concept by Natasha Logan."

For "I Need You Near Me", however, Shay would be listed as the lyricist, since they were using her exact words from the novel. The song would be published as written by "Logan and James", which thrilled Shay to pieces.

When Shay got to the description of the one gospel song in the novel, "He Carried Me," "Five," as Shay also had begun to call him, grimaced.

"I'm really stuck on that one," Five confessed. "I've written gospel music before, but I want *this* one to have a really original sound, and everything I've come up with so far sounds too much like something that's been done."

Shay debated speaking up, but then shyly admitted, "Well, Quin...er, Five, I've...I've written some music for that song."

Ric and Five stared at her as though she'd just announced there was a bomb in the room, "You've...you've *what*?" Five finally asked.

Shay felt like a fool and was sorry she had even mentioned it. "I...wrote some music, and words too, for that song. I've always loved gospel music. I sang in the church choir at home all my life. And while I was writing the book, I sort of composed a song in my head to go with the title of that song."

Five looked at Ric, and Ric looked at Five, then they both looked at Shay. "Well," Five said softly, "let's hear it."

Shay was flabbergasted. "*What*? Five, I said I just put something together in my head. I never committed anything to *paper*. I play piano a little, but I'm not sure I *could* write it down, even if I wanted to."

"I didn't say let's *see* it. I said let's *hear* it. You can sing it for me and Ric, can't you?"

"Well, yes, but..."

"Go ahead, honey; sing it for us," Ric urged. "We're really stuck on this one, and maybe what you've got 'in your head' will give us a little inspiration."

Shay couldn't believe they were serious, but they both sure *looked* serious. Loathe as she was to sing before these two musical giants, she cleared her throat and began. They both listened intently; at a couple of points looking at each other with unreadable expressions, as she went through the song.

When Shay finished, neither man said a word. Five went over to the nearby piano. He was still for a moment, a frown of deep concentration on his face then started to play. It was unquestionably the melody Shay had just sung, but his embellishments of an upbeat rhythm, harmony, and counterpoint made it sound totally new, even to Shay.

Ric nodded in time to the music for a few bars, then went over near the piano, and began to sing. To Shay's absolute amazement, he got right most of the words he had just heard for the first time a few moments before.

Shay had been in awe of these two talented men even before she had met either of them. Now she was in near shock.

Anyone who has ever doubted that these two deserve the heap of awards they've both received over the years ought to be here now, she marveled.

When they reached the end, both men started laughing and gave each other a high five.

"All *right*!" Ric cheered.

"You know it, man!" Five whooped back. He turned to Shay, his face glowing, "Hope you like the sound of 'Words and Music by Natasha Logan'."

Shay felt light-headed, "What...what did you say?"

"This is perfect," Five exclaimed. "Just what I've been

shooting for! I'll tell the record company they're going to have to amend your contract for proper credits—and payment—for this song. Have your agent and lawyer contact them. That voice of yours ain't bad, either." He bowed forward twice, arms outstretched, giving Shay a salaam. "Miss Logan, you are one-of-a-kind!"

Ric looked at Shay proudly, "I coulda told you that, man," he said emphatically.

Once again, Five looked from Ric to Shay, and back again with perplexity in his eyes, then just shrugged.

Shay looked at Five in stupefaction, "Are you *serious*?"

"As a heart attack," he succinctly replied.

"But...Five...what you and Ric just did...I didn't write *that*," Shay protested, going over to him. "Well, the words I wrote, but that little melody I sang for you sure didn't sound as amazing as what you just played. I didn't write all that!" she stammered.

Five took Shay's hand and gently pulled her down to sit next to him on the piano bench.

"Honey, what do you think a song *is*?" he asked patiently. "It's a melody. Even words are not essential. I grant you, my arrangement improves how it sounds, but arranging other people's melodies is one of the things I do best. Arranging a song, and creating it are two very different things, Shay." He looked at her closely, "You don't *object* to us using your song for the movie, do you?"

"Lord, no!" Shay proclaimed. "I'm just knocked off my feet!"

"Well, that makes two of us. You can sing up a storm, Shay."

"Make that three of us," Ric put in. "I'd heard you were a singer, but I never dreamed you were *this* good," he added in amazement.

"Well, Ric, I think we're over the last big hurdle," Five told him. "With this song settled, we've pretty much got all our basic material. Now I can concentrate on instrumentation and arrangement."

"Oh, so you've already finished the music for 'I Need You Near Me'?" Shay asked Five, standing, and going back to her chair.

"No, *I* haven't. But Ric has."

Shay turned to Ric in bafflement, "*You* wrote the music?"

Ric gave her that dazzling smile, "Yes. The melody just came to me one night. Don't look so surprised, baby. I *have* written a song or two in my time, you know." He took a step closer to her, "And I had some mighty potent inspiration for this one," he added softly.

Ric nodded to Five, who started to play again. This time the beat was leisurely and magnetic; the harmonies delicate and intertwined. Ric looked at Shay, and began to sing:

Something about you captured me right from the start.
Something about you found its way inside my heart.
Just like the shore is destined to be by the sea,
I need you near me.

Came unexpectedly; caught me by surprise,
But then I saw my future there, deep within your eyes.
So though my stubborn heart at first refused to see,
I need you near me.

The stars would be astray anywhere but in the sky.
The valley all alone without the mountain high.
A flower without rain would wither soon and die.
And just that fundamentally
I need to have you close to me.

I guess I never knew what love was all about
Until you came along and turned me inside out.

And so I'll tell you, girl; tell you on bended knee,
That I will always need you near to me.

For always...I need you near me.

Shay felt like her heart had stopped, her breathing ceased, and all time stood still as Ric sang. His eyes never left hers as the words she created, words that were embedded in her heart, came back to her reborn, delivered by music *he* had created.

The feeling of unreality, of having her fantasy come to life, once again hit her like a lightning bolt. The thought of Michael, her glorious Michael, singing this song to the woman he loved had filled her mind, filled her dreams, more times than she could remember.

But the song had no life, no melody, not even in her vision. She couldn't associate any of the simple ditties that flitted through her mind with *this* song. They didn't do it justice. But now it had substance; it was alive, through the haunting, mesmerizing music Ric had married to her words.

The electric tie that bound Ric and Shay was unmistakable now. There was a deafening silence when Ric finished the song. Even Five seemed in baffled awe of the almost tangible tether between them.

Finally, Ric asked, almost too softly to be heard, "Do you like it, Shay?"

Shay was unable to speak at that moment, so she merely nodded, blinking back the tears that threatened to spill from her eyes.

The room grew silent again with Ric and Shay just staring at each other. Five mutely watched then, clearly wondering what the hell was going on. At last, Five spoke up, "Unless I'm very mistaken—and when it comes to music, that's not often—you two have got yourselves a very possible Grammy *and* Oscar winner there. Wood is going to be tickled to death."

Five could see something very unexplained was happening between Ric and Shay. And like most people connected with the movie, he had assumed something was going on between *Woody* and Shay. Five had deliberately dropped Wood's name to see their reaction.

There wasn't one. The two of them just kept staring at each other as though Five hadn't spoken at all.

"Words and music by Logan and Weaver," Ric finally whispered.

"Logan...and Weaver," Shay echoed.

"Ahem...ah, Ric, your shooting schedule is tighter than my grandmother's corset," Five interjected after a long silence. "We better try to get some work in this afternoon, while we have the chance. Shay, why don't you stick around and watch?"

That brought Shay back to reality, "No; no, thanks, Five. I've got a lot of work to do at home; re-writes and what-not." Shay deliberately avoided looking at Ric as she stood up, "Guess I'll be on my way."

"I'll walk you to your car," Ric told her.

"No, Ric. That won't be necessary. It's the middle of the afternoon, and..."

Ric took a step closer, "I'll walk you to your car, Shay," he insisted, looking into her eyes. He turned to Five, "Be back in a minute, man."

Neither of them spoke as they walked down the corridor to the parking lot. Shay didn't trust herself to speak. She was too shaken by Ric's song...*their* song...and by his nearness.

Outside the rain had turned into a downpour. "Wow! Wait here a minute, Shay. I'll go see if anybody has an umbrella."

"Don't bother, Ric. I'll just make a run for it."

"Then I'm going with you."

"There's no need to get yourself all wet for nothing. My car's right over there, and I can..."

Suddenly Ric burst out the door, racing for her car, "Last one there is a rotten song-writing egg!" he shouted.

"No fair!" Shay took off after him. "You hooked a head start!"

Ric did beat her to the car, but it did him little good since all he could do was just stand there in the rain until she arrived to unlock the door.

They jumped into the car, Shay under the wheel. "Shay, honey..." Ric began.

"I'll drop you off at the door," Shay said quickly, turning the ignition. But instead of the engine coming to life, all they heard was a series of clicks.

"What in the world?..." Shay began; then saw that the dashboard lights were on, but very faintly. "Oh, damn! I left the lights on! The battery's dead." She pulled out her cell phone. "Got to a call a tow truck for a jump."

"I can take you home, Shay. The Toy is right over there."

"The *what*?"

"The Toy—my Toyota."

"But what about *my* car?"

"I'll have my mechanic replace your battery, and drive it out to your house later—no problem."

"But, Ric, there's no need for..."

"Stay here! Be right back!" He jumped out of the car and sprinted off towards the Toyota. In minutes he was back, pulling the passenger side of his car alongside her driver's door. Shay quickly hopped between cars, and they were on their way.

"Ric, there was no need for you to go to so much trouble. And Five's waiting for you at the studio."

"Let him. And as for trouble," he smiled at her, "finding any excuse to be near you is no trouble at all." He stopped smiling, "'I Need You Near Me'...Shay."

Shay quickly turned to look out the window.

"Did you really like the song?" Ric murmured.

"Yes. It's...it's how I always knew in my heart it would sound...*should* sound. Your music will make it a classic, Ric."

"It just came to me. After all, you did write the words for *me*, didn't you?" He chuckled softly, "I know it's stupid, but I'm starting to get a little jealous of Michael. He's accomplished something I haven't been able to do—find his way into your heart."

Shay didn't answer him, and they rode on in silence, with only music from the tape deck, and the thunder from the storm for accompaniment.

As they approached her house, Shay pawed through her purse a few moments, then said, "Damn!"

"What's the matter?"

"I left the garage door opener in my car! And it's pouring out there!"

"Well, baby, we're both more than slightly wet already. A little more soaking sure ain't gonna hurt *me*. But I don't know about you," he grinned as he pulled as close to her front door as he could. "Sugar melts."

"So does salt; so watch yourself," Shay threw back at him, as she opened her car door. Ric jumped out of the car also and they raced together to her front door. But in spite of their speed, they were both drenched from head to toe by the time they reached it.

"Oh, Ric; just look at you! You didn't have to see me to the door. You look like something that drowned!"

Ric gave her a soggy aristocratic bow, "And you, my dear, look like the puddle I drowned in!"

They both started laughing. "Well, I can't send you on your way squishing like that," Shay told him, unlocking the door. "Come on in, and I'll find something for you to wear."

Shay opened the door and flicked the light switch that was just inside. Nothing happened. "Must be a downed power line somewhere," Ric surmised, as they stood in the gloom of Shay's entryway. Ric looked out one of the tall windows along each side of Shay's front door. "This thing started off slow, but looks like it's gonna turn into a whopper." A strobe-like flash of lightening lit his face momentarily.

"I hate thunderstorms!" Shay said. "When I was a kid..."

All at once there was a boom of thunder so close and so deep the floor vibrated under their feet. By reflex, Shay jumped into Ric's arms, trembling, "Oh!..."

The next moment, his lips found hers, as his arms encompassed her tightly. "Shay," he whispered hoarsely, "it took an act of God to do it, but I have you back in my arms again."

"Ric, I don't..."

He kissed her again, and this time the yearning she felt was not to be denied. They sank slowly to the floor; the sound of the thunder, and the drum of the pelting rain mingling with their cries of passion.

Much later, as they lay huddled together on the living room floor, Shay started to shiver. The light whose switch Shay had flicked earlier Suddenly came on. "Electricity's back on," Ric noted.

"It's been on in *here* all afternoon," Shay commented naughtily.

Ric chuckled, stood, and offered his hand. "Be that as it may, you're going to catch your death lying here wet and naked on the floor, honey," he said as he helped her up. Ric bent to pick up the packet of condoms that Shay had insisted upon, even in the midst of their passionate haste.

Shay went into the bathroom. When she emerged Ric said, "Here; put this on." Ric came up behind her with her terry cloth robe and held it out as she slipped her arms into the sleeves. Then he took a towel and gently dried her hair. She turned. He had on another of her robes, a loose flowing African print she had gotten on vacation in the

Virgin Islands the previous year. It practically swallowed Shay but was just a fit on Ric.

"Is there anything you don't look good in?" Shay stood back to appraise him. "In that, you look like an African prince."

He put his palms together and gave her deep bow. "Thank you, my princess," he intoned in a deep voice.

Shay fetched their wet clothes from the entryway where they'd left them before rolling onto the living room carpeting. She went through the kitchen to the laundry room, where she started them on a wash cycle.

Shay went back into the kitchen. Ric told her, "I started some coffee brewing."

They took a tray with the coffee set, and a bottle of Grand Marnier, into the living room. The storm had diminished, but it was still cold and rainy.

"This would be a great night for a fire," Ric said, looking at the fireplace. "Is this thing a working model?"

"I've never fired it up, but my real estate agent assured me it was, and that it had recently been cleaned. I've never had a fireplace before, and I've been afraid to mess with it, but there are logs, and an irons, and stuff in that cabinet," Shay pointed.

"Uh...that's 'andirons', love," Ric corrected her with a smile, going to the cabinet.

In no time at all he had the fire going. Shay had started some soft music playing, and they leaned back on the sofa sipping their augmented coffee. Shay swung her feet into Ric's lap, and he casually draped one hand across her legs.

"I think this is where I came in," Shay noted wryly.

"What?"

"The night you gave me the foot massage?"

Ric grinned, and put down his coffee, "Would you like another one?"

"That's the least you could do.." Shay said, wiggling

her toes, "after dragging me around in a typhoon."

Ric started massaging her feet, "And what's the most I could do, my princess?" he asked suggestively.

"Ummm...I'll think of something."

The telephone rang then, and being closest to it, Ric handed it to Shay.

"Shay! You're home! Are you all right?" Shay tensed at the sound of Wood's voice.

"Yes, Woody, I'm fine," she cautiously replied. Ric stopped his massage and just looked at her.

"Thank God! I've been trying to call you for hours. I heard there was a power outage in your part of town; guess some of the phone lines were down, too. Didn't you hear your cell phone ringing? I've been worried sick about you. If I hadn't gotten through this time, I was going to head on out there to make sure you were all right"

Shay shivered at the thought of Wood popping up at her door just *then*.

"I would have been out there already," Wood was continuing, "but I called the recording studio, and Five told me you left there with time enough to get home before things got really bad."

And Five was apparently discreet enough not *to tell you I left with Ric—and that Ric never came back* Shay thought.

"Yes, Wood. I got home right after the power went out. It's back on now."

"I stayed at the studio late, talking with Holly and her manager. She's promised to go into detox, and get her act together, so she'd staying on the movie. But anyway, I got caught in the worst of the storm, trying to get home. When I got here, there was a small fire in the woods behind the house, from a lightning strike. Man, this has been one wild and wooly day!"

"*That's* for sure," Shay said with feeling.

"Anyway, I can come out there now, if you want me

to, Shay." His voice lowered, "I know how you hate thunderstorms, baby."

A dagger pierced Shay's heart. This sweet, wonderful man; he remembered everything she'd ever told him about herself. Nothing was too much for him to do for her comfort or well-being. The thought of hurting him with the news about Ric and herself was more than Shay could take at that moment.

"No, Woody; I wouldn't dream of having you come out on a night like this. I'm fine, really. You've had a tough enough day as it is."

"You know I wouldn't mind, Shay," Wood replied softly.

Shay's eyes squeezed shut in pain at the devotion in his voice. "Yes, I know, Wood. But it's all right. I'll talk to you tomorrow. Good night."

"Good night, sweetheart."

Ric sat silently by, watching the fire while Shay was on the phone. He looked at her as she hung up. "You're got to tell him *sometime*, Shay," he said softly.

"I know, Ric; but I just couldn't tonight. And I don't want to tell him over the phone. I want to tell him face to face."

"Do you want *me* to talk to him?"

"No; no, Ric. I've got to tell him myself. I owe him that."

"Well, look; there's nothing we can do about it tonight, darlin'." He stood, pulling her up with him. "You've worn me out. Let's turn in."

"I've worn *you* out? *You're* the one who couldn't wait to go into the bedroom. I've got carpet burns from here to..."

"I know, baby, I know. And Ric will kiss every one of them, and make it all better."

"Is that a promise?"

He gave her that heart-breaking grin, "You know it."

While Ric was seeing to the fire, Shay went into the laundry room, and put their clothes in the dryer. By the time he entered the bedroom Shay had lit several candles and was lying in bed in her sexiest negligee.

"Damn, woman!" Ric exclaimed when he saw her. "Are you out to kill me, or what?"

"Oh, I think you can handle it." She crooked her finger, "Come here."

Several passionate kisses later, Ric suddenly stopped, and just held her close. "Shay?"

"Yes, honey?"

"Look, I've been out there on the wild for a long time now. I guess you know that."

"Yes, Ric, I do," Shay replied quietly.

"I've done a lot of things I'm sure not proud of." He looked at her intently, "I saw you talking with Simone. Do you know about her?"

"Yes. And I was surprised she's still working for you after you broke off with her."

Ric laughed softly, "I didn't break it off with her. She broke it off with *me*."

"She *did*?"

"Yep. Things got started one time we were traveling on tour. We were both away from home, and lonely and... Well, one thing just led to another. Hell, it would probably *still* be going on if she hadn't stopped it. I like Simone; she's easy to talk to..." He kissed Shay's forehead, "like you. And she's a beautiful woman. I *like* a woman with a little meat on her—skinny ain't my thing.

"But when we got back from the tour, I kept on with my same old ways, and she laid down the law. Either I cut it out, or we were through. I wasn't willing to be a one woman man, and she absolutely refused to be 'one of the crowd.' So she took our relationship back to where it was—professional only."

"She's quite a lady," Shay said, meaning it.

"Yes, she is," Ric agreed. "Which brings me back to my point. Shay, I've cut a pretty wide swath. You're going to run into a lot of my used to be's because there *are* a lot of them. But that's all over now, honey. Now I've found you. And I know *you're* not going for that stuff."

Shay looked him in the eye, "No, Ric; I'm not."

"That's history now; if you'll have me. One on one is the way I want it…with you."

"I can't live with it any other way," Shay told him straightforwardly.

"I know, hon. I know you. And it will be that way. I promise." He kissed her tenderly, "It won't be hard, my princess. I don't *want* anyone but you."

Ric took Shay in his arms once again, and they spent the night listening to the sound of the rain, and the beat of each other's heart.

CHAPTER 10

DANGEROUS LIAISONS

The sun shone brilliantly through the sliding glass doors. Shay drifted to consciousness slowly, feeling warm...and achy, but pleasantly achy. She rolled to her side, to wake Ric with a kiss, but was amazed to find herself in bed alone.

No! Not again! I can't believe this is happening again! I was so sure. He seemed so sincere. And like an idiot, I believed him.

Shay pounded the pillow as she buried her face in it. *How could I be so stupid? How could I fall into the same dumb trap twice?* Tears of bitterness filled her eyes as she lay there feeling numb—and used.

"Ta-da!" came Ric's voice from the doorway. Shay's head snapped up to see Ric entering the room with a bed tray.

"Madam's breakfast is served. And Ric's Cafe serves the finest spread in town!" He looked down and saw the tears in Shay's eyes. Ric hurriedly put the tray on the dresser, and sat down on the bed next to her, "Honey! What on earth is the matter, baby?"

"I thought...when I woke up, and you were gone, I thought...."

"That I'd pulled another disappearing act...right?" Ric asked gently.

"Yes." Shay blinked, and a fat tear ran down her cheek.

Ric leaned forward, and tenderly kissed the tear away, "You're not getting rid of me that easily, lady." He took her hand and kissed it. "This time I'm here to stay, Shay."

Shay smiled at him through her tears, "Poet and know it," she whispered.

Ric kissed her forehead, "Now...breakfast awaits." He got up to retrieve the tray and placed it on her lap as she sat up in bed. "Better eat this stuff while it's hot," he said, looking at it dubiously. "Cooking is not one of my strong suits. If it gets cold it might not be fit for human consumption."

Shay looked down at the tray. Indeed, it did not look like cuisine that could pass any gourmet taste tests. But Ric looked so proud, Shay knew she'd eat it no matter how much force of will it took.

"Ooops! Forgot the coffee! Be right back, baby." He took off for the kitchen again just as the telephone rang.

Somehow Shay knew before she answered that it would be Woody.

"Morning, sunshine! How are you today?"

"I'm fine, Wood. You?"

"Going through the usual convolutions with my crew of talented lunatics. If it's not one of them, it's the other. This morning Mr. Wonderful has popped up missing. He was due in makeup an hour ago. I called his house, but he's not there. And he's not answering his cell phone. I can only hope he's on his way. Where else could he be?"

Shay began carefully, "Woody..."

Just then Ric stuck his head in the door, "I can't find the coffee cups, baby. Where do you keep them?" he called out.

Shay sighed. There it was. There was no way Wood couldn't have heard that. And no way he would think Ric would be there that time of the morning other than the obvious reason; he'd been there all night.

"In the cupboard above the coffee maker, Ric," Shay softly replied.

There was dead silence on the phone as Ric again left the room. "Woody?" Shay asked reluctantly.

There was silence again for a moment or two, then Wood said bluntly, "Well, guess *that* mystery is solved."

"Wood, listen; I didn't want you to find out this way. I..."

"Tell Ric I'll shoot around him today, Shay," was all he said.

"But, Wood..." But she was listening to the dial tone.

Ric came back with two cups of coffee. He took one look at Shay's face, and said, "Woman, are you going to look like you've lost your best friend every time I come back into the room?"

"I *have* lost my best friend, Ric; at least one of them. That was Wood on the phone just now."

Ric's face showed his concern, "And you told him?"

"I didn't have to. *You* did. He overheard you."

"Oh..." He sat down on the bed again. "I'm sorry, honey. I barely realized you were on the phone at all. That was pretty thoughtless of me."

"It's not like you did it on purpose, Ric. And he had to find out sooner or later. I'm just sorry it had to happen this way. I care about him, Ric. He means a lot to me, and I just can't bear knowing I hurt him this way."

Ric took her hand, "Shay, the sad fact of the matter is you could not avoid hurting one of us. That's just the way this hand was dealt." He looked deeply into her eyes, "Would you rather the one hurt had been me?" he asked anxiously.

Shay returned his gaze, searching his eyes, "No," she finally whispered, leaning forward to kiss him.

When they broke apart, Ric said, "I was due at the studio an hour ago. Guess I better call to let them know I'm on my way."

"Wood said to tell you they'd shoot around you today," Shay told him in a subdued tone.

"That's probably for the best. I don't think there's any way Wood and I could accomplish anything even semi-constructive today. It's going to be hard enough from here on out without pushing it.

"So, tell you what; we've got a whole day to spend together, just you and me. Let's make the most of it."

And the day was wonderful. They spent the morning just lazing around the house, making love. Then they went out for a late lunch and wound up on Rodeo Drive, shopping. Shay bought Ric a fabulous pair of gold cuff links, and Ric bought her a stunning emerald pendant necklace.

"And I don't want to hear no stuff about me buying you expensive presents," he said sternly as he placed it around her neck. "After all," he leaned forward to gently brush her lips with his, "you're my woman, now, Shay."

They stopped by a grocery store, and despite the near riot Ric's presence caused, managed to get provisions for dinner. Back at her house, Shay cooked him a down home soul food dinner, complete with black-eyed peas, collard greens, and cornbread.

"Have mercy, girl!" Ric declared, patting his stomach. "From now on *you* do the cooking." Shay just smiled in return, but inwardly heartily agreed.

They turned in early. Ric had an early call at the studio, and anyway, they were both eager to be in each other's arms. Shay lay half asleep on Ric's shoulder, her heart bursting with joy, but there was a shadow across it— the shadow of Woody's anguish. He had kept coming into her mind all day.

If only there was some way this could happen without hurting Wood. He's such an extraordinary, beautiful man. He deserves better. How can I be truly happy knowing my rejoicing is rooted in his despair?

Ric stirred, and his arm tightened around her, "What's the matter, baby? Did you say something?" he asked fuzzily.

"No, I didn't say anything, honey. Go back to sleep," Shay drowsily replied before drifting off herself.

The telephone rang. Shay sleepily answered it,

"Hello?"

"This is Martha," came Marty's terse response.

"Marty?" Shay said, looking past the still sleeping Ric to the bedside clock. "Marty, it's past midnight! What's the matter? Are you all right? Is something wrong?"

"No," Marty replied in the same clipped tone. "Nothing's wrong." Shay had never heard Marty speak that way, except when mightily ticked off, and that usually in the midst of a hot and heavy negotiation.

"I just called to let you know, *Miss* Logan," Marty continued with the same frosty inflection, "that as of now, you are no longer represented by Martha D. Tibbs."

"*What*?" Shay sat straight up in bed, suddenly wide awake. Her outburst woke Ric, who groggily inquired what was wrong. Shay shushed him, and continued into the phone, "Marty! What in hell are you talking about?"

"Just what I said," Marty curtly replied. "Effective immediately, you are no longer a client of the M.D. Tibbs Literary Agency."

"Marty, I don't understand! What's happened? What have I done? How could you feel this way?" Shay snapped on the bedside lamp. Ric was watching her closely but didn't speak.

Has she already heard about me and Ric? Is that what's going on? Woody is Darnell's best friend. But Marty wouldn't put me down like this because of that. I know she wouldn't. And Darnell wouldn't ask her to. So what's going on here?

"Look," Shay went on aloud, "you and I are going to have to sit down and talk this over, girl. And not over the phone. Tomorrow morning I'll be on the first flight to New York I can get, so we can talk about whatever it is face to face."

"My plane will take you, honey," Ric whispered. "It can be ready within the hour to take you anywhere you need to be." Shay gave him a grateful glance.

"I'm not *in* New York," was Marty's brusque response.

"Well, I'm coming where ever the hell you are," Shay shot back. "Marty, we're not just talking about a business contract here. You're my friend; one of the best friends I have in this world. We're got to talk about this, Marty! Besides being one of my dearest friends, you're my agent, for God's sake! Who in the world could I trust to represent me like I trust you?"

"How about Martha D. *Franklin*?"

In her agitated and confused state, it took Shay a few seconds to digest the message in Marty's answer. Then she leaped out of bed. "*What*!"

"I said 'Martha D. Franklin', Miss Logan," came Marty's giggle. "As of yesterday, Martha D. Franklin is your literary agent, my dear."

"Aaahh!" Shay screamed. "Marty! I don't believe it! You don't mean it!"

"Yes, I do mean it," Marty laughed. "And if you don't believe me, you can ask *Mr.* Franklin." Her voice softened, "He's sitting right here beside me."

There was the sound of rustling fabric, and some muffled undertones, which Shay assumed to be caused by Mr. Franklin assuring his wife he'd be only too happy to confirm anything she wished.

"Darnell and I were talking on the phone yesterday evening," Marty eventually got back on the line, "saying for the umpteenth time how much we missed each other; how hard it was to be together when we lived on opposite sides of the continent.

"Suddenly, my ultra-romantic man said, 'To hell with this! I love you. You love me. You wanna get married, or what?' And before I knew it, we were both flying to Las Vegas to get hitched."

"Oh, Marty, I'm so happy for you! I'm so happy for *both* of you! Where are you now, still in Vegas?"

"Nope. We're in Darnell's...I mean_*our* car—right

outside your front door."

Shay dropped the telephone to the floor as she snatched up her robe.

"Honey, what in the world..." was all Ric got out before Shay went flying out of the bedroom.

She ran headlong for the door, ran into it while skidding to a stop, and flung it wide open. There stood Mr. and Mrs. Franklin, both beaming from ear to ear.

"Oh, Marty, I could just *kill* you!" Shay exclaimed, hugging Marty with all her might. "How could you scare me like that! Get in here!"

"Careful, sugar," Marty laughed, holding out a huge bunch of flowers. "You're going to crush my bridal bouquet, and after I saved it just to throw to you."

Shay turned to Darnell, and just flung herself around his neck, "Darnell, I'm so happy for you! I hope you know you got yourself one fabulous woman!"

"And I hope *you* know that's my husband's neck you're draped around, honey. Don't squeeze all the hug out of him. I kinda had plans for him later along those lines myself!"

Shay wrapped an arm around each of them, and walked them into the living room. She suddenly remembered Ric. She had half expected him to follow her to the door, but he hadn't made an appearance as yet. "Look, this requires a toast. I've got some champagne in the vegetable bin. Get it out, and some glasses. I'll go throw on some clothes."

"Some clothes? What for? I've already seen everything you've got, and Darnell has seen a woman in a robe before." She looked over at Darnell, arching an eyebrow, "I know that for a certainty."

"Well, I don't know, hon," Darnell dissented. "Maybe she should. We haven't told Hollywood yet. Maybe the three of us could ride over to his place, and scare the hell out of him, too!"

"Uh...I'll be right back; Okay?" Shay said as she dashed from the room. As she left she caught Marty and Darnell giving each other a look, but they didn't say anything.

In the bedroom, Ric had gotten dressed and was sitting on the edge of the bed. "Ric, It's my friend Marty. She and Darnell got married!"

"So I overheard."

"Why didn't you come out, honey?"

"I wasn't sure if I should. I wasn't sure if you wanted me to."

"Why *wouldn't* I want you to, Ric?"

"I don't think either of them will be too thrilled to find me here. I'm sure Darnell wouldn't. He knows how Woody feels about you. He and Woody have been best buds for years."

Shay sat down next to him and took his hand. "Ric, they're my friends, but you're my man. Did you plan for us to keep our relationship a secret?"

"Hell, no, baby; I want the world to know."

"Well, an important part of my world is out there in that living room. And I want another important part of my world—*you*—out there, too, by my side."

Ric smiled, "All right, baby; you got it. Let's go."

"Just a sec," Shay said, going to the closet. "I'd feel awkward being the only one not dressed."

"I got a feeling *this* would be awkward even if you were dressed for the opera," Ric opinioned as Shay slipped into a bra and panties, and a light cotton dress.

"You're probably right," Shay agreed, "but let's just act like it isn't, okay?"

Darnell and Marty were sitting on the sofa. Darnell was just about to open the bottle of champagne when Shay and Ric walked into the living room holding hands.

As if they'd planned it, the newlyweds' eyes went in unison from Shay and Ric's faces, to their clasped hands, and back to their faces again. It would have almost been funny if their looks had not been of shock and total dismay.

Darnell spoke up first, "I see we're not the only ones with a surprise this evening." He wasn't smiling.

Ric stepped forward, and offered Darnell his hand, "I hear congratulations are in order. You're a lucky man, Darnell."

It was touch and go for a second as to if Darnell was going to shake Ric's hand or punch him in the nose. The handshake won, but it was about as half-hearted as they come.

"Best wishes, Marty," Ric said to her, wisely deciding the traditional kiss for the bride would not be exactly a good idea *this* trip.

"What are we waiting for?" Shay asked with almost believable merriment. "Let's bust open that champagne!"

"Allow me." Ric stepped forward and finished opening the bottle. Marty and Darnell came to life long enough to hold up their glasses as Ric poured.

"To the bride and groom," Ric said, holding up his glass. Then he stopped, and gently put his glass down on the coffee table, looking around the room. "I've never seen three more uptight faces in my life."

He turned to Shay with a sad smile, "This just ain't gonna work, honey."

He turned back to Marty and Darnell, "Look, you guys. This is your celebration. It should be one of the happiest days of your lives. And I just don't feel right casting a pall over the whole thing.

"I would never stand between Shay and her friends. You want to share your happiness with her, and I don't blame you. So if she wants to go with you to Woody's to celebrate, it's all right by me." Shay started to protest, but Ric stopped her, "No, baby, really; it's all right."

He looked back to the newlyweds, "Whatever you think of me," he picked up his glass again, "I sincerely wish you all the happiness in the world." Ric drained his glass and put it back on the table. "Now, if you'll excuse me..." he started for the bedroom.

"Ric..." Shay started toward him, but before she could, Marty stepped up to him; one hand on her hip.

"Excuse me, but I'm the bride here, mister. Do I get a kiss, or what?"

Ric looked tentatively at Darnell, "It would be my pleasure, as long as your old man won't try to introduce me to the carpet for doing it."

Darnell looked fierce a moment, then just sighed, and threw up his hands, a resigned look on his face. "You heard the lady."

That broke the ice. Things didn't get exactly chummy, but it was at least sociable, with the four of them sharing a toast and light conversation. Darnell had them cracking up, describing the hard of hearing minister who performed the ceremony. "And I'm not sure this thing is even legal. I think a dude named Darryl married some woman named Bertha."

After a while, Marty rose from her seat. "Shay, let's go into the kitchen," she suggested, "and get some more of this marvelous bean dip."

"There's still plenty right here, honey," Darnell informed her with a perceptive grin.

"Then we'll put it up, my angel," Marty replied sweetly, taking the dip. "Come on, Shay."

In the kitchen, Marty swung the door closed behind them and turned on Shay. "How long has *this* been going on?"

Shay sat down at the kitchen table, "Since yesterday. Look, Marty, do you think it's safe to leave those two out there alone?"

"Sure. Ric's not high on Darnell's hit parade, but he was impressed with how Ric handled himself just now. And so was I. Ric doesn't seem like the same man I met a month or so ago. Is that your doing?"

"I don't know, Marty. So much has happened so fast that I..."

"Does Woody know?"

"Yes, he knows."

"What does he have to say about it?"

"Well, we haven't actually...discussed it...yet."

"You haven't discussed it? Then how did you tell him?"

Shay related the morning's events. Marty shook her head, "Poor Woody. And what a way to find out!"

"I know, Marty. I'm just sick about it. I want to talk this over with Woody; to explain to him what happened, if I can. And I miss him, Marty. He's become such an important part of my life that it just doesn't feel right now that there's this rift between us."

"What about Ric?"

"Well, he and Woody still have to work together, and..."

"No, I don't mean that. I mean how do *you* feel about Ric? Are you sure about this?"

Shay lifted her chin, "Yes, I am. Marty, I tried to stop this from happening, tried to stop thinking about him, but I can't. He says his feelings for me are for real. And I believe him."

"I have to admit, he sure acts like they are." Marty touched Shay's hand, "I just don't want you to get hurt, little sister."

Shay laughed, "I wish you would make up your mind. First, you were Mama, then you were my auntie, now you're my sister. Now, which one is it, girlfriend?"

Marty laughed, too, "This a multiple choice quiz. The correct answer is 'D: all of the above.' "

"Look, honey" Shay put in, "in case you've forgotten, you're a newlywed. Don't you and Darnell have more important things to do than worry about me?"

"A valid point."   But Marty's eyes held her apprehensions, "But I'm still going to worry about you." She paused a moment, "I think we will run by Woody's, to tell him in person. Do you want to go with us? Ric said he wouldn't mind, and it might be a good time for the two of you to talk about this."

"Uh-uh. Ric was right; this is a time for celebration. I know Woody's going to be overjoyed for you two, and I don't want to dampen it by throwing this in his face at the same time. I'll talk to him sooner or later, but not tonight."

Things settled into a pattern over the next few weeks. Wood and Ric were indeed able to continue working together, so successfully that only a few sensed the strain between them.   Shay did her script revisions at home. Woody had Sherry, his assistant director, call Shay to discuss future needed changes, and Shay sent them to the studio via email.

Ric and Shay began to spend more and more time at his house, rather than hers.   His lavish, sprawling ranch provided every amenity, including a bowling alley, and a movie theater.

Ric didn't have a butler. He had a housekeeper named Clementine, who treated him like a son. Every time she got on Ric's case about something or the other, he started singing, "Oh, my darlin'...oh, my darlin'…oh, my darlin' Clementine," all off-key, a la the rendition made famous by Huckleberry Hound. And Clementine would start beaming, like all the other millions of women who found Ric's charm irresistible.

Clementine abundantly approved of "Miss Shay," seeing right away Shay was not at all like most of the other women Ric had brought home. She thought Shay was just what Ric needed, and embarked on an open campaign to get them to the alter.

Woody was really pushing hard now to finish the picture, shooting until much later in the day.   Ric's evenings at home became fewer and fewer, as he stayed late to get a scene 'in the can', or work on some of the musical numbers with Five.

Ric called Shay at what was rapidly becoming *their* home late one afternoon. "Babe, sorry; gotta work late again."

"*Again*? Ric, that's the second time this week. And Clementine fixed us a special dinner since I'm going to be away for the next week."

"I'm sorry, honey, but what can I do?" A smile crept into his voice, "I mean, it's not like I can call in sick, now is it?"

Shay had to laugh in spite of her disappointment. "No, I guess not. But come home as soon as you can, honey. My flight leaves at ten tomorrow morning, and I want us to have *some* time together before I go."

"Will do, princess. Keep it warm for me, okay? And I'm not talking about dinner."

"E.T., you are a *very* nasty man...and I love it. Well, 'phone home' if you run into another delay."

Ric was calling from his trailer at the studio. He was dressed in only a bathrobe, having just showered. Booker was with him and was staring a Ric with unconcealed disgust.

Ric stared back at him, "What's your problem?"

Booker just snorted. There was a knock at the door. At Ric's "come in", it opened, and Holly Benson stuck her head inside.

"All right, Hot Stuff; I'm finished for the day. Are you ready?"

Ric grinned at her, "Be out in a minute, baby." After she gave a tentative glance at Booker, who was shaking his head in disbelief, Holly left.

Booker started for the door. "Excuse me, man, but I need some fresh air." He suddenly stopped. "I don't like you very much right now, Ric."

"What's got a bug up *your* ass?"

Booker abruptly turned to face him, "The way you're cheating on Shay. Man, have you no shame—and no sense—at all?"

"Who died and made you guardian angel for my lady friends?" Rick bristled.

"*Lady* friends?" Booker grumbled. "Calling those skeezers you've been banging the past few years 'ladies' requires a very elastic definition. Other than Simone, Shay is the only 'lady' *you've* had more than a nodding acquaintanceship with in ages."

Ric turned from the mirror to glare at Booker. "I don't recall asking you to critique my relationship with Shay. Or with anyone else, for that matter."

"Well, you damn well should have. It's obvious you can't do it yourself." He stepped closer to Rick, "The problem with you, old son, is that you've started to believe your own press releases. Contrary to popular—and your own—belief, you are not God's gift to the female populace. Shay's the best thing that's happened to you in ten years, and you're too blinded by your own manufactured radiance to see it."

Ric turned back to the make-up mirror, to all outward appearances totally unruffled, "Book, why don't you take a hike," he said coolly. "You're starting to get on my nerves."

"It's mutual, E.T." Booker slammed out of the trailer without another word.

Ric went back to combing his hair. Abruptly he stopped and just sat staring at himself in the mirror for a long time.

Shay went to Detroit, and then to Chicago for her week of publicity and book signings for *Challenges*. But when she got back, she was frequently lonely. She saw Marty often but had no other really close women friends in California, and Ric's frequent absences left her with many a solitary evening.

On one such occasion, Clementine came to tell her Woody Hollister was there to see Mr. Ric. Ric wasn't home, having called yet again to say they were shooting late. Shay was confused as to why Woody would be there. A bolt of fear shot down her spine. Had something happened to Ric? She went anxiously downstairs to the music room, where Woody was waiting.

Woody was standing with his back to her as she entered the room. He was staring at the picture of Shay in a silver frame on top of Ric's grand piano.

"Hello, Woody," Shay said softly.

He turned quickly, obviously startled, "Shay! I didn't know you were here. I thought the housekeeper was going to go get Ric."

"Ric's not home, Woody. Would you like to wait for him? Won't you have a seat?"

"Shay, I'd better not." He started for the door, "I really need to talk to Ric, though. When he comes in, would you tell him..."

Shay stopped Wood with a hand on his arm, "Wood, *I* really need to talk to *you*. Won't you stay? Just for a moment?"

Wood had trembled when she touched him. "I...I don't think that's a good idea, Shay," he replied unsteadily. "If Ric came home, and found us together... Well, this *is* his house, and I don't want to start anything."

"Ric trusts me, Woody, and I trust him," Shay said and was instantly sorry she did when a look of heartache flashed across Wood's handsome face. "And he knows I've been meaning to talk to you," Shay rushed on. "I...I just didn't know how to approach you. Please; sit down."

Wood gazed at her a moment, then said softly, "I've never been able to deny you anything, have I? All right."

He sat hesitantly on a sofa, while Shay sat on the sofa across from him.

"How...how have you been, Woody?" Now that they were face-to-face, Shay didn't know how to begin.

Wood gave her a piercing look, "How have I *been*? I guess I should be a good loser, and tell you I've been fine, but I'm not in the mood for playing make believe." Once Wood started, it seemed he couldn't stop.

"How do you *think* I've been? I've been going through hell. Having to look Ric in the face every day; knowing when he leaves he's coming home to you. Lying in bed at night knowing that the two of you..."

He stopped suddenly, seeing the anguish on Shay's face, "Oh, Shay, I'm sorry. I...I didn't mean it."

"Yes...you did," Shay murmured, eyes downcast.

Wood stood and paced a moment, "Okay; it *is* true," he said turning quickly. "But I didn't mean to say so; not to you. I don't blame you for what happened, honey."

He came to stand next to her, "I don't think there's anything in this world that could make me resent you, or feel any malice toward you. Not even this."

Shay was trying with all her might to maintain her composure but was dangerously close to tears, and Wood seemed to sense it. He went down on one knee.

"Shay, there's only one way I could ever feel about you." He gently took her hand, "And not Ric, or your relationship with him, or anything else, will ever change that."

"Well... Ain't *this* just a touching scene." Neither Woody nor Shay had noticed Ric's entrance. Now Ric slowly ambled toward them, a strange combination of anger, arrogance, suspicion, and confusion on his face. "I'm not interrupting anything, am I?"

Wood unhurriedly stood, not backing down one inch. "No, you're not interrupting anything. It was you I came to see."

Ric looked at Woody, then at Shay, then back at Woody again, "Sure don't look that way to me," he said belligerently. "And there *is* a slick little device they have now called a telephone if you needed to talk to me so urgently."

"I need to talk to you face-to-face on this one, Ric," Wood straightforwardly replied, clearly not in the least cowered by Ric's threatening posture. "Since we quit shooting so early today, I thought sure I'd find you here...or at Shay's"

"You stopped working *early* today?" Shay asked Wood in confusion. But she was looking at Ric.

"Well...yeah," Wood answered her. "The set for the next scene wasn't right; so I just let everybody call it a day this afternoon about one o'clock. Why?"

"Okay, look, man," Ric said quickly before Shay could respond, "you're here now, so why don't you just get to whatever it was you had to discuss with me so tough?"

Woody looked at Shay, "I need to talk with Ric privately for a minute, Shay. Would you excuse us?"

Shay started to rise when Ric settled next to her on the sofa and flopped his arm around her shoulders. "Whatever you have to say, man, you can say in front of my lady."

Wood recoiled at Ric's words and action. Shay was ashamed of Ric. *Why does he have to rub it in?*

But Wood's next words were spoken calmly, "I think it might be better if she left the room, Ric," he suggested, taking a seat again on the sofa across from them.

"While we appreciate your concern," Ric shot back sarcastically, "Shay and I are able to make our own decisions about these things, without your input. Thank you very much."

Shay could have smacked Ric. Why was he being such an ass?

Woody's face hardened, "Okay, have it your way." Woody leaned forward, staring straight at Ric, "Holly

Benson tried to kill herself this evening."

Shay peripherally felt a tremor run down Ric's arm that was still around her, but she was too shocked to really notice. "Oh, Woody, no! What happened? Is she all right?"

"Honey," Ric rapidly put in, "maybe it would be better if you *did* take off. No use for you to get upset by all this."

"No, Ric; I want to know. How is she, Woody?"

"It was a close call, but it looks like she's going to make it. She took an overdose of sleeping pills. She's finished most of her scenes for the movie, so she wasn't due on the set today. If her sister hadn't just happened to go by her place and find her, it would have been a different story."

"Oh, the poor thing! What could have happened, Woody? She seemed to be doing so well once she went through detox. She came by here a few days ago with some other people from the cast. Shay turned to Ric, "Remember?" Ric didn't answer.

Shay shook her head, "She seemed like a new person. She was so happy, even bubbly. Said she felt like she had a new lease on life. I can't imagine..."

Shay's voice trailed off once she realized how Ric and Wood were staring each other down. "What's going on here?" Shay turned to Woody, "Wood, why was it so important you discuss this with *Ric*?"

"Get outta here, Shay," Ric almost growled at her. But he was still staring at Woody.

Shay looked Ric up and down, "I'm not going *anywhere* until I find out what this is all about!"

"All right, hotshot," Ric challenged Wood, "what *is* this all about, man? If you've got something to say, spit it out."

"I don't have something to *tell* you; I have something to *give* you." Wood reached into an inside jacket pocket, pulled out a pale pink envelope, and wordlessly handed it to Ric.

The envelope was sealed and had simply "Ric Weaver" written on the front in a very shaky, but obviously feminine hand.

"So what the hell is *this*?" Ric demanded.

"I don't know what's in it. It hasn't been opened, as you can see. I don't read other people's mail. Holly's sister found it. And wisely, for Holly's protection—and yours— she slipped it into her purse before the authorities arrived. When I got to the hospital, she gave it to me."

Wood stood, "I'll be on my way now.   He contemptuously added, "See you at the office, Ric."

Woody's eyes softened, "Goodbye, Shay." He left the room without another word.

Shay turned slowly and stared at Ric as if seeing him for the first time.

"What?" Ric asked nervously, fingering the envelope.

Shay slowly stood, "Do you think I'm crazy? Do you think I don't understand what this is all about? Holly tried to kill herself over *you*. That envelope is a suicide letter addressed to *you*." She looked at Ric in loathing, "You lying, cheating bastard!"

Ric jumped up from the sofa, "Baby, you're jumping to a lot of outrageous conclusions here! Give me a..."

"Chance?" Shay finished for him. "Seems like every time I do, I wind up regretting it. Don't lie to me, Ric. You've already cheated on me and almost cost that pitiful, unstable girl her life. Please don't add to it by insulting my intelligence! You were having an affair with her, weren't you?"

"It...it wasn't an *affair*, Shay; it was...was just..."

"And today you told her it was over, didn't you? That's where you were when you told me you were at the studio! And that's why she tried to kill herself! And I, like an idiot, told Wood not 15 minutes ago how much I trusted you!"

Shay started for the door. "Holly really is mixed-up, to

think you were worth a second thought, let alone her life!"

"Shay! Baby! Where are you going?"

Shay turned, and gave him a scorching glance, "Home."

CHAPTER 11

LADY SINGS THE BLUES

Shay was tempted to run to Woody when she fled Ric's house.   But just as she approached Wood's estate, she abruptly turned and headed the opposite way.

No. I won't cheapen Wood or myself by going to him now. Everybody warned me about Ric, even Woody— especially Woody. And even though Wood wanted me with him, I know his motives were not self-serving.   But I wouldn't listen. I had to let Ric into my life. All right; if I was woman enough to decide to be with Ric on my own, I'll have to be woman enough to handle things blowing up in my face on my own, as well.

Shay sighed. *And what makes you think Woody would even want to be with you now? He's probably lost all respect for you at this point, despite what he said earlier. And I sure don't blame him.*

The telephone was ringing as Shay entered her door. She went to the phone and just listened as the answering machine kicked in. It was Ric, pleading with her to call him back.   She just stood there as his message was recorded, then moved closer to the machine.   There were four messages in all.   And all of them from Ric.   Shay didn't touch the machine as they were played, allowing them to be automatically erased.

I just wish I could erase him from my heart as easily, she thought.

Shay starting shivering, the impact of what had just happened fully registering. And it also registered that, in spite of Ric's betrayal, she missed him.

What is this hold he has over me? Am I in love with him to the degree I'd let him mistreat me, and still want him back? Am I in love with him at all? Or the better question is: is he in love with me? He's never come out and said so.

How could he love me and do this to me—to us? *Is this what love is? If so, I don't want any part of it.*

The telephone rang again. Another message from Ric. She again allowed it to be recorded, played, and erased. *This is nuts. I'm exhausted, dazed, outraged, and confused. Ric and I have to talk, but there's no way I'm going to talk to him tonight. I'm going to bed.*

Shay took one of the sleeping pills she seldom used, took the phone off the hook, and did just that; she went to bed.

Somewhere in the night she heard the doorbell ringing insistently but had no inclination to go to the door.

If he's bad enough to break it down, let him, Shay thought woozily, as the drug again dragged her down to sleep.

Shay awoke the next morning feeling at least physically refreshed. But waking in bed alone brutally reminded her of the previous night's heartbreak. She was so used to waking in Ric's arms. To having him pull her close, and kiss her, and starting off the day with the flaming intensity of his loving.

And I said Holly *was mixed-up. How crazy does it make me to lie here aching for that man's embrace after what he's done? How can I still even stand the thought of making love to him? Am I that weak for him; that defenseless against whatever Ric wants to put me through?*

Just as tears yet again began to fill her eyes, another voice inside her answered sharply *I wish you* would *try to lie around here, mooning like a sick calf. You get your behind out of this bed right now, and get on with your life!*

Shay jumped out of bed and went into the kitchen to start a pot of coffee. She took a shower while it was brewing. Going back into the bedroom in her robe, coffee in hand, her eye fell on the telephone, still off the hook. She put it back on. *All right, world. I'm ready to face you now. Give me your best shot.*

Shay jumped when the telephone rang almost before she could take her hand off the receiver. *Be careful what you wish for, girl* she thought wryly *you just might get it.*

She took a deep breath. *I'm all right. I can handle this,* she thought. But still, her voice was hesitant as she whispered, "Hello?"

"Shay! Thank God!" It was of all people Darnell. "Where in hell have you been? I've been trying to reach you all night. I even came by there! Are you all right? What in God's name is going on?"

"Slow down, Darnell," Shay said, sitting on the bed. "I'm fine. But I have absolutely no idea what you're talking about. Are *you* all right? Where's Marty?"

"Marty had to fly to New York unexpectedly yesterday. Some client of hers that she said was committing professional suicide. And what I'm talking about is the entire Western seaboard—and Eastern too, for that matter—calling here looking for you."

"What?"

"Ric's called three times. I told him Marty was out of town, and that I didn't have the least idea where you were. I don't think he believed me, although I give less than a damn about that.

"Hollywood called, wanting to speak to Marty, and when I told him she was in New York, he apparently called *her* at her hotel. The next thing I know, Marty's calling me, on the run on her way to a meeting, with just time enough to tell me to find you, and have you call her there.

"Then I called Wood back and told him the hell off for calling my wife and getting her all upset. And over something that he didn't even tell me—his best friend. That's when he told me about Holly, and that you were tremendously upset by the whole thing."

"Yes, Darnell, I was," Shay said cautiously.

"So why's Ric turning the city upside down looking for you?"

"We...we just had a little argument, Darnell. That's all," Shay lied.

"Come on now, Shay. Wood was very discreet in telling me about Holly, but I gathered she OD'd on something or the other. And right after that you jump up and leave Wonder Man, with him and Wood both frantically searching for you. Now, I ain't the smartest man in the world, but I can put one and one and one together. Whatever happened to Holly had something to do with her and Ric messin' around. Am I right?"

Shay sighed, "Yes, Darnell; you're right."

"How can I help, Shay? Wood wanted me to call you because he wasn't sure you'd want to see him right now, but he's worried to death about you. Is Ric pestering you? Just say the word, and I'll go straighten *him* out. You want to come stay with us? Marty should be home this evening, but I'll come by for you right now if you want."

"No, Darnell; but thanks. I'm all right. Ric's been trying to call me, and I thought he was at my door last night, but I guess that was you. But anyway, I'm all right here."

"It could have been me—or Woody. He came by there last night, too. Wood wants to see you, Shay. Is it all right if he comes over? You know, he's feeling pretty low, too, with this business about you and Ric. And he's always felt responsible for Holly."

"He has? Why?"

"Holly's fascination with Woody is no joke. She's really in love with him. She has been for years. She's been in love with Wood even before she started with the booze and whatnot, back when all three of us were waiting tables and parking cars waiting for our big break.

"Wood likes Holly, but he's never felt *that* way about her. When she started getting high, Wood felt as though it was at least partly his fault, because of her hang-up on him. I told him that was ridiculous, but you know our soft-hearted, soft-headed friend."

"Yes, I do," Shay quietly acknowledged. *That explains a lot,* Shay thought. *Sweet, tenderhearted Woody. He would feel responsible.*

"Anyway, Shay, Woody really wants to see you. I like I said, he came by there last night, too."

"I'm...just not up to seeing Wood just now, Darnell. I'm ashamed to face him after..."

"Woman, are you crazy? That man would walk a bed of nails to be with you. It would take more than this to turn him off to you, Shay; much more."

"I just can't talk to Woody right now, Darnell. Tell him I'll call him later today, or tomorrow, okay?"

"All right, Shay. Marty's been trying to reach you, too. If she doesn't get you before she leaves for home, she'll call when she gets in. And you know I'm here if you need me. Hang in there, girl."

"I will. Thanks, Darnell," Shay told him gratefully, thinking how lucky Marty was to have this light-hearted, endearing man who could turn serious at the drop of a hat when a friend needed him.

There was almost no food in the house since Shay had spent most of her time for the past several weeks at Ric's, and she was hungry. She threw on jeans and a T-shirt and decided to go to the grocery store.

As Shay was backing out of the garage, she looked up to see Booker standing at her front door.

"Yo, Shay," he called to her, walking toward the car. "Got a minute?"

Shay stopped in the driveway. "I don't think so, Booker. Whatever Ric sent you to tell me, I don't want to hear."

He had reached the car door. "Ric didn't send me. He doesn't even know I'm here. I came on my own. I just want to talk to you personally."

"What about?"

Booker looked exasperated, "What do you think?"

"Book, whether he sent you, or you came on your own, it's the topic I find objectionable. I don't care to discuss it right now—period." Shay started backing up the car again.

"Shay, are you prepared to make a decision about you and Ric—without knowing all the facts?" Booker said quickly.

Shay stopped the car again, "What facts *don't* I know?"

"Look, can't we go inside? Standing here bent over, peering in this car window, is playing hell with my sacroiliac. And I don't think you want your neighbors listening in on this conversation."

Shay's property wasn't so small that a neighbor could hear what was being said unless she and Booker started yelling at the top of their lungs. And Shay didn't think that was very likely. Since their conversation at the studio, Booker had treated her in a respectful, almost fatherly manner, and she'd actually come to like him very much.

Still, his point was well taken. If they were going to talk, the driveway was hardly the place to do it. And his comment had piqued Shay's curiosity. "Okay, Booker; you win," Shay said, stopping the car and getting out. She started for the front door, "Let's go inside."

Once in the house, Shay asked if he'd like coffee.

"I'd love some. And I need some. I've been up all night," he wearily replied.

"Why?" Shay asked, leading him to the kitchen.

"I've been up with Ric. He's gone plumb loco, Shay."

Shay's face hardened, "At this point, Booker, my suspicion is Ric's always *been* plumb loco. I just didn't know it until yesterday." She poured a cup of coffee and handed it to him.

Booker chuckled as he sat at the kitchen table, "Oh, come on, Shay. Don't play the man that shabby."

"Why not?" Shay asked bitterly as she sat down with a cup of her own. "He played *me* about as shabby as it gets."

"Yeah; I guess he did, honey," Booker sadly admitted, both hands around his coffee cup. He looked down into its swarthy depths as if searching for the right words.

"Shay, I've known Ric since he was ten years old. There's a lot you don't know. A lot of things that might help you understand why he is the way he is."

"Are you talking about how he was raised? About him not knowing who his father was? And...and about his mother?"

Booker's head snapped up in surprise, "He *told* you that stuff?"

"Yes, he did."

"Man! He *must* be hooked on you," Booker said, looking at Shay in wonder. "I've never known him to tell that to a living soul."

"Well, he told *me*. Is it true, or was that just some yarn he ran on me to get my sympathy?"

"Oh, it's true, all right. I ran a neighborhood nightclub in Chicago where he was raised. I know. And since *you* know, Shay, can't you understand how messed up it was for him growing up that way?"

"That's not what he told me. He told me in spite of everything, his mother loved him dearly, and he hardly knew what was going on until he was much older. He said everything seemed normal to him, despite the constant night-time 'visitors' ".

Booker looked Shay in the eye, "That's only partially true. His mother *did* love him..." he looked away, "just like I loved her."

"You did?"

He smiled sadly, "Yes, I did. In spite of what she was doing, I loved her. I even asked her to marry me, but she turned me down flat." He stared back into the coffee cup again for a moment. "I don't think Camilla ever loved any man except Ric's father."

"Did you know *him*?" Shay asked solemnly.

He looked up again, "No. I didn't move to the neighborhood until Ric was ten. His Dad was long gone by then. I don't think Camilla ever really got over him. And she was left feeling so empty, so worthless, by the way he treated her, she just didn't care about herself anymore. But she *did* care about Ric.

"But if he told you he didn't know what was going on as a kid, that's not true. He's told me a hundred times how he used to lie awake in bed at night, listening to the mother he loved in the next room, in the arms of one stranger after another.

"Can you image how that must feel for a kid? Can you image what's it's like to go to school, and have some kid tell you 'My old man humped your Mama last night'? Or have one of your classmates ask if your Mama would give him some—for his lunch money?"

Shay was shaken right down to her very soul. Why hadn't Ric told her the whole truth? Had he been too ashamed to divulge it, even to her?

A question popped into her mind, and although it had nothing to do with the current situation, she had to ask, "Booker...you say you loved her. Did you ever... I mean, did she and you ever...."

"Was I one of the 'Uncles?' " He shook his head, "No. I didn't want her that way." He lifted his chin, "I loved her, Shay. I tried to get her out of the life. And anyway, she wouldn't have gone for that herself. She told me 'I need you as a friend, Book, not a customer. I've got plenty of customers, but not a lot of friends.' "

The two of them just sat there silently for a moment. Then Booker started again, "Anyhow, I ran into Ric again when he was 19. I used to have some local groups do gigs at my club on the weekends and whatnot. Ric was trying to establish himself as a singer and asked if I'd book him and this little combo he had gotten together. Well, one listen, and he had himself a job. Ric inherited his mother's talent, as well as her good looks. In fact, Ric's looks were what got him over."

Shay was astonished to hear Booker, of all people, say that. "Book, what are you talking about? Ric's got one of the most incredible voices ever recorded. And most of the songs he's written are classics. How can you say he's a star just because of his looks?"

"That's not what I said, Shay. I said his looks got him over; got him his shot. Sure, he wouldn't be the star he is today without talent, which my man has in abundance. But when he was first starting out, it was his looks—and women's reactions to his looks—that got his foot in the door."

Booker stopped, and took Shay's hand, "And that's another thing I want you to understand, honey. Ric comes on like gangbusters, like confidence personified, but inside, he's always had this doubt; he's always felt...unworthy. And even with all the Grammies and whatnot he has lined up on the shelf, he's never overcome that.

"I think that's why he plays around so much. He needs the...validation, if you will. In his mind, he's tied up his worth as a person so much to his lover boy image that he needs to have it constantly reaffirmed."

Shay looked out the balcony doors, "I think I understand him now, even more than before. And I appreciate you telling me all this." She turned to look at him intently, putting her hand over his, "But I can't live that way, Book. I can't give my love to a man I have only as a...a partial stockholder."

"Shay, I've known Ric a long, long time. I know more about him than any person alive. Ric loves you, Shay. For the first time in his life, I think he's really fallen in love.

"But old habits die hard. Lord help him as he gets older when his looks start to fade. I don't know what's going to happen to him then...unless something comes along to show him he's more than just a twenty-first century Don Juan.

"I think he could give up all that running around—for you—if you give him the chance. Don't leave him, Shay. He loves you—and he needs you. "

Shay just stared at Booker a long moment before whispering, "Where's Ric now, Booker?"

"At home, asleep. Like I said, we've been up all night, talking, drinking. Hell, we came by here twice. I just barely stopped him from breaking the door down! He's called all over the city looking for you. He even called Woody!"

"He *did*? What did Wood tell him?"

"To go to hell," Booker said wryly. "Shay, didn't you get Ric's messages?"

"Yes, I did, but I didn't want to talk to him."

Booker's shoulders slumped, and then he stood, looking expressively down at Shay. "You've got to talk to him sometime, Shay," he said quietly.

Shay sighed as she stood, too, "Yeah, Book; I know."

Shay saw Booker to the door. "You're a sweet, beautiful woman, Shay. I hope you're not offended by this, considering what she...was, but you remind me a little of Camilla."

Shay felt her eyes misting, "I'm not offended in the least, Book. Since she was the woman you loved."

Shay opened the door for him. Booker stopped in the doorway, "Shay, I wouldn't lie to you. If I didn't think Ric could change...would change, I'd tell you to run like hell. But I really think Ric *will* change—for you."

He leaned forward, and kissed her forehead, "Just think it over, honey; all right?"

"I will, Book." Shay lightly kissed his lips. "Thank you for telling me...and for caring—about both of us."

Shay closed the door a moment too soon to see Ric's Toyota come flying down the street, and pull into her driveway so fast it almost hit her car.

"Book! What are *you* doing here, man?" Ric jumped out of the car. "Why didn't you wake me up? Is Shay here?"

"I didn't wake you up because you passed out. I told you not drink so much. And, yes; Shay's here."

Ric looked closely at Booker's face, and then his own face screwed up in an ugly grimace, "So I see," he whispered menacingly. He then hauled off and punched Booker spang on the jaw.

Booker fell on his back in the grass, "What is *wrong* with you, boy?" Booker exclaimed, rubbing his jaw. "Have you totally lost your mind? What did you do *that* for?"

Ric stood over him, fist still clenched, "Because I can see why you couldn't wait to get over here without me! You've got her lipstick all over your mouth, you low down, back stabbing, old dog!"

"What! Ric, are you crazy?"

"Not crazy enough to miss what's been going on here! You've always had the hots for Shay; I could see it in your eyes. You just couldn't wait to try to get next to her, to put your bid in, could you?"

Booker calmly reached into a jacket pocket and pulled out a handkerchief. He lay right where he was on the ground, contemplating Ric, as he wiped the blood from the corner of his mouth. Then he got to his feet, "Ric, I want to ask you a couple of questions. Do you think Shay has the hots for me?"

"*Hell,* no! Are *you* crazy?"

"Am I the kind of man who would force himself on a woman?"

Ric stood panting, just staring at Booker for a moment, then grudgingly answered, "No."

"Then I think you've got the answer to your question," Booker started down the driveway toward his car.

"Hey, Book! Wait a minute!"

Booker turned but didn't speak.

"Man, look; I'm...I'm sorry. I don't know what got into me. I'm not thinking straight right now." Ric walked toward Booker, offering his hand, "Forgive me, man."

Booker looked him up and down, then said, "Tell it to your new manager."

"What do you mean?"

"Just what I said. That's it. I've had it. I'm outta here."

"Outta here? What do you mean? You *walking* on me, man?"

"You got it."

"Now wait a minute, Booker. I think we've let things get out of hand here. You can't walk on me, man. We've been together since times were so tough we had to share a Big Mac for dinner. Hell, you sold your business to finance my career. We've had fights before. I told you I was sorry. You can't let a little misunderstanding come between us."

"This is not a little misunderstanding, Ric. What you just did is an insult to Shay *and* me. Yeah, I *do* love her—like a daughter. But then, I guess you can't understand a man having feelings for a woman that don't involve trying to get into her panties.

"Anyway, it's just the straw that broke the camel's back. Fact is, I just don't like you anymore, Ric. I don't even know you anymore. And I sure as hell ain't gonna work for you anymore."

"You don't *work* for me, man," Ric said nonplussed. "You're my friend; my best friend; the only friend I have that I know will tell it to me straight."

"You're right; I am. But you don't listen to me anymore, Ric. Your head's so swelled up it's blocked your hearing.

"We've long since passed being in it for the money. You *were* in it for the music. And you've always had the talent; I give you that. But now the music's become secondary to the care and feeding of your ego, and to be honest with you, old son, you turn my stomach. I don't need this crap." Booker turned and again started for his car.

"All right, then; go! Go ahead!" Ric bellowed after him. "Who the hell do you think you are, anyway? I don't need you! I'm Eric Tyrone fucking Weaver, and I don't need you...or anybody else!"

Booker opened the door to his car, then stopped, "I sure hope you're right about that, Ric," he said softly. "Because they way you're headed, you're not going to *have* anybody else."

After seeing Booker out, Shay had returned to the kitchen to put up the coffee things, when she heard Ric yelling outside.

She ran to the front door just in time to see Booker get into his car, slam the door, and tear off down the street. Ric looked dejectedly after Booker's car for a moment, then turned, and ran up to Shay's door.

Shay jumped back quickly from the door window, not wanting Ric to see her, and she continued to stand there while he repeatedly rang the bell, not certain if she wanted to talk to him or not.

Ric began banging on the door, "Shay! I know you're in there! Open the door! Open the damn door, I said!"

Shay was really inclined not to talk to him then. He sounded totally out of control. She was positive Ric would never do anything to physically harm her, but she'd never seen him like this. All of his laid back cool was gone. The always polished and impeccably dressed Ric Weaver stood at her door with his hair uncombed; his clothes looking like he had slept in them. Shay didn't know *what* he might do. She was just about to go to the telephone to call Darnell, or Woody, or somebody when Ric suddenly stopped banging on the door and turned around as if to leave.

But he didn't leave. He just stood there with his back to the door.

What on earth is he doing? Shay wondered.

All at once his shoulders slumped. He bowed his head and put a hand over his face. Shay could see his shoulders begin to heave.

Why, he's... I don't believe it... He's crying! Shay realized in astonishment.

Although part of her said to just turn and walk away; to leave him alone, Shay just couldn't. She was so unnerved by the sight of this proud, powerful man in tears that she opened the door before she knew what she was doing.

He seemed not to hear the door open. He didn't turn around.

"Ric?" Shay called softly.

He abruptly stiffened, and quickly wiped his hands across his face before turning around, "Hi, Shay," he said simply, looking dazed and disoriented.

Shay looked him over in confusion. "Hi, Ric," she finally replied.

They stood there awkwardly for a moment before Ric said, "Can I come in? I need to talk to you, Shay."

"Ric... I don't know... I...."

"Please, Shay." His eyes, all red and bleary, were pleading. "For the sake of what we've meant to each other over the past few weeks...please...just let me talk to you."

Shay slowly stood back and motioned him in. They went into the living room, where Ric wearily sank down on the sofa. "Shay, can I have a couple aspirin?" Ric asked. "My head is killing me."

Shay went into the kitchen and came back with the aspirin and a glass of water. She silently handed them to Ric.

"Thanks, babe. I feel like hell."

Shay sat in the chair opposite him, "You look like hell, too," she observed.

He looked down at his rumpled, disheveled clothing, "Yeah, I guess I do. I got drunk last night after I couldn't find you."

Shay just continued to look at him.

"Okay, Shay, look; I'll just get right to it. You were right about me and Holly. We did have a thing going on. Don't ask me why I did it. I don't really understand why I did it myself. All I can tell you is that it will never happen again. I want you to forgive me, Shay—and come back to me."

"And you think it's that simple? That you can just say 'I'm sorry', and that's all it takes?"

"Honey, what else can I do? It happened. I wish to God it hadn't, but I can't undo it." He lowered his head. "I'd give anything if I could," he whispered.

"Ric, let's forget about you and me for a minute," Shay put in. "What about Holly—or even Simone? What about them? It was all fun and games for you, Ric, but you *hurt* them; really hurt them. Can't you see how wrong it is to lead a woman on, let her think there's a future for the two of you, and then drop her like a bad habit?"

Ric looked up sharply, "Like you did Woody?"

Shay recoiled as though he had slapped her. "That's not fair, Ric." Her eyes narrowed, "That wasn't the same thing, and you know it. How dare you compare what you've been doing to what happened between me and Wood. My heart bled over Woody, as you know better than anyone."

Shay turned away from him. "You never miss a chance to hurt me, you know that, Ric?" she whispered.

He didn't reply at first, then whispered back, "Then I guess what they say is true: you always hurt the one you love."

"You've taken that to new heights."

"Did you hear what I said, Shay?"

"What do you mean, did I hear what you said?"

"I said 'you always hurt the one you *love*.' "

He left the sofa, and kneeled in front of her chair, taking her hand. "I love you, Shay," his eyes searched hers.

"And for all the lines I've given women over the years, that's the *one* thing I've only said to one other person in my entire life." Shay knew without him saying so that he meant his mother.

"Ric, I..."

"And I think you love me, too. At least you did. Have I killed *all* your love for me, baby...or is there at least a spark left?"

"It's not that I don't care, Ric." She looked away again, "I do. If I didn't, I never would have opened the door just now. If I didn't, I would just walk away and not look back. That's not the problem. The problem is that you've shaken my trust in you to the foundation. You want to party. I want something more."

He moved closer to her, "We both want the same thing. I want you to be my woman, baby."

"You want me to be *one* of your women, Ric. There's the difference. I don't want to be one of a harem. One and only is my style."

He reached into his pocket and pulled out a small black velvet box. Inside was a diamond solitaire; the most beautiful piece of jewelry Shay had ever seen. She gasped in surprise.

"Shay, this is about as 'one and only' as it gets," Ric whispered. He kissed her hand and looked up into her eyes. "Will you marry me?"

Shay just stared at him, dumbfounded.

"They also say 'silence gives consent,' " Ric smiled tentatively. "So if you're not saying 'yes,' you better speak up."

"Ric," Shay finally choked out, "to me marriage is a very serious thing. Do you know what you're saying? Do you honestly understand what it means?"

"Yes, darling girl. I do."

"It means each of us being true—being *faithful*—to each other only, for the rest of our lives."

" 'Forsaking all others...clinging only one to the other...as long as ye both shall live.' Yes, baby; I know. That's what I want. And that's what I pledge you, from the bottom of my heart."

He leaned forward and kissed her gently. "Please come back to me. I don't know what I'll do if you don't. I want you. I need you. I love you. And I want to spend the rest of my life proving it to you. Will you marry me, my only love?"

Shay was unable to look away from him. His heart was in his eyes, and his eyes were inexorably drawing her back into his world, back into his life, back into his arms.

"As long as you truly give me your promise, along with this ring..."

"I do," Ric whispered.

"Then...yes."

CHAPTER 12

TRADING PLACES

Over the next several weeks, Shay came to understand that the somewhat specialized fame she experienced as a romance author was nothing compared to the full-blown rendition.

She thought that through her association with Woody, Darnell, and of course Ric she was intimately acquainted with how it felt to be world famous. But she rapidly found out that kind of fame can only be understood from the inside out; not from the outside looking in. Shay felt sudden empathy for Princess Di, Oprah, and Michael Jackson, and came to know what a heavy burden it is to lose one's privacy.

Due to the front page tabloid stories and T.V. snippets about her and Ric, Shay couldn't even go to the grocery store now without a crowd gathering, or an inquisitive cashier asking, "Come on, now; when's the wedding?" That question was rapidly becoming as frequently asked as "Does this make me look fat?"

Shay would have lost her mind without Marty. They talked almost daily.

"Marty, now I really appreciate the hassles you went through when you married Darnell," Shay told her about a week after she and Ric announced their engagement.

"It's outrageous, isn't it? But don't worry. Most of the truly insane stuff will start to die down after a while. It has for us. Most of the media probe on me was just to satisfy people's curiosity. Life will never be the same, but once that's done with, the worst is over."

"Do you know this morning I caught a photographer trying to take a picture through my bathroom window?"

"Well, no wonder, honey. He could get big bucks for a picture of the bod that finally snared Ric Weaver. You know half the women in the world want your secret."

"I couldn't care less what 'half the women in the world' want. It's my family *I'm* worried about. My father almost punched a reporter in the nose because the dude had the gall to ask Pops, 'Is your daughter pregnant, Mr. Logan?' Stop laughing, Marty...that's not funny," Shay scolded, suddenly seeing the sick humor in the situation herself, and joining in.

"Shay?"

"Yeah?"

"Well...you're *not*, are you?"

Shay sighed heavily. "Marty, please!" she feigned exasperation. "Not you, too! If you nut out on me, there won't be a single soul on this planet I can have a sensible conversation with!"

"Well, girlfriend, I just wanted to be sure."

"Anyway, Ric was right. I can just forget trying to live here, even on a part-time basis. I'm going to have to move in with him now. We're there more often than we're here, anyway. And Ric's place has security; mine doesn't."

"Shay, are you sure that's what you want to do?"

"Of course I'm sure. Marty, I'm going to be married to him as soon as the movie is finished, and you and I can rearrange my book signing tour."

There was a beat of silence before Marty softly asked, "And are you still sure about that, too?"

Shay was really annoyed this time, something that very rarely happened in her friendship with Marty. "How many times are you going to ask me that? Yes, Marty; I'm sure."

"I'm sorry. I don't mean to keep harping on this, girl, but I'm...I'm *scared* for you, Shay."

"Ric loves me, Marty. I know he does. He's told me his running around days are over. And I believe him. People *can* change, you know."

"I know. But don't you think it would be wise to give it a little more time for him to *show* you he's changed before you get married?"

"No, I don't. The way I see it, it's like that old joke about being 'a little bit pregnant.' Ain't no such thing. Either you are, or you're not. Period. So either I trust him, or I don't. And if I didn't, I never would have accepted his proposal in the first place."

"Shay, I always wondered about that. What *was* it that caused you to change your mind so quickly after the...the thing with Holly?"

How can I explain it to her? How can I tell her I know why Ric's priorities are...were so screwed up, without telling her about the pain and shame of his past? And I can never tell her that. That's something Ric entrusted to me, and me alone. I'll never divulge that to anyone, not even my best friend. It would have to be Ric's decision to share that with anyone, not mine.

And how can I tell her how I can be so sure he loves me without telling her I saw that strong, willful man cry tears of desperation when he thought he'd lost me? There's no way I can ever explain it to her without telling her things that are too personal, too private.

Since she felt she couldn't tell Marty the whole truth, Shay said the first thing that popped into her head. "Why does any woman accept a man's proposal? Because I want to be his wife."

"Wrong answer, Shay," Marty said tersely.

"What do you mean 'wrong answer'? Well, if *that's* the wrong answer, what's the right one?"

"The right one is...'because I love him.' "

"Well, Marty, of *course,* I love him! That goes without saying. That's *why* I want to be his wife."

Shay stayed away from the movie set as much as possible. The tabloids didn't help; bribing some members of the movie cast and crew for their "stories" concerning her and Ric. As if any of them *had* one except Woody...and Holly.

But Holly was still hospitalized, and all Wood had to say to the press was "I wish them all the happiness in the world." Although Vanessa was of course only too glad to supply the media with 'helpful' information…on a situation she knew nothing about.

When Shay was on the set, she tried to stay in the background as much as possible. Her respect for the professionalism of both men escalated even further when she saw for herself that Ric and Wood were still able to work together in a productive manner. But there was a tension there, just under the surface. And Shay made herself as scarce as she could, not wanting to be the spark that triggered a blow-up.

And she couldn't bear running into Simone again. Simone had approached Shay on her last visit to the set. "Ric's a handful, Shay," Simone told her, "but there's a hell of a man inside that's just been waiting for the right woman to bring it out." Simone touched Shay's arm gently, "I'm glad he's finally found her. I wish all the best for both of you."

Shay was so deeply moved by Simone's unselfish kindness all she could respond with was a shaky, "Thank you," as Simone sadly smiled and walked away.

Ric was looking for a new manager. He didn't need one immediately, his work on the movie and the soundtrack album would be taking up most of his time for the next several months, but he'd already started considering various people.

On one occasion when they were discussing it, Ric said, "Maybe I ought to give Gabriel Lamont a call." He laughed nastily. "I already took Woody's woman; maybe I can take his manager, as well."

Shay stared at him in stunned disgust. "That was a hateful thing to say, Eric Weaver," Shay scolded him. She often marveled at how this man who was usually so magnanimous could at times turn so needlessly vicious with no warning at all.

And it bothered Shay that Ric wouldn't tell her what had caused the break with Booker. "We just didn't see eye to eye anymore," was all she could get out of Ric. But Shay knew how close they had been, and she knew it had taken something very grievous indeed to break them apart.

Unknown to Ric, she called Booker at his new home in Florida to try to talk sense to *him*, but he wouldn't hear of it.

"Shay, Ric and I had a long run, but all good things come to an end. It was just time for us to go our separate ways, that's all."

"Book, don't hand me that. I know just how much you care about Ric, and how much he cares about you. You two had much more than just a business arrangement. In a sense, you were like the father he never had."

Booker chuckled sadly. "Shay, sometimes you care about someone, but it just doesn't work anymore, you know? And I think that's what happened between me and Ric. But, look, honey, that doesn't mean that I don't wish you—*and* Ric—all the best."

Shay sighed, "You know, it's really ironic that just when you helped get Ric and me back together, the two of you fell apart. He needs you, too, Booker. Nobody could possibly look out for Ric's interests the way you do."

"Don't worry about Ric, honey. He's a hell of a businessman; he'll be all right. And as for me, retirement suits me. All that ripping and running around was getting to be a little much for me, anyway. And thanks to managing Ric, I'll never have money worries as long as I live. Not bad for a guy who started out with a jook joint on the South Side of Chicago."

Wood had finally finished with all the sound stage

shooting when one afternoon Marty called Shay, all excited about a Brazilian publisher's offer to translate Shay's books into Spanish.

"Here we go, Shay. This could open up a whole additional segment of the international market for you!"

"Marty, a *Brazilian* publisher wants to translate my books into Spanish? Dear heart, they don't speak Spanish in Brazil. They speak Portuguese."

"That's right—and they know how to make a whole lot of money. Sugar, I know they don't speak Spanish in Brazil, but they export books to countries that do, capisce? And get *this*; they want us to come to Rio de Janeiro to discuss the deal, and do some preliminary publicity!"

"*Rio*! When? And for how long?"

"Within the next couple of weeks. We'll probably be gone for a week or two."

Shay discussed it with Ric in bed that evening. "Honey, that's fantastic!" he exclaimed. "I wish I could go with you. You're getting to be more famous that I am. I could paraphrase John F. Kennedy, and say 'I'm the man that accompanied Natasha Logan to Rio!' "

"Oh, Ric," Shay laughed.

But they both knew there was no way he could go. In fact, she had been preparing to travel with him. The sound stage shooting completed, Wood was preparing to take the cast on location shoots to cities where the action took place in the script. He wanted the authenticity of actual sites in Atlanta, Detroit, and Chicago to lend to the scope of the movie.

"We haven't been separated this long since we've been engaged, Ric," Shay said somewhat mournfully.

"I know, baby; but given the professions we're in, we might as well get used to it." He reached for her, "Now come on over here, and show me how much you're going to miss me while we're apart."

So Shay and Marty, with Darnell as their escort, went

on to Rio. And it was fabulous. Shay had never been to South America before, and although she was there on business, still had plenty of time to sight-see. But she missed Ric and lamented he couldn't be there with her. *Well, maybe we can come back here for our honeymoon,* she consoled herself. They talked daily, Ric first being in Chicago on location, and then Detroit.

It took slightly longer than Marty had anticipated for them to complete the business end of things. Shay had been in Rio three weeks, not two, before all the details were nailed down, and her appearances completed. Ric had just gone to Atlanta a few days before for the last location shoot, ironically the first few scenes of the movie, where Michael and Alicia meet. As the three of them were making travel arrangements to return to the States, Shay got the bombshell idea of not going straight back to LA, but flying to Atlanta, to surprise Ric.

"Marty, are you sure you and Darnell don't want to come with me?" Shay asked.

"You love birds will be much too busy to pay much attention to us old married folks," Marty replied. "When it comes to these kinds of reunions, three's a crowd, and four's even worse. We're going home. We'll see you guys when you get back to LA"

Shay didn't try to change her mind. She knew Darnell had made every attempt to get along with Ric, for the sake of Marty's friendship with Shay. But he and Ric would never become buddies, and both Marty and Shay knew it.

Anyway, Marty was probably right on the other score, as well. On the flight over, Shay shivered in anticipation of being with Ric again, and she had planned a very special evening for the two of them. Shay had sent most of her luggage on home with the Franklins. Ric would only be in Atlanta a couple more days; she would only need one bag.

Although Darnell for some reason didn't think it the best idea in the world for Shay to *surprise* Ric, Shay insisted.   But she did call ahead to notify Ric's hotel of her arrival, with strict orders for them not to inform Mr. Weaver.

When Shay arrived at the hotel, she didn't need to identify herself.   The whole country knew of her engagement to Ric. After the copious bowing and scraping he apparently felt appropriate to the situation, the manager informed her that Ric was not in.   But he personally escorted her to Ric's suite.

Shay took her suitcase into the bedroom and was too impatient to unpack. All she did was take a moment to plug her cell phone in to charge because its battery was low.

Room service came to the door with the bottle of champagne on ice and two glasses she had ordered. She hid them behind the bar.

Shay put several CDs of soft music, of course including Ric's, into the CD player, but did not turn in on. She didn't want anything to tip Ric off to her presence and spoil the surprise.

Returning to the bedroom, Shay put her suitcase on a chair and pulled out the slinky negligee she'd gotten in Rio, just for this reunion. She quickly undressed, tossing her purse and her clothes on top of the suitcase, too excited to take the time to hang them up. Ric would be returning soon, and she wanted to be ready. She lay down on the bed to await his arrival.

About twenty minutes later, Shay heard the outer door to the suite open. She smiled to herself thinking how surprised Ric would be when he came into the bedroom and found her there waiting.

The voices coming from the living room were muffled. And Shay suddenly realized there were *voices*—plural. Ric wasn't alone.

Now, who in the world could he have with him? Shay peevishly thought. *I hope he didn't bring back a whole bunch of the crew. Well, if he did,* she snuggled back cozily into bed, *as soon as he finds out* I'm *here, he'll send them on their way fast enough. But who in the world is that out there?*

Suddenly she heard a woman's laughter, followed by Ric's. Then came the unmistakable sound of a zipper being undone.

Oh, no. This can't be happening.

"Hey, baby," Ric's voice came through the closed bedroom door, "hold on a second! Let's at least wait until we get into the bedroom, okay?"

"That's not what you said in the shower this morning, sugar pie," came the coquettish reply. As if the situation wasn't bad enough already, it suddenly worsened as Shay realized the woman's voice belonged to Vanessa Sweet.

There were more sounds; the rustling of clothing, steps approaching the bedroom door. Shay was too stunned and shocked to even move. She just sat in the middle of the bed in dread and watched as the doorknob slowly turned, and the door flew open.

Ric stood there with his jacket in his hand, his shirt unbuttoned. Vanessa stood next to him with her high-heeled shoes in one hand, her purse in the other, and her unzipped dress half off one shoulder. They were kissing and rubbing against each other; too engrossed to even notice Shay— at first.

Seeing movement out of the corner of his eye, Ric turned slightly and glanced toward the bed. Then he jerked his head around so quickly a long red trail of Vanessa's lipstick, which already covered his lips, smeared in one long guilty streak across his cheek.

"*Shay! Oh, my God!*"

Shay looked from Ric to Vanessa. Vanessa momentarily looked shocked, then shifted her body and stood there hip shot, the hand holding the shoes cocked over one shoulder, with an "I shot the sheriff" smirk on her face.

Shay looked back to Ric. She could almost see the gears in his head turning as he tried to calculate some way of explaining the whole thing away.

"Shay...What...What are you...doing here?"

A cold, icy calm settled on Shay. She was hurt; she was humiliated, but the tantamount emotion coursing through her body at that point was anger. Bitter, white-hot anger. It kept her calm, and it made her strong.

"What am I doing here? Catching my soon-to-be *former* man about to cheat on me, evidently," Shay coolly replied. "And from what I just overheard, not for the first time."

"Honey...now...look...I can explain this. It's not what you think..."

Shay rose from the bed, and just stood there, the silky folds of the negligee caressing her feet. She stood silent and still, stiff as a board, eyeing them both.

Vanessa sucked her teeth and said, "Well, after all, honey, what did you expect? You've been away from the man three whole weeks. And to tell the truth, darling, I never *did* understand just what he saw in *you* in the first place."

"Shut up, Vanessa," Ric hissed between clenched teeth.

"You can't tell me to shut up!" Vanessa shot right back at him.

"She's right, Ric," Shay smoothly agreed, closing in on Vanessa. "You can't tell her to shut up." Shay leveled Vanessa with a look, "That's *my* job. Shut up, Vanessa."

Vanessa bristled, "Let me tell you something, you..."

"Excuse me," Shay icily interrupted. "I don't believe this involves you. This is a private matter between me and *him*," Shay jerked her thumb in Ric's direction, not dignifying him with the use of his name. "So frankly, I give less than a damn about any comments you have to make..."

"Oh, you don't?" Vanessa sputtered. "Just who the hell do you..."

"...so I advise you to pull up your panties, zip up your dress, and shake your narrow behind right on out of here."

"What!" Vanessa was outraged. "How dare you, you little bitch! Well, I never..."

"No, I bet you haven't," Shay was continuing. "But you damn sure will if you don't haul ass to the other side of that door before I have to tell you a second time!"

Vanessa checked out the wild look in Shay's eyes and knew she meant business. In no time at all, Vanessa was gone.

Shay stood transfixed, staring at the outer door until it closed behind Vanessa. Then she excruciatingly slowly pivoted her body and focused her gaze on Ric.

"Now, honey...now, wait a minute, Shay..." Ric started again.

Without a word, Shay grasped the single bow holding the negligee together and pulled it loose. It fell in a billowing puddle around her feet.

Ric's eyes widened in surprise, and then his famous slow, lazy grin slowly spread across his face, almost as if in triumph.

"*That's* my baby!" he said, walking toward Shay. "You know I love you, baby. That didn't mean anything. I knew you wouldn't let a little..."

Shay abruptly held her right arm out stiffly, palm-outward, like a traffic cop. "Hold it!" she commanded in a voice that even Ric had to acknowledge brooked no nonsense. "I just wanted you to get one long last look at what you're *not* going to have any more!" she continued, eyes flashing fire.

With that, she swept her recently shed clothing off the chair, dashed into the bathroom, slammed the door, and locked it.

Ric was immediately on the other side of the door

pleading with her. "Shay, come on, honey! We gotta talk about this! Open the door, baby!"

Shay totally ignored him, going to the wall phone above the toilet. She called the front desk and asked for the manager.

As soon as he came on the line, Shay said in her most imperious voice, "This is Miss Logan, in Mr. *Weaver's* suite. There's been an emergency, and I must leave immediately. Would you be so kind as to send a couple of bellmen to assist me? I will need *two* bellmen. There's quite a *load* of... things I've collected from Mr. Weaver. And I need the bellmen immediately. My flight leaves within the hour. Please have a car waiting for me, as well."

Shay waited a beat, then added, "Mr. Weaver would not be at all appreciative if there was a delay, and I missed my flight..." She listened to the manager's profuse assurances. "Oh, thank you so much."

During the brief telephone conversation, Ric's protests had gotten louder and more adamant. "Shay! Open this damn door right now! Right now! Do you hear me?"

Shay rapidly dressed. Just as she was buttoning her jacket, Ric started to pound on the door. "Natasha! If you don't open this door right now, I'm gonna to kick this mother in! I mean it, Shay!"

Just then, Shay heard the door-bell. She snatched opened the bathroom door. Ric was standing there looking wild and crazy, but he jumped back in surprise when the door opened so quickly.

"I don't think such a macho display will be called for, Ric," Shay informed him. "As you can plainly see, the door *is* open."

Shay grabbed her purse and her bag and made it out the bedroom door into the living room before Ric caught up with her. "Where are you going?"

When she didn't stop walking, Ric roughly grabbed her arm, causing her suitcase to drop to the floor with a bang.

"I said where do you think you're going? You can't just walk out like this!"

Shay's stare was cool fire, "*Can't* I?"

"We've got to talk this over, Shay! You can't leave me like this, baby!"

"Just *watch* me," Shay hissed, trying to wrest her arm away from him. "Let go of me!"

"No, damn it!" He grabbed her other arm as well, holding her so tightly it hurt. "Damn it, Shay! You're going to stay right here, and we're going to talk this out, right now!"

"We're not talking *anything* out, Ric! Now or ever! I'm through talking."

He held her even tighter. "I don't think you're going anywhere right now!" he said with a lunatic look in his eyes. "You can't go unless I *let* you go. I don't think you're bad enough to get away from me!"

Shay quickly snatched one arm free, grabbed a vase of flowers on the desk beside her, and smashed it to the floor, breaking it with a shattering crash.

"What the hell did you do *that* for?" Ric panted, totally mystified.

"There are two employees of this hotel standing right outside that door," Shay told him in an eerily quiet voice. "So unless you want to get the headline of every tabloid in this country... Unless you want the evening news saying 'Superstar Ric Weaver Jailed for Beating Lover, film at eleven,' I think you better let me go. I can scream *real* loud, Ric."

Ric looked wounded to his heart, "Shay, God knows I've done a lot of things in my life I'm not proud of, but I've *never* raised a hand in violence to a woman." Ric reluctantly let go of her other arm. "And after what happened to my mother, I never could. You *know* that, Shay."

Despite her anger, Shay softened a bit toward him,

"Yes, Ric; I *do* know that. I'm sorry. Threatening you with something that ugly, and that untrue, was uncalled for; even now.

Shay lifted her chin, "But I'm leaving, Ric. I'm walking out of here, right now. Please, for both our sakes, don't try to stop me."

Ric pulled back in confusion. "Don't do this, baby; please, I'm begging you."

Shay picked up her bag again and quickly crossed to the outer door. The two bellmen were craning their necks, trying to look into the room.

"Sorry to have kept you waiting, gentlemen," Shay said sweetly. "They sent *two* of you? Oh, I only have one bag. Is there a car waiting for me?"

"Yes, ma'am," one said, looking alternately at Shay, the breathless Ric, and the smashed vase on the floor.

"Then I'd better get going. Oh, and please tell the manager that we are *so* sorry, but Mr. Weaver accidentally bumped against the desk, and broke that absolutely beautiful vase. Be sure to tell him we insist the cost be added to Mr. Weaver's bill, don't we, darling?" Shay asked sweetly, turning to Ric. She blew him a kiss and walked away, the bellmen following.

Shay's anger kept her in control all the way to the airport. Fortunately was able to get a flight to L.A within an hour. But once on the plane, her bravado caved in. She was glad she didn't have a seatmate as she pulled a tissue from her purse, and began to weep.

Oh, Ric... How could you to this. Why did you do this?

But in her heart she knew why. Ric did love her, at least he *thought* he did; of that she was still certain. But since Ric was a selfish man, his love was a selfish love. And that love wasn't strong enough to overcome his basic doubt in his own self-worth; his need for constant reinforcement. And all at once, Shay knew in her heart that it never would be.

He can't find himself though loving me—or anyone else. Only he can define what Eric Weaver is as a person. And until he does, Ric isn't capable of real love. Not until he's able to understand—and love—himself.

Shay looked down at her engagement ring, still glittering on her finger. She took it off, wrapped it in a tissue, and put it in her purse. *I forgot to give this back to him. Oh, well. I'll send it back tomorrow.*

A voice from somewhere inside her suddenly piped up:

So he plays around a little. Do you think you're the only woman in the world who has to put up with that? You know damn well Vanessa means nothing to Ric. You're the woman he loves, in spite of everything. You better think about this twice, girl. There are women who would kill to be in your shoes. What does it matter if he has a little something on the side as long as you're number one? As long as you have his name, live in his home, have his...children?

Shay sat back in her seat, and closed her eyes, resting her head against the seat cushion. Then a voice from deeper inside replied:

Don't fool yourself. You couldn't be happy with that kind of life. And the more unhappy you became, the more he'd cheat on you, using that as an excuse. And the more he played around, the more despondent you'd get, in a vicious circle, until finally, you'd just come to hate each other. No. It's over.

Having come to that painful but resolute decision, Shay felt some degree of peace. She closed her eyes again and soon fell asleep.

It was after sundown when Shay arrived at her house. She was grateful the legion of reporters had stopped hanging around there since she had been living at Ric's. She stood at the front door, feeling through her purse for her keys, as the taxi she had taken from the airport roared away. She suddenly rudely remembered she didn't *have* her keys.

"Damn!" She'd been all but living at Ric's for the past several weeks. She sure didn't need keys there, not with his huge household staff. At her house, she had once had a weekly cleaning service, but she'd even discontinued that, and they had returned the key. Shay hadn't even thought about taking her keys when she left for Rio. How could she have known she'd be returning *here*, rather than to Ric's, the place she had just begun to think of as "home"?

Well, I'll just have to call another taxi and go...where? She thought about going to Ric's, just long enough to retrieve her keys. *The hell with that. I'll just go call a locksmith to let me in. I've got ID galore showing this is where I live. That shouldn't be a problem.*

Then she remembered what *was* a problem. In Atlanta, before her hasty departure, she had managed to grab up all of her belongings—except one. *My cell phone! I left it in Atlanta, all plugged in and charging. I forgot all about it!*

She picked up her bag and started down the driveway. *Okay, I'll walk over to a neighbor's and...*

Just as she had almost reached the street, Woody's Bentley turned a corner and approached her.

Oh, God! What is Woody doing here? I thought he was in Atlanta! I'm not strong enough yet to face him right now. All right, girl, stay calm. He couldn't know about you and Ric yet. Just play it off like nothing's wrong. And you can use his phone to call a locksmith.

Woody pulled the car into her driveway. "Woody," Shay called to him as calmly as she could manage, "what are you doing here?"

"Looking for you," Wood answered, stepping out of the car. "I'm glad I found you."

"I meant, what are you doing in LA? I thought you were on the location shoot in Atlanta."

"No, I didn't go. The editing crew at the film lab was running into all kinds of problems, so when I left Detroit, I just flew back here. I let Sherry take over the shooting in Atlanta. It's only a couple of scenes, and she's getting better at this than I am. But the question on my mind is, what are *you* doing here?"

"Well, I just got back from my trip to Rio," Shay lied, showing him her bag.

"You only took one bag for a three-week trip?" he asked.

"Uh...I feel like such an idiot," Shay replied, sidestepping his question. "I forgot my cell phone and I forgot my keys. Could I use your phone to call a locksmith?"

Wood silently opened the car's passenger door for her, put her bag in the back seat, then walked around, and got in the driver's side.

"Isn't this silly?" Shay babbled, reaching for his telephone. "I can keep my belongings together all the way to another continent and back, but I get home and find I've lost my keys. I swear, I think sometimes I'd forget my head if it wasn't..."

Wood reached over and took the telephone from her, and wordlessly returned it to the holder.

"Woody, what are you doing?" Shay prattled nervously on. "I need to get somebody out here to open the door. I only hope they..."

"Shay," Wood calmly interrupted, "when are you going to tell me what's *really* going on?"

"What do you mean, Woody?" Shay attempted a laugh. "What's going on is that I can't get into my house. I..."

"Shay, Darnell called me. When he and Marty got home, there was a frantic message from Ric waiting for them, asking if you were there, or if they'd heard from you. Darnell couldn't understand that since he said you left Rio on your way to Atlanta—to be with Ric.

"Then Sherry called to tell me Ric was insisting on leaving Atlanta, even though they're not finished shooting there. She had to threaten to sue him for breach of contract to keep him there.

"So I came here, only to find you looking like a lost waif. Why did you come *here* in the first place? You've been at Ric's for weeks now."

He reached over, and took her hand, saying softly, "What happened, Shay? You can talk to me. And whatever it is, I'll do my best to help." Woody looked deeply into her eyes, "That's why I'm here, Shay. Not to judge you, honey, but to help you, if I can."

Shay looked into his eyes and saw all of his love and devotion still intact, even after the way she'd treated him. And she knew Wood was prepared to do anything in his power for her, whatever the trouble, based solely on that.

And then she could no longer hold back the tears of betrayal, and shame, and anger, and regret. Woody just put his arm around her, and let her cry, her head on his shoulder.

When her sobs started to subside, he handed her a tissue, and started the car, backing out of the driveway. They'd been traveling for several minutes before Shay sniffed, "Where are you taking me?"

"Home. To my house."

"Woody, I can't impose on you that way. All I need is just a way to get into my house, and I'd be..."

"Shay, whatever has happened, it's obvious you need a friend right now. And although you still don't seem to realize it..." he turned to give her a melancholy version of that lopsided grin, "I'm the best friend you've got."

Richmond met them at the door. "Good evening, Mr. Hollister. Miss Logan! Uh...Good evening, Miss." Even the reserved, dignified Richmond could not keep the surprise out of his voice, seeing Shay enter with Woody.

"Good evening, Richmond." Woody handed Richmond Shay's bag. "Miss Logan is going to be staying with us for a while. Please prepare the room next to mine for her, and tell Stephan they'll be two for dinner."

Richmond took the bag. "Yes, sir. At once." He gave Shay one last baffled glance as he left.

"Come on, Shay," Woody said. He put his arm around her and led her into his study.

Shay collapsed on a sofa, while Woody went over to the bar. He returned with two glasses and handed one to Shay. "Here."

"Woody, I don't know if I should. I could probably use a bracer, but you know I'm not much of a drinker."

Woody smiled, "Mine is vodka. Yours is just Perrier."

Shay looked at the glasses a moment, then reached for the one Wood had prepared for himself. "Well... maybe I need a little something to help calm me down after all."

Woody chuckled, then sat down next to her. "That's what *I'm* here for." He took her hand, looking at her attentively. "Tell me what happened, Shay."

"Woody, I'm...I'm ashamed to tell you." She looked away, "Of all the people on earth, I'm most ashamed to tell you."

"Now that's a pity," Wood said, squeezing her hand. "Because of all the people on earth..." he gently placed a finger under her chin and turned her face back toward him, "I'm the one person you don't have to be ashamed to tell anything. Come on, now, Natasha; spill it."

Seeing the tranquil, devoted acceptance in his eyes, Shay no longer hesitated. Her heart was bursting to unload this burden; to share it with someone she knew would truly care. She painfully told Wood of the morning's events in Atlanta. He interrupted briefly once or twice, asking questions to clarify something she'd said. When she finished, he just sat there, holding her hand.

Finally, he asked gently, "What are you going to do now, Shay?"

"Now? What can I do? I'm just going to put this behind me and get on with my life. That's all I can do...now."

"I meant, are you going back to...to Ric?" Wood asked, softer still.

Shay looked Wood in the eye, "No. No; that's over with now. There's no way I could ever trust Ric again, no matter *what* promises he made."

She looked away, and said in a whisper, "I know sooner or later he's going to come after me. He's going to fall on his knees, and tell me how sorry he is; that it will never happen again. But I'm going to be ready for him when he does."

Shay looked back to Woody, "I can't live that way, Wood. I *won't* live that way."

There was a knock at the door. At Wood's come in, Richmond entered.   "Dinner is ready, Mr. Hollister, whenever you wish it served."

"Have you eaten yet today, Shay?"

"Not since breakfast, on the plane—from Rio." She looked down at their hands, still clasped, and on Wood's knee. "I didn't want lunch when they served it on the...the other flight."

"Well, you need to eat, and I'm starving." He turned back to Richmond, "We'll have dinner shortly. Would you serve on the terrace, Richmond?"

"Certainly, sir. All will be in readiness within 15 minutes."

"No need to rush, Richmond. I think I'll have a cocktail, first, and Miss Logan would like to freshen up."

As Richmond left, Wood told Shay, "You'll feel a lot better if you get out of that suit and those heels. Let me take you up to your room."

He led the way upstairs, to a beautifully decorated, airy suite, with a balcony overlooking the lake. The bed had been turned back, and her suitcase unpacked. The few clothes she'd brought with her were hanging in the closet, and her toiletries placed on the dresser and in the adjoining bathroom.

"Take your time changing, honey. I'll wait for you downstairs."

"Thank you, Woody," Shay said gratefully. He just smiled as he left.

Shay quickly showered, and changed into a loose top and matching leggings. Woody was right; she felt a hundred percent better. And she knew it wasn't just the shower that had done it. Being with Woody, and having his unruffled, unquestioning support had smoothed away the madness of the day. She felt like herself again; confident, and able to face tomorrow, whatever it held.

She suddenly thought about Marty. She and Darnell must be worried to death. Shay sat on the bed and called them.

"Marty, it's me, your favorite problem child," Shay told her. "I just wanted you and Darnell to know I'm fine. I'm at..."

"Woody's. We know. He called a few minutes ago."

"Marty, I'm sorry to be such a pain in the ass for all of you..."

"Girl, don't be ridiculous," Marty laughed. "You're my sister/niece/daughter, remember?"

Shay had to laugh with her. "Well, I'm mighty glad I am," she said sincerely.

"We were worried sick about you, but it's all right now; now that we know you're in the best possible hands. Get a good night's rest, and we'll talk all this over tomorrow, all right?"

Shay went downstairs then and found Woody waiting for her out on the terrace. A round table had been laid with two place settings, in the finest linen, silver, and crystal. Wood had his back to her, sipping a drink, looking out across the lake.

"This is magnificent. Are we expecting the royal family?" Shay asked.

Woody turned and grinned at her, "Yes, I am; American royalty, anyway, Milady Natasha," He held out a chair for her with a courtly bow. "Natasha…wasn't there a Russia's czar's daughter named that?"

"Yes," Shay replied with a laugh, taking her seat. "That's how I got it. My mother's a history teacher, and she's a nut about the Russian Revolution; don't ask me why." She made a wry face, "I almost got named Anastasia."

"Whoa—I think Mama made the right choice," Wood gave her a sly smile, taking his seat.

They had a quiet, peaceful dinner, talking about Rio, which Woody had visited in the past. They very deliberately avoided talking about the movie, or *The SuperStar's Lady*, or anything else that would remind Shay of Ric.

After dinner, they decided to take a stroll. They wound up near the lake, and Woody headed toward the same stretch of beach that had witnessed Shay's confrontation with Ric all those weeks ago. Shay flinched as they headed that way, but Woody didn't notice.

Wood stood there looking out over the water, "Beautiful, isn't it? I think this view was what decided me on buying this place, more so than anything else."

"Uh-huh," Shay said uneasily. "Wood, let's go back to the house. I'm cold," she added, turning to go.

"Cold? It's almost tropical out tonight!" He reached for her arm, "Shay, how could..." He stopped, and took her other arm, as well. "Why, you're trembling like a leaf! And from that anguished look in your eyes, *not* from being cold. You were so at peace a moment ago. What's the matter?"

Tears started to fill Shay's eyes, but she didn't speak.

"Natasha, this is me; the guy you can tell anything," Wood said softly. "There's already been too much holding back; far too much 'smoke and mirrors.' Tonight we're going to put all our cards on the table."

He sat down on the sand, pulling her down with him. "Now I know something's wrong. Tell me," he urged.

Shay told him about the night of the party; about how Ric had pursued her throughout, and confronted her at this very spot, professing his captivation with her.

"But I thought you said nothing happened the night you went to the awards party with him," Wood probed.

"I...I haven't been honest with you, Woody; not from the beginning, in telling you about me and Ric."

And Shay proceeded to tell Woody about that first night with Ric; about what *really* happened. And she finally told him about the connection between Ric and the character Michael. Of how she had based Michael's outward persona on what was—at that time—her impression of Ric Weaver.

"Of course, I didn't actually know him then, Woody," she went on. "And there was no reason then for me to think I'd ever actually meet him. But I needed a...a structure for the kind of 'superstar' I was creating in my book."

Wood paused a long moment. "So *that's* what's been going on," he said reflectively. "Now a lot of things I didn't understand fall into place."

"Yes. Woody...I'm sorry. I'm so ashamed of myself for lying to you."

Wood gave her an impish smile. "Well, let's not call it *lying*. You didn't lie to me...exactly. Although it was one hell of a good case of uh...misdirection. But, baby, I ain't mad at ya. And I'm glad you finally told me."

"Oh, Woody, I feel like such a fool."

"Shay, you're not a fool. That scum-bag got you drunk, and then he seduced you."

"I can't put the blame all on him, Wood. It's not like I put up much of a fight. I'm no starry-eyed school girl. I'm a grown woman. I should have been able to see what he was doing that night. I should have been able to see through him all along."

"Honey, has it ever occurred to you that Ric's hold on you had very little to do with Ric himself, and much more to do with the connection between him and Michael in your mind? Ric's no Michael, Shay."

"That's for sure," she whispered emphatically.

"Have you ever told *him* this? That the character Michael was based on him?"

"Yes. I told him that first night."

"I've become very intimately acquainted with that formidable imagination of yours, lady. Shay, I think you had the two so mixed up in your mind you didn't even see the *real* Ric Weaver. And I think he knew that and used it to win you over, and hold on to you."

That had never occurred to Shay before. "You really think so?"

"Yes, I do. And now that I know it," he put his arm around her, "...I'm even more encouraged about *our* chances."

"Woody, I'm not ready yet for..."

He suddenly pulled her to him in one swift, firm motion, holding her close, and kissed her, his lips insistent and demanding.

Shay pushed back from him, "Wood! Woody, what are you doing?"

"Something I should have done a long time ago. If I had, maybe that low-life never would have gotten his hands on you in the first place."

He kissed her again. Shay struggled with him, but feebly. Her common sense told her this was wrong. That it was too soon after her break-up with Ric for her to be in another man's arms, even Woody's. But it didn't *feel* wrong.

"I love you, Natasha," Wood whispered hoarsely. His eyes burned down into hers, like two brown suns, and she was charmed. She couldn't have looked away, even had she wanted too.

"You know I love you, honey. You've *got* to know that I love you."

"Woody, I..."

He kissed her again, smothering her protests with his lips. His lips were so soft, and she whimpered a little when he slid his tongue into her mouth. His arms tightened around her, and one hand wound itself in her hair.

She pulled away again, "Woody, stop..." she panted. "I want you to st..." He smothered her words yet again. Shay found herself lying on her back on the sand, with Woody hovering above her.

"Natasha," her name was a velvety caress the way he breathed it in a muted whisper. "I love you so."

Shay looked into his eyes and knew it was true. She knew that he loved her, that he meant every word he said. The strongest feeling of warmth overcame her. It was as though his love had thrown a blanket of sanctuary over her. She was moved by the strength and honesty of his love; soothed by it. It felt right in his arms, as though it were where she belonged. She reached up, and gently touched his cheek.

Woody's eyes searched hers a long moment. Then, to her great surprise, he released her. Woody stood and offered Shay his hand. "We'd better stop now," he said breathlessly, "while I *can* still stop."

Shay took his hand, and he helped her up. "I want you, Shay," he whispered. "I've wanted you since the day I met you. But I won't take advantage of the situation; of your vulnerability. It's too soon to expect you to make a decision like this, and it's not fair of me to ask you to. I want you, but only when—if—you're sure you want me, too."

"Woody, I..." Shay began, at that moment so confused she didn't know *what* she felt.

"Let's go back to the house," Wood said quickly, leading her away.

They slowly walked back, brushing the sand from each other's hair and clothing as they went. "We don't want to scandalize poor Richmond," Woody teased.

It was getting late, and it had been a long, physically and emotionally draining day for them both. They held hands and slowly went up the stairs. They stood outside Shay's bedroom door. Wood didn't embrace her or even touch her. It was as if he was afraid to. He bent forward and kissed her lips tenderly. "Good night, my love," he whispered softly as she closed her door.

Shay got ready for bed, her mind in a whirl. She lay down and snapped off the bedside light. Lying in the shadowy room, Shay stared at the ceiling that was lit only by moonlight. Sleep would not come. She got up, and went over to the balcony door, and stood looking out over the lake. Suddenly Shay turned and walked swiftly out into the hallway. She walked to Wood's bedroom door and hesitated only a moment before softly knocking.

Wood came to the door almost immediately. Apparently, he hadn't been able to sleep, either. He didn't say a word, but the question was in his eyes.

"May I come in?" Shay asked shyly, eyes downcast.

Woody lifted her chin so that she was looking into his eyes. His eyes spoke of his desire, of his longing, of his need, but also told her he was willing to wait. She knew, as he had told her, that he would "wait the rest of my life, if I have to".

And Shay immediately realized she didn't want him to wait. *She* didn't want to wait. She wanted to be with him.

She wanted to be in his arms; to share the warmth of his love. Shay returned his gaze, and simply whispered, "I'm sure, Woody."

Wood put an arm around her waist, and she put her arm around him in return. As they slowly went into his room, Woody quietly closed the door behind them.

CHAPTER 13

48 HOURS

The sun shone brilliantly through the sliding glass doors. Wood drifted to consciousness slowly, feeling warm...and achy, but pleasantly achy. He rolled to his side, to wake Shay with a kiss, but was amazed to find himself in bed alone.

There was the sound of water running, and Shay appeared in the bathroom doorway, stretching and yawning, wearing only Wood's pajama top. She smiled radiantly when she saw Woody was awake, "Good morning."

"Morning." Wood perched on one elbow, "When I woke up, and you were gone, I thought...I thought that..."

"That I had run off?" Shay finished for him with the weirdest sense of deja vu. "Not a chance, mister," she added, coming over to sit on the bed next to him. "After last night..." she gave him a wink, "I can barely walk, let alone run. Although..." she touched Wood's cheek with a seductive smile, "had I known last night what a wild man I was with, I might have."

Wood drew her down to the bed, next to him. "Did I hurt you, honey?" he looked down with deep concern. "I didn't mean to get so...so energetic with you, baby. It's just that I've wanted you so bad..." he nuzzled her neck " for so long, that I..."

Shay silenced him with a finger across his lips. "That wasn't a *complaint*, Woodington," she whispered. Shay wrapped her arms around his neck and pulled him down to kiss her, making it unquestionably clear her comment was just the opposite.

"Natasha," he breathed against the hollow of her throat. Shay had never liked her name until she heard Woody say it. No one had ever said it the way he did; like an adulation, like a breeze on the wind. That sultry look came back into his eyes again as he began to leisurely unbutton the pajama top.

The night had been boldly sensual but at the same time...tender. This morning the tenderness factor ruled supreme, as Woody lovingly caressed every inch of her body with his hands, and his lips as he made love to her. As she had the night before, Shay was left limp and breathless in his arms as he held her close afterward.

"Shay," he whispered into her ear, "you don't know how many times I've lain here in this bed, not able to sleep, thinking about you; longing for you. I thought I had lost you forever." He looked down into her eyes. "And now you're here; in my home, in my room, in my bed, in my arms..." he kissed her, "in my heart." He paused a moment, "This is where you belong. And where you're going to stay... Shay?"

"Yes, Woody?"

"I was thinking about something while you were sleeping last night; something you said."

"Well, you sure couldn't have thought about it very long," Shay teased. "We didn't go to sleep until sunrise."

"Whose fault is that, insatiable woman?" Woody grinned as he needled her back, then turned serious again.

"Shay, I'm glad we had that talk last night. Glad we both felt the need to be honest with each other about...about our histories. Now that we know we've both always practiced safe..."

"I'm glad, too, Woody. Now that we know and ..."

"Shay..." Woody interrupted her, "what you said about Ric...." He could feel Shay tense in his arms. "About him coming after you. He *will*, you know."

"Yes. I know. But my mind is made up. I'm not going back to him. Things were never really right between us. And they never could be. I'm convinced of that now."

Woody looked at her left hand, "You gave him back

the ring?"

"No. We parted in so much turmoil I forgot to. But I took it off on the plane; it's in my purse. I'm going to send it back to him today."

"You're that sure?"

Shay looked him in the eye, "Yes, Woody. I'm that sure."

Wood cleared his throat. "Shay...there's one way Ric *can't* marry you."

Shay looked at him in confusion. "What? If I put a contract out on him?" She laughed naughtily. "I don't want him *dead*, Woody. I just want him to leave me alone."

Wood laughed, too. "No, I didn't mean killing him..." he raised one eyebrow, "although that *is* a thought." Shay poked him playfully in the ribs.

Wood took Shay's hand, clearing his throat once again. Then he looked into her eyes and said, "Shay, Ric can't marry you...if you're already married to somebody else."

Shay was sure hadn't heard him correctly, "Huh?"

Wood squeezed her hand, "Will you marry *me*?"

She looked at him in surprise, "*What*?"

"I want you to marry me, Shay. Will you marry me?"

"Woody, we...we can't get married."

"Why not?" He gave her his lopsided grin, but the fervor remained in his eyes. "We're both free, black, and over twenty-one. And I've got the price of a marriage license."

Shay sat up, "Marriage is not a subject to joke about, Wood."

He sat up too. "I'm *not* joking. I never meant anything more in my life."

"Wood, you can't marry me just to shield me from Ric. That's no reason for two people to get married."

"I didn't say I want to marry you just to shield you from Ric. I said that would be one consequence of me marrying you. But that's not why I want to marry you."

Wood took her in his arms, "I want to marry you, Natasha, because I love you. Because I want to spend the rest of my life with you." He kissed her tenderly, "*That's* why I want to marry you. Will you marry me, Natasha?"

Shay was speechless.

"Wait a sec!" Woody said suddenly, jumping up from the bed. He went over to a dresser, opened the bottom drawer, and took something out. When he returned to sit on the bed, Shay could see it was a small red velvet box.

"I've...I've had this for weeks," Wood said slowly, looking down at the box. He looked into Shay's eyes, "I was going to ask you to marry me the night I got stuck getting Holly out of jail; the night you went out to dinner with Ric. I guess that was the *real* reason I went on the nut that night."

"Oh, Woody..." Shay was so surprised, and so touched, that was all she could say.

"Even after you became engaged to Ric, I couldn't bring myself to return it. So you see, baby; this isn't an idea that's just popped into my head. It's something I've been thinking about for a long, long time. Something I thought had become impossible...until now."

"Oh, Woody," Shay repeated, her eyes misting over. She touched his cheek, "I don't deserve a man like you."

"You're right," he kissed her hand, "you deserve ever so much better. But you're stuck with me, anyway."

"Wood, think what you're asking. I mean, twenty-four hours ago, I was engaged to another man."

"So what? Twenty-four hours from *now*, you'll be married to *me*."

"*What!*"

"If we're going to do this, honey; let's *do* it. Now. Today. We can fly over to Vegas, and get married this evening, like Darnell and Marty."

"But Woody..."

"Or do you have your heart set on a big wedding?"

"No, Wood, that's not important to me; but what is..."

"Good. But I promise you the biggest damn wedding reception party this town has ever seen!"

"Woody, slow down. Now, you know how deeply I care for you; how deeply I've always cared for you. And I have to admit..." she tenderly caressed his cheek again, "last night added a whole new dimension to our relationship; a wonderful new dimension. But I don't think we should rush into anything. We've got all the time in the world. Why don't we just..."

"Shay, I want to ask you just one question. That night; the night things got all messed up, the night I *was* going to propose to you... If things hadn't gotten so off track; if they had gone the way we planned, and I *had* proposed to you that night..." his eyes drilled into hers, "would you have said 'yes?' "

Shay saw the sincerity in those eyes. She knew this man was laying his heart at her feet, and that she could do no less than be as honest as he. She thought back to that night, before Ric re-entered the picture. Shay remembered how she had carefully planned every detail; remembered how she had shivered with anticipation of being with Wood, consummately with him, at last. When she finally answered, it was as though her words came of their own volition; not from her lips, but directly from her heart.

"Yes," Shay replied almost too quietly to be heard. "Yes, I would have."

His frown of anxiety melted away. His eyes seemed to glow, and his beaming smile lit his face with sunshine. "Well, honey, can't we just start back up there? Can't we forget all the turmoil since then, and just go back to that night?" He paused a moment. "If that night had jumped off the way we planned," he whispered, "we'd be married right now, Shay."

Wood stood, pulling Shay along with him. "I've asked you three times already, and I still haven't got an answer. I never asked a woman to marry me before. Maybe I'm not doing it the right way."

He put his hands on her shoulders and guided her to sit on the edge of the bed. Then he went down on one knee at her feet.

"Natasha," he said, taking her hand, looking up at her in undeniable adoration, "I love you from the bottom of my heart. If you'll be my wife, I'll spend the rest of my days doing everything in my power to make you happy. Will you marry me?"

And Shay's heart melted, with this sweet, wonderful man on his knees before her.

I'm *the one who should be on her knees, after all the hell he's been through for my sake. I'm lucky to have him even still want to see me, but here he is, still offering a love that I know will never desert me. And I'm not going to disappoint him this time.*

Once again her heart spoke for her before her brain could stop it, "Yes, Woody."

He caught his breath, his eyes wild with joy and wonder. "What! Really? You mean it?"

Shay had to smile at his delight, "Yes, Wood; I mean it."

"Are you *sure*?"

"Yes; I'm sure." Shay laughed gaily, "You asked me three times, and now I've said yes three times. Have you changed *your* mind?"

Wood hopped up beside her and took her in his arms. "No, ma'am," he said emphatically, as his lips descended on hers.

Woody then opened the box. The ring was not a diamond. It was a brilliantly beautiful ruby.

"I know it's not traditional, honey," Wood said hopefully, "but I saw this one, and it just seemed so right." He looked at her lovingly, "That fire reflects my love for you more accurately than the iciness of a diamond, and I know red is your favorite color. But it you don't like it..."

Shay looked at the twinkling radiance of the ruby, like a miniature red sun. "I love it, Woody," she breathed, as he slipped it on her finger.

That afternoon Marty and Darnell tried their honest best to talk them out of it. They were, of course, overjoyed at Woody and Shay finally fulfilling the promise their relationship had held dormant for so long. But they were troubled about the two getting married right away.

The Franklins came over as soon as Wood called to tell them their plans. Darnell marched Wood out of the library into another room to talk sense to him, while Marty moved in on Shay.

"Shay, do you two know what you're doing?"

"*We* think so, Marty."

Marty stood up and began to pace. "Shay, I know you're had feelings for Woody right from the start. I mean, I was there when you met him. The chemistry between you two was undeniable, right from the get go. And, of course, I think Wood is the second most wonderful man in the world.

"But because I care so much about him—*and* you—I don't want either of you to get hurt. Shay, this time yesterday you were engaged to Ric. Don't you think part of the reason you want to marry Woody is to get back at Ric? And to protect yourself from being tempted to go back to him?"

"No, Marty; I honestly don't. Woody and I talked about this. There's no way I'd ever go back to Ric. No way, even if Wood *wasn't* in the picture. And I'm not trying to hurt Ric." Shay looked away, "He does a good enough job of hurting himself without my assistance," she finished so softly Marty barely heard her.

"All right, then," Marty reasoned, "if that's the case, why don't the two of you wait a while? If Ric really *is* out of your life for good, what's the rush?" Marty suddenly looked alarmed, "Shay, you're not..."

Shay cut her eyes, "Martha Tibbs Franklin, if you ask me that again, I'm going to smack you! No, I'm not!"

"Then why the big hurry?"

"I...I think Woody needs that from me, Marty. After all that's happened, he needs me to make that degree of a commitment. He needs to know I'm for real. And I'm perfectly willing to make that commitment, because I *am*."

Shay went over to where Marty was still pacing, "Marty, I'd never marry Woody just to get back at Ric. I'd never use Woody that way. He means too much to me. I *need* Woody, Marty. Just as much—or more—than he needs me."

"But, girlfriend," Marty asked softly, "do you love him? *That's* the question. Wood deserves a wife who will love him just as much as he loves her. Do you? Can you?"

Shay thought back to all the wonderful times she'd shared with Woody, and added in the new heights their relationship had achieved just the night before. "Yes, Marty. I can. I will," she answered firmly.

There was a knock at the door. Darnell stuck his head in, "Are you ladies finished talking? Can we come in now?"

"Yes, honey; come on in," Marty told him. "Are you two finished already?"

"*Already*?" Darnell snorted as he and Wood came into the room. "We've been finished for half an hour, since all I could get out of *him*..." he nodded to Woody, "was 'I love her, man.'"

"Well, what else did I need to say..." Wood put in, walking over to Shay. One look in her eyes told him she hadn't changed her mind either, "...since that said it all?"

He turned to Marty and Darnell, "So are you two going to Vegas to stand up with us, or are we going to have to get that hard of hearing minister and his wife to do it?"

Eight hours later, Shay and Woody stood on the same Las Vegas penthouse balcony where they had stood so many nights before. Although the night was warm, Shay shivered, as she had on their first visit there. But this time Wood couldn't offer her his jacket. He wasn't wearing one. All he had on was a pajama bottom and a robe.

"Cold, baby?" Woody was behind her. He wrapped both his arms around her, savoring the silky feel of her negligee, but thinking it didn't come close to the velvety softness of her skin.

"No, not really. It's just that it's all beginning to hit me now. We're actually..." she looked down at the ruby and the slender gold band on her finger, "actually..."

"Married?" Wood finished for her, burying his face in her hair. "But we're not, you know."

Shay swiftly turned to face him, "What?"

"There still remains one little matter to be taken care of before we are indeed lawfully, indisputably married." That impassioned look came into his eyes as he swept down, and picked Shay up, cradling her in his arms. "And I, for one, can't wait."

He kissed his bride tenderly, "This is what I should have done the *first* time we were here; pick you up in my arms and carry you off to my bed," he whispered. Shay's arms encircled his neck before she knew it.

"Fortunately..." he started inside with his bride in his arms, "I don't make the same mistakes twice."

Shay was aware of Wood's arm around her as she drifted to consciousness. His arm tightened as she contently snuggled closer to him, and opened her eyes. Wood was already awake, lying there looking at her. *This*

man is my husband. The reality of it hit her like a lightning bolt.

Woody and Shay had spent their wedding night at the hotel in Vegas while Marty and Darnell flew back home. Woody promised Shay an extended trip to the Caribbean for their honeymoon, but it had to be postponed a few weeks until Wood finished post-production work on the movie. So, the afternoon following their wedding, Shay and Wood had flown back to LA and Shay had just spent her first night as the mistress of her new home.

"And just who do you think you're staring at, sir?" Shay playfully asked with a shaky smile.

"Why, I'm just admiring the beauty of Mrs. Woodington James Hollister, III, ma'am," he whispered back.

Somehow, he always knew exactly what to say to touch her heart. "Okay..." Shay put her arms around him, "long as you've got the name right."

"You know, I need to ask you something," Wood murmured softly as he nibbled her ear. "I just thought about it. We've been married a whole day and a half now, and I realized I don't exactly know." He pulled her closer and looked into her eyes. "How would you feel about a...a Woodington James Hollister—the fourth?"

Shay looked deeply into her husband's eyes. Things had happened so fast that she had never thought about that before, either. But then she did, and a gentle reverence suddenly enveloped her. She answered spontaneously, "I'd feel like about the happiest woman in the world."

"I see," Wood said simply. He kissed her forehead, then lightly kissed her lips. "I'm glad."

"Well..." Woody started to slip her nightgown down, and began to kiss her shoulders, "how about getting started along those lines right now?"

"That's about all we *have* been doing ever since the wedding," Shay teased while running her fingers through his hair.

"Practice makes perfect, baby," Wood whispered from between her breasts.

"In that department, Mr. Hollister..." Shay replied, gasping from the ecstasy of his touch, "you're already perfect."

Wood moved over her, enveloping her in his arms. "And Mrs. Hollister..." he panted, as his lips took hers, "sometimes you talk too much."

A couple of hours later, Wood was dressing to go down to the film lab. "What are you going to do today, baby?" he asked.

"There are so many things that need doing that I don't exactly know where to start. I guess I'll contact Marge about selling the house, and start lining up some movers to get my things over here, especially my computer. And if we're going to have our reception two weeks from Saturday, I'd better start working on that, too."

"Don't forget about contacting my...I mean, *our* travel agent to make arrangements for our folks to come out that weekend."

Shay gave him a jittery laugh, "I wouldn't dare forget that. I just barely kept *my* folks from flying out here yesterday, when I called and told them I was married...but not to the man they thought I was engaged to. I'm sure they think I've lost my mind, Woody; that I'm totally out of control."

"You can sure *get* out of control when the mood strikes you, Mrs. H.," Woody said with a wicked leer. "And am I glad!

Shay went over to him, and put her arms around his neck, "How was I to know I was marrying a love machine?" she teased.

Wood smacked her on the rump, "You can handle it." He held her close as he kissed her, then whispered, "You know, this is the first time we've been apart since we've been married, sweetheart. You gonna miss me?"

Shay looked at the sweet, sentimental man she had married. His love for her shined from his eyes like a beacon. For the past thirty-six hours, they'd been in a world of their own, just the two of them. She had thought she'd known this man well, but the past day and a half she'd been privileged to see into his heart, into his soul, which he bared to her openly; freely.

She saw there a man of strength, of honesty. A man who thought before he spoke. A man as natural and unaffected as a mountain stream; who could, no matter what, retain the ability to laugh at the world, and at himself.

And she saw there, in his deepest of hearts, that which she could only now truly sense; now that she was his wife. She saw the enormity, the width and the breadth of his love for her. And the force of it took her breath away.

Thoughts of Ric had been few. The tempestuous relationship she had with him was rapidly fading in comparison to the tranquil oneness she now felt with Wood.

Shay kissed Woody in return. "Yes, honey; I will miss you," she answered sincerely; the unfamiliar term of endearment toward him starting to feel comfortable to her tongue. She was rewarded with that famous lopsided smile.

Woody reached for his jacket. "You know all hell is going to break loose once word that we're married gets out; don't you, baby? I mean, with all the hoopla that was raised about you being engaged to Ric, it's really gonna start up a stir when it gets out you're married—to me."

"I know, Wood," Shay replied pensively.

Wood took her in his arms again. "It's gonna be all right, honey. Don't worry about it. There'll be a big burst of hype for a while, but then it'll die down and they'll leave us alone. And as for Mr. Weaver..." he tipped her face to look into his eyes, "don't worry about *him* either.

Whenever he shows his face, *I'll* handle him."

"Wood," Shay was suddenly alarmed, "You're not..."

"That's up to him," Wood replied grimly. "No, I'm not going to start anything with him, baby. But I'll do whatever I have to do to protect you. I know Ric, Shay. He's not going to let a little thing like a marriage license stop him from going after you. It wouldn't be the first time Ric set his sights on a married woman." A fierce shadow came over Wood's face. "But if he makes a move on *my* wife, it'll damn sure be the last."

"Woody, don't talk like that. You're scaring me," Shay said with a shiver.

Wood's expression instantly changed, "I'm sorry, baby. Here I am telling you not to worry, and then I start talking like Dirty Harry. But it's a good thing shooting for the movie is all finished. Our working relationship was strained as it was. Now I think it would be pretty close to impossible; professionalism be damned."

He looked at his watch. "I better get going. You know how to reach me if you need me, honey. And if you need anything done around here, Richmond will take care of it."

Shay giggled, "You know, I never saw Richmond smile until you told him we were married last night."

Wood laughed, too. " Yeah. He's been with me for six years, and that's as close as I've seen the old boy come to losing that imperturbable cool of his. He's really crazy about you, Shay." His eyes softened, "But then, who isn't?"

"I think you're biased in that assessment, mister."

"You're right. Nobody knows just how wonderful you are as well as I do. Nobody else has ever been married to you." He kissed her tenderly. "I'll be home about four, honey. See you then." And he was gone.

Shay called downstairs and had Richmond bring breakfast to the sitting room, reminding herself to start doing her wifely duty and start nagging her husband about not eating breakfast himself. After eating, she made a couple of calls to check on movers before taking a shower.

She had just come back into the bedroom when there was a sudden a commotion below, followed by footsteps on the stairs. Shay could hear Richmond arguing, "You can't go up there, sir! Stop at once, or I shall call security!" There was the sound of doors opening and slamming, and a man's voice was calling, "Shay! Shay, where are you?" It was Ric.

Shay snatched up her robe, threw it on, and was going through the parlor to the outer door, but it flew open just as she reached it. Ric stood there with his hair in his eyes, panting. Richmond was right behind him.

"Beg pardon, ma'am. Mr. Weaver told the guards at the gate he was here for a business appointment. When I opened the front door, he rushed in right past me," Richmond was panting, too.

Ric ignored him. "Shay, I've got to talk to you!"

Richmond grabbed Ric's arm, "Sir, really! I must insist! How dare you!" Ric tried to snatch his arm back and glared at Richmond with a look Shay recognized. Ric wasn't going without a fight.

"Richmond, it's all right. I'll see Mr. Weaver... "she scowled at Rick, "despite his colossal lack of manners!"

"Very well, ma'am; if that's what you wish," Richmond replied apprehensively. "Would you like me to wait in the corridor?" he asked, reluctantly releasing Ric's arm but continuing to glare at him.

"Yes. Yes, I think you'd better," Shay told him, still frowning at Ric.

As soon as the door closed behind Richmond, Shay crossed her arms, and demanded, "What are you *doing* here? Have you lost your mind?"

"*Me*? Have I lost *my* mind? Shay, what the hell is going on?" He started toward her. "What are *you* doing here?"

Shay didn't back off, "I happen to *live* here."

Ric stopped then. He looked her over in confusion, then sank into a nearby chair. "Then it *is* true," he whispered.

"That Woody and I are married?" she shot back defiantly. "Yes...it is."

Ric just sat there for a moment, then looked up in bafflement. "A messenger brought the ring back. Then there were all these rumors, but I kept telling myself it was too crazy to be true."

"Oh; so it's 'crazy' for a man to marry me, huh?"

He shook his head sadly. "No, Shay. Of course, I don't think *that's* crazy. After all," he looked sadly into her eyes, "I asked you to marry *me*; remember?" His head snapped up, "But I think it's insane for you to up and marry Wood!"

"Why?" she challenged. "My...my husband..." she stumbled over the unfamiliar word, and the feeling of unreality hit her all over again. "My husband and I see nothing insane about it," she finished.

"See! You can't even *say* it without stuttering. Shay...Shay, honey...how could you do this?" he moaned. "How could you do this to yourself? How could you do this to *me*? Did you need that badly to hurt me back?"

"Do this to *you*? Hurt *you*? That's the problem—that's *your* problem, Ric. You think this—and everything else— is about you; about what you want; about your needs. Well, I've got a news flash for you, buddy. This time it's about what *Natasha* wants; what *Natasha* needs!"

"And Natasha needs to be married to a man she doesn't love?" he asked quietly.

Shay looked him in the eye. "I do love Woody."

He stood quickly, and strode over to her, "No, you don't. I know you don't." He took her in his arms. She struggled with him, but he wouldn't let her go. "Because I know who you do love..." he whispered, pulling her closer. He looked into her eyes, "You love *me*," he murmured, as his lips smothering her protests.

Shay was immobilized for an instant, transfixed by his closeness; the sensual familiarity of his kiss. But then she furiously pushed him away and slapped him—-hard.

"Who the hell do you think you are? Woody would break you in two if he knew you were here!"

"He'd *try*," Ric said with a smirk, rubbing his cheek. "But not him, his stuck-up butler, or anybody else around here is going to stop me from going after what's mine."

"*Yours*? Look here, dream-man, nothing you see around here belongs to you. *Nothing*. This is Wood's home, this is Wood's bedroom...and I'm Wood's wife. Nothing you're likely to say or do will change any of that in the slightest."

Shay marched to the door and flung it open wide. "Now you get the hell out of my house before I call the National Guard to help you along!"

Richmond and three burly guards were waiting just outside the door. Hearing Shay's words, the guards tensed. They were angry at Ric already, for tricking them to gain entry. They were more than eager to show the new lady of the house the National Guard wouldn't be necessary. And Richmond looked only too glad to pitch in on that effort, should it be necessary.

Ric saw the four men standing there and apparently decided the odds were not in his favor. He started for the door but turned just as he reached it.

"This isn't over, Shay," he said softly. "You might try to pretend it is, but you know it isn't. Sooner or later, you're going to come back to me."

Shay was shaken and was starting to feel drawn in by those eyes when she suddenly realized the four men in the corridor where waiting for a signal from her to act.

Shay crossed her arms again, turned her back to Ric, and scathingly replied, "Don't hold your breath!"

Ric seemed to crumple. But he rallied and gave Shay

one last jolting look before silently leaving the room.

The four men in the hall started to follow Ric, when Shay called out, "Richmond? Would you step in here for a moment?"

Richmond entered the room as the three guards escorted Ric out. "Mrs. Hollister, again, my deepest apologies for...."

"It's not your fault, Richmond. And I appreciate your efforts to protect me. Were you hurt?"

A ghost of a smile skirted around his lips, "Just my feelings, ma'am."

Shay smiled in spite of the situation, then turned serious. "Richmond, under no circumstance is Mr. Weaver to be allowed on the grounds in the future. Would you talk to the guards about it for me?"

"Yes, ma'am. That would most be my absolute pleasure."

In spite of the gravity of the situation, Shay was tempted to smile again. The usually unflappable and impeccably dressed Richmond was standing there with his hair all mussed, and his clothes hanging awry from his tussle with Ric, clearly still in the mood to go kick some butt.

"And Richmond...please...I don't want Mr. Hollister to know anything about this. I don't know what he would do... Correction: I *do* know what he would do if he found out. And I don't want to start married life with my new husband in the morgue or in jail."

"Yes, Mrs. Hollister, I understand perfectly. I'll speak to the staff about that as well. You can rely on me, ma'am." He bowed and withdrew.

Shay began to tremble as she stood there trying to pretend to herself she wasn't shaken to her very soul, remembering words Woody had said to her on their wedding night.

"Shay, I've never asked *why* you decided to marry me.

I'm not sure I want to know. But I know why I married you." He looked deeply into her eyes, "I married you because I love you, Natasha Logan Hollister. And I always will."

He chuckled cheerlessly, "You know what, baby? We've been married six whole hours now, and you've never once said 'I love you'."

Shay's eyes misted; she reached out and touched his arm, "Woody, I..."

"Nope." He put a finger across her lips. "I want to hear you say you love me more than anything in this world." He looked out the window at the moon, "I lay awake earlier, with you asleep in my arms, praying you'd open your eyes and say 'Woody, I love you'."

He turned back to Shay. "But I don't want you to say it out of obligation or loyalty. I only want to hear it if you *want* to say it. When—and only when—you know in your heart you mean it."

He cradled her head on his shoulder, and kissed her forehead, "Until then, honey, it's enough for me to love you."

CHAPTER 14

THE TOWERING INFERNO

Wood was right. The breaking out of "all hell" was exactly what happened when word of their marriage was released. Which didn't take very long. The first whispers and "unconfirmed rumors" started the day after the wedding. Before long an enterprising reporter unearthed a copy of their marriage certificate. Then it was everywhere; in every newscast, in every newspaper, in every tabloid. The telephone rang incessantly. And the question on everyone's lips was "What happened with Ric Weaver?"

Woody and Shay held a brief press conference, hoping that would help defuse some of the furor, but it only made things worse. Shay found there was no way she could answer questions like "How could you be engaged to one man one day, and married to another man the next?" without revealing the innermost workings of her heart; things that were too private to share—and nobody else's damn business, anyway. The questions she and Woody ignored or answered "no comment" just added fuel to the fire.

And Ric's handling of the situation astounded Shay. She felt sure Ric would play the whole thing off as it being *he* that had dumped Shay, and she—poor heart-broken thing—turning to Wood as a second-rate substitute.

Instead, Ric openly admitted he had been the one "dumped." He told the world he still loved Shay, and wanted her back, even after she wounded him to his very soul by breaking their engagement and running off with another man. And, Ric hastened to add, this other man was none other than someone he had worked with daily; a man he trusted; and this man had gone behind his back and stolen his woman.

Ric's past history made *that* story a little hard to

swallow for many. But a lot of others bought it, and thought was Shay a two-timing hoochie Mama, and Woody a back-stabbing "playa."

One consequence of the whole brouhaha was that sales of all three of Shay's books went through the roof. People everywhere were buying the books to see if they would give some clue into the heart and mind of the woman at the center of this famous—rapidly becoming *in*famous—love triangle.

The movie had already been eagerly anticipated by public and critics alike, but now Wood had to post all sorts of security around the film lab, where the final editing was being made, to keep unauthorized advance "snippets" from being leaked.

The album accompanying the movie was finished, and the executives at the record label had staff working day and night to release it earlier since the public was practically tearing their door down waiting to buy it. The first single from the album, "I Need You Near Me", had just been released, and entered the charts at number one.

"Well, Five predicted this whole thing was going to make us all a lot of money," Shay lamented to Woody late one evening. "But I sure never thought it would be *this* way."

"Neither did I, honey. But in the end, after the dust dies down, the movie and the album will either stand or fall on their own merits. After the curiosity factor is satisfied— and believe me, that won't take long—people will judge them on how good they are. I still have faith in them both. The movie and the album are both dynamite, and no amount of hype is going to change that.

"As for your books, all of them were already bestsellers before this whole thing came up. And they got to be bestsellers because of your talent." Woody gave her that grin. "Not because you are 'the heartbreaker of the century,' to quote some of your most recent press."

Wood paused a long moment, then asked, "Did he call today?"

Shay shook her head, "No, Wood. No calls, no notes, no flowers, no messages, not for almost a week now. Maybe...maybe he's given up."

Wood laughed bitterly, "Don't count on it."

Shay and Woody kept to themselves, avoiding the hype as much as they could, and decided to go ahead with their wedding reception as planned. "We don't have anything to hide or be ashamed of, baby," Wood said firmly.

They really did try to keep it reasonably small, but Shay had a large family, and so did Woody. Shay had a lot of friends, and so did Woody. And Shay had an abundance of business associates, and so did Woody.

And then they got together with Marty and Darnell one night. The Franklins, who had also eloped, had not yet had their formal wedding celebration, either. It somehow got decided the party would be a joint one, for the four of them. And Marty had a large family, and so did...well, suffice to say the party did indeed turn out to be "the biggest damn wedding reception party this town has ever seen!" as Woody had promised.

Constraining the guest list proved to be impossible. With Woody and Darnell, two of the most popular entertainers in the world, marrying two beautiful, talented, and well-known women, an invitation to the party became the most sought after one of the season. Shay had originally planned to have the party at her new home. But as the guest list grew and grew, she had to finally admit that plan was out the window. She and Marty put the catering and other arrangements for the whole shebang into the capable—an exorbitantly expensive—hands of the Beverly Hills Regal Country Club.

Shay's parents had flown in early and had a couple of days to meet—and assess—their new son-in-law before the party. Shay knew her parents were already apprehensive about her change of groom in such an abrupt about-face. And they were skeptical about her whole new "Hollywood" lifestyle, anyway. But by the time the party rolled around, Shay's Dad had taken to clapping Woody on the back and calling him "son".

"Your Daddy is just in seventh heaven, girl," Mama whispered to Shay at the party, while Shay's Dad was making a toast.

"And what about you, Mama? Come on, admit it. You like Woody, too—don't you?" Shay teased her.

"Well, to tell the truth, I *did* have some qualms about this whole thing, but now that I've *met* Woody..." Mama just silently lifted her glass along with all the other guests, but there was a twinkle in her eye as Woody came over to Shay, and gave her a kiss, while their guests cheered.

Wood's father and brothers were equally as taken with Shay. Wood's younger brothers were all still single, and thought their new sister-in-law was "*too* fine, man!"

"After raising three knucklehead boys..." Woodington James Hollister Jr. told Shay with a kiss, "I've finally got myself a daughter!" Tears came to her eyes when he presented her with a bracelet that had belonged to Wood's mother.

"This was one of the first things Wood bought when he first started making a name for himself. He gave it to her about a year before she died," Dad said, with a faraway look in his eyes as he fastened the bracelet on Shay's wrist. "I know she'd want Woody's wife to have it," he finished softly.

In spite of the tremendous crowd, some of whom she didn't even know, Shay felt cherished and content with her family and closest friends...and her husband...nearby. In the past weeks, the devotion between Shay and Woody had deepened day by day. She watched Wood now as he smoothly maneuvered the crowd, making his way back to the head table where she was sitting with Marty and Darnell. His eyes met hers across the room, and he smiled, suddenly causing everything else to fade into the background, as the memory of their days together—and the sweetness of their nights—enveloped her.

But their gaze was rudely broken when Vanessa Sweet grabbed Woody by the arm to give him yet another congratulatory kiss.

"That heifer!" Shay started to rise from her seat, "I'm going to..."

"You're going to sit right there in your seat like the sweet, blushing bride you are," Marty ordered, seeing the situation, and pulling Shay back down. "Anyway, *you're* the one who told Wood to let her stay after she crashed the party!"

"Yes, but I didn't think she was going to try to spend the evening slobbering all over my husband!"

"Shay, *ten* Vanessa's wouldn't have a chance with Wood, and you know it." Marty sucked her teeth, "Everything girlfriend's got is fake, starting with her personality. When she goes to bed, I bet she leaves her hair, her nails, those light-brown eyes, her boobs, *and* her teeth on the nightstand!"

"Honey," Darnell told her with a straight face, "you really need to stop beating around the bush, and learn to just speak your mind."

The three of them burst out laughing at that, just as Woody joined them, "What's the big joke?"

"Your leading lady," Darnell said, nodding toward where Wood had left Vanessa standing in the middle of the floor.

"My leading lady's last name is Hollister," Wood replied, taking the seat next to Shay. "Which reminds me, ma'am; may I have this dance?"

Shay smiled tenderly at him, and they were just about to rise when all of the sudden, the music trailed off, and the room grew silent.   Shay and Woody looked around, wondering what had happened.

"Oh, no," Shay breathed softly as she looked toward the stage. Woody twirled around, following her gaze.

Ric had mounted the stairs to the stage and was approaching the mike.

"What the hell...?" Wood muttered.

"Ladies and gentlemen," Ric was saying into the mike, "May I have your attention?" That was certainly overkill. You could have already heard a pin drop in the silence of the room.

"I'd like to do a song today..." Ric was smoothly continuing, as though four hundred people weren't staring at him with their mouths open, "for one of the happy couples; two of my most recent...and *dearest...*" he added snidely, "co-workers."

Ric turned and said something to the band leader. The guy just stood there, staring at him. Ric then gave the man a rough shove. Several of the guests gasped. Ric's look to the band leader clearly said, "Do it—or else". The dude hurriedly whispered something to the musicians, and they started to play.

Shay recognized the song from the brief introduction, even before Ric started to sing. It was "I Need you Near Me".

"That son of a bitch!" Wood exploded, snatching his napkin from his lap, and hurling it down on the table. "I'm going to have him thrown out of here on his ass! Better yet, I'm going to do it myself!"

As Wood started to jump up from his seat, Shay stopped him with a firm hand on his arm.   "No, Woody, don't! There's a better way to handle this! Look around you!"

Wood did. It was obvious from their faces the vast majority of the guests were totally appalled by Ric's audacity and tactlessness. Most were also surreptitiously glancing at Shay and Wood, too; checking out their reaction.

"He's only making a damn fool of himself, Woody," Shay leaned over to urgently whisper. "Don't you see? And it wouldn't help any for you and me to make even bigger damn fools of ourselves. Just sit tight, hon," Shay tightly gripped Wood's hand. "Let him finish."

They stared straight ahead as Ric finished the song. A million emotions were coursing through Shay, but strongest of all was the devotion she felt for the man beside her. Although she felt like crying, like fleeing the room in mortification and bewilderment, she struck fast by Woody's side, determined to make it clear to all just where her loyalty lay.

But as Ric poured his heart out to her in the song, Shay could not help but hurt for him—hurt *with* him. She ached with the memory of the first time he had sung that song for her; of when love for him was just beginning to bloom in her heart.

Ric's voice had never been so hauntingly exquisite, so poignantly expressive. Shay reflected what a tragedy it was that the finest performance of his life should be done in this way; at this time.

At the end of the song, the silence continued, after being momentarily broken by a few clueless die-hard Ric Weaver fans, who at first broke out in wild applause. But that quickly subsided under the stony glares of their more discriminating neighbors.

As the hush re-established itself, Ric stood boldly center stage, legs wide apart, staring a challenge down to where Shay and Wood were seated.

Shay slowly stood, unflinchingly returning Ric's stare, and began to slowly, lifelessly applaud. Wood stood and joined her. The room followed their example, joining them in what had to be the most artificial, half-hearted ovation Ric had ever received in his entire career.

Before Shay could stop him, Wood walked away from her, and slowly approached the stage. The mock applause faded away as the guests watched Wood's advance. Ric watched him, too; with a look of absolute defiance, as if to say, "Come on, man; I'm ready for you!"

Wood walked right up to the edge of the stage, his eyes never leaving Ric's. Then, in one swift move, he put one hand in his pants pocket and withdrew a handful of change. With a disdainful glare, Woody flung the change on stage—at Ric's feet. There was a collective gasp from the guests. Then, without missing a beat, Wood turned his back to Ric and walked away.

The crowd erupted in a spontaneous chorus of laughter and cheers. Ric looked angry, confused, offended, and hurt, all at the same time. He looked around, disoriented for a moment. Then, ignoring the steps, Ric leaped down from the front of the stage, and fled the room, ruthlessly shoving people out of his way as he went.

Wood, who was by then back at Shay's side, watched Ric go. "I've got some business to tend to, honey," he said to Shay, his eyes still following Ric. "Be right back."

"No, Woody!" Shay pleaded, holding tightly to his arm. "Please, just let it go! He's gone now; let things be!"

"No, baby," Wood replied, gently but firmly removing her hand. "A confrontation is long overdue. He's just begging for a showdown. And he's damn sure gonna get one."

"I'll go with you, man," Darnell said wrathfully, as Marty put her arm around Shay.

"Thanks, my brother, but that won't be necessary. I don't need any help disposing of the likes of *him*. Just stay here, and take care of my lady."

"Woody, please!" Shay begged softly. "Honey, I..."

Wood kissed the hand he was still holding and looked deeply into Shay's eyes. "This has to be done, Natasha," he gently replied in a tone that told her there was no changing his mind. "Now wait here, baby; I'll be right back."

The entire assemblage watched as Wood left the room in the direction Ric had taken, a look of grim determination on his face.

Out in the hallway, Richmond approached Wood apologetically, "Mr. Hollister! I had no idea Mr. Weaver was here! Our regular guards would have never admitted him, but the extra guards we hired for this event didn't know, and..."

"It's not your fault, Richmond—it's his. Don't worry about it. Did he leave?"

"No, sir. He went into the men's room, just there," Richmond replied, indicating a room across the corridor. "We were just about to go in there," Richmond had gathered three guards, who were standing with him, at the ready, "when you..."

"I'll handle it," Wood said shortly.

"Sir, don't you think it would be wise for us to go with you?" Richmond advised.

"No, I want to talk to him alone. But if you hear me groaning..." he gave Richmond a wink, "don't be shy about joining us."

Richmond seemed relieved to see Woody's sense of humor kick in, even at a time like that. He smiled, "Never fear, sir; we shan't."

Wood squared his shoulders as he went to the men's room door. He was grateful for the short interlude with Richmond. It had helped calm him down; helped him focus. He paused to take a deep breath before resolutely pushing the door open and entering.

Ric was standing in front of a huge mirror with both hands on a sink, shoulders hunched, head bowed. But his head snapped up when the door opened, and a malicious grin materialized on his face when he saw Wood's reflection in the mirror. "Well...I thought you might show up. I've been waiting for you," Ric informed him.

"I figured you would be," Wood replied, "that is, if you had the nerve to show your face after that disgraceful stunt you just pulled."

"Nerve is one thing I have in abundance," Ric shot back, turning around. "As Shay could tell you," he added cuttingly.

"Natasha *has* told me. She's told me everything about her relationship with you—*everything*. Especially how it started."

That revelation seemed to unsettle Ric's confident pose, and Wood forged on. "I'm going to say this one time, and one time only, Weaver; and I suggest you listen up; your health may depend on it."

"Oh, so you're *threatening* me now, man?"

"You can call it a threat. I prefer to think of it as a promise. Are you listening? Natasha Logan *Hollister* is my wife. You got that, man? I'm sure dealing with irate husbands is something you do on a regular basis, but let me assure you, you ain't seen nothing like the hell that's gonna to bust loose if you keep messin' with *my* woman.

"If I catch you in Shay's face *one more time*..." Wood took a step forward, and scalded Ric with his eyes, slowly and crisply biting off each syllable "I'm going to hurt you *real* bad."

Ric drew himself up and laughed scornfully "I'm not scared of you, man," he replied in a dangerously quiet tone, evenly returning Wood's stare. "If that's what it comes down to, so be it.

"You're getting kind of heavy handed with that 'husband' routine, anyway, blood. This ain't *1912*. The woman's free to do whatever she wants with whomever she wants."

"You're right." Wood told him. "She can. She does. And if Shay ever decides to come to you of her own volition..." Wood couldn't help but wince at even the thought of that alternative, "I won't try to stand in her way.

But it has to be *Shay's* decision, and I'll be damned if I let you or any other man on earth embarrass her, or pressure her, or force himself on her against her will."

"We'll see about the 'against her will' part," Ric retorted.

"Indeed we will," Wood came back. "This is all some sort of macho game to you, isn't it Ric?   That's the difference between us. This is literally survival to me. I love that woman down to the bottom of my soul, and I'll move heaven and earth to keep her by my side."

Ric leaned back against the wall, crossing his arms and giving Wood a smirk, "You're pitiful, Wood; you know that?   You know damn well Shay married you on the rebound. That's what it took for you to get her; catching her at her weakest point. Did it ever occur to you, my man, that you wouldn't have to try so hard...if Shay loved you?"

Wood was visibly rocked for a moment, but quickly bounced back, "And did it ever occur to you—Dream Boy—that if you *had* tried, you wouldn't have lost Shay to me in the first place?"

Ric turned dark with anger but didn't have a reply.

Wood looked him up and down contemptuously, and started to walk away.

Just as Wood reached the door, Ric called out, "You know what, buddy? Keeping me away from Shay is not your problem. Your problem, my friend, will be keeping *her* away from *me—Woodrow*."

Woody just confidently gave Ric his lop-sided smile. "Don't fool yourself. If your stuff was all *that* airtight, Shay wouldn't be *my* wife, to begin with.   You keep 'dreaming.' " He started to leave again, then turned back, "And by the way, chump—my name *ain't* Woodrow."

Wood walked out of the room without another word. Richmond was standing anxiously nearby. "Is everything all right, Mr. Hollister?"

"Just fine, my man," Wood answered, straightening his

tie. "I'm going back into the ballroom now. Just leave him alone—but stay by the door. When he comes out, have the guards make sure he heads for an exit and follow him out. If he tries to come back in where we are, stop him—and let me know ASAP."

Wood turned to head back down the corridor to the ballroom when there was a colossal rumble, and floor suddenly became unstable beneath his feet. Some of the flowers vases on tables lining the corridor fell over and smashed to the floor. Down the hall in the ballroom, the band stopped playing, and a troubled murmur replaced the conversation and laughter of the guests: "Earthquake!"

Wood turned back to Richmond and the guards, "Forget Weaver! Come with me! We've got to get my wife out of here!" Just then there was an enormous boom as a section of the wall not five feet from where they were standing imploded. The impact of the detonation shattered the large glass window on the other side of the corridor, and they were showered with large shards of glass.

Two of the guards looked at Woody, and then at the shattered glass, and turned tail, running for the outer exit door.

"Come *back* here!" Wood yelled after them. But they were gone. Wood turned back to Richmond and the remaining guard, "All right, fellas, it's just us. You with me?"

"We're with you, sir," Richmond stoutly maintained. The one remaining guard looked scared to death, but he nodded shakily and stood his ground.

The three men started down to corridor toward the ballroom, but they were going against the tide. The screaming, panicked guests were pouring from the room in a torrent, and Wood and his party were going against the flow.

A burly male guest roughly pushed Richmond out of his way, in his hysteria to escape, and Richmond was violently thrown against a wall.

Wood rushed over to him. "Are you all right, man?" Wood called to Richmond above the furor.

"I..I think I've broken my arm, sir," Richmond answered faintly, but rallied, "But I can go on."

Wood clapped him on the shoulder, and they continued their struggle to enter the room. Woody saw Darnell carrying an unconscious Marty over his shoulder. "Darnell! What happened to Marty? And where's Shay?"

"I don't know, man!" Darnell shouted back. "We were looking for Shay when some behemoth broad knocked Marty over a table. She's out cold! Let me get her out to safety, and I'll be back to help you find Shay!"

Just then a large painting on the wall above Woody was jarred loose and came careening down, the heavy frame hitting Wood squarely on the head. He crumpled in a heap as though shot.

Richmond gasped one of Wood's arms with his uninjured hand. "Take his other arm!" Richmond yelled to the guard. "We'll have to drag him out to the parking lot!"

"But what about his wife?" The guard asked, puffing as they dragged Wood's dead weight between them.

"A rescue squad has arrived outside. I'll tell them Mrs. Hollister is still inside. There's nothing the two of us can do now but get *him* out of here!"

Shay wasn't in the ballroom. She had slipped down the corridor to the women's room. Worried to death about Woody, shaken and shamed by Ric's shenanigans, she needed to get away from all the staring, probing eyes long enough to compose herself.

Shay was refreshing her lipstick when the earthquake began.

Why can't I get this stuff to go on straight? she wondered. *Am I so shook up I can't even keep my hand steady?*

Then she realized it wasn't just her hand; the whole

room was shaking.   The mirror she was looking into
suddenly came loose, and smashed to the floor, breaking
into a million pieces. *What the...?* Being relatively new to
California, it took her a few seconds to fathom what was
going on.

Oh, my God! An earthquake! I've got to find Woody!

Shay ran to the door and flung it open, but the exit was
blocked by a ponderous section of oak paneling with some
furniture fallen across and behind it. Shay pushed against it
with all her might, but it was too heavy for her to budge.

"Help! Help! I'm trapped in here!" she cried through
the tiny opening left near the top of the paneling. All she
heard in response were the screams and cries of people
trying to escape the building, and the rumbling of the
building all around her, joined shortly afterward by the
sound of sirens.

Nobody can hear me, she realized. *And nobody knows
I'm in here. I slipped away without even telling Marty.* She
smelled smoke. *I've got to get out of here!* she realized in
panic.

Shay started to kick the paneling, trying to force it
forward enough for her to slip through the opening, but she
couldn't budge it. Something heavy was blocking it from
the other side. She screamed out in terror as she continued
to futilely kick and pound against the barrier blocking her
way to safety, when a voice suddenly called out, "Shay! Is
that you in there, Shay?"

"Yes!" Shay almost swooned with relief. "I can't get
out! Something is blocking this thing. I can't move it!"

"Hold on!" the voice answered.

Shay could hear the man's grunts, and the sound of
something massive being laboriously pushed aside, the high
pitched screeches testimony to the deep grooves it was
leaving in the floor as it went.

After what seemed like an eternity, a bloody hand
inserted itself along the edge of the piece of paneling as the

grunts renewed.

"It's too heavy! I can't tip it back! Push it from your side, too, Shay! On the count of three. One! Two! Three!"

On the count, Shay pushed with both hands and one foot as hard as she could. The unwieldy piece of oak tottered for an instant, then fell away from the open door with a resounding boom. And there stood Ric.

"Ric! What..." Ric's white dinner jacket was ripped in several places, and he was speckled from head to foot in soot. The dirt on his face was smeared with blood from several freely bleeding cuts.

"No time for questions now." He grabbed Shay's hand and helped her climb over the precariously leaning partition. "We gotta get outta here!"

Still holding Shay's hand, he pulled her along, running down the smoke-filled corridor, in the direction of the ballroom, and the outer exit.

"Ric! I won't leave without Woody! He's got to be here somewhere!"

"He's safe. I saw the butler and some other guy carrying him out."

"*Carrying* him out?" Shay stopped short and snatched her hand from Ric's. "He was *hurt*? Ric, what..."

Ric stopped and took Shay by the shoulders, "Look, girl, I don't know how bad Wood was hurt, okay? But I *do* know they got him outside where he'll get medical attention. I also know you and I better haul ass with a quickness, or no medical attention on earth is going to do us any good. You dig?"

Shay nodded rapidly in reply, blinking in the ever increasing smoke.

Ric took her hand again, "All right, then. Let's go!"

They took off again down the corridor. They could see firemen down at the very end of the hall and were almost to them when a huge section of burning ceiling caved in before them. It was so close a segment of it touched the hem of Shay's evening gown, and the delicate fabric burst into flame.

"Oh, God! Ric! I'm on fire!" Shay twirled in terror, only causing the flames to spread.

"Hold it! Shay, stand still! You're only making it worse, baby!" Ric flung Shay to the floor, beating the flames with his hands until they were extinguished.

He quickly helped her to her feet, "It's out now. Are you all right? Did you get burned, baby?"

"Just a little. But, oh, Ric!" Both Ric's hands were burned and blistered.

But Ric was waving and yelling to the firemen, across the barrier of flames.

"We can't get to you!" a fireman yelled in reply. This exit is blocked! Go back down the corridor in the other direction! We'll try to get to you that way!"

Without another word, Ric snatched Shay's hand again and took off for the other end of the corridor. He stopped briefly at each door they came to, touching it gingerly with his seared hands.

"Ric, what are you doing?" Shay choked out as the swirling smoke began to fill her lungs.

"Trying to find a room the fire hasn't reached," he told her," going to yet another door. "Yes! This door is cool. Stand back, Shay!"

Ric cautiously opened the door. It was some sort of meeting room. It was full of smoke, but the smoke here was not as intense as the smoke in the hallway. Even through the haze, they could see a door on the far side of the room.

"Mrs. Hollister, I think we've got our ticket out! Come on!"

They entered the room, Ric carefully closing the door behind them. They ran over to the door on the other side. It wouldn't open. It was blocked, or locked, or *something*, but they couldn't open it, not even with both of them trying.

"Okay, no problem.   We'll just regroup," Ric said confidently, leading Shay back to the hallway door. But when he opened it a gush of flame greeted them, and he slammed it shut again instantly.

Shay's eyes were wide with fear as she just stood there, looking up at Ric. "We're trapped, aren't we, Ric?" she asked softly.

"The fat lady ain't sang yet, honey," Ric replied, looking around the room. He went over to a vase of flowers, and took off his jacket, soaking it in the water from the vase. Then he stuffed the wet garment in the crack under the corridor door.

Still looking around, he spied several tiny windows up near the ceiling. Shay's eyes followed his gaze. "Ric, those windows are so small we couldn't get through them even if we could reach them."

Ric ignored her and flipped several tablecloths from the tables all about the room. "Start tearing these into long strips, Shay!"

No knowing what else to do, Shay started ripping the table cloths for all she was worth. Ric began to knot the torn strands together, and in a short while declared, "That ought to be long enough."

There was a small microphone in a short stand on the lectern.   Ric threw the microphone to the floor, and wrapped the end of the rope of cloth around the heavy stand over and over again, then secured the wrapped cloth with a double knot.

"Stand on that, Shay!" he shouted, pointing to the other end of the makeshift rope. He began to twirl the encased stand around his head using the rope's other end. It took three tries, but he finally succeeded in hitting one of the windows. The glass broke, and the stand went flying out, trailing the cloth behind it.

"Success!" Ric shouted. "Hey! Don't let *that* fly out, too!" He dived, just in time to snare the remaining end of the rope, which had come loose when Shay moved. He secured it by tying it to a table leg.

Ric turned to see Shay staring at him in frightened utter bewilderment.

"That's a marker, baby!" he told her. "That'll let them know where we are! See?"

"Oh..." Shay said, finally comprehending. "I see now. And am I glad. I thought you had lost your mind."

Even though the smoke and the pain, he gave her that slow, easy smile, "Can't lose what I never had, baby."

"So...so...what do we do now?" Shay asked faintly.

Ric put his arm around her shoulders, "We wait." They sat on the edge of the room's small stage. "Don't worry, honey; they'll find us. They already knew what part of the building we were in. Now they know which room. They'll get to us in...in time."

They were silent for a moment, then Shay asked, "Ric, how did you know where I was? How did you know I was in the women's room?"

"When the earthquake started, Wood forgot all about me. I was standing nearby when he told his boys they had to go find you. He didn't know it, but I was right behind them. I was sure he wouldn't turn down even *my* help if it meant getting you to safety. When he got knocked out, I knew it was up to me. I just kept asking everybody I saw if they had seen you until finally some woman told me you came into the ladies' room just as she was leaving."

There was another rumble, and the floor shifted. "Oh!" in her fright, Shay threw herself into Ric's arms.

"The man upstairs is looking out for me again." He wrapped his arms around her and pulled her closer. "That's the second time an act of God brought you into my arms, Shay."

Ric bent, and kissed her tenderly, "I was beginning to think I'd never do *that* again," he whispered softly. "Shay, doesn't it seem like fate keeps pulling us together? Maybe that's the way it should be, honey; the way it was destined to be."

Ric looked away a moment, "Shay, forgive me for...for what I did this evening." He then looked back into her eyes, even more intently. "I couldn't seem to stop myself. I was hurting so bad that I wanted to hurt you, too—*and* Wood. But after I did it... I've never been more ashamed of myself in my life. Can you forgive me, honey?"

"After you've gotten yourself burned, and bruised, and put your life on the line to save mine?" Shay touched his arm softly. "How could I not?"

"If you were to die, I wouldn't want to live," Ric replied gently. "I'd rather see you walk away in the arms of another man than have to go on living in a world without you in it." He cupped her face, "Letting you get away from me was the biggest mistake of my life. I love you, Shay."

Ric kissed her again, and in spite of the smoke and the danger, in spite of everything, Shay felt her heart melt in his embrace.

But it was different now. There wasn't that wonder, that magic. There was just a vast tenderness for this flawed man and for the considerable good inside him despite those flaws. And Shay felt a bittersweet sympathy for the man he *could* have been.

Ric is only the outward *manifestation of my ideal man,* Shay realized; *the smooth, sexy, talented exterior. But that's not the part of Michael that won my heart.*

I fell in love with the inner man; his tenderness, and compassion; his humor, and strength...and...and I've met that *man, too!* Shay was rocked by this staggering revelation. *I'm* married *to him!*

The smoke was becoming much thicker now. Shay could hardly catch her breath.

"Ric..." Shay could hardly croak out, "Ric, I'm getting so...so...sleepy."

"Me...too...honey." Ric's voice sounded sluggish and

slow. "We...need to...stay awake...stay...alert..."

They leaned against each other, Ric's arm still around Shay's shoulders.

"Ric...I..."

"Don't...talk, honey," Ric said weakly. "Breathe as... shallowly...as you can. They'll...be here...any...minute. Just... hang on...Shay...Just..."

But Shay's eyes had already closed.

"Shay? Shay, baby; can you hear me? Open your eyes, honey. Please, just open your eyes."

"Woody?" Shay asked woozily, sure she was in some vapor induced dream. Then she opened her eyes, and there he was before her. She instantly sat up, and flung her arms around him, "Woody!" She delicately fingered the bandage around his head, "Woody, you're hurt!"

"No, I'm all right baby. I'm too hard-headed for a bump on the noggin to do me much damage. But they just gave you oxygen. Are you all right now?"

Shay looked around her. She was lying on a bed in the back of an emergency medical vehicle. A fireman with a face mask and oxygen tank in his hands was at Woody's elbow.

"How do you feel, Mrs. Hollister?" the fireman asked. "Are you okay? Can you sit up?"

"Yes, I'm fine," Shay told him, swinging her legs to the floor. "I feel a little dizzy, but...." Shay suddenly remembered and looked up, her eyes wide with fear. "Wood, where's Ric?"

"Right here, Shay." The fireman moved and stepped out of the truck, and Shay could then see Ric, seated on a bed on the other side. Someone had washed the blood and soot off his face. It was covered with scratches and bruises, but none looked too serious. But his hands! Both his hands were swaddled in bandages.

Shay moved over to sit next to him, putting her arm around him. "Ric! Oh, Ric; your poor hands!"

"They'll heal, baby." Ric smiled, "I just won't be playing the piano for a while."

Wood stood stiffly by for a moment, then cleared his throat. "Look, man; there's been a lot of bad blood between us, but I thank you from the bottom of my heart. If you hadn't gone after her..."

Ric looked him in the eye, "I *had* to go after her, man..." he said quietly, "for the same reason you did."

Wood looked back and forth between them; Shay still sitting with her arm still around Ric's shoulders. Then Woody sighed heavily and said, "Well, guess I'll be on my way." With that, he turned and quickly left the truck.

"Woody?" Shay called, rising. "Woody, where are you..."

"It's better this way, honey," Ric said, gently pulling her back down. "We can straighten out all the legal stuff later, and..."

Shay jumped to her feet and started down the steps from the truck.

Ric climbed down after her, "Shay! Shay, where are you going?"

Shay turned to look up at him. "I think you know where I'm going, Ric," she said frankly.

"Shay, okay; you're married to Wood now. But divorce courts are open every day of the week, baby. You were in love with *me*. I know you were."

Shay looked up at him in complete honesty, "Yes, Ric; I was. At least I was *beginning* to fall in love with you. I might have gone all the way—had you let me."

Ric awkwardly took both her hands in his bandaged ones. "I know. I didn't understand that then, but I do now. And Shay..." he stepped closer, "I think I've finally grown up enough to for it to happen now—this time—if you give me another...."

"I believe you. I believe you truly mean it this time; you risked your life for me. But..." she turned to look in the direction Wood had gone, "it's too late, Ric." She turned back to him. "I'm already in love—with the man I married."

She released Ric's hands gently, "And if you'll excuse me, I'm a few weeks late telling him so."

Shay started for the parking lot, the way Woody had gone. "Shay!" Ric called after her.

She turned.

"You're sure?"

Shay nodded firmly, "I'm sure."

Ric seemly to slump, but rallied and gamely smiled. "Much as I hate to admit it, Wood is one remarkable dude, and God knows, far more worthy of you than I am. But before you go, I want to...to thank you."

"*Thank* me? Shay was puzzled. "Thank me for what?"

"For teaching me *how* to love." He gave her a dejected smile, "Forrest Gump had one up on me. Even *he* knew what love was. I didn't. Not until now. And now that I *do* know; maybe there's a chance I'll find it again someday. And I have you to thank for that, Shay." He again took her hand into his bandaged one and kissed it. "Take care of yourself, baby. I wish you only the best—you deserve it."

Shay smiled tenderly, "Thank you, Ric." She gently kissed his wounded cheek. "See you around, all right?"

"Yeah." Ric smiled sadly as he winked at her, "See you at the movies."

Shay dashed madly across the parking lot, finding Wood just as he reached his car.

"Wood! Woody!" she called out as she ran to him.

He turned quickly, clearly astonished to see her. "Well...What a surprise. Did you forget something?" Woody was trying his best to sound caustic, but the pain in his eyes showed in his voice as well.

"Yes," Shay gasped, as she reached the car. "I forgot to tell you something."

Wood laughed bitterly, "Is there anything left to say?"

"Yes, my husband; just one thing." Shay stood on her toes and wrapped her arms around his neck. "And I'll tell you..." she murmured with her head on his shoulder, "as soon as you take me home."

Wood looked deeply into Shay's eyes, then kissed her joyfully, lifting her off her feet and spinning her around. He opened the car door and helped her inside.

"Wood," Shay said worriedly once they were on their way, "our families; Marty and Darnell... Where are they? Are they all right?"

"All our friends and family are fine. There were a lot of cuts, bruises, and burns, and a few broken bones, but by some miracle, none of them got seriously hurt. Our families are at our place. Your Mom lost it when you got trapped inside. Your Dad thought it was best she wasn't here if...if...well, anyway, they went home. But I've called them; they know you're all right."

"And your family? Marty and Darnell?"

"My folks stayed until you were found, then they went on home, too. Marty and Darnell are at the hospital. Marty fainted."

"Oh, my God! Wood, maybe we better go there! I hope she's all right!"

"She's fine. She just got all hyped up over you being trapped, and passed out again when we got word they had found you." Wood grinned over at Shay. "Too much excitement can do that with pregnant women, they tell me."

"Pregnant! Marty's *pregnant*? And she didn't tell me?"

"They were going to surprise everybody with an announcement tonight," Wood chuckled. "But she's fine. Darnell just wanted her to get checked out, to be on the safe side."

"Pregnant! Huh! Just wait 'til I see *her*! After all the hassle she's been giving *me,* asking if *I* was..." Shay looked out the window at their surroundings, "Wood, where are we going? This isn't the way home."

"I know. We've got a house full of guests, and probably a legion of reporters at our door. So we're not going home. We're going to a hotel."

"A hotel?"

"Yep. I want it nice, and quiet, and *private*, so I can be sure to not to miss whatever it is you've got to tell me."

Shay smiled at him tenderly. "You do?" she asked softly.

"Yes, darling girl," he grinned at her happily; "and I think I'm going to need a lot of privacy for an appropriate response, as well."

EPILOGUE

IT'S A WONDERFUL LIFE

"And entering now, that Oscar *and* Grammy-winning couple, the multi-talented Woody and Natasha Hollister!"

Shay and Woody stopped a moment to wave to the crowd, who cheered and applauded in response.

"Well," the reporter continued, "I must say, it is a bit of a surprise to see the two of *you* here. After all..."

"That's all in the past; ancient history," Shay interrupted. "We're here because the bride *and* the groom both called to invite us, and we were thrilled to accept their invitation. We couldn't be happier for them."

Shay's firm reply, and the "back off, dude" look in Woody's eyes told the reporter *that* subject was closed, so he moved on to other things.

"It's been over three years now since *The SuperStar's Lady: The Movie* walked away with multiple awards at both the Oscars and Grammies. And of course, no one will ever forget the posthumous Oscar won by the late Vanessa Sweet, who tragically lost her life during that last great earthquake."

"Yes," Woody answered him. "The world lost a great actress."

"Well..." the reporter continued, changing gears, "what are the two of you working on now?"

"I just started casting for my next movie, 'The Quest'— original screenplay by Natasha Hollister," Woody smiled down at Shay.

"And I'm just finishing my fifth novel," Shay put in.

"But to tell you the truth," Wood went on, "*this* production..." he reached over to lovingly pat Shay's bulging tummy, "is our top priority right now."

"And when is the happy event?" the reporter probed.

"Any day now," Shay told him with a little wince.

"I'm almost a week overdue."

Wood asked the guy to excuse them, and they approached the entrance to the country club.

As the Woody and Shay walked away, the reporter looked into his camera and continued. "This reporter is *most* surprised at the Hollisters appearing here today. As I'm sure you will recall, Woody Hollister, the then Natasha *Logan*, and Ric Weaver were the key players in one of the most talked about love triangles..."

Wood looked over his shoulder, "I oughta go back and pound that guy," he said with a mischievous grin.

"Now, now; that's no way for a wedding guest to act. Behave yourself," Shay chided with a grin of her own.

The club was festively adorned with flowers and ornaments in bride's colors of red, white, and black.

"Boy, this is something!" Wood remarked as they were shown to a table, right up front.

"Yes," Shay agreed as they took their seats. "And the wedding was simply exquisite."

Wood took her hand, "Sorry you missed out on a big one, honey?"

Shay shook her head happily, "Uh-uh. I got what I wanted from my wedding," she squeezed his hand. "A lifetime with the man I love."

Two hands suddenly covered Shay's eyes. "Bet you can't guess who!" a man's voice declared.

"You'd lose your money," Shay answered with glee, bouncing up, as well as she could, to give Booker a big hug. "Book! Oh, Book, it's so wonderful to see you! What a wonderful surprise when *you* turned out to be Ric's best man!"

"Now you know I couldn't let my problem child get married without my blessing," Booker said while shaking Wood's hand. "And, anyway, haven't you heard? I'm Ric's 'best man' again in more ways than one. I'm managing him again, you know."

"No, I *didn't* know! When did that happen?"

"About two months ago. I opened my door one day and there he stood. We talked a long, long time, and...well, here I am. And here's another surprise. See the guy over there talking to Five?" Booker indicated an extremely handsome older man who somehow looked familiar to Shay.

"Yes, but I can't place where I've met him before."

"You haven't met him before...and neither had Ric until about six weeks ago. That's Eric Tyrone Johnson— Ric's father."

Shay's eyes misted, "Oh, Book, you mean Ric finally..."

"Yep. *She* asked him to do it. She lost both her parents years ago, and told Ric his Dad was the only grandparent their children could ever know. Frankly, I think Ric has always longed to contact his father, but his pride stood in the way.

"And it seems Eric senior knew Ric was his son all along. He wanted to meet with Ric, but he was ashamed of the past and didn't think Ric would want to meet *him*. They've got a lot of things to work out, but at least now they're *trying* to work them out.

"But look, the receiving line's getting shorter now. Anyway, you two can take cuts." Book looked at Shay's extended mid-section and offered her his arm. "I can't imagine anybody insisting on making *you* stand in line."

"I hope not," Shay said, faltering a bit as she took his arm. "I couldn't take much standing just now."

Book led them over to the reception line, where Wood and Shay greeted a few other members of the wedding party before reaching Ric and his bride. Shay watched Ric as they approached him.

Some people are saying it won't last. That Ric will go back to his old ways sooner or later. But I don't think so. He really loves her. I know. Because he's looking at her the way he used to look at me.

When they finally reached the newlyweds, Ric's face broke out into a luminous smile, "You came!" He put his arm around Simone, looking at her with his heart in his eyes, "Shay and Woody are here, sweetheart."

Ric turned to Wood, "Mind if I give the incipient Mama a kiss, man?"

"Not if you don't mind me kissing *your* wife," Wood replied with a grin, kissing the beaming Simone.

Ric turned to Shay, lightly placing his totally healed, but permanently scarred hands on her shoulders. "Thank you, Shay," he whispered as he gently kissed her forehead.

As she looked into his eyes, Shay felt the last shadow to her happiness float away. Woody was the man she loved. Of that, there was no doubt in her mind or her heart. She never regretted the decision she made on that frightening, unforgettable night.

But Ric's pain, his suffering, had troubled her. Now she could see for herself he suffered no more. She remembered Ric's "thank you" from that horrible night, and knew he had finally found happiness with the woman he *now* loved.

Shay turned to Simone, "You look absolutely radiant!" Shay lowered her voice to a whisper as she touched her cheek to Simone's and said, "I wish all the best for both of you."

Simone's eyes grew misty then, for only she and Shay knew the history behind Shay's words. Words Simone herself had spoken when their roles were reversed. And she knew Shay's good wishes were just as sincere as her own had been all those months ago.

Simone hugged Shay, then patted her swollen tummy. "Is it a boy or a girl?"

"We don't know," Shay laughed. "My *doctor* does, but we wouldn't let him tell us."

"We wanted to do this the old-fashioned way," Woody

added with a wink.

"Well," Simone laughed, "maybe if I touch you here, it'll be catching, and I can join you at the playground in the next few years!"

Ric's arm tightened around Simone's waist, as he leaned over to kiss her, "Count on it, honey!"

"Auntie Tay! Auntie Tay!"

The unmistakable voice of Mr. Darnell Franklin, Jr. was heard in the land. Shay looked down at her godson, who was tugging on the hem of her dress. "Auntie Tay, where you been?" he demanded, both hands on his three-year-old hips.

Marty came rushing up, "Yes, 'Auntie Tay,' just where *have* you been? This hellion has been asking for you for the past half hour!"

"Well, I'm here now, DJ," Shay said to the child, "and my back hurts. So let's go sit down, and Uncle Vood can go get us some ice cream, all right, honey?"

After excusing themselves from the Weavers, they joined Darnell, who was seated at Shay and Woody's table.

"Where the hel..." Wood looked down at DJ, "heck have you all been, man? We didn't see you when we came in."

"His Majesty got restless, and we took him out for a walk in the garden out back." Darnell looked at Marty, "*Told* you certain people would get fidgety at this shindig!"

"Don't start with me, Franklin," Marty told him with a kiss. "It's not my fault *certain people* are just like their father!"

"Shay? What's the matter, baby?" Wood had abruptly noticed the distress on her face.

"It's nothing, honey. These false labor pains are at it again. They've been bothering me ever since the wedding. But they're usually not this bad, and...OH!"

"You've been having these pains for over an hour?" Marty asked, leaning forward with concern.

"Yes, but they usually go away in a little while, and..."

"How far apart are the cramps, Shay?" Wood asked, standing as he spoke.

"Every few minutes or so...now..."

Marty jumped up from her seat as well, "Mrs. Hollister, I got a funny feeling ain't nothing false about those pains *this* time!" She turned to Woody, "I think this is it, Dad. We gotta get her to the hospital, pronto!"

"Daddy, Auntie Tay having her baby now?" DJ asked his father.

"Yes, DJ; sure looks like it, man," Darnell told his son before popping up himself, looking like he had seen a ghost.

Ric appeared by Wood's side, "What's the matter?" Seeing them all standing around Shay, Ric and Simone had come over to find out what the problem was.

"Shay's in labor, man!" Wood told him. "We gotta get her to the hospital!

"Okay...okay," Ric stammered. "Now, stay calm...everybody stay calm. We'll just...we'll just...ah..."

"Where's your car?" Simone quietly inquired.

"Outside...somewhere!" Wood excitedly told her. "I'd...I'd better go see if I can find my driver, and..."

"No, I'll go, man," Darnell said, tripping over a chair. "Just stay here with Shay and I'll..."

"Look, our limo is right outside the front door." Simone gently put her arm around Shay and helped her to her feet. "Can you make it to the door, honey?"

"Yes...OH!... Yes, Simone, but...but we can't take *your* car!"

"Yes, you can," Simone said calmly. "It's the closest one. Ric and I are going to be here for a while longer. So our driver can take you to the hospital, and just come back for us; all right?"

Shay slowly made her way to the door with Woody supporting her on one side and Darnell on the other, and they were off.

At the hospital emergency room bay, two gardeners were tending the flowers beds when they saw the white stretch limo covered with streamers and a big "Just Married" sign on the back roar into the driveway. A man in a tuxedo leaped from the car and helped a very pregnant, moaning woman in white into the wheelchair a nurse had rolled out.

One of the gardeners whistled. "Man! *They* sure cut it close!"

They didn't name the baby Woodington James Hollister IV.

"We'll just have to wait a year or two for her baby brother to come along," Shay told Woody as he sat there on the bed next to her, holding his daughter in awe.

OTHER BOOKS BY RAYNETTA MANEES

eBooks / Digital Books

All For Love
(The SuperStar Series: Book One)
Available as Kindle Nook
Paperback
Re-release date May 14, 2013

All For Love: The SuperStar
(The SuperStar Series: Book Two)
released Sept. 23, 2016
Available in Kindle, Nook, and
paperback format

Fantasy
released July 2014 ISBN: 978-0-
9855324-0-6
(re-release of paperback edition)

All The Way Home
released May 2012 ISBN: 978-0-9855324-1-3
(re-release of novella from paperback book "A Mother's Touch")

Follow Your Heart released April 2012
ISBN: 978-0-9855324-0-6
(re-release of paperback edition)

My Alzheimer's Diary
released June 2015 ISBN: 978-0-9855324-5-1

Classic Paperback Books

All For Love
released September 1996, ISBN 0-7860-0309-X
rated 5 stars on both Amazon and B&N

Wishing On A Star
released August 1997, ISBN 0-7860-0423-1
rated 4 ½ stars Amazon   5 stars B&N

Follow Your Heart
released September 1998 ISBN 0-7860-0560-2
rated 5 stars on both Amazon and B&N

Fantasy
released August 1999 ISBN 1-58314-030-1
rated 5 stars on both Amazon and B&N

Heart Of The Matter
Heart of the Matter, released January 2002 ISBN 1-58314-262-2
rated 5 stars Amazon   Not yet rated on B&N

A Mother's Touch
A three author anthology containing Raynetta Manees'
novella, "All The Way Home"
released May 1999 ISBN 1-58314-015-8
Rated 5 stars on both Amazon and B&N

ABOUT THE AUTHOR

Raynetta Manees is a best-selling, award-winning author. Her books are in both digital and print editions and she is traditionally published and self-published. She's done it all! She has written several five-star Black romance novels as well as a non-fiction book about #Alzheimer's. All Raynetta's books are on Amazon and B&N.

Her landmark first-person novel, **All For Love**, first released in 1996, is now considered a Black romance classic. An updated e-book edition of the novel was released in 2013. This book is now Book One of *The SuperStar Series.*

September 2016 marked Raynetta's 20th anniversary as an author. She celebrated this milestone with the release of Book Two of *The SuperStar Series*, **All For Love: The Superstar** in Sept 2016. The book is a finalist for the 2017 Emma Award for the Best Contemporary Romance of the year. The Emma is the premier award for black authors of romance.

Raynetta is the very first recipient of the Award of Excellence from RomanceInColor.com for her novel **Follow Your Heart.**

She is currently working on Book Three of *The SuperStar Series*, **All For Love: The Superstar's Daughter**, which will be released in 2018.

Raynetta's author page on Amazon.com is www.amazon.com/author/raynettamanees

All of Raynetta's books are rated four/five stars by readers on Amazon.com and BN.com (Barnes and Noble).

Raynetta Manees is a graduate of Wayne State University, with a degree in Mass Communications. She retired as a Federal government executive administrator after a 28-year career. Raynetta now writes full-time. Her love of the media arts is reflected in her novels, whose characters are involved in some aspect of entertainment/media.

Raynetta has been a solo vocalist since childhood. Her stage name is "Rayne," and her first CD, "Singing in the Rayne," a collection of smooth jazz vocals, was released in December 2012.

The author is an accomplished actress who has appeared in numerous stage productions and in TV and radio commercials. As an on-air radio personality, she was known as "Shalimar Brown, the baddest girl in town" on AM 1180 WXLA.

Raynetta stepped away from her career as a notable romance novelist in June 2015 to pen her first non-fiction work, **My Alzheimer's Diary.** The book explores Alzheimer's effect on her family and her own journey of diagnosis.

Raynetta welcomes your comments at her website www.RManees.com. She can also be reached via email at RManees@aol.com (Please show "Reader" and your name in the subject line.)

You may also reach Raynetta via:
Facebook: Raynetta Manees, Author
Twitter: @raynettaman,
Pinterest: Raynetta Manees Author on Pinterest
Instagram: ms.manees
Mail: P.O. Box 3203, Southfield, MI 48037
Goodreads Author Page:
goodreads.com/author/show/21931.Raynetta_Manees

www.ingramcontent.com/pod-product-compliance
Lightning Source LLC
Chambersburg PA
CBHW031253170626
46807CB00001B/127